When Memory Dies

Book Two of *Tales of Tasimu*

By

Celu Amberstone

WHEN MEMORY DIES

First edition. February 29, 2024.

ISBN: 978-1990581199

Written by Celu Amberstone.

Note to the Reader:

When Memory Dies is a work of fiction and I hope you'll read and enjoy it as such. Though I've drawn material in the abstract from places I've lived and from my own mixed-race background, any resemblance to people, places, languages and cultures, Indigenous or otherwise existing in our world is purely coincidental.

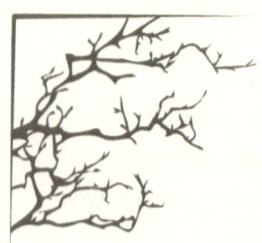

Dedication

This book is dedicated to all the refugees and displaced indigenous peoples around the world. It is also dedicated to my children and grandchildren. Not being a woman of material wealth, my writing is my legacy to both them, and all the children who are our cherished future. Also in dedication, I offer my eternal gratitude for the traditional teachings of my grandparents, aunties, and the other Elders I've met over the years who have taken the time to teach me. The wisdom and strength of my Elders has always been, and will continue to be, an inspiration in my life.

Acknowledgements

I would like to thank for their support, my four sons, my daughter, and those of my friends who were there when I needed them. Paula, Lila, your friendship and help with proof reading, book covers, and other important book related things, was greatly appreciated.

I would also like to thank the folks at Kegedonce Press for their dedication, hard work, their vision, and their fearless determination to encourage Aboriginal writers of all types.

A Short Summary of Book One: *Taste of Memory*

Tasimu is a boy with inherited magical gifts, but he is also troubled by the mystery surrounding his parentage. Some of his friends taunt him, claiming that he isn't truly human. Before he can discover the truth, soldiers from the Empire come north with orders to remove his people from their arctic home, when gold is discovered on their land.

Along their journey out of the northern mountains, his people face hunger and many hardships. But Tasimu meets another man of power who knows of his heritage and can teach him, if Tasimu will agree to pay his price.

He agrees and learns how to see events from afar by weaving magical patterns with a child's toy, a loop of string, and to call upon spirits to save his family lost in a storm.

But he is also an unwitting agent for a sickness brought into the refugee camps by his mentor who seeks vengeance against the converts to the Empire's new religion, for they are the ones who signed away the tribe's land.

Fearing that he might unwittingly be the cause of his baby cousin's sickness and death, Tasimu chooses to give up his lessons with the man his grandfather claims is an unsuitable teacher. But by choosing family over magic Tasimu also fears he has lost any chance of continuing his studies and contacting the enigmatic Seal man that is his father.

Book one ends with the death of Tasimu's young cousin and his people nearing the end of their terrible journey to the Empire's Tribal Preserve.

Rushton Archives: pg. 346, Second Interview with subject 297

To the Empire and her great lords all Indigenous peoples they found when they took our lands were alike, no matter where we lived and the different languages we spoke. We were just savages and dirty zaunks. It only made sense to them to put us all together on the Tribal Preserve. It was more cost-effective and easier to administrate, they argued.

The Preserve, I discovered by listening to my relatives' ration day gossip, was a large arid basin hollowed out between a western and eastern mountain range. At its southern tip a briny, undrinkable lake created a bleached desert of salt and other minerals. Most of the Kukiya, the tribal peoples who were native to the desert region, and therefore some of the first to be relocated, had been settled in that hot southern land.

Further to the north-east where our agency was located, the land was harsh and water starved—by our standards—but not as unkind as by the salt lake. But the dry desert land to which they brought us was also land their own people didn't want, and so alien to our northern home. It is no wonder we didn't thrive there.

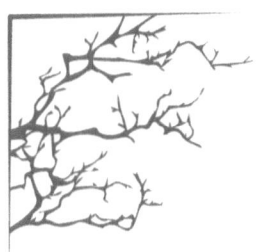

Part One
Chapter One

The smothering cloud billowed about the column of soldiers, wagons and my weary relatives trudging among them. Dust. It stung my eyes and sucked the last drops of moisture from my lips and tongue. There was no escape from the torment. It was everywhere, pale as the bones of the dead we'd left beside the trail, and just as dry.

"So, this is the glorious new land the traitors, May the Unseen Ones curse them, sold our ancestral home for?" Uncle Tli ended his words with a bitter laugh that soon changed into a fit of coughing.

Plodding along behind my mother, I glanced over at the skeletally-thin man doubled over, the dry hacking sound making my own throat hurt. Who was he talking to? Why had he bothered to speak at all? I felt dizzy, my head pounding; the sun's glare in this barren land nearly blinding.

I glanced up and saw Grandmother and Tli's wife Shilshigua watching him anxiously from their place in the jostling wagon. "There is room in the wagon for you, Son," Grandmother called. "Come sit beside us and rest."

Mother stopped and offered her brother her hand. Still coughing, he waved her away. With a grimace of pain he spat out a dark gob of phlegm and blood. Ignoring his wife and mother's further coaxing, he straightened himself and kept walking.

"You should listen to the women and ride for a time in the wagon, my son," Grandfather coaxed putting a hand on Tli's shoulder.

With an angry gesture Tli brushed his hand away. "I'm fine. Leave me be. I don't need to ride like an invalid with the women and old people."

Grandfather sighed and stepped away. The women and Grandfather exchanged troubled glances.

"Stubborn Man," Mother walking beside me muttered under her breath.

Tli wasn't fine; he knew it and so did everyone else, but there was no point in arguing with him. The farther we traveled from our northern home by Big Ice Lake, the more withdrawn and angry my Uncle had become. His young wife, Grandfather and all my female relatives were worried about him.

I suppose in part I shared their concern, but I also understood his resentment. Finding the yellow rocks they valued so highly by the shores of our lake, the Chamuqwani's emperor sent his soldiers to force us from our homes. We had no choice but to go with them—or die.

And the harshest dregs of this bitter draft to swallow, was knowing that some of our own Qwani'Ya people, those blundering fools who had converted to the newcomers' religion, signed the emperor's treaty. And this treaty bound all Qwani'Ya People. They had given away, not only their own, but all our homelands, lands belonging to Convert and Traditional alike—forever.

"Uncle Tli is right to curse them," I said to my cousin Samiqwas. "The Tribal Preserve the Chamuqwani promised us seems to be nothing more than waterless brown hills of sage, rabbit brush and cactus. When I turned my head I could see the violet snow-capped peaks of the mountains we'd descended to come here, looking cool and inviting on the eastern horizon.

"And I'm baking in this heat," I grumped, wiping dust and sweat off my face with the cloth covering my nose and mouth.

Samiqwas snorted. "It's still winter, yet it's already hot and no snow. We're going to fry like bannock on a hot stone come summer," he complained.

I had no extra breath or the energy to lower the cloth I'd replaced over my nose and mouth and answer him, so I just shook my head and kept moving.

My people's Qwakaiva, our spiritual power, had always been immersed in the essence of water.

"Perhaps the ones who came for us didn't know how leaving our land would torment and shrivel our souls, maybe even the old drunkard of a priest in our community didn't understand," Grandfather said, as if thinking out loud.

"But the Chamuqwani god and his black sorcerers knew," I growled, glaring at him.

Like my former mentor Chumco, I believed with all my heart that the empire wished us dead, so that no power would be left to challenge their dominion over the land. And also I now knew to my own bitter regret that Chumco was right about other things...

We were at war with these strangers. And like a mewling pup whining after its mama's tit, I had heeded Grandfather's entreaties, abandoned my studies with Chumco and most likely forfeited my chance to help my people survive.

Allowing my unwary tongue to voice some of my thoughts, I heard myself say, "I wonder if they knew how much sending us to a desert land would break our spirits? Did their priests and rich lords plan so cunningly the torture above all others that would shatter our souls?"

"Wherever there is life there must be water, Grandson. And water is everywhere there is life. Lake, river or desert seep, we can drink from its Qwakaiva and grow strong," Grandfather said in a tired voice. He waved a hand vaguely in the direction of the gray and brown bushes through which the wagons were rolling. "These plants are dormant now but rain must give them life at times. We, too, will survive—even here."

Tli snorted with disgust. "Yes, look at those plants; most of them covered with thorns. Even they don't want us here."

For just a moment I saw the hurt in Grandfather's eyes, then he forced out a laugh. "I know that isn't much of a comfort, my children. My soul too feels as if it will shrivel up and blow away in this heat. But the water's Qwakaiva is here. I feel it flowing deep within the rock. With a little coaxing, it will come to us."

"And will Qwa'osi the Otter swim that dangerous underground water to come and lend you his Qwakaiva?" I couldn't resist taunting him.

"Water underground," Grandmother scoffed, "black water belonging to Kunai and his Aseutl relatives. Since when do you put your trust in those unpredictable creatures?"

Grandfather opened his mouth as if to argue, but dust swirled around his face and he coughed instead. Grandmother knew little of the ways of power, but there was some truth in her words. Most of our northern Qwakaiva was lost to us when we left the well-spring of our power by Big Ice Lake.

I stared at him incredulous. Did he actually believe he could call upon his soulmate Qwa'osi and draw The Otter's power from these deep pools under the earth? His eyes met mine for a moment then he looked away. Perhaps not. Perhaps the old man was only trying to cheer us, because he made no further comment on the subject. A hunter and fisherman born, that hot dry land must have challenged even his Qwakaihi's great power.

Examining him more closely for the first time in a long while, I saw how this terrible journey southward out of the mountains had aged his strong work-hardened body. A shiver of fear sliding down my backbone, I suddenly realized that my beloved grandfather had aged without my paying attention. He had transformed into a shrunken old man.

An old man who one day soon would die...

OUR USUAL ROUTINE ALONG the march was to stop in late afternoon. A cai herd beast would be slaughtered and rations handed out. This allowed the stragglers a chance to catch up before dark. But there were no more herd beasts to slaughter, hadn't been for several days, and that day we continued on long past our usual time for camping without the soldiers offering an explanation.

The sun was just sinking behind the purple mountains to the west, when we climbed a brushy slope and looked down at a muddy ribbon of water winding through a dusty valley. When asked, the soldiers told us this place was our final destination.

At the end of the trail we were following, was a Chamuqwani settlement and some fenced enclosures for their herd beasts. Maybe a half day's walk further down the creek, sprawled other encampments of tents and brush shelters. Like other encampments we'd seen on our way here, I was certain this one would be filled with ragged and hungry strangers. People from other tribes, speaking unknown languages, but like us, condemned to exile in this terrible place.

Like the settlements we'd passed before, the Willow Creek Agency proved to be nothing more than a cluster of log buildings set in the bend of a nearly dry streambed. I recognized among them a soldiers' barracks, a long building with a roofed porch, and some smaller structures which I later learned were the homes of the agency people.

Off to one side, the foundations of what looked to be the half-finished temple dedicated to Mighty Djoven the Thunderer squatted ominously in the shade of a few drooping trees. I shuddered and felt a knot of fear tighten in my gut. The lightning bolt emblem over the doorway, the symbol of the temple's power, had drawn my eyes like an evil charm.

Had the vision granted to Chumco by the Great Aseutl been true? In the back of my mind Chumco's departing laughter echoed, twisting the knot in my gut even tighter. I had been warned, but I had chosen and now was abandoned to face the enemy alone.

Swaying on my feet with thirst and exhaustion, I was too tired to worry about what retribution might befall me if the evils lurking within its walls discovered my presence. Only the need for water, food and sleep could hold my interest. None of which would soon be offered us, I discovered as our weary band arrived.

When we finally halted at the agency, a short Chamuqwani man with a large belly and a red face came hurrying from the long building that held the crown and crossed long knives of the Emperor's crest above the doorway. He took a long look at the convoy of wagons and ragged people stumbling along beside them and his face became even redder.

Shouting for the column to halt, Captain Mu'Dar, the commander of the soldiers who had guarded us on our journey, rode past us with some of his officers. The soldiers dismounted in front of the squat official and put fists to chest in a thumping salute.

Content to close my eyes and lean against the wagon nearest me, I would have probably fallen asleep where I stood, but a sharp jab in the ribs jolted me upright, my eyes flying open.

Samiqwas grinned and made a motion towards the head of the column. Grandfather and our headman Tsanqwati were pushing through the crowd with the rest of the Elders to hear what the soldiers and the agency officials were saying.

"Hurry up before Grandmother notices we are following," Samiqwas whispered.

Tired as I was, I reasoned that I was nearly a man-grown, so, I figured I had a right to be apart of such things. I was also just plain curious and didn't want to be left out.

As we huddled small behind the Elders, hoping not to be noticed and sent back to our female relatives, I peered from Grandfather's side and saw Captain Mu'Dar speaking to the fat little man. Tall and dark-skinned, Mu'Dar managed to look proud and commanding in spite of the dust of travel that coated his gray uniform. I knew him to be hard and ruthless when his rules were defied, but he was also an honorable and just man in his way.

He had followed his emperor's orders and forced us to leave the north, but he was also not a cruel man. Watching the red-faced official dressed in brown that was now yelling so disrespectfully, I wondered if we would fare better or worse if left here under his rule.

By this time other inhabitants of the agency were coming out of the buildings to gawk at us and listen to the shouting going on between the two men. A blue-robed priest and another high-ranking soldier dressed in brown joined the men's conversation.

The new soldiers at the agency wore brown uniforms with a blue lightning bolt on the right shoulder. These men had the blond hair and ruddy skin the paler Chamuqwani often get when exposed to hot sun for long periods of time. Lord Hiram's soldiers, who had brought us from the north, through the mountains and rolling farmlands to this place, wore gray uniforms. They had shared our hardships in some ways and knew our suffering. Even the most hardened among them I believe came to pity us before the journey ended.

I saw no compassion or understanding in these hard-faced men's eyes. To them we were no more than "filthy zaunks," ignorant, lazy, and bound to give them trouble if they showed us any kindness. Already we had come up against this attitude on our journey in the settled Chamuqwani country through which we had traveled.

Zaunk, I had no idea what this foreign word meant to them but they spoke it with contempt. It was an ugly word, and I hated the sound of it. When they flung it with all the power of a curse, I felt small and ashamed. The epithet stuck to my spirit like a leech on a white fish, sucking away my strength.

Samiqwas risked being noticed and gave me a lopsided grin. "That fat man doesn't look happy to see us."

"I'm not happy to see him either." I glanced around the dusty square; my throat was so dry that even the muddy water in that creek looked good

"Maybe he will make the captain send us home." There was a wistful note to Samiqwas's words as he said them, though I'm sure he knew that wasn't going to happen. "I would walk on bloody stumps if they would let us go back."

We will go back one day, I silently promised him.

Samiqwas looked at me strangely, as if he had heard my unspoken thought. He opened his mouth to say something more but never got the chance, because just then the argument was concluded, and then the soldiers drove us into some large corrals that not long before must have held herd beasts of some kind, the sand still littered with their dung.

As she stepped from the wagon my grandmother grabbed one of the soldiers' interpreters by his coat sleeve and demanded to know what the captain and the fat man were saying about us.

"That man is the youngest son of Lord Joper," the interpreter said to my grandmother and the crowd gathering around them to listen. "The Emperor, may he live long, has appointed him the new agent for this portion of the Tribal Preserve. He is angry because there are too many people here already and he doesn't have enough supplies and cai beasts for you here. He wants to send you further west, but Captain Mu'Dar says his orders were to bring you here so this is where he has brought you."

"What will they do now?" Someone asked.

The interpreter shrugged. "We will have to wait and see. Messages will be sent to the proper officials. They will speak to other officials and then other officials. Someone will decide and send word back here to tell the lord's son and the soldiers what to do."

"How long will that take," Grandmother demanded.

He shrugged and pulled out of her grasp, stepped out of the enclosure and slammed the gate closed. "Who can say? You must wait and see."

When settled in our pens for the night, we were given buckets of muddy water and hard-cake by the brown-clad soldiers. Now the sun had set and the chill of its absence enfolded the land. Tired people wrapped in their blankets lay beside smoky fires of animal dung, but the flames gave little protection from the chill. Wrapped in my dirty blanket I leaned against a fence post and opened my senses to the night around me and tried to rest.

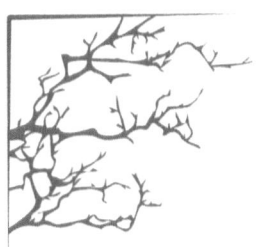

Chapter Two

With the sun next morning came a delegation of brown-skinned people dressed in dust-coated Chamuqwani clothing from one of the settlements up the creek. With the other Elders Grandfather left our smoldering cook fire to join Headman Tsanqwati in greeting these newcomers, hoping to learn what they could about the new land and the Chamuqwani stationed here.

More interested in the oat-mush starting to thicken in the tin pot resting on stones atop the hot coals, I ignored Samiqwas' suggestion to go exploring when he wandered over to our fire. Instead I settled myself near my mother and Grandmother, shaking my head. Samiqwas too glanced to the cook pot. He might have waited for me, sharing our meal, but a call from Matoqwa made him wave a farewell and move in that direction.

Samiqwas was my cousin and best friend. Until his mother, my aunt Tuulah, ran away with one of the Chamuqwani soldiers, he had lived in Grandmother's household like the rest of the family. Now that Tuulah was gone Samiqwas was spending more and more of his time with his father Ko and his paternal relatives. I missed him, but I saw the logic in his defection. Ko's widowed mother's health was failing. She had no daughters to care for her and a young strong boy would be a great help to those people.

Not long after he left, we were joined by Uncle Tli, his wife Shilshigua and their baby daughter. When the mush was done, my mother lifted the big tin can off the fire. Grandmother left a portion in the pot for my absent grandfather, then poured the rest of the can's contents into a wide shallow birch bark bowl to cool and sat it down between us.

Intent on quelling the ache in my belly with the tasteless steaming gray mass in Grandmother's bowl, I was only vaguely aware of either the excited cries of reunited family members or the ominous angry mutters, going on around me. Instead I focused on scooping the sticky mass of oat-mush onto my fingers and cramming it into my mouth, until Grandmother's soft words halted my gluttony.

"You must eat, my son."

Startled, I glanced at Uncle Tli squatting with his hands still resting upon his knees. Tli by nature was a tall lean man with piercing eyes and a sharp wit and tongue to match. But over the moons of our journey his naturally lean frame had become cadaverous in its thinness. I'd heard the women talking; they feared for his health if he didn't put on more weight soon.

Tli glanced around the fire and saw everyone looking at him. Reminded once again of their concern, he grimaced and muttered, "I will eat when it is time."

I glanced longingly at the depleted mound of mush, then at my uncle. Plastering what I hoped was a cheerful smile on my face. I licked my fingers clean and made sounds of enjoyment. "Mm, Grandmother, that was so good, but I am so full I cannot eat another mouthful. Thank you very much for the good meal." Murmurs of agreement came from mother and Shilshigua following my lead.

Tli gave me a sour scowl. He knew we were lying. But before he could voice a further protest, Shilshigua murmured in a soft, yet firm voice, "Please eat, my dear one." Tli grimaced as if the thought of food pained him, but under both his wife and mother's stern glares he reluctantly began to eat.

I was about to wander off to find Samiqwas and the rest of my friends when I caught sight of Grandfather returning to our fire with a stranger in tow. The man was short and thick-bodied like many Qwani'Ya people. He wore his black hair close-cropped in the Chamuqwani fashion. His patched and dusty woolen trews and jacket were also Chamuqwani. I could see little under his broad-brimmed hat, but there was something about his features that looked vaguely familiar.

Stopping beside Grandfather, he studied each of us for a moment, then took off his hat and smiled. "Hello, Amima." He nodded to his sister and brother, then his glance lingered for a moment on my face and his brown eyes widened. "And is that little Tas? My how you've grown. May the Thunderer be praised you made it here safely."

Grandmother stared in stunned silence with her mouth open for a long moment, hesitant and confused, then she rose silently to her feet. Letting out a strangled sob she held out her hands to him. Stepping to meet her he folded her trembling body into his arms.

On our way through the dry basin of this new Tribal Homeland we had come across other encampments of refugees and their soldier guards and imperial agents. It had never occurred to me before that moment that the camp we'd seen from the rise yesterday could be composed of northerners like ourselves. I should have guessed, and yet the knowledge came as an unwanted shock.

Then, without warning, I felt my temper ignite. Damn the converts and all the Emperor's men! If this barren rock valley had to be my home, I didn't want to share it with traitors. My own emotions in turmoil, I turned away from the family reunion and happened to catch a glimpse of Uncle Tli's scowling face.

He hadn't joined the others. But remained standing beside a worried Shilshigua, who held tight to their sickly daughter. The food we had coaxed him to eat a short time before seemed to have soured his digestion to judge from how he held a hand to his stomach. Our eyes met, and then the sending took me like a punch in the gut.

I staggered at its force, a pounding like horses' hooves thundering inside my skull. I heard war cries and somewhere the sound of women screaming. Then a fountain of red exploded across Tli's chest. Trembling I closed my eyes trying to blot out the vision, drive away the fear.

<<Kunai, please help me! Don't let such a bad thing happen.>>

Gasping for breath, I willed the vision to fade, and as it did, the ache in my head eased. I followed Tli's gaze back to the newcomer's face. So this man was my grandparents' eldest son, Uncle Da'wabin. While the women exchanged their greetings with the newcomer, I studied my Grandfather. Had he sensed the surge of Qwakaiva that had caused my Spirit Sending?

No, perhaps not. He seemed too intent on Tli's radiating hostility that Da'wabin, too, was slowly becoming aware of.

Like me and many others in the encampment Grandfather had heard the angry mutterings of those who planned vengeance against the headmen who signed the treaty, giving away our land.

In the stillness that settled like a heavy blanket of dread over our little group, I saw Shilshigua take her husband's arm, urging him to come away with her. Tli shrugged off her touch, and hissed something that caused her eyes to fill with unshed tears.

Disengaging himself from the women, Da'wabin's round face sobered as he slowly came around the fire to stand in front of his younger brother. Though younger in age Tli was the taller of the two, Da'wabin favoring the shorter, rounder proportions of Grandmother's lineage while Tli and Amima favored Grandfather's family.

"Well, little brother, have you no words of greeting for me?"

Tli folded his arms across his chest and glared down at his brother, red spears of rage shooting from his Spirit Fire. Grandfather must have been viewing Tli with his spirit sight, too. His own aura radiating concern, he took a cautious step in their direction.

Tli's smile was as cold as a blade made of glacier ice. "A greeting is it you want from me? I have no greeting to offer a traitor—save for that of a war spear in the gut."

Da'wabin stepped back surprised by the intensity of his brother's words. Then he flushed a deep purple. His hands balling into fists, he took a step closer to his still smiling adversary.

Before the brothers could come to blows, Grandmother let out a growl and charged between them like an angry mama bear. Her whole body quivering with emotion, she snarled, "Stop this right now. You are brothers—blood kin—and there will be no violence or bad words spoken between you. I will not allow it. Tli apologize."

Tli gaped in astonishment. "Apologize? Me?" A flush darkening his features he fell silent, his mouth opening and closing several times before he could force the words out once more. "Mother, if you care about our family—our people—how can you defend him? You know what he has done—"

"—Care about my family? How dare you speak to me so rudely!" she snapped. "It is because I care that I say that Da'wabin is your brother. That is all that is important."

"Well, not to me," Tli shot back. "One niece lying dead along the trail, the other and my older sister lost to our lineage—I say I have no brother. This traitorous convert malicer is no kin of mine, he has sold away your daughters' and granddaughters' inheritance. Amima, he is a traitor—to all the Qwani'Ya people. Can't you see that?"

"I am no traitor, you fool," Da'wabin cried. Trembling now with his own growing fury, Da'wabin swept his hand round to encompass their surroundings. "Open your eyes and look around you, brother, can't you see and understand the strength and might of these Chamuqwani?"

"Yes, I know their power. But that doesn't change the fact that you and the other treacherous converts didn't have the right to sell my birthright and that of my children for your own advantage. We could have fought them. Our Qwakaiva—"

Da'wabin let out a harsh laugh. "—Your Qwakaiva is nothing, little brother—nothing. The Chamuqwani Empire and its soldiers are too strong for us. We can't fight them. Living on Big Ice Lake you couldn't have seen—but I have. You wrong me and the other headmen down the Socanna River when you imply we signed away our homeland for our own selfish reasons."

"Do I? I think not. You only compound your guilt by lying."

Suddenly Da'wabin let go his anger, shaking his head his voice softened with sadness when finally he spoke. "No, Tli, you're wrong. But I suppose many of the Qwani'Ya people will think as do you. We had no choice. The Father-Emperor wants our gold. To resist would have meant death for all of us. Here in this new place at least the Chamuqwani will leave us alone. Here we have a chance to save ourselves—to build a new life for ourselves—survive."

Tli glanced from his brother to his mother's flushed face, finding no support. Next his gaze traveled to his father and saw only indecision in his eyes. His lip curled with disgust and he turned his back on them.

As he led his wife and daughter away, he flung back over his shoulder, "Da'wabin, if you think the Chamuqwani will leave us alone you are more the fool than you think me to be. "They will never stop until they have destroyed all that we are. "Your own conversion to their alien religion tells me that they will continue until we have lost not only the graves of our ancestors and our land, but the very souls of our children."

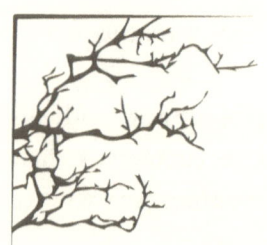

Chapter Three

After Tli was gone, my breakfast felt like it wanted to come spewing back up. I was angry, split in two, torn apart by the discord growing among my relatives. In the confusion I slipped away to find Samiqwas without telling anyone.

I found him at Matoqwa's family fire with our hunting pack of friends. I'm not sure what Samiqwas saw on my face as I approached, but he stood up quickly and hurried to meet me. Touching my arm, he murmured, "What's wrong, Tas, you look so—so—is anyone hurt or sick?"

Hurt? Sick? The family's harsh words whirled about in my head with images of a blood-covered Tli and a smiling Da'wabin, making it impossible for me to understand his meaning. Then in a voice that sounded frightened, even to my own ears, I heard myself say, "Uncle Da'wabin is here. He came with the people from up the creek. He and Uncle Tli almost got into a fight."

Samiqwas's eyes widened at that revelation. He would have liked to pester me until I told him everything, but I was given no time to explain in detail, for at that moment the gates were opened and the soldiers began shouting and gesturing with their thunder weapons for everyone to assemble in front of the Agent's office.

There was no time to wander about looking for mother or the rest of my family, so I hurried after Samiqwas and our friends as they dodged through the milling people, pushing and joking with each other. Halted at last by the press of bodies in front of me, I shifted my weight from one foot to the other, anxious and frightened of what might happen next.

A round ball of white fire Sun climbed some distance into the cloudless blue sky, while we sweated and waited in the dust. The air was thick with the smells of sage brush, horse dung and burnt kafa. Down by the creek desert doves called to one another in the branches of the willows.

Hoping to see familiar faces among the soldiers, I peered through the gaps in the crowd. All I saw were the red-faced men in brown uniforms that belonged to the agency. With a sinking feeling in my gut I suddenly realized that Captain Mu'Dar and his men were gone.

"That building with the long shaded porch, reminds me somewhat of the trading post back on Big Ice Lake," I heard Cohasi, Matoqwa's brother say.

Matoqwa snorted. "That fat man isn't going to give us any candy, though."

Samiqwas chuckled. "Not likely. Probably saves it all for himself."

Candy... As I stared through the open door into the agency post's dark interior, I fantasized I could hear Trader Jombonni's cheerful booming laugh. I smiled to myself thinking of the many times back home his son Kutima and I had stolen candy from the store's wooden barrels and gotten away with it.

But my happy musings shattered when two soldiers pushed through the entrance, carrying a heavy wooden table between them. They set the table beside the door, then went back inside for chairs and the big books like I'd seen Trader Jombonni and his clerks use. When all was in order, the agent we learned was named Daglish, flanked by the blue robed priest Intercessor Karl and the red-haired Commander Forggal, stepped out onto the porch to speak to us.

The heat, the dust, the grim-faced men, nothing here was like home. How could I have imagined such foolishness, even for a moment? I had no home. And my family...?

Intercessor Karl, a middle-aged man with a big nose and stern lines about his mouth shouted for quiet in our language. As the people settled, the big-bellied agent wiped his sweaty face with a dirty cloth he took from his pocket and turned to a sullen breed-man with sly eyes named Abe, standing at his side. Speaking through this interpreter, Agent Daglish said, "The land in this portion of the Tribal Preserve has been allotted to all the Northern peoples and a few of the desert bands native to this land."

"Stupid Chamuqwani," Matoqwa muttered. "Those wolf clan People living by the Copper River Falls aren't even our relatives. We can barely understand them."

"Shut up, dog fart," Samiqwas hissed, "before someone hears you. The Father-Emperor and his soldiers don't care about the opinions of a zaunk boy or his relatives. Haven't you figured that out yet?"

That the Chamuqwani considered all the people living along the Socanna River and her lakes, deer people, fish people, wolf people, to be the same frustrated not only me and my friends but our Elders as well. Time and time again we had tried to explain to these ignorant southerners, but they just didn't listen. To the Emperor and his rich lords, living in their far away villages we were all the same, savages and "filthy zaunks."

Matoqwa's scarred face darkened and he raised a threatening fist. Samiqwas grinned and dodged. Things might have progressed to a friendly tussle, but Aunty Qwatsitsa told them to be quiet so she could hear the fat man, and they immediately stopped and apologized, their expressions sliding into ones of innocent attentiveness

"...As the cai and building supplies promised in the treaty arrive," the interpreter was saying, "you will be given your share. Your children will be registered and attend the new school that will be built for you. There they will learn to read, write and the other skills that will help them become prosperous citizens of the Empire.

"It is my hope that you will all work hard and appreciate the gifts and opportunities you are being given by the Father-Emperor and Lord Joper."

Looking with my spirit sight I could see gray and muddy streaks of color churning in the Spirit Fires of these stern officials. My stomach knotted with fear, my mouth suddenly dry. This soft big-bellied man with his petulant mouth and watery blue eyes was lying about something.

"What supplies will the Father Emperor be sending us?" An Elder from Broken Shell Mound village wanted to know. "There is not much water here. How long must we wait?"

"You must wait and see," was the repeated response, no matter the question directed at the menon the porch.

Impatient with the endless stream of talk, finally Agent Daglish made a cutting motion with his hand and the interpreter announced that there would be no more time for questions that day. "Everyone must line up now and be registered in the agents big book," Abe said.

As our names were entered on the tribal roles, the male head of each family would receive a metal disk hung on a cord that was printed with a number. Abe warned us not to lose or trade these disks, because the father of the family would have to show the disk on every ration day or no rations of food or supplies would be granted—no matter how dire the family's need.

Though we'd been expecting some such, this news too rankled, because unlike Chamuqwani custom, among the Qwani'Ya peoples it was the women who were the heads of their families. The Elders had tried to explain this to the government officials many times in the past, but they never seemed to listen to that, either. Things would be done the Chamuqwani way and no other, and that was that.

"Their ignorance is boundless, and they are proud of it," I heard Grandmother say in disgust. "Every sensible person knows that children belong to their mothers. And it is only logical to inherit from your female relatives."

"After your family is enrolled," Abe continued, "then you will receive several days' food rations and other camping supplies. Behave yourselves and do what you are told, for you must still walk to your allotted area and set up your shelters or you will spend the night with the coyotes and the rattlesnakes out in the cold."

"Who wants to go to land where the converts are," a young man shouted. "I'd rather sleep out with the animals than spread my blanket next to that of a traitor."

The voice wasn't Uncle Tli's but it sounded familiar. There were several murmurs of agreement to that thought and I craned my head to try and see who had spoken. Tli was standing with his brother-in-law Chugai, Matoqwa's older brother Qwati and several more young men. Tli said something I didn't catch and the whole group began laughing.

Turning away from them to hide my own smile, I noticed that Commander Forggal had taken note of my uncle and his friends, too, and he didn't look happy about what he was seeing. Calling the interpreter over to him, the commander said something to him and the interpreter nodded.

His lips curving into a mean smile, Abe stepped to the edge of the porch and raised his voice to be heard. "The Captain says you young buckies can sleep anywhere you like, but don't stray far from the agency. Every seven days every man must return here to pick up supplies for his female relatives and children or they will starve."

Uncle Tli and his friends stopped laughing and stood glaring at the interpreter. Abe swallowed and glanced back at the commander for assurance. He received a nod and Abe's smile widened.

"You must do this to assure the soldiers that you haven't run away. If you try to run away, the soldiers will come after you and shoot you with their thunder weapons. Then you can sleep with the buzzards. Maybe you would like that, eh?" Abe laughed loudly at his own joke—though no one but he thought it was funny.

While still trying to absorb all this new information, soldiers began bawling orders and shoving confused people into a semblance of an orderly line. Whispering to Samiqwas that we should probably get back to our family, I turned and began slipping through the milling people looking for mother and Grandmother. I thought Samiqwas was right behind me, but when I turned to joke with him about how funny the priest's big nose was, I found he hadn't followed me.

Surprised, I started back to look for him, and then I spotted him standing with his father and his paternal grandmother. I wanted to run up to him and ask him why he was fooling around. Grandmother would be angry with us both if we didn't hurry.

He saw me and I motioned with my chin for him to come. For the briefest moment he met my eye, then he turned, said something to his father and ignored me. the revelation of what his actions meant hit me like a rock between the eyes. Feeling as though the world was coming apart around me, I staggered against Aunty Qwatsitsa and nearly fell.

Grabbing my shoulder to steady me, the old woman looked into my eyes, frowning with concern. "Are you all right, boy? Did one of those soldiers hit you?"

My throat suddenly choked with grief and unable to speak, I shook my head and lurched away to find my mother. In this new order that the Chamuqwani were imposing upon us, Samiqwas was no longer a part of my family. He belonged to his father and his paternal relatives.

And what of me? what would happen to me—and Amima? She had no husband. And the Qwa'Nayhi Seal man who had fathered me was hardly likely to appear in this desert to enrol his name in the agent's big book.

In spite of my fear for our future, the image of Star Swimmer rising out of the muddy water in the creek, violet light shooting from the tips of his flippers, destroying all the soldiers' weapons, then calmly shape-shifting into human form and asking to be enrolled as the head of the family in Agent Daglish's big book, such a ludicrous fancy made me want to laugh, even as the tears pooled in the corners of my eyes.

"There you are, Grandson, come stand with us while we wait our turn," Grandfather said.

When I looked in the direction the voice had come from, I saw Amima and Grandmother standing with Grandfather and Uncle Da'wabin. I hurried over to them, taking my place by my mother's side. She must have read the concern in my eyes when I glanced up into her face, because she gave me a reassuring smile and smoothed the tangled hair off my forehead.

"Don't worry, my son, for now we will go with your grandparents to live near uncle Da'wabin."

"But what about Samiqwas, and, and Uncle Tli, Amima? Where will they go?" Mother shook her head and squeezed my shoulder for silence.

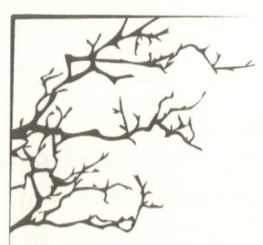

Chapter Four

With Uncle Da'wabin there to help us through the process, our enrolment and ration collecting went smoother than it did for other families that day. Then, it was another dusty walk in the heat and the sagebrush to the convert settlement up the creek.

As I trudged along behind Amima and Grandfather, with the blanket roll and sack containing a share of our supplies over my shoulder, a shiver of dread touched me. Over and over, I heard in my mind the new Chamuqwani name I had been given by the agent.

From then on I was to be called Martin by everyone, Martin Fishspear. Mar'teen. Ma'ar'tin. I repeated the name under my breath, trying out its sound. But no matter how I pronounced the foreign-sounding word, it left a chill in my heart. It felt to me as if by naming me anew, the Chamuqwani magic had stolen away a part of my soul.

Martin. Like slime clinging to lake weed I didn't like its alien sound, and I wanted to know what my new name meant. But when I had asked in my best Chamuqwani, the man writing the name down in the big book shook his head impatiently and the soldier standing by the table frowned and motioned for me to move along.

How could the priest or the new agent know what kind of person I was, by just looking at me? Was the priest's Qwakaiva that strong? Had he fasted and prayed and been gifted with that knowledge? I doubted it. That wasn't the Chamuqwani way. And the men seemed to be laughing and joking among themselves too much to be giving the naming the respect such a sacred duty deserved.

I knew enough of their language to know they thought the names only as an amusing way to get through the long tedious process of registering so many people. They cared little for the meaning behind their words, a meaning that would echo down the generations for those afflicted with its power.

If a person's personal or family name didn't translate into their language well, someone chose one for him. Samiqwas became Sammy Mushy, his father Ko became Joh Mushy. Matoqwa was now Peter Blueshirt and his brother Cohasi was Tony Blueshirt.

We had been fortunate, I suppose, because Uncle Da'wabin had gone through this ceremony moons before and had had time to choose his family name carefully. He had claimed for himself a word in the Chamuqwani tongue that had meaning and Qwakaiva. And being related to him through Grandfather, Amima and I, too, became part of the Fishspear lineage.

The converts had settled nearest the agency in a ragged line along the river. Having been here the longest they had had time to begin building mud and stone houses for themselves under the shade of the trees. Sprawled further out along the valley floor the waterless land was available to the newcomers without convert kin already here. Or for those wishing to live apart from the ones they believed to be the traitors of our people.

The Fishspear settlement sheltered within a grove of cottonwood trees in a favored spot by the river. It consisted of a collection of smaller shelters clustered about their chief's house, a larger dwelling of mud and stone with a roof of dry grass. Nearby another larger half-finished building squatted with a symbol of the god's lightning bolt painted above the framed doorway.

Our approach was noticed and by the time we reached Uncle Da'wabin's encampment, people in the nearby dwellings had stopped what they were doing and gathered with the rest of uncle's family to stare at us. All these people proudly displayed upon their chests the metal lightning bolt emblem of the Thunderer's followers.

When I looked at these strangers with my Qwakaiva I saw no hostility, only curiosity, but their gaze slowed my steps, making me shy. I wished it had been night when we arrived, so we could have just crept into the village and settled in without drawing such interest.

Uncle Da'wabin saw me looking at the squalid collection of tents and brush-covered lodges that made up the bulk of the settlement, and came over to me. I'm not sure what he read in my expression, but he plastered a smile upon his face, and said, "Martin, I know our new home doesn't look like much now. But when the supply wagons come in the spring with our treaty goods, we will all have fine houses of flat wood boards painted red with glass windows. Just like the Chamuqwani dwellings you must have seen on your journey here."

Still smiling he put an arm about my shoulder and began walking towards the large unfinished dwelling. "You would like that, wouldn't you? Won't it be grand to live in a house with fine glass windows, so you can see everything even when it's too hot, or cold to go outside?"

Live in a house with glass windows? I had never considered such a novelty before and the prospect neither excited nor dismayed me. To please this uncle I barely knew, I smiled and nodded, but secretly I wondered why things like glass windows meant so much to him.

Da'wabin's family, or Uncle Royston as I must remember to call him, stepped forward from the onlookers as we halted. Two women with similar features dressed in black shawls, long blue skirts and puffy sleeved shirts in the Chamuqwani fashion, smiled and held out their hands in greeting.

One had grey beginning to show in the twisted knot of black hair she wore on the top of her head. The other a younger version of her mother had bright bird's eyes and a wide mouth. Uncle introduced them to us as his wife Marika and her mother Tani.

The stern hawk-nosed man with sloping shoulders and scarred hands by the older woman's side was uncle's father-in-law Eagan and the agent's appointed headman for this group of about a hundred people. The frown that seemed to permanently drag down the corners of his mouth, deepened into a scowl when he was introduced to Grandfather.

There were many more in-laws lined up and introduced, but I lost track, their faces and names a confused blur in the growing heat of the afternoon. None of the children were presented to us except for Royston's young son Hathin, a three year old with green snot dripping from his nose, and his daughter, Thonna, a tall bony girl of about my own age with her mother's wide mouth and sullen dark eyes.

The mauve shadows of the cottonwoods were long across the dry ground when greetings over, we were shown to a well-made shelter thatched with grass. Announcing that the evening meal would be served in the chief's unfinished house, they left us to settle in and rest.

Uncle also told us that the morning and the evening meals the family cooked and ate together. We would also be expected to show up for the prayers preceding the meal. I saw the surprise in my grandparents eyes when Royston implied that Eagan, who had control of all our rations, allowed no person to be fed unless they were present for the grace.

When Uncle and his wife were out of sight Grandmother dropped her blanket bundle and snarled, "Refuse to feed hungry relatives! Who does this ugly old man think he is to order others about like disobedient children?"

Grandfather sighed and set down his own pack. I could see the orange flames of irritation swirling about in his Spirit Fire, but his words to us when he spoke were calm and controlled.

"For our son's sake, my dear one, let it be. We are newcomers here. We must be patient like the fox by a mouse hole until we know more about this place and what will be expected of us."

Grandmother snorted and sat down by the empty fire pit, giving him a disgusted look. Someone had thoughtfully supplied our new lodge with a mound of dry grass, gray sage and rabbit brush. During their talk mother had been busily shaping the softest of this vegetation into a low platform on which to lay the old people's blankets. She looked up and studied her parents thoughtfully.

"Ati, I see the wisdom in your reasoning, but I also saw how my brother's father-in-law looked at us—especially you. We aren't his relatives and I think he doesn't like the idea of us being here at all."

"He makes me feel uncomfortable," I added. "Maybe we should find Tli and live with him—" I broke off speaking when I saw a scowl cross Grandmother's face.

During the registration ceremony that morning, Uncle Tli had refused to acknowledge his father or brother. Remaining hostile and silent when the agent spoke to him, Tli was given the name Jimmy Shoeless instead of being acknowledged as a part of our Fishspear lineage.

Grandfather patted Grandmother's shoulder in a comforting gesture, before she could rebuke me for interrupting. "It is too soon to consider moving even though Eagan does seem like a hard man. Perhaps once we get to know each other all will be well, Grandson. Don't worry."

"I'd rather live with Tli," I muttered as I shook out my own blankets.

I hadn't meant to speak loud enough for anyone to hear, but apparently I had, because Grandmother snapped, "Well, it isn't up to you, so be quiet, rude boy."

Startled I looked up. Both the old people were frowning at me, so I murmured a hasty apology and went back to fussing with my blankets. When I had my bed to my liking, I lay upon my blankets and studied Grandmother with my Qwakaiva through half-closed eyes. Seeing the tremors of grey uncertainty in her spirit fire, I realized that in spite of her angry words earlier she didn't want to leave the convert settlement.

Maybe she had missed her oldest son and welcomed this chance to be near him again. And in spite of the barrier of Uncle's new religion that had grown between them maybe Grandfather missed his son too and was willing to compromise.

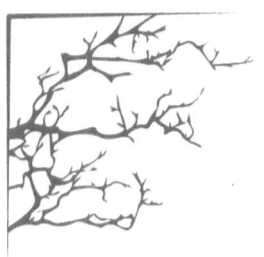

Chapter Five

The crier shouted for the people to come eat as the evening stars grew bright in the night sky. Huddled in my blanket, I trudged after the others into the stone house and sat next to mother and the others gathered around the central hearth. To conserve fuel the fire was small, giving off only a weak glow and little warmth. Blue smoke wafted lazily upwards to disappear among the shadows.

When we were all present and seated, Eagan, with a ragged blue priest's scarf draped about his neck, stood. Thonna, sitting on my other side, jabbed me in the ribs with her elbow and mouthed something I didn't catch.

"Don't do that, stupid girl," I snared under my breath.

"We're going to pray now, stupid boy."

"I knew that, stupid girl."

"Oh really? Well, you'd better bow your head before my grandfather sees you. He likes to smack disrespecting heathens upside the head."

There was a gloating tone to her whisper that made me think she might enjoy seeing the old man hit me. Hastily I ducked my head and folded my hands upon my chest like everyone else.

His eyes focused upon the silver stars poking through a gap in the roof, Eagan raised his hands above his head, and intoned, "Oh, Mighty Djoven, Lord of the Heavens, have pity on the poor sinners gathered here tonight to give thanks for your bounty and praise your holy name."

Give thanks for the god's bounty? Not hardly. If the Thunderer was so great and powerful, then why didn't we have more to eat than lumpy mush? I'll thank him with all my heart if he gives me nice fat moose meat to eat, I thought, feeling miserable, and sorry for myself.

Grandfather Eagan's prayer droned on and on, but I didn't listen. I tried to curb my impatience and keep from fidgeting. Then my rebellious stomach grumbled in complaint. Thonna stifled a giggle at the sound, and I felt the heat rise into my face. Several people stared in my direction, displeased by the interruption.

Much to my relief, Eagan finally lowered his hands to his chest in conclusion. The Converts murmured, "Amen'neh," in response as the old man sat. At last Marika and her mother rose to pass around the food. All this praying seemed like a lot of fuss for a couple spoons of lumpy gruel and a few fried strips of the very salty meat the Chamuqwani called bac'con. Conversation I discovered wasn't permitted at mealtime, so I ate my share along with the rest in silence, longing for more.

Before we were dismissed for the night, however, the old man singled out my family for his vitriolic attention. Looking Grandfather in the eye, he said, "I have yielded to my son-in-law's entreaties and will allow you to remain among us. An old man and his wife, an unmarried daughter and her bastard son alone in this harsh land, the Mighty Thunderer considers charity a virtue when not overly indulged.

"But you need to understand that we are a moral, god-fearing community and I won't tolerate any heathen conjuring or loose sexual morals among my people. Do you understand me?" Eagan's stare shifted from Grandfather to mother.

Mother's mouth dropped open in surprise, a rosy flush mottling her cheeks. She spoke not a word, respecting our traditions by not arguing with an Elder, but that prohibition didn't apply to *her* mother.

Grandmother had turned an even deeper shade of red than her daughter. And being an Elder herself, she spoke her mind as always. "Insulting your guests like an ignorant Chamuqwani, didn't the women of your lineage teach you any manners? You know nothing about the women of my family. How dare you say such hateful things about my daughter?"

"The Mighty Thunderer teaches that a woman's place is to be silent and serve men. I will expect you to hold your tongue in future, woman," Eagan roared. "And as for your daughter's morals she has no husband and I can see the fruit of her fornication sitting beside her."

Fornication? Mother and I exchanged puzzled looks. That Chamuqwani word was unknown to us, but the old man's tone implied that it meant something shameful.

Eagan might have said more cruel things, but Uncle Royston cut in, "Father-in-law, please don't judge my sister so harshly. She is a good woman. Once she has had the opportunity to hear the teaching of the true god she will see the error of her past sins and repent of her weaknesses."

Grandfather rose, pulling Grandmother and mother up with him. Hiding in the adult's shadow I scrambled to my feet. In a quiet and controlled voice, Grandfather addressed our tormentor, "We have no wish to bring disharmony into this settlement. If you wish us to leave, so be it. In the morning we will take our share of the rations that were collected in our name and find another place on this Preserve to live."

Take back our share of the food? I saw the horrified expression that passed between Marika and her mother at that pronouncement. The older woman jabbed Uncle in the ribs and he rose to follow us out into the night.

"No, Father, don't do that. The honored Elder didn't mean that at all." Royston's words tumbled out of his mouth as he tried to keep up with us and explain at the same time. "It's just we have rules here. We all share our food and supplies and pray together—like in the old days.

"Everyone must work if they wish to eat, and there is no drinking waskyja or fornicating—having a sexual contact with someone who isn't their partner in the God's holy marriage. This is a good way to live—surely you can see that? Please don't go. I truly want you to stay."

We had reached our grass hut by this time. Mother hurried inside without a word, but the old people turned back to face him. In the dim light Uncle's smile was tentative, a pleading in his eyes when he studied his parents' faces.

"I will speak to my father-in-law. You will see; everything will be all right. Don't do anything rash, please."

Grandfather breathed in and let his breath out in a long sigh. "We will talk more in the morning, son, then we will see. Good night."

I caught the glint of tears in Grandmother's eyes as she patted her son's hand and followed her husband into the hut. Royston let out a long sigh of his own and headed back to the warmth and laughter coming from the stone house.

Fearful of Eagan or Uncle's regard, I slunk off to gather fuel for our night's fire as soon as it was safe to come out of the shadows where I'd been hiding. The spectre of these people's god followed me out into the darkness.

The skin on the back of my neck tingled as I picked up abandoned sticks among the rocks. Cradling the bundle in my arms, I sensed the regard of unfriendly eyes watching me. Already I knew I wasn't going to like living in this place.

When I returned with the last armful of brush, the old people were rolled in their blankets across from the tiny fire mother was nursing in its stone circle. Hoping not to wake my grandparents I lowered the wood softly to the ground near the hearth and went to sit by mother.

Studying her face in profile for a time in the flickering light, I finally worked up the courage to voice some of my fears. "Amima, I don't want to live here with Uncle Royston. Can't we go live with Uncle Tli and Shilshigua—or just by ourselves with Ami and Ati?"

She let out a low chuckle and tousled my hair, pulling me close. "It may come to that, my little Rock Squirrel, but life might not be any better if we did move away."

"I don't see how that could be possible. That hateful old man said terrible things about you—he's a devil—and Uncle Tli would—"

"Hush now, my son. Eagan did say terrible things, but we may have to put up with many irritations to avoid worse suffering."

"I don't understand; like what?"

"Think, Tas, we are two old people, a boy and an unmarried woman. Without the help of our kin or a strong man to hunt for us and protect us how will we survive, hmm?"

"Grandfather is—"

"Is an old man, son, haven't you noticed? Our journey here has drained him of much of his Qwakaiva. He gave all he had to help the People along the way. Now his strength and health are failing. He can't hunt for our food, or take care of us. We have to take care of him—both the old people, don't you see?"

Well, actually I hadn't noticed, hadn't wanted to think of our situation in that way before. Her words twisted a knot in my gut, but I could see the truth in her words, now that she'd called my attention to our situation.

Grandfather, Grandmother, they were old—maybe old beyond their years, and we were responsible for their care. A part of my mind still didn't want to recognize that fact. I still wanted to have things like they'd been back home—never changing.

I hated this new hostile world that had ensnared us like a wolverine trap in its steel jaws. It was grinding the life from our souls. Without much expectation of success, I tossed out my last argument, hoping to sway her.

"But I'm nearly a man grown, Amima, if we leave here and go find Uncle Tli I can hunt with him and take care of you and the old people."

She gave me a warm but pitying smile. "I know you would like to do just that, my son. Your heart is strong, but in body you are still too young for a man's responsibilities. And Tli—Tli... I pray for him and Shilshigua every day. He is a very troubled man, and right now he has his own path and his own burdens. He isn't strong enough to handle any more, I fear. No, unless we have no other choice, we can't ask this of him."

I wasn't sure I agreed with her. Like most children my own concerns were of most importance to me, so I grumbled, "But it's so terrible here."

She chuckled and kissed my forehead. "I know, my dear one. So, you must be strong—like a man, hmm?"

Whatever she saw in my face brightened the teasing light in her eyes. "Go to sleep, son, and don't despair. Who knows, I might find a new husband to my liking and move us far away from these people and their angry god. Would you like that, my little Rock Squirrel, hmm?"

"Yes, I would—and don't call me that baby name any more, Amima!"

She rose and headed for her blankets. "Oh, sorry, I forgot."

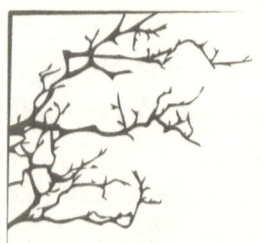

Chapter Six

The next morning I was still tired when mother woke me to gather brush and dung for the morning fire. The upsetting confrontation of the night before wasn't mentioned at breakfast—or later. Everyone pretended that it never happened. Dark currents of fear and mistrust might be churning in the depths of our souls, but on the surface people smiled and made an effort to get along.

After hauling water from the creek to the cook fire, I headed back to the creek with a pouch of throwing stones and a coil of nettle twine wrapped about my arm, looking for something edible. That morning's half dipper of mush left me feeling grumpy and still hungry. I craved the taste of meat. Like a ravenous wolf I longed to sink my teeth into rich bloody flesh and gorge myself till my belly was near bursting.

I snorted a laugh at such a fancy, then rubbed a finger across my aching gums and spat out a mouthful of blood. Sink my teeth into anything tougher than hard-cake soaked in tea and they might fall out.

Well, I didn't have to worry; there were no moose or caribou in this dry hot place. And even if there were, I had no bow or thunder weapon to kill such prey. No, I would have to settle for rabbit, grouse, or even gophers—if I could find them. If boiled into a nice thick broth, I thought I could manage to chew such dainty prey.

The eastern sun was warm upon my back, the sky overhead as blue as glacier ice. The air was dry and chill carrying little but the musty odours of last summer's lifeless vegetation and creek mud. I ambled along the stream, searching for likely spots to set my snares. In the distance I could hear the noises of the settlement, but here by the shallow creek I felt the tensions of the camp draining away into the earth.

I found a few likely spots for my snares, set them, then waded the creek at a muddy shallow ford, and headed up the other side to the sage and rabbit brush covered rocky land beyond. Constant hunger had stolen away my strength; I'd been walking for a while by then and I was tired. As I climbed the farther bank, I cut strips of bark from a cottonwood shrub and stuffed them into my mouth, chewing slowly till they became a gluey mass. I was so hungry....

Finding a sandy spot in the sun at last, I sat down and focussed my Qwakaiva. <<Oh, Guardians of this land,>> I prayed. <<Have pity on a stranger. Bless my hunt. Let me bring back food for my People.>>

As I finished, a soft breeze touched my face, bringing with it the smell of sage and juniper. I felt content; some kindly Spirit had heard my prayer.

As I sat waiting for the little ones to find my snares and make their gift to me, my mind wandered and the sadness and worry I'd earlier felt returned. What had happened to Uncle Tli; was he safe and well? Where was Samiqwas? The one who had always been my best friend and companion, I deeply missed him most of all.

With him beside me, living with Uncle Royston's in-laws wouldn't be half so bad, I decided. But he belonged to his father's kin now. I felt lost without him by my side.

Where were they, those missing ones I loved...? Without consciously being aware of what I was doing, I took the woven cord from around my neck and looped it over my hands in the familiar string pattern of "The Seer's Pool." Mother had given me the cord after Grandfather forced me to end my studies with Chumco. It was braided from a mixture of her own and my father's hair, and so had a special significance to me.

To those unaware of its power, it appeared no different than any other looped cord children amused themselves with by making string figures. Just a child's toy, but under my mentor's tutelage, I had learned to focus my Qwakaiva and conjure something magic. In its patterns I could see images of people and events from a far.

My longing calling him, an image of Samiqwas easily formed in the centre diamond of the pattern...

He was somewhere out on the flatland to the east of the agency. Arms full of sticks and grass, he walked towards a smoky fire. Behind him I saw a ragged canvas lean-to with someone lying wrapped in a blanket under its shade—probably his paternal grandmother, she wasn't well. His father Ko sat by the fire, drinking something in a battered tin cup.

As I watched, Ko's brother Gagayii and two men I didn't know joined him. Seeing Samiqwas tore at my heart, but I also felt relief, knowing he was safe. I allowed the cord to slip from my hands, releasing the magic. Then, I reformed the pattern anew. What of Uncle Tli, how was he fairing...?

Tli's camp was to the north, much farther away from the agency and the converts' settlements along the creek. His wife Shilshigua and their stick-thin baby girl were sitting by a smoky fire, eating some kind of boiled roots. A bunch of her relatives camped nearby. The land they'd chosen looked desolate and barren compared to the lush growth of Uncle Royston's settlement. With only brush lean-tos and dirty ragged blankets to protect them from the night's chill, they looked forlorn and miserable.

As I watched, Tli approached his wife's shelter, carrying a skin bucket of water. Walking beside him, Chugai hauled a similar burden. Skeletally thin, his steps were slow and laboured, but at last Tli hung his burden on a tripod of poles, then doubled over coughing. The spectral image of Death's Raven perched on the lean-to's cross pole, eyeing both Tli and his daughter hungrily. Like a blow to my gut, a wave of anger and pain slammed into my body from the sending. The truth of my mother's words hit me like a flung stone. Truly, Tli wasn't well.

"What are you doing?"

I jerked as if I'd been stung by an insect, then gasping I fell forward over my legs, the string falling from my hands, its magic shattered. Still gulping for air, I looked up. My new coshelah cousin Thonna was standing with her hands on her hips staring at me. I blinked and took a deep breath to calm my pounding heart. In a voice that shook only a little, I demanded, "What are you doing here? Were you following me?"

She continued to stare, her head cocked like a bird, an amused smile, playing about her wide mouth. "Maybe."

"Well don't do it—ever again," I snapped.

"Or you'll do what?"

"I'll, I'll—" By the ancestors of my lineage what would I do? Nothing really, though an annoying girl, she was coshelah to me, my sort-of cousin by marriage. I couldn't abuse my gift and harm her. Her speaking to me so abruptly had caused me pain when I was ripped from the trance so abruptly, but it was my own fault for not creating a shield to protect myself—not hers.

"Oh don't look so murderous, little coshelah cousin. Mostly I needed a break from babysitting, so when I saw you on the other side of the creek, I crossed to see what you might be doing." She reached for the cord lying on the ground between us. "So what were you doing, hmm?"

Just before her fingers would have touched it, I snatched the cord and hastily pulled it over my head and tucked it safely under my tunic. "I wasn't doing anything interesting, just making string figures like the Raven's Nest and Sled Dog Running—just passing time."

She cocked her head again and studied me with one eye closed. An image of a northern jay peered at me from the luminous swirls in her Spirit Fire. "Oh? I've never seen someone making the string patterns become so oblivious to his surroundings. I wasn't sneaking up on you, you know? I was just walking normally. You should have heard me."

"Well, I didn't. Maybe I was asleep—or nearly so." Before she could ask me more uncomfortable questions, which I would have to refuse to answer, I stood. "Come on. I set some snares in the willows down by the water. Let's see if the Spirits of this land have blessed my hunt."

Her eyes widened at the mention of Spirits, but she willingly followed me down to the creek. "Don't let Father or Grandfather Eagan hear you talking about heathen spirits, or you'll get a beating," she taunted.

Feeling the flush darkening my face, I spun round, making her step back wide eyed. "And are you going to tell them?"

Thonna hesitated, then grinned. "Not if your hunt is successful." Stepping past me, she lifted her skirt and waded the creek, leaving me staring at the ropy braids hanging down her back. Reaching the other side, she glanced back over her shoulder, a ghost of a smile still playing about her lips. "Well, what are you waiting for? Come along."

Much to my relief, we found two rabbits and a small brown bird for which I had no name, in my snares. I doubted if Thonna would have actually told her father of my prayers to the Spirits if the snares had been empty, but I knew so little of her nature, I was glad not to have to test that assumption.

We were talking companionably together as we took the well-worn trail to the settlement, when suddenly four boys popped up out of the brush in front of us, blocking our way.

My head half turned, I'd been telling her a joke, when I saw a startled look cross her face. I jerked round, then without thinking I thrust the thong holding our meat into her hands and stepped in front of her.

"Well, well, brothers, what have we found here? Could it be a dung-eating heathen savage?" A pale-skinned boy in ragged Chamuqwani cast-offs growled.

They were silhouetted against the light, so I didn't recognize them at first, but by his voice alone I knew him. These convert boys were the same ones that had tried to push me into the shitter back in the Fort Protection stockade when we'd been waiting to march south. At that time, Matoqwa Samiqwas and Cohasi had come to my rescue. When they'd showed up at my back, these gutless cowards hadn't liked the odds and had slunk off.

Now, however, I was alone....

"What are you doing here, witch boy?" The stocky full-blood boy raised his fist and shook it at me. "We don't want any slime of a heathen smelling up our homes, so it's time you got out of here."

Ah, I remembered that one too. I'd been surprised that a full-blood of the People could hold such anger in his heart to one of his own kind. I sighed, mentally preparing myself for the beating I was sure to come. "What am I doing here? I live here, same as you, apparently."

A mean smile curving his cracked lips, the breed boy said, "Not for long, though."

Fists ready, I stared at each boy in turn. I was angry now, a cold rage filling my veins with ice water. "I remember you from the stockade. Even then it took the four of you banding together to find enough courage to attack one boy alone." I pulled my lips back into a wolfish grin. "Come on, see if you can do it right this time."

My show of bravado startled them. The smallest of the four took a step backward, then caught himself and resumed his place. I didn't care what happened to me by then. My fear, my hunger, my loneliness all sought an outlet in violence. I wanted blood—theirs—mine, I was beyond caring.

"If you have a problem with my coshelah cousin living in our settlement, you'd better take it up with my father, Charlic," Thonna shouted.

"Coshelah?" That gave them pause. The breed boy's eyes widened.

As fierce as a mama bear protecting her cubs, Thonna had tossed our rabbits into the willows and come up to stand beside me. "That's right, you big pile of dog shit, he's my cousin, so, are you calling my family dung-eating, heathen savages, Charlic, Kiethrap? Well if you are, then you'll have to fight me, too."

Inwardly I groaned. Out of the corner of my mouth, I growled, "Coshelah, don't—please—you are only making things worse. Go back—stay out of this."

She snorted and remained where she was. "And let them beat you? No way, stupid boy."

"It's written in the Holy God's big book that women and girls should be silent and know their place—or be beaten till they learn a woman's proper behaviour," Charlic declared, glaring at Thonna.

Thonna bristled and might have thrown the sharp-edged rock she picked up, if the full-blood she'd called Kiethrap hadn't chimed in, "We don't want to hurt you, chief's granddaughter, but you don't understand how truly evil this witch boy is. He likes to insult the God's holy women and he and his grandfather placed a curse on the Good Intercessor Raymonel and made him ill."

Thonna turned to me with eyes wide. "Did you really?"

From the tone of her voice I couldn't tell if she was awed or horrified by the prospect of my power. Either way, my gut twisted at the thought of trying to answer that accusation. So, instead I kept my attention focused on their leader, the breed Thonna named Charlic.

The wolfish grin was back on my face, as I said, "If I can do the things you claim, making priests have accidents and fall ill, aren't you a bit worried about your own safety if you harm me?"

It was comical to see that realization bloom in their tiny minds. I could have laughed, but didn't dare. "Ah, but there's no such thing as witchery, is there? Didn't the intercessor tell you that, time and time again? So, what are you waiting for?" I balled my fists and took a step towards them. "Come on; let's get this over with."

They didn't exactly run away, but they backed down. I let them leave with as much dignity as they could salvage from the encounter, grabbing the irate Thonna's arm to prevent her hurling rocks at their departing backs.

"Calm down. Let them go. It will only create more trouble and probably get us both bloody if you anger them further."

"Beat me? Teach me my place? I hate them, especially that nasty dog fart Charlic. And if Grandfather thinks I'll ever marry him—well I won't—ever. I'll kill myself first."

Now it was my turn to stare with mouth agape. But before I could put my questions into words, she vented her pique on me. "Why don't you send bad Qwakaiva against them? They deserve it."

Tempting, oh so tempting, but no. the boys accusations had been aimed too close for my comfort. I had no wish to do evil, either unwittingly, or knowingly—ever again—or so I kept telling myself. "No, cousin, they don't deserve it. And if I had such power—which I'm not admitting—I wouldn't use it to cause harm. I don't want to be that kind of Qwakaihi."

She studied me for a long moment as her temper cooled. Without a word she retrieved my kills from the brush and followed me back to our family's encampment.

Adding to my sombre mood, a furious Aunty Marika and her mother were waiting for us as we walked into camp. They berated Thonna harshly for abandoning her babysitting duties and even my displaying my catch for the evening meal, and praising Thonna for her helping me catch them didn't placate their anger.

"Hunting is men and boy's duty. Child-minding and cooking are a woman and girl's tasks," I was told in a firm voice by Aunty Marika. Then to my horror my poor cousin received a beating with a willow wand for her abandonment of her brother.

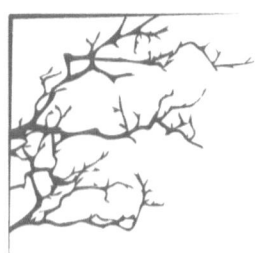

Chapter Seven

It was difficult for me in the convert encampment. Some of the northerners that had traveled south with us remembered the rumours of witchcraft that were whispered about Grandfather and me by Celibress Vomica and others. The accusations never stopped, even though Intercessor Raymonel himself, the victim of Chumco's conjuring denied our involvement.

Grandfather was both feared and shunned by everyone except my close family and I was singled out for special torments by the boys, whenever they thought no adult was around to scold them. They often tried to sneak up on me and hit me with mud balls and other offal, but by using my Qwakaiva, I could usually sense their intent and slip away without harm. Unfortunately my evasions only seemed to enhance the rumors of my unnatural powers.

I might have been tempted to do more to discourage their pestering than slip away from their ambushes, except for the fact that I truly feared the Chamuqwani god's punishment if I were caught. And discovery wasn't an unfounded childish fancy on my part. Eagan whether he would admit it or not, did have Qwakaiva. Though probably untrained, his power could be formidable in both the physical and unseen worlds when focused.

Early in life he had thrown in his lot with the newcomers to our land and had dedicated himself to their god. He thought it his holy duty to root out and destroy all evidence of our ancient traditions and those who still practiced them. For this reason I had a healthy respect for his temper and tried to stay out of his notice.

I didn't think Grandfather would let his malice go as far as to physically beat me, but the tensions in our family circle were strained and I had no wish to add fuel to the flames of simmering discord among us.

Uncle Royston's disciplines were a different matter, however. Though I didn't agree with his assumption, he saw himself as my father in the

Chamuqwani fashion, and both Chamuqwani law and our traditional customs, as my maternal uncle, lent weight to his discipline and supervision over me.

To be fair, Uncle Royston tried his best to include me in his family, but I would have none of him, slinking away into the desert whenever I wasn't set some task.

At first he would talk to me of an evening, trying to convince me of the wisdom in his signing away our people's northern lands, but like Uncle Tli, I hated him for his treachery, and though I never spoke my mind, he could sense my feelings and was both hurt and angered by my sullen refusal to see his way of thinking. Over time he talked less and became very strict with me whenever I broke any of the community's rules.

Thinking myself very clever the day our resentment boiled over, I left the settlement early to avoid the ambush I had seen with my Qwakaiva Charlic and his band of convert boys planned for me along the creek, where I usually set my snares. So I was surprised when I returned late in the afternoon with several rabbits strung over my shoulder to find a grim-faced Uncle Royston waiting for me.

"Uncle, what's wrong?" I stopped, watching him through down cast eyes. In my mind I quickly retrace the events of the day, wondering what I'd done now to displease him. I could think of nothing. I held out my string of rabbits, hoping to placate him for whatever it was he thought I'd done. The converts had so many new and confusing rules given to them by their Chamuqwani god I couldn't keep them all straight in my mind.

Uncle's face darkened and he took several deep breaths trying to control his anger. "Don't try to lie to me, boy you know what's wrong."

I had no idea what he was talking about—and I was no liar. Stifling down my resentment I continued to silently stand, not raising my eyes for fear he would see how much I was growing to hate him.

"Look at me, disobedient boy, and confess!" he growled.

My head snapped up and I looked him rudely in the eye. "Confess to what? I don't know what you are talking about."

For answer he held up the axe he'd been carrying unnoticed at his side. Startled I stepped back, unsure what he was planning.

He saw my fear and gave me a triumphant smile. He pointed to a big nick in the shiny blade. "Did you think you could get away with damaging such a valuable tool and not suffer for it? Have you no respect? We all have to share this axe until our treaty goods arrive. If it is damaged or lost..." his face contorted just thinking about such a terrible disaster. "Confess now and maybe I won't beat you."

"Beat me?" I cried, my voice loud with my indignation. I was angry now myself at such an unjust accusation. We were starting to attract a crowd of onlookers but I didn't care. "Uncle, I'm no liar. And I haven't even used the axe today. And when I do, I know how to take care of an axe properly—"

Uncle made a cutting motion with his free hand. "Charlic saw you!" he roared.

So that was Charlic and his followers' new game. If they couldn't ambush me and beat me, they would lie and get me in trouble with my relatives—damn them! Well, two could play at that game, I told myself.

"He saw me?" I held up my string of meat. "I've been hunting up the creek since early this morning. But being one of the Chamuqwani god's converts of course he would never lie, eh?"

My smart mouth earned me a slap across the face. But before Uncle could carry out his threat to beat me further, Grandfather intervened.

"My son, stop! It isn't the Qwani'Ya way to beat a child. Have you forgotten everything your mother and I taught you when you converted?" Grandfather looked so sad and disappointed with his oldest son that Uncle let his hand fall and dropped his eyes.

"If Tas had damaged the axe, I'm sure he would admit his wrong and do his best to repair it. There is no reason to threaten him with a beating," Grandfather said.

"You may believe this treacherous heathen boy but I do not," a harsh voice said to Grandfather. We all turned in that direction and saw Chief Eagan step out of the shadows; he stood with his arms folded across his chest, and a scowl on his flushed face.

"As I've said before, Elder Eagan, if you want us to go we will leave, because I think it isn't a boy's misdeed that is the real problem here, is it?"

Eagan snorted. "No it is not, witch—"

Suddenly this confrontation was taking a dangerous and unexpected turn. I saw it on Uncle's horrified face. "Father-in-law please, my father is no malicer. Mighty Djoven as my witness, I swear it. I'm sorry we disturbed you." Uncle sent a pleading look my way. "Whether my nephew damaged the axe or not I'm sure he will be willing to repair and sharpen it. Won't you, Martin?"

Martin? It took me a moment to realize he was referring to me. I started to protest, but then I saw Grandmother's anxious face among the onlookers and I nodded my head in agreement.

Eagan glared at us for a long moment then relented and agreed. "Give him the axe." Then turning to me he growled, "You will have no food tonight until it is done. And tomorrow instead of running off to laze around up the creek 'hunting' you will stay in camp and haul water to the men working on our meeting hall and do other chores needed around camp."

At my sullen expression Eagan smirked and walked away.

When he was gone I took the chipped axe Uncle handed me and sat down, pulling out my sharpening stone from my belt pouch. To no one in particular I grumped, "I'm no liar." My empty stomach rumbled. I keenly felt the injustice of this punishment, but to restore harmony in the family I would sharpen the axe—if it took me all night... and it just might; it was a deep nick.

At that moment I hated my Uncle and vowed I'd run away—someday. I'd show him he couldn't treat me so cruelly—I'd show them all!.

IT WAS LATE; I WAS sitting by a tiny fire still working on the axe, empty stomach growling and complaining, feeling miserable, when a sound from the darkness set a shiver down my back.

I kept on working, my Qwakaiva, and all my physical senses alert. Images of Charlic and his pack creeping up to ambush me had been tormenting my imagination throughout the evening. Luckily for me there had been too many people around, praying and singing in the unfinished meeting hall or doing other chores for them to risk bothering me. But that wasn't true now. Most of the settlement's inhabitants were in their own lodges asleep, or nearly so.

I was almost done with the axe and had had enough of their games..."If you're planning to attack me, mangy dog, just remember I still have the axe—and I will use it to defend myself."

The rustling behind me paused, then I heard a girl's soft chuckle and Thonna stepped into the firelight and then crouched in the tree's shadow beside me. My mouth dropped open and she chuckled again. "Close your mouth, stupid boy. Did you really think I was Charlic?"

I closed my mouth, suddenly grateful for the dim light that was hiding my flushed face. "What are you doing out here, stupid girl? You're going to get both of us into trouble," I whispered.

Thonna smiled. "I couldn't sleep because your empty belly was making too much noise."

I snorted. Then to give truth to her words my belly made a loud groaning noise at that moment—though she couldn't possibly have heard its earlier complaints from inside her parents hut.

"So," she continued, "I decided if I wanted to get any sleep tonight I'd better bring you this." From under her shawl she handed me a small cloth-wrapped object that when I opened it turned out to be a large piece of rabbit meat inside a chalky white griddle cake.

Once again my mouth dropped open in surprise.

"Close your mouth, stupid boy, before your teeth fall out."

I closed my mouth and stared, feeling a lump of gratitude form in my throat. She had risked much to defy her Grandfather's punishment to bring me food. "Thank you," I stammered, finally remembering my manners.

She motioned for me to eat. I needed no further urging.

"It was nothing, stupid boy. You are one of our best young hunters. We can't afford to lose you to a wasting illness because of that lying dog fart Charlic—who is too lazy and stupid to hunt even a sand turtle. I don't know why my father thinks he will make a good husband for me. All my children would starve if I married him."

Wolfing down the last of her gift, I asked, "Uncle really wants to marry you to that piece of dog shit?"

to come up with a reason on my own. Grandfather wouldn't help me and that only added fuel to my resentment.

THE BIG NOSED PRIEST and two other Chamuqwani churchmen arrived in a cart pulled by two brown mules, when the sun was high in the southern sky. A crier ran along the settlement paths, calling the people to gather at the stone meeting house to hear the priest and pray.

My throat felt dry and a knot of dread tightened in my empty gut, hearing the news. Using the excuse of getting more water as a ploy, I picked up an empty bucket and started for the creek, hoping to put off the moment of going to hear the priest as long as possible.

I had just started down the trail when an amused voice at my back stopped me. "You can't get out of going that easy, you know?"

Feeling the heat rise onto my cheeks I turned slowly to face the speaker. The wet hem of her skirt now tucked into her belt to keep it out of the dirt, Thonna leaned against one of the big cottonwoods. A full bucket of water set on the ground by her bare brown feet. A smirk curled at the corners of her wide mouth. She motioned with her chin towards the full bucket. "I've already gotten the water."

I snorted, turned my back on her and began walking again. Over my shoulder I shot back, "They may need more—for kafa—or tea."

She laughed, the sound low and mocking. "Sure they will. Don't get lost, Little Coshelah-Cousin. If you do, Father will only come looking for you, and my grandfather will be furious when hebrings you back. Maybe he will beat you this time. Poor, little cousin, I will make you willow bark tea to sooth the pain if he does." She laughed again, picked up her bucket and headed for the cook fire.

Beat me? Let Uncle or that mean old man try—I'd show them—I'd run fast as a deer—or fight them!

"...Bossy girl, what do you know, anyway?"

"Yes, he does," she snarled, jabbing a twig viciously into my tiny fire. "He says it will have a great advantage for our family, because Charlic was favored by the old priest in our village up North. The intercessor was already teaching him how to read the Chamuqwani's sacred books. He says I am smart—though not very pretty—so once I go to school and learn to read as well, it will be good for both families if we marry."

Her voice thick with emotion, she took a deep breath and rushed on, "But that is never going to happen, because I will not marry him. I will run away—become a soldier's cloocha-whore—or kill myself first."

Thonna fell silent after that fierce declaration. I couldn't see her face in the shadows, but I sensed she was fighting back tears, so I too remained silent, allowing her time to get herself back under control.

From what I had already observed living in the convert settlement I knew—sometimes to my own discomfort, that my new cousin was a person of strong emotions and opinions, but I hadn't realized how frightened and troubled by what she perceived to be her future she truly was.

"You deserve much better than that lying, cowardly dog fart," I told her. "And I will run away with you—whenever you want to leave."

Stifling a sob she stood up, turning her back on me. "I have to go before I'm missed. As she disappeared into the darkness, she said. "It was Tomson that damaged the axe then left it lying on the ground by the stump. I told Appi that but he didn't believe me, either."

IN SPITE OF MY EVER-present exhaustion I couldn't sleep that night. Hunger still gnawed at my gut even with Thonna's generous gift to ease its emptiness. I'd been keeping track of Uncle Tli and Samiqwas in the Seer's Pool, and my worries for them plagued me nearly as much as my belly.

The air in the hut was warmed by the fire, but the rustling of small animals crawling through the tied grasses over my head kept me wakeful, giving me time to nurse my feelings of injustice. Finally I rose and crept as silently as I could out into the night, so that I wouldn't disturb anyone.

Even though there was no snow in that desert land the nights grew quite chill, water freezing along the edges of the creek before morning. Outside our hut the waning moon was a shrinking crescent in the eastern sky, dappling the ground under the bare trees with spots of silver. Somewhere in the camp behind me a baby cried, then settled. Moving cautiously through the shadows under the trees, I headed for the bank overlooking the creek.

Shallow with its winter fasting, the muddy creek below made only a soft murmur as I walked out from the trees and sat on a patch of dry grass, my blanket wrapped about my shoulders. Clumps of thorn bush and brush dotted the rolling hills of grass and sage that spread out to the west beyond the stream. The sky was black above me; stars like gleaming shards of a broken waskyja bottle were scattered across its expanse.

Somewhere in the night one of the little wolves the people here called coyotes howled a questing song at the moon. Its howl was answered by another of its kind in the hills to the east. Resting my head on arms crossed atop my bent knees, I sighed. What was I doing here in this dry alien land?

A sound by the stone house made me turn, but I could see nothing in the gloom. I shivered as if a malignant presence watched me from the shadows.

The Chamuqwani priests will take you away to the special prison they have for children. What will you do when they try to steal your soul? My old mentor's words whispered anew their warning in my mind.

I should have gone back north with Chumco when he offered....

Angry at myself, then, I hurled a stone over the bank and into the stream below. These morbid thoughts were pointless. Why torture myself with what wasn't to be? I'd made my choice. I couldn't change the course of my life's river now.

I closed my eyes and listened to the breeze blowing through the dry brush across the creek. The feathery touch of its breath cooled my brow, caressed my cheek and whispered incomprehensible, alien words in my ear.

<<Hello Spirits of this land,>> I said in the mind speech of the Unseen Ones. <<I am a stranger here, but I mean you no harm. Bless me and guide me in this dry place so far from my home.>>

Around me in the blackness, I sensed the Spirits of the land pause, listening, observing then drifting away without contact. I felt neither acceptance nor hostility in their contemplation of me, but their indifference made me feel unbelievably sad and abandoned.

Without the wisdom of the Unseen World to guide us how were we, as a people, and me personally, going to survive in this desolate place? Would the Chamuqwani god truly take care of us as Uncle Royston and the priests assured us? I feared not. So far in my young life I had seen no evidence to make me trust in their words.

Cresting on the wave of my fear and self-pity, I suddenly saw the violet eyes and brindle fur of a lake seal appear before my inner eye. This magical, shape-shifting being that was my father I had seen only once when the steamboat carrying us south had to pass through Drown Canoe Rapids.

The river was dangerously low; the fear for my life and that of my relatives helped me to strengthen my Qwakaiva and contact him through the veil that separates our worlds—though I hadn't known ahead of time that my conjuring would bring a lake seal's help.

My mother had never told me my father's identity before our meeting, and the revelation when it came was quite a shock. Our touch had been fleeting, but his guidance and protection through those dangerous rapids saved the boat from crashing, and filled an empty place in my heart. I realized after he left me, that in spite of my relatives' affection, all my life I had longed to know and be loved by a father of my own.

<<Oh father, when you helped us through the rapids, you should have stayed, should have listened to me. Why did you leave me? I need you so much!>> Tears blurred my vision, silently running down my face. I couldn't stop their flow, but a part of me was angry at myself for the self-pity and the waste of my eyes' precious moisture.

<<Why do you weep, foolish boy,>> the unseen spectre whispered. <<Your Uncle Royston would be like a father to you, if you'd let him. Surrender your soul to me, little human, and let me take care of you. I will give you power as I have done for the others. You need not be alone>>

A cold tingling clutched the nape of my neck. The voice that had spoken to me had come from behind me, not from the Spirits I'd heard in the wind and rocks across the creek a few moments before. Slowly I turned my head, trying to see into the shadows by the unfinished meeting hall. Its nearest wall cast an impenetrable shade across the ground in that spot. I sensed something crouching there, but the darkness hid it from my sight.

<<Go away. Leave me alone, I won't give you anything.>>

The spectre mocked me, the sound like wind rustling dry grasses. <<You will—in time—I can wait for such a tasty treat as you.>>

In spite of my attempt to remain silent, I must have made some noise in protest, alerting another wakeful person to my presence. "Grandson, what's wrong? Why aren't you in bed?" I heard quiet footsteps then Grandfather crouched beside me and touched my shoulder.

"Nothing's wrong, Grandfather." I scrubbed a hand across my eyes and looked up. His face was only a soft blur in the starlight; I couldn't read its expression. Had he felt the malignant Spirit that was tormenting me just moments before, or was I truly alone? "I'm sorry, Grandfather, I couldn't sleep. Did I wake you?"

"No, no, Grandson. I couldn't sleep either. I was just coming back from a little walk of my own."

Trying to avoid further confrontations with Eagan, Grandfather acted more like a ghost than living man. Keeping to himself, he wandered far out into the desert searching for medicines and anything edible. I think he would have gone to live with his nephew Lynx Hunting, or another of his own kin, if it weren't for love of Grandmother and his eldest son.

"I was trying to call the Spirits of this land. I have been trying since we came here, but none will come to me." I let out a deep sigh, feeling discouraged by my failures. "Have the Unseen Ones in this dry land spoken to you on your walks, Grandfather?"

He crouched beside me and rubbed a hand across his face. Using my Spirit-Sight I saw the black ribbons of discouragement entangled in his Spirit Fire's luminescence, but when he at last spoke, his words gave no hint of his inner doubts. "We must be patient. We will learn the flow of the seasons and touch the heart of this land in time. We will search out its sacred places and find new guides. The Spirits will come to know us. Our Qwakaiva will be strong and we will prosper once again. Don't fear."

Why was he lying to me? He knew I could see the truth in his Spirit Fire. "Don't fear? Easy words for you to say, much harder for me to believe," I said.

He sighed and patted my hand. "I know, my dear one, I know."

But oh how I wanted to believe him. I wanted to curl up in his strong arms and drink in the acceptance and comfort given a child, but when I reached for him I felt only the thin brittle bones of an old man.

Mother had been right in her observations—he couldn't take care of me and protect me. The solid, powerful Qwakaihi and hunter my heart remembered was no more.

The ordeals of our torturous journey had aged him beyond his years. In spite of my youth, I wasn't a child any more. Too much water had flowed over the rocks, too much had happened to me along our journey, and neither his words nor his embrace could comfort me.

Perhaps because I felt that lack, mourned my lost innocence and was afraid, I irrationally blamed him for my troubles. And so, my words were bitter and cruel when I spoke again.

"The priests and Grandfather Eagan say that the Thunderer is a jealous god. Do you really believe these mean converts will let us find peace and harmony here? Or will the traitors and the Chamuqwani demand our obedience, no matter what we would prefer?"

In a stray shaft of moonlight I saw his stricken face and was ashamed of my harsh words. Ever since my apprenticeship with Chumco was severed, relations between Grandfather and I had become strained.

Fearing that by aiding my mentor in his conjuring I had unwittingly helped caused the death of my young cousin Seicu, I had chosen of my own will to break off the contact with a Qwakaihi of questionable practices who knew how to teach one such as me.

I loved my grandfather, but I also resented him for forcing me into having to make a choice between my apprenticeship and my family. Grandfather's affinity for the Power was so different than mine that he couldn't teach me.

Chumco had been the one man I'd found who could truly help me to learn how to use the gifts given to me by my unique heritage. I blamed grandfather for the loss of my teacher and my eventual hope of contacting my father with my Qwakaiva.

Then, feeling ashamed, I stammered out an apology. Hadn't I just reminded myself that he was old and not strong? I had no wish to cause him unnecessary pain. So I smiled and added, "Who cares what the Thunderer's priests and these converts think, right? I'm a foolish boy."

"I'm sure your words are true. Once the spirits of this land get to know us, they will gift us with their Qwakaiva as they once did back home."

He accepted the gift I offered with what seemed to me to be relief. We were companionably silent for a time, taking in the wonders of the night together. Then I jumped when at last he spoke.

"Though my power has little affinity with the ancient stone beings, I sense that like our home, the rock of this dry land is very old. Hidden within its substance are many memories that have the power to guide us." He pointed with his lips towards the snow-capped mountains hugging the far horizon to the northwest. There should be caves in those mountains, caves containing crystals of power and wisdom. We will need such gifts if we are to survive in this new land."

He picked up a stone from the ground by his feet and rolled it between his fingers, lost in his own thoughts. I was about to leave him to his pondering, when he startled me by speaking once more.

"The Aseutl under the earth, those mighty ones who push up the mountains from the mud, are kin to the Aseutl of the dark waters. As one whom Kunai has favored, you might seek a renewal of your power in the bones of the Earth, Grandson."

"Will you take me to find these caves?"

"Perhaps when the weather warms. There will be much snow there now. We will ask your Uncle Tli to come with us perhaps."

Tli. The knot of worry tightened again in my gut. Would Tli still be alive by then? Grandfather hated to talk about my Spirit Benefactor Kunai. My affinity for the Aseutl's magic I'd inherited from my shapeshifting seal father, whom he disliked above all men. I knew it cost him dearly to offer me this thread of hope, and for that reason I chose to share with him what I'd seen in the Seer's Pool about Tli.

To my dismay, my news fell like another heavy weight upon his shoulders. What was a matter with me; would I never learn? I still wanted him to take away my worries and make everything better. Thonna was right—what a stupid baby I was!

"I don't know if the Raven was waiting for Tli or his daughter—she has been very sickly, you know. Tli is a strong young hunter. He has Qwakaiva; he won't die. It was the girl Death's Messenger watched, not Tli. Don't worry about him Grandfather."

He touched my hand to reassure me that all was well. "Don't trouble yourself on my behalf, Grandson. Thank you for telling me." Soon after that we parted, each seeking our beds back in the shelter.

As I drifted towards oblivion, I thought of black water under the earth, and Kunai, Master of Enigma, the one to whom I had pledged my soul. The Great Aseutl was the source of my Qwakaiva and only he could swim the dark currents under the earth and save me, binding both my past and future together in a unified whole.

I shivered, fearing his regard. And yet I knew that someday I would humble myself and seek his aid once more.

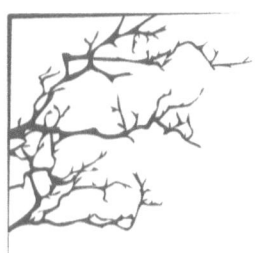

Chapter Eight

The winter dragged on with everyone cold and hungry most of the time. We settled uneasily into the encampment's routine. Mother and Grandmother joined the women of Uncle's extended family in preparing the meals and doing other household chores.

Children fetched water from the creek and fuel from the surrounding countryside. The boys with hunting skills set snares and hunted with small hand-made bows and arrows along the creek and up into the surrounding hills.

Uncle Royston and the rest of the convert men seemed to spend a lot of time praying and meeting in council, but they did gather rock that would be used in finishing up the various building projects that had been started in the settlement last autumn.

Truth be told, no one put much effort into these projects, however. They expected to have fine new homes of flat wood, like the Chamuqwani once the wagons carrying our treaty goods arrived.

And when would that blessed day be? No one seemed to know—not even Agent Daglish. All we got when the Elders asked were evasions and promises, promisesthatleft a bitter taste in the mouth, and were hard to swallow.

Chief Eagan and Uncle never seemed to be discouraged by the agent's evasions, however. They only counselled the people to pray harder and the god would provide. I hated them for their lies. Sometimes when my hunts for rabbits and other small game were particularly successful, I kept back some of the meat for myself.

I felt like a thief, stealing from my relatives, but anger and resentment had found a home in my spirit. The promised Cai beasts never arrived. And other supplies like flour beans and oat-mush were bug-infested, never enough and often late. The Chamuqwani were liars and monsters, and my Uncle was a fool, I told myself to justify my feelings.

The sixth day of the ration cycle got to be called "Do nothing day," because by then we were out of the rations we'd been allotted seven days before. Do nothing day, I drank willow bark steeped in boiled water and tried to sleep as much as I could.

Sleep wasn't easily found if I stayed in our shelter, though. The thin brush walls didn't blot out the impatient shouts of hungry people who had nothing to do but argue with one another, and Hathin's monotonous whining.

Being a favored boy-child it became abundantly clear to me that Hathin had been hopelessly spoiled. His loud screaming temper tantrums and shouted demands to any adult within sight would never have been tolerated back home in our village on Big Ice Lake.

Once I overheard Marika apologizing to Grandmother for her son's bad behaviour, explaining that he was a sickly boy and couldn't help what he did. I think Grandmother might have given the young mother a piece of her mind on the subject, but Marika's sister called to her at that moment and grateful for the interruption she hurried away, the screaming Hathin still straddling her hip.

Hathin had a true knack for making himself a nuisance, poking his snot-nosed face and grubby fingers into everything. I tried to avoid the little brat as often as I could. And being a male I was for the most part excused from babysitting, something I'd never been allowed to get away with back home.

But my poor cousin Thonna wasn't so lucky. Though I was often the brunt of her sharp tongue, I felt sorry for her and sometimes saved her little treats from my hunts, which seemed to please her.

Piling up the last of the brush I'd gathered one morning, I dusted off my hands and followed Grandfather into the unfinished stone house. My stomach growled in anticipation. The women of our combined family were just finishing the cooking of the morning meal.

When everyone had arrived and was sitting quietly, Grandfather Eagan rose and lifted his hands to offer up another of his monotonous prayers. Feeling grumpy and cold, I paid no attention. I was a rock grounded into the streambed of a swift-moving northern creek. My mind conjured up the image and I allowed his words to flow over and around me, deaf to their meaning.

Then, as he paused for breath, my stomach growled again. Eagan scowled in my direction, and continued praying. From across the circle Thonna hid a grin behind her hand. Heat rose into my cheeks. I huddled into my blanket next to Grandfather and tried not to draw any further attention to myself.

At last the sticky mush was set down in a low flat bowl for us to share. Everyone ate in silence, shovelling in the goo with a grim determination. The tasteless grey mound was quickly demolished, too small a portion to feed so many people. My belly ached for more, but Uncle's youngest had been allowed to lick the bowl clean.

As the family rose to go, Eagan announced that the priest from the agency, Intercessor Karl was coming later in the morning for a special ceremony. I didn't see why this news would be of interest to me, until I heard Uncle Royston tell Grandmother that the priest would expect us to stay for the temple assembly along with everyone else in the converts' encampment.

Ever since that first night when Eagan had openly raged against heathens living among them, I had heard the grumbling of Marika's family and other converts. Though they valued the extra rations and wild foods that came with us and our labour, we weren't welcome. It was only their regard for my uncle that had prevented trouble so far.

Like Grandfather, I tried to stay out of everyone's way as much as possible. I hunted, gathered fuel for the cook fires and jumped at any excuse to be out of the encampment. I glanced sharply at Grandfather, hoping he would make some excuse for our absence.

Coming back with a load of brush earlier, I had told him that I'd seen more of the little brown birds and rabbits down by the water. I wanted to hunt, not sit around the stone house listening to more prayers.

Grandfather nodded to Uncle and stepped out into the sunlight. I was sure he could sense my disappointment, but he refused to meet my eye or acknowledge my silent plea for deliverance.

As I followed him out, I risked a glance at the formidable old man, a tingling running down my spine. Eagan was a dangerous enigma. But if I wanted an excuse to avoid the afternoon's tiresome proceedings, I would have

...Little coshelah-cousin indeed. I probably was a few moons older than her—and, and I was taller, too. I bet I was. "...And the people would need the water for kafa—yes they will."

Thonna tried to boss me around like she did her little brother and the younger convert children in the village, but I ignored her, or hid across the creek where she'd been forbidden to go whenever I could.

Such a ploy was cheating—and she let me know it when next she cornered me, but I didn't care. I needed every advantage I could muster, if I wanted some peace. I tried to avoid her and her cutting remarks when I could, but I couldn't find it in my heart to hate her. She just made me feel uncomfortable, but in truth I pitied her.

Her mother, aunties and grandmother were constantly scolding her for her wild ways, urging her to be quieter and retiring, like the priest said all women and girls should behave.

During these sessions Thonna listened with eyes cast down, promised to be a good girl, but I could see the red spears of anger erupting from her aura, all the time the women chastised her. With a stubborn resignation, she ignored their words and her grandfather Eagan's occasional canings with a willow wand, and did as she pleased.

Like a lynx caught in a steel trap, willing to chew off her own leg to get free, I feared that someday Thonna might do something equally drastic like she'd told me the night I sharpened the axe, rather than surrender to their will.

But on that day, if Thonna had been hoping to get me into trouble, I refused to give her that satisfaction, so setting aside my earlier plan to do as I suspected she hoped I would, I didn't get myself lost—on purpose. I filled the bucket in a deep pool up stream and came right back to the encampment.

The people were just gathering by the stone house as I set the bucket down by the cook fire. Aunty Marika smiled at me. "Thank you, Martin. That was very thoughtful of you."

I dropped my eyes and murmured something, feeling a guilty flush heat my face. I looked forward to when the new temple was finished and people would have to go to the agency for these ceremonies. I was certain I could find many more opportunities to lose myself among so many at the agency or along the way.

But until that happened, the priest and his minions traveled to the people, timing their visits just after ration day, so we would be forced to use some of our meagre food supplies to feed them.

Intercessor Karl brought always with him a wooden statue of The Thunderer. It lay wrapped in blankets in the wagon, nestled in a bed of straw. Uncle and four other men from the settlement carefully lifted out the statue and gently carried it into the unfinished stone meeting hall. They placed it against the back wall on an earthen mound that had been flattened and smoothed to resemble an altar.

At the God's feet, Chief Eagan built a tiny fire in an iron brazier. Soon the resinous odour of incense filled the air. The assembled people quieted and bowed their heads.

Intercessor Karl conducted a similar service to the ones I attended while growing up by the Big Ice Lake. Though my family had never been bathed in the god's holy smoke as converts of the Chamuqwani's new religion, we'd attended the temple on feast days back home. I knew what was expected of me. I folded my hands upon my chest and bowed my head like the rest of the assembled people when the ceremony began.

The priest could speak our language passably well, his voice rich and compelling, and he used its timbre to full affect. At moments its pitch would drop to an insistent rumble like an approaching storm in the mountains, then, when we were lulled into a sense of well-being, it would boom out like peels of crashing thunder, warning us of the pit of torments that awaited those who earned the God's wrath.

At such times I shivered and squirmed within my skin, remembering the fearsome stone monsters I'd seen chained to the great temple walls when we passed through the river town where Train lived. I had reason to fear this angry god's punishment. Hadn't I aided Chumco in injuring one of his priests?

No, I wouldn't think about such things. *Our thoughts have power*, so the old people always said. I wasn't going to give these mean people and their vengeful god that kind of hold over me. Bad enough the Chamuqwani could starve me and maybe kill me, but I wouldn't allow them to plant the seed of fear in my mind. I had Qwakaiva—

<<Qwakaiva? Ah yes, but will it be enough? Surrender to me, for I too can protect you and give you power.>>

I shuddered, unsure what Spirit had spoken. But it didn't matter; I wouldn't listen. I was son to a Sealman. I would not give up my soul so easily. I'd pay no attention to the mocking laughter in my mind—I-I would fight them.

When the priest finished praying, I edged towards the open doorway behind me. Freedom, I could almost taste its sweetness upon my tongue. Grandmother saw me and clamped a hand on my shoulder before I could escape. An aisle opened up between the people and the next thing I knew Grandmother had taken mine and mother's hand and was steering us toward the front of the gathering near the altar.

When she stopped we were standing right in front of the priest. Chief Eagan and Uncle Royston moved up to stand on either side of him. Feeling the panic bubbling up, I glanced over my shoulder searching the congregation for Grandfather. He was standing at the back of the assembled people where we'd left him. I tried to catch his eye, wondering if he knew what was happening. But he turned away and slipped outside as soon as our eyes met.

I took a deep breath and tried to control my fears. I didn't know what they planned, but surely Grandfather wouldn't let anyone hurt me—surely not. <<*What will you do when your grandfather betrays you?*>> Unbidden Chumco's prophetic words echoed in my mind.

I turned and Uncle smiled down at me. He touched my shoulder then addressed the people.

"Brothers and sisters, this is a joyous day for me; one which I have awaited for some time. I would like you to welcome my mother, my sister Jannia and her son Martin into our congregation. In the Holy God's name I have asked Intercessor Karl to come here and perform baptisms for my relatives and the other newcomers who have joined their relatives in our settlement."

Baptism! I stared open mouthed, feeling both trapped and angry. I was still considered a child, under the care and protection of my clan Elders, but surely they knew I didn't want this. My eyes darted around the room, searching for—escape—Grandfather!

And then, once again Chumco's mocking words echoed in my mind. He had warned me that Grandfather would betray me—many times.

Grandfather wasn't of our lineage, had Uncle singled out only his blood-kin for this *honor*? Maybe my uncle was more of a traditional than I thought. Or maybe Chief Eagan was too afraid to force this indignity on one who claimed a Qwakaihi's power. Suddenly the scraps of argument I'd heard over the past few days made more sense.

I turned away and glanced at my female relatives out of the corner of my eye. Had they known of Eagan and Uncle's plan; did they approve? To counter the grumbling and encourage harmony, maybe they did. Mother's expression remained serene. She had probably retreated into a light trance, where none of the world's unpleasantness could touch her.

Grandmother's expression on the other hand, was stern but content. Then it hit me like a hammer blow. Hadn't I seen the longing in her eyes whenever she looked at her oldest son? Was this the price of his love? Was this baptism what Eagan had demanded to allow us to stay among them?

I suspected it might be true, and I hated him for what he was doing to my family. I doubted that she had thought of this idea on her own, but when Uncle Royston had proposed it to her, as the matriarch of the family, she must have willingly agreed.

Uncle and the priest continued to speak, but I paid them little attention. Grandfather had left the gathering, Grandmother craved the love and acceptance of her eldest son above all things—and Amima? A woman with no husband, she had no power here. Once more I faced the unknown and the enemy alone.

As the worm of self-pity began to gnaw, I could almost hear Chumco's voice in my mind once again. <<Have you forgotten everything I taught you, little Seal? You have a warrior's courage and Qwakaiva. Use them!>>

Qwakaiva. One of the first lessons my mentor had taught me was how to shield myself from Convert Magic. To please Grandmother I would surrender my body to their ritual, but inside I would form a glowing shield about my soul. I would keep faith with our old traditions.

Head bowed I knelt alongside Grandmother and Amima when the time to be bathed in the holy smoke came. Through half closed eyes I stole a glance at the stern old man who was behind this violation. Wearing a self-satisfied expression, his hard eyes swept over the people as if searching for someone or something.

Was he looking for Grandfather, hoping to taunt him with his power? I rejoiced in Eagan's frustration when he couldn't find him.

Being a Traditional, Grandfather wouldn't consider himself as part of our clan. Before coming to this Tribal Preserve, we claimed our lineage through our mother's kin. I doubted that he'd approved, but he wouldn't have opposed Grandmother if she had her mind made up about this baptism ceremony. He might have concealed his opinion to promote family harmony, but he wouldn't stay around to witness the act either.

Shifting my perception to see Eagan with my Spirit-Sight, I gasped and jerked my eyes away, before the skeletal creature clinging to Eagan's shoulder saw me. My mouth was suddenly as dry as sand. I took a deep breath, trying to control my trembling.

Grandmother squeezed my hand and smiled her reassurance. I tried to smile back, but I doubt my expression was very convincing. She didn't know; she couldn't see the horror that whispered into the old man's ear.

The creature reminded me of the Temple's stone monsters. It had a misshapen face, all hard red eyes and teeth, bony hands with long claws. Was it sent from their terrible god, or was it kin to some evil, and masking its true nature from its host? I had no way of knowing the truth, but I did know that I would have to be careful—be alert and watchful.

With a vision of a white hair crouched in a winter snowdrift, as a talisman in my mind, I breathed in the clawing smoke and tried not to flinch when the priest laid his hand on my head and prayed over me.

When it was over a smiling Uncle raised me to my feet. "Is it not written in the Mighty Djoven's book that blessed are the children who have bathed in his holy smoke, and there by been cleansed of their sins and blessed by his mercy?"

"Haya, it is so, Brother," the Converts chanted in response.

Reaching into his shirt pocket, Uncle drew out a small silver pendant shaped like a lightning bolt and hung it around my neck. "Welcome to my home and my community, Martin, my son. With this baptism I stand before the people gathered here and promise to protect you and instruct you in the paths of righteousness. You are one of the God's own chosen now and blessed in his eyes."

In the front row Thonna caught my eye her expression unreadable. Blessed? No, I didn't think so. The pendant's cord hung like a choking weight about my neck, cutting off my breath. I wanted to snatch it from my neck and fling it into the fire. Breath, I needed air! I staggered against mother, feeling suddenly faint. What was happening to me? Then I happened to look in Chief Eagan's direction.

The skeletal thing grinned at me, displaying sharp white teeth. <<Mine, sweet little human, now you are mine.>>

Refusing to give into my terror, I asked myself, what would my father do when taunted by such a one?

...I angrily defied it. <<Another might dispute your claim, Demon. Have you heard of the Great Aseutl Kunai?>> The fear I saw in its malignant red eyes gave me strength. <<I think you have. Foul Creature, Kunai has already claimed me. Leave me alone, before I call him!>>

With a muttered threat, the spectre vanished. Though besting it had been momentarily satisfying, its departure left me with a knot of worry in my gut. Djoven's talisman hung like a leaden weight about my neck. I'd been bluffing, and the demon—or whatever it was would figure that out soon enough.

I shuddered, wishing my father was here to protect me. Deep in my soul I feared I wasn't strong enough or brave enough to defy the creature forever. And asking Kunai to help me would have its own consequences.

As my grandfather had often warned me, Aseutl were capricious beings. If I asked for his aid, I wasn't certain I would be pleased with the result.

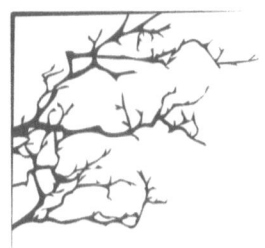

Chapter Nine

Grandfather didn't return that night. I was worried about him, but when I voiced my worries to mother, she reassured me. "He's fine, my son. He just went to visit his brother's oldest son Lynx Hunting, living up the creek. He recently married a woman in that camp with two little girls. One is sick. Lynx Hunting came over to ask him to come earlier. He has probably just stayed the night to help care for the child."

Her explanation sounded logical, but I knew there was more to his absence than that. He was avoiding me—and I hated him at that moment for his betrayal and his cowardice.

Grandmother had curled up in her blankets not long after the evening meal ended. Mama and I were sitting by the dying fire in our lodge. I could hear Hathin's monotonous whining coming from Uncle's dwelling, the murmur of women's voices trying to sooth him.

In the desert beyond a coyote howled. As she placed another branch on the flames, mother's new amulet flashed, a bolt of reflected lightning in the firelight. The silver pendant about my own neck hung like a burning stone, its menace lurking at the edge of my consciousness, sapping my strength.

Glancing at the motionless lump in the shadows to assure myself that Grandmother was sleeping, I boldly asked, "Amima, have you truly forsaken our traditions and converted to the foreigners' religion?"

Collecting her thoughts, she sipped at her cup of juniper tea before answering, but finally she said, "No, not really. The memory of your father's love still claims a special place in my heart. I could never betray his memory by forsaking our traditions. In my heart I am true to the Unseen Ones."

"Then why did you do it?"

She set down her cup and stared earnestly into my eyes. "I agreed to take the Thunderer's baptism to please my mother who is old and has lost so much. And to please my brother who has generously offered us shelter."

"Do I have to ware it? Even if Uncle is allowing us to stay here I'm no traitorous convert—and never will be," I grumbled.

She sighed, and holding up her pendant she examined it as if seeing it for the first time. "Tasimu, the pendant is no more than a piece of shiny metal. It has no power to hurt you, or change what's in your heart.

"I know this is difficult for you, but growing up is often about learning to make hard choices. Agreeing to wear the amulet was a harmless concession on my part, but if by doing so I help create harmony in our family, it was worth it. I advise you not to make a fuss about it."

Ah, but I feared that she was wrong about the ceremony and wearing Mighty Djoven's symbol being harmless. In the Unseen World that surrounds us all, such acts have power. That was why Grandfather hadn't agreed to his own baptism—I was sure of it.

I believe in her heart Mother knew it, too, but she had chosen to deny her feelings for the sake of giving Grandmother and me a home. There was no point in arguing with her, so instead I chose another approach.

"Why can't we leave and go live with some other relatives until you find a new husband? You promised to find a new husband once we got to the Preserve, you know? You aren't going to choose one of these mean convert men are you? If you do, I swear I will go live on my own."

She laughed softly and told me to go to bed. She promised to take my concerns for her new mate into consideration when the time came.

I went to bed but also resolved to remove the hated pendant whenever I was away from the settlement hunting and food gathering.

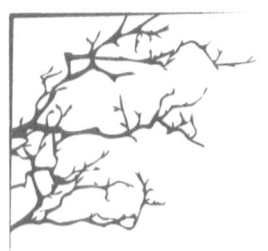

Chapter Ten

A s the moons passed, we saw less and less of Grandfather. Though he and Grandmother hadn't officially divorced, he was often away from our hut. As head of our household according to the agent, he still showed up on ration day to collect our share for us.

I would have liked to have accompanied him on his trips to explore the desert, or when he was called to other encampments to perform a healing, but Grandmother forbade me to go and he was reluctant to take me without her permission. And so, I withered in Uncle Royston's encampment, weighed down by his discipline, drowning in loneliness and harassed to near madness by Charlie and his friends.

And then as the days lengthened into spring, the blizzard came, with its waist-deep snow, blocking the trails to the agency. We had no snowshoes or sleds to go for food and medicines and we nearly starved before a horse drawn sled came to deliver our share of the meager rations. Who would have thought that such a dry hot land could have a fierce storm, like the ones we had known in our northern home?

Along with the extreme cold and freezing winds, the storm also brought a new and deadly sickness that burned the body until small red spots popped out all over the sick one's face and chest.

Constantly tormented by the spectre lodged in the Thunderer's talisman about my neck draining me of my Qwakaiva when I had to remain in the settlement, I, too, fell victim to the disease's merciless power.

<<THERE IS NO ESCAPE,>> a harsh voice rasped. <<You belong to me, body and soul>>

No escape... <<No, no, not true! Go away leave me alone!>>

"His fever is rising again. Bring more of the willow tea, Daughter."

Who was that speaking, Grandfather? No, it couldn't be. He had gone home to Big Ice Lake, leaving me alone. Alone...

My hand tugged weakly at the strangling cord around my neck. I had to fight, had to...

Mocking laughter. <<Too weak now. You will die soon if you don't surrender your Qwakaiva to me and become my slave. Do you want to die, little human?>>

"There have been so many deaths... Tasimu has been sick for several suns now. Will he be all right, Appi?"

"I don't know, Daughter. The source of the evil causing this sickness eludes me. I will pray for the Spirits to aid in his healing."

"Look he is pulling on the pendant's cord again as if it pains him. Maybe we should take it off if it bothers him so."

Yes, yes, take it off. Mother save me from its evil—

"Don't be foolish, sister. It's only the power of the Great God that protects him, and the others who are ill in the settlement from some malicer's power. The evil flies all about us on the cold wind, spreading sickness and death. Like Father Eagan says, we must pray."

Listen to the wind, yes I must listen—the Wind will blow my words to those with power to hear me. <<Spirits of this land, help me I need your protection....>>

<<No one is listening, little human. Why don't you call on your great benefactor to save you, Hmm? Are you afraid of what price he will exact for saving your miserable life? I will be a much kinder master.>>

No wind now—silent. <<O Spirits have mercy. I'm no convert to the foreigner's faith—no matter what my Elders wish. I will honor the ways of my new land, if you but open to me and grant me your protection.>>

Hearing only the pounding of my heart loud in my ears, I tried to disappear into its rhythm—blot out the mocking laughter. I had to hide from the evil monster trying to devour me. My lungs ached. I couldn't breathe. Fire, I was on fire, the burning ache centred in my chest under where the talisman of silver metal rested.

"Be easy now, Grandson, Your uncle has gone and your mother is sleeping. I will take off the Thunderer's talisman for a while if that will ease your mind."

Someone gently lifted my aching head and slid the strangling cord from around my neck. Far away in a corner of my mind the skeletal phantasm screamed its curses at the one who had rescued me from its power. Cool and sinuous as lake water the healing gift of respite flowed over me, quenching the fire that was killing me.

The ache in my lungs eased and the burning in my body subsided. With a grateful sigh I swallowed the tea offered me and sank into the depths of restful sleep.

I floated in a dark place for a time, content just to drift, grateful for the absence of pain. Then, as I sank further into the Dream, an unfamiliar whirring noise mingled with those of my heart and breath, urging me to follow the sound deeper into the earth. Down through the flinty ground, down into the rivers of black water, down, down in search of its source....

Finding sanctuary at last, I rested on cool ground in a hidden place—safe. The whirring was louder here. It reminded me of the tiny rattles—the kind some Qwakaihi use when doing a healing. I smiled, had someone come to save me from the evil one hungry for my soul? Behind my closed eyes the sound seemed to move, enclosing me within a circle.

After a time I also began to hear words in my mind. <<Come, brothers and sisters. I shake my rattles to guide you. Come see what swam in the dark water under the earth and climbed out of the sacred spring to lie in this holy place.>>

I cracked open an eye to see the speaker. A soft golden light illuminated the brown and tan snake with dark diamond-shaped spots down its back. Beyond us lay only the blackness. I could smell a cave's musty dampness, and from somewhere deep in the shadows water dripped. The snake had coiled its mass beside me, the tip of its tail vibrated, the source of the whirring noise. Its flat triangular head was raised, watching me. Its long forked tongue flicked out, tasting my scent upon the cool air.

I lay perfectly still. Some of the Chamuqwani soldiers on our march to the agency had warned us about these fearsome creatures. Their bites were lethal. Maybe it hadn't come to heal me, as I'd hoped.

As I pondered what to do I heard the sound of wings and a giant golden eagle landed nearby, folding its brown wings about its body. Its curved beak snapped shut and it cocked its head to one side fixing me with one yellow eye. <<What have you found, Sister, hmm?>>

<<Shall I bite him with my poison?>> Rattlesnake asked Eagle.

<<No, not yet. We must know more before we decide what to do with such a strange creature.>>

<<Is he the one the Night Wind has been whispering about?>>Antelope asked. Her hooves clicked upon the stony floor as she walked forward into the light. Bending over me, she took an experimental sniff. Her warm breath smelled of fermenting grass as it blew across my face. <<He smells like a young male of the Humans.>>

<<Don't be silly,>> Cougar growled. <<None of those unpredictable creatures have flippers like a Seal.>>

Flippers? I slowly tried to curl my fingers and found I couldn't. The bones were now buried under a webbing of firm hard membrane and skin.

<<True enough,>> she agreed, <<but Seals have fur all over their bodies, and this being doesn't. Except for the flippers at the ends of his limbs, he appears like a man-child.>>

<<He does have an odd odour to him, though,>> Coyote said. He took a large sniff, the nostrils of his moist black nose flaring with my unfamiliar scent. <<Smells a bit fishy if you ask me.>>

<<No one did, so be quiet,>> Eagle said.

<<He must have great power to find his way to this sacred place,>> said Owl.

Rattlesnake's sinuous mass uncoiled and flowed across my arm to resettle herself upon my chest. <<He is warm to my touch. It would be a comfort to sleep next to such a one on cold desert nights.>>

Coyote snorted. <<Until he rolled over on you and squashed you.>>

Rattlesnake hissed and shook her rattles at him. <<Come closer and I will bite you.>>

<<Enough of your foolishness, Joker,>>Eagle warned. <<No one is going to squash anyone. I won't tolerate you trying to make trouble.>>

Coyote tucked his tail between his hind legs and crawled on his belly in a submissive posture. <<Sorry, oh so sorry, Mighty Chief of the Skies.>>

Cougar glided forward and peered down at me. He reached out a large paw and ran it down my arm. I could feel the tips of his claws lightly graze my skin. A trickle of blood dripped onto my flippered hand. He bent and took an experimental lick. <<Mm,>> Cougar purred. <<It has very thin skin like a human. I think we should eat it.>>

<<Don't you be silly,>> said Bat to Cougar. Hanging upside down from the rocky ceiling it eyed me quizzically. <<We need to find out what it is first. Then we can decide what should be done about it coming to our sacred cave uninvited.>>

<<Look, see its eyes are open,>> Mouse gibbered excitedly. <<Someone ask it a question.>>

<<What are you, creature, Human or other?>>

<<I am both Human and lake Seal,>>I said. <<My mother is a woman of the Qwani'Ya Tsa'adi, but my father is a warrior of the Qwa'Nayhi, who usually takes the form of a lake seal in our world.>>

<<Hmm. That explains much,>> Eagle said. <<But not how you came to be here—or what you want from us.>>

Very slowly I sat up, cradling the snake in my lap. << I heard a sacred noise and followed. Unknowing, I came here in my Dream.>>

<<As I suspected,>> Owl said. <<This young one has much power.>>

I bobbed my head in acknowledgement of the Bird's compliment.<<As to what I want, I'm a stranger to your land—I seek knowledge of its mysteries. Evil men have taken me and my people from our home by Big Ice Lake. We had no choice. And now we are hear with no Spirits to help and protect us. I come on behalf of my People, asking for your teachings, asking for protection.>>

<<You already have a Benefactor,>> Eagle said. I can see the mark of the Great Aseutl upon you, why do you wish another Guardian?>>

<<It is true that I have pledged myself to Kunai, but his home is far from here. I need to understand this new and dry land where my people and I now live. I ask for a guide and protector with knowledge unique to this desert. Would someone of your Spirit Council help me? For I truly need your protection.>>

<<The Great Aseutl is the one best suited to protect you from the alien spectre that stalks you,>> Cougar said.

With a sinking feeling I suspected that the big cat was right. I had pledged my life to him, and only he could protect me from the foreigners' god or his demons. And yet...

<<It's true that the Great Kunai is very powerful, but all are needed in this struggle to protect the Earth Mother and Her traditions. You should be warned—if you don't already know—my enemy is yours as well. The foreigners and their god seek dominion over all in this land. They will destroy its beauty and harmony if not stopped.>>

The Spirit Beings gathered by the sacred spring were silent for along time—pondering my words—deciding my fate. At last Eagle spoke, <<We've heard your words, child of two peoples. You are wise for your years and have given us much to consider.>>

I lifted my arm, changed my flipper back into a hand and allowed it to lightly caress the dry scaly skin of the being lying in my lap. <<If you would share with me your Qwakaiva I will willingly share my warmth with you when you need it,>> I told her.

<<You must go back now, before your spirit is parted from your mortal flesh.>> Eagle said sternly, before Rattlesnake could reply.

Hearing the desperation in my own voice, I begged, <<But I need your wisdom. I am here in this desert and I must acquire the power rooted in this land if I am to help my people survive. We sicken in this place and without Qwakaiva we will die. Won't you help us—help me?>>

<<Be easy in your heart, young one. You will be contacted in your dreams when the Council has pondered your request and made our decision,>> Eagle said. <<Listen for Rattlesnake's call and follow where the sound takes you. Then you will know our answer.>>

I heard no more, for I was swept away, spinning round and round on a mighty wind. A dark wind that carried me back to a world of cold, hunger and despair among the living.

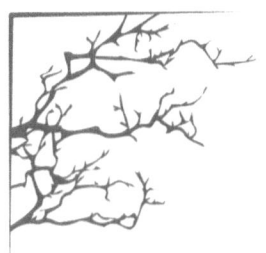

Chapter Eleven

I was weak for quite some time after my fever broke and the ugly spots disappeared from my skin. Grandmother too had been very ill. Though her mind often wandered, her body was recovering with the return of early spring's warmer weather, and we all hoped she would get better in mind and spirit as well. Mother and Grandfather looked gaunt and haggard, but had managed to come through the worst of the evil with only light fevers.

Though I was shielded from the knowledge during the worst of my weakness, Uncle Royston's son Hathin and many others in the settlement hadn't survived the cold, the hunger and diseases of that terrible winter.

I hadn't cared much for the whiny little boy during his short life, but his death saddened me. I'd been too ill to attend his funeral, but I grieved with Uncle and his family when Amima told me the news.

When I was well enough to hobble about the encampment, Amima gently suggested that I resume wearing the Thunderer's talisman. Prior to that time its removal had been Grandfather's and her little secret. Now, however, people would begin to notice its absence and ask unpleasant questions if they didn't see it.

"I probably don't have to tell you that with so many dead over the past few moons, tensions all over this Tribal Preserve are nearly bubbling over," Mother said as she held out the pendant to me one morning.

I took the cursed thing, but hesitated before putting it back on. "Do I really have to, Amima?"

She sighed and suggested, "I know you don't want to, but it would be better—and safer for you if you did. Everyone is looking for reasons why this evil happened to us.

"Oh I know many, even among the Converts, blame the Chamuqwani and their lies—as well they should, but some around here would be more than happy to make an accusation of witchcraft at anyone not wearing the god's talisman."

I stared at her open mouthed. "But I almost died of the evil—how could they think—"

"People are afraid; they will believe whatever suits them to believe if it will ease their fears," she counseled. "And our family..." she left the rest of her thought unvoiced, but I knew what she meant.

Swallowing down my unease, I returned the pendant to its former place around my neck. Occasionally I heard the demon's whisper in my mind or saw its malignant red eyes in my dreams, but then I would hear Rattlesnake's tail whirring, and I gained strength from the sound.

And she was right about the accusations of witchcraft, too. Not long after I regained enough strength to resume my hunting up the creek Charlic and his band of scavenging weasels ambushed me when I was returning back from a successful hunt.

Still weak from my long illness I wasn't paying enough attention to my surroundings, my mind focusing on a warm fire and roasting rabbit when they jumped me.

Stepping in from behind the large boy named Kiethrap grabbed my arms, forcing them painfully behind my back. The next thing I knew Charlic and the others were punching and kicking me, calling me "witch boy and other foul Chamuqwani names, accusing me of causing the sickness.

"But I was sick, too, stupid dog turds!" I choked out in between their blows. "If I did what you claim, why would I make myself sick? My grandfather said I almost died, smelly fish guts—leave me alone!"

"Who believes that dirty old man?" Someone behind me snarled and punched me hard in the ribs. He's a malicer, too."

Then a bit later when I was getting desperate, I croaked, "And I wear the Thunderer's talisman—same as you. All of you saw my uncle and the priest baptise me in the holy smoke. What's a matter with you—are you mad dogs? Stop!"

Some of the boys hesitated at my words, but Charlic gave me a murderous glare and punched me hard in the gut. With a groan I puked up the slim contents of my stomach on the ground at his feet.

With a Chamuqwani curse he hopped back, snarling. "You're lying, witch boy; you're not one of us and we both know it."

Well he was right about that, the sly dog turd, but still— Fortunately, I had put the charm back on before I started for the settlement.

Breathing hard with the exertion of beating me, he suddenly voiced what I believed was his real reason for their ambush. "Stay away from my betrothed, Thonna! She belongs to me—me, dog turd, do you hear me? And I don't want her ruining her reputation by spending time with a God-cursed malicer, like you."

If my jaw didn't hurt so much by that time it would have fallen open with shock. "She's my coshelah cousin, I'm not going to marry her, stupid dog fart."

Then thinking about his words a little more I got angry, and blurted, "Thonna belongs to you! You? Since when does one of the Qwani'Ya People own another? You are a disgusting pile of fish guts to even say such a terrible thing. What's a matter with you—all of you, if you would consider dishonoring any woman or girl so!"

"The Great God teaches in his Blue Book that a wife belongs to her husband, and I will have the right to beat any other notion out of her when we are wed."

I sat up, wiping the blood dripping from my nose and mouth onto my sleeve. Angry beyond any sense of caution and self-preservation, I taunted, "Have a care; Thonna is my coshelah cousin and I won't stand by and see my relative hurt by a bully and coward like you. If I am the witch you think I truly am, you might be sorry if you hurt her."

Charlic swore a vile Chamuqwani oath then hit me so hard I must have blacked out for a moment. When I regained my senses enough to pick myself up off the ground Charlic and his pack were gone—along with my cord of game.

Too sick and hurting to face any questions about my appearance if I followed them back to the settlement right then, I crawled off into the brush like a wounded wolf to lick my wounds in private.

It was nearly dark when Thonna and my mother found me. Helping me to my feet they half carried me back to the settlement. "I saved you some of the meal," Thonna murmured, as she helped Mother lay me on the blankets.

"I knew that carrion-eater was lying when he claimed he had caught so many rabbits. And then when you didn't show up for the meal..." Choking on a sob she left the rest of her thought unvoiced.

Mother sent her for more water and fresh willow bark for tea at that point. Not long after that I drifted off into a troubled sleep while she washed and bandaged my wounds.I would be grateful for the food later, but right then all I wanted was to escape the pain.

Grandfather gave me healing herb teas to drink when he returned, but I remained close to our hut for several days after the attack, wary about being caught alone again until I regained my strength. I don't know what Mother or Thonna told Grandfather and Uncle Royston, but nothing more was said to me about the incident.

And, Charlic and the other boys as far as I knew were never punished for what they did to me. The beating was a good lesson, however, for it taught me to always be on my guard. It was a lesson that would serve me well in the years to come.

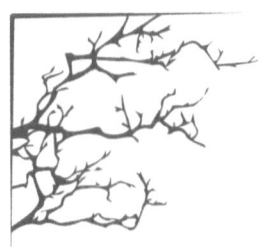

Chapter Twelve

Unlike the slow awakening of spring I'd grown used to in the north, this desert seemed to burst with life as soon as the white sun began to climb higher into the blue sky each day.

Bright green buds appeared overnight on the aspen and cottonwoods along the creek. The silver furry buds of willow gleamed against their branches' red-brown bark. Birds sang in the grey sagebrush and hawks and golden eagles soared with wings out stretched, riding the warm air currents, searching for unwary prey.

The sun was a welcome and comforting warmth, lifting everyone's spirits, but there was little or no rain to raise the water in the creek. Like my Elders, I feared the sun's power when full summer came to this land. But I tried not to dwell on what I couldn't stop or change.

In spite of the recent beating I was healing, growing stronger with each day. I nibbled on green buds and shoots like the deer, and resumed setting my snares along the stream. I was learning the rhythms of my new home; I would adjust in time.

On the ration day after the full moon, I asked to go to the agency with Uncle Royston, Mother, Chief Eagan and others from the settlement who had recovered enough for the trip. We were in desperate need of our allotment of bac'con, grease, course flour, oat-mush, kafa, sorgum-lases, and hard white beans.

As the winter moons had dragged on the rations allotments had been cut, then cut again, because the promised supplies never arrived. In spite of the better weather, a cloud of sadness hung above the settlement, weeping women and the men's prayer chants a constant din in my head. I welcomed the next trip to the agency as a break to the monotony of our days, so even though I was still weaker than I cared to admit, I begged to go.

Up at dawn, we left as soon as we'd gulped down a cup or two of juniper tea. Our settlement wasn't far along the creek, but it was far enough that the sun would be climbing high into the clear blue sky before we neared the agency.

Though I'd been looking forward to seeing my friends, my footsteps began to drag before we'd traveled only half the distance to the agency. I hadn't made the journey with the family for a number of ration-day cycles, and I was surprised how weak I felt.

"Are you well, Grandson? You can return home if you are still too sick to make the journey. The agent won't give us much, I think. I can carry your portion and my own."

His gentle words jerking me out of my misery, I looked up from the path where I'd been concentrating on putting one foot in front of the other. I saw the retreating backs of my relatives at the top of a small hill some distance ahead. Thonna turned her head as if searching for me. Probably laughing at me, just waiting to tease me for my laziness, I thought.

Though she had been very ill last fall soon after the Converts came to the Tribal Preserve, during this last sending of the evil, Thonna had remained untouched by the fevers that had swept through the Preserve.

Since my recovery from my illness and Charlic's beating she had been unusually kind to me, doing some of my chores and bringing me food treats whenever she could. I suspected she was doing it to annoy her betrothed, but in the misguided thinking of the young, I also thought she was doing it to let everyone know how weak and babyish she thought me, as well.

I gritted my teeth and looked away, my resolve renewed. I was no baby to stay home with the grannies and sick children. I was nearly a man, wasn't I? Forcing a smile for Grandfather's sake, I shook my head and kept walking. "I'm all right, Grandfather. You don't have to worry about me."

He narrowed his eyes and I knew he was looking at me with his Spirit-Sight, but I didn't care. I was going to the agency and carry my share of our supplies, and that was that.

At last he nodded and fell into step beside me.

When we neared our destination at last, I was dizzy from the growing heat and exhausted, but I soon forgot about my own miseries when I noticed the new encampment of ragged tents and grass shelters that had sprung up around the outskirts of the agency since my last visit.

Some of the tents and people looked vaguely familiar, but my sluggish brain couldn't make sense of what my eyes were telling me. My empty belly cramped, my bones ached and it was all I could do to put one foot in front of the other and keep moving.

Finally curiosity pierced the fog clouding my mind and I asked, "Where did all those people come from? Did the Chamuqwani bring some new people here—more of the dust-eaters?"

He frowned at my use of the derogatory name some of the Converts called the tall darker-skinned Kukiya desert tribesmen that the Chamuqwani had also confined to the Preserve with us.

Glancing in the direction I was pointing, he shook his head. "No, Grandson, those are our relatives. See, there's Aunty Qwatsitsa's eldest grandson holding one of the soldier's horses. Don't you recognize him?"

I did, now that Grandfather had drawn my attention to him. But I couldn't be blamed for not recognizing him. Lake Jumper had changed. Dressed in dirty Chamuqwani cast-offs and as thin as the post by which he was standing, he no longer wore a proper hunter's braid. His hair had been hacked off unevenly at the shoulders and what remained was streaked with premature grey.

Then I recognized other relatives and friends and my spirits lifted. Was Samiqwas living here; could I come live here too? But as we drew nearer I began to see the world around me more clearly. True, this was no gathering for ration day feasting and trading; it was a permanent settlement—a settlement of the broken and lost.

The camp had a squalid occupied look that reeked of apathy and despair. Sullen, hollow-eyed women sat cross-legged on the stony ground holding irritable, unwashed children. People coughed and spat blood onto the ground as they moved aimlessly from one place to another. The stench of urine and feces stung my nose as I turned away.

We were sick, hungry and without most necessities in the convert settlement, necessities that I'd taken for granted at home, but Chief Eagan and his council would have never tolerated the filth and the neglect that I witnessed. I scanned the encampment with an inner disgust that I hoped couldn't be read in my expression, and prayed silently that I wouldn't find Samiqwas here.

Unable to keep silent any longer, I blurted, "This is terrible. Why are all these people living here? Surely the agent has given them land elsewhere in this vast preserve?"

"Yes, they probably do have allotted land elsewhere, Grandson, but it may be too far away for them to walk to and come back for their rations. Look about you, my dear one. Most of these people are sick and starving. They have nowhere else to go."

Bleached bones lying in heaps on a rocky hillside, hot swirling wind coating them with dust as red as dried blood, the sending made me gasp with its power. Nowhere else to go, yes I could recognise the truth in those words. Trapped in this hot dry land—none of us had anywhere else to go—but to our graves.

With such thoughts, Mighty Djoven's pendant suddenly dragged at my neck as if it weighed as much as a moose. I staggered then grimly continued walking. Enhanced by my own fear, I'd fallen prey to an illusion—nothing more. Mocking laughter swirled in my mind and a dry voice whispered, <<Surrender to me. Only I can save you from this.>>

Ignore it! The foul creature has no power unless you give it some. Its words disappeared in the whir of a snake's warning rattle. To distract myself, I asked, "Is this where you come when you disappear from our shelter, Grandfather?"

He sighed and looked down at me. In a voice barely above a whisper, he said, "Sometimes I come. I look for medicine in the desert to help them."

"Why won't you let me come with you? I could help you." My hand trembling I pulled the hated pendant from my shirt and held it out to show him. You know I hate living at Uncle's. When we first came you talked about going with Tli to the mountains in search of caves where the ancient teachings of this land could be found. What has happened to change your mind? You yourself have chosen not to wear the enemy's brand. How could you let them do this to me?"

We walked in silence for a long moment, before he answered. "I am an old man. I will die soon. As much as I dislike to admit it, my eldest son is probably right. We must accept the Chamuqwani way now. Our old ways are dying and we will die with them if we can't learn to change. Accept what has been offered you and let go of the past, Grandson."

I stopped in the path to stare at him as if he had just sprouted moose horns from the top of his head. When the words came, I couldn't keep the bitterness from my voice, and didn't try. "Knowing who my father is and the gifts I have inherited from him, how can you say such evil words to me?"

My accusation sparked red spears of irritation in his aura and a harshness in his voice to match my own. "It's precisely because I do know these things about you that I tell you to forget about your father and what Chumco taught you."

"Leave me to be swallowed up by the demon that has eaten Chief Eagan's spirit? Chumco warned me, you would betray me; do you remember?"

His face paled at my accusations, but he remained silent doggedly continuing to walk down the dusty trail.

His words about my father had been like bright steal knives slicing my heart, leaving me speechless. He hadn't dared look at me, knowing perhaps the shock and hurt he would see in my eyes. At that moment I wanted to cry out more hurtful words, *If your hatred of the Qwa'Nayhi who fathered me is more important to you than your love for me or my well-being, then I will go my own way and not bother you again.*

I didn't, of course, he was my Elder and the teachings of respect that had been drummed into me since my babyhood couldn't be ignored so easily. So I swallowed my bitter words, kept my mouth shut and hurried ahead to walk beside my mother.

By the time we arrived at the long two-storied building that served as the agency's office and trading post many people were listlessly sitting on the ground in the growing heat, waiting for the rationing to begin. No one was talking much, just waiting with their sacks and willow baskets clustered about them.

I scanned the growing crowd, searching for Samiqwas, at last spotting him sharing a smoke that he must have gotten from one of the soldiers with Matoqwa and some of our friends. Though dirty and ragged, my old hunting pack joked and aimed mock punches at one another as they always had. My heart ached at the sight of them, and I longed to leave my place beside Uncle and Grandfather to join them.

I would have made the excuse of using the privy to get away, but just then the fat agent came out of his office door and took his place behind the long table on the porch. He opened his big book and motioned for Abe the interpreter to announce he was ready. Without needing to be told, the waiting people formed a line to receive their ration vouchers.

When it was my family's turn, I took my place beside Grandfather and Mother and stepped up onto the porch. Just ahead of us in line, I heard Uncle give the name of his dead son and his wife's younger sister to the agent when it was his turn to collect his family's rations.

Startled, I glanced at Grandfather. He put a hand on my shoulder and squeezed gently, warning me to keep silent. Confused, I dropped my eyes to the dusty planks of the porch and kept moving.

When I focused my attention once more, Chief Eagan was saying to the agent, "The weather is warming and the water is rising in the creek. It will soon be time to plant the seeds the Father Emperor has promised us for the gardens he wishes us to grow. My people are hungry, and will be more so by next winter. Where are the seeds and the farm tools we will need to dig the holes for them, so we can plant them in the earth?"

Flushed and sweaty even in the shade of the porch, when Abe translated Eagan's words Agent Daglish's face became an even deeper shade of red. "The wagons are coming," he snapped, motioning with an impatient hand gesture for Eagan to move along. The old man ignored the gesture as if he hadn't understood and continued to wait. "You will get the supplies as soon as they arrive, now move along. They are coming."

As the news was passed down the line I could hear a chorus of angry muttering. This red-faced Chamuqwani was fat while others starved. Maybe he was stealing our rations and keeping them for himself. Someone in the line behind me snorted. "The supplies are coming? He has been saying that for moons and still there is nothing for us but mush and salty bac'con—and little enough of that."

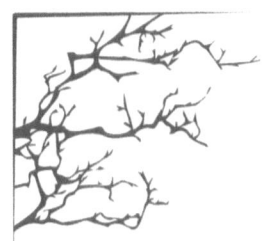

Chapter Thirteen

When Grandfather showed the agent's servant his medal with the numbers on it a mark was made beside his name in the agent's book. Then, he was given a few small pieces of paper with colored pictures and Chamuqwani writing on them. The interpreter had told us on the first ration day that this paper was called "script." With Script we could go to the next door on the porch, which was the trading post's door and exchange the paper for our allotment of rations.

Unlike the good smells of smoked fish and peppermint candy that I associated with the trading post on Big Ice Lake, this store had a musty unpleasant odour. It stank of dirt and putrefying meat.

Grandfather handed the bald trader our Script and he marked down our ration allotment. While he did this, another trader put small sacks of oat-mush and flour, a can of grease and two tiny pouches of kafa and sorgum-lases on the counter. While he was doing that, the bald trader measured a smelly lump of bac'con on his measure scales.

When he wrapped it in dirty cloth and tried to place it with the rest, Grandfather put a hand out to stop him. In his best Chamuqwani, he said, "No want. Meat bad—make mans sick."

The trader's mouth hardened into a thin line. "It won't make you sick," he growled. Grandfather said nothing, rudely staring the man in the eye. The trader was lying and they both knew it.

The meat, in spite of its coating of salt from the storage barrel stank of rot. With my Spirit-Sight I could see the brown slime crawling over and within it. As hungry as I was, the thought of eating that particular meat made my stomach cramp.

"No want bad meat," Grandfather repeated stubbornly.

The trader called Grandfather a bad word in his language and slammed his hand down on the counter. "Take it. It's a little ripe that's all. It's still good."

"No. Me want hard beans—no bad meat," Grandfather insisted.

"Listen, you stupid zaunk you take the meat or nothing. No beans! Beans all gone. No beans, you hear? No beans."

Grandfather started to walk away, but mother stopped him. "Take it, Appi. Tasimu can use it as bait for his deadfalls. Maybe he can catch a weasel or coyote and we can trade the hides next time we come."

Grandfather picked up his supplies—including the meat and we walked back out into the noon day heat.

Once more outside the noon day pounced upon us like a hungry lynx. Mother fanned herself with a piece of rag and complained to Marika's eldest sister, Ashiqwa, about the heat. Marika herself had stayed home to tend the sick and my ailing grandmother. The two women moved to the shade of the building and joined some other women they knew from Broken Shell Mound village back home.

I followed them and set down my carry-pack beside Mother. Then seized with an idea that would get me away from their watchful eyes for a while, I offered to go to the pump in the stable yard and bring them back some cool water.

"That would be very thoughtful of you, my son," Mother said. She rummaged in her sack and drew out the soot-stained and battered tin can that we used as a tea pot. She handed it to me and smiled.

I was thirsty, but my real reason for getting the water was to have a look around while I was doing so. I'd lost track of Samiqwas when I'd gone into the post with Grandfather, and I was anxious to find him before Chief Eagan and Uncle decided it was time for us to leave.

Those who lived further up the valley often camped at the agency overnight, catching up on the gossip and visiting before heading back into the desert. Chief Eagan and Uncle never indulged in what Eagan considered "idle foolishness." Our trips to the agency were confined to business and a quick return to our own encampment.

Passing by the soldier's wooden barracks, I spied Samiqwas by the stables. He and Matoqwa, Cohasi and a couple boys from the Kukiya desert tribe were lounging against a pole fence idly watching his father Ko, his brother Gagayii and a few of the brown uniformed soldiers posted at the agency playing a gambling game with square painted rocks they called dice.

As I waited in line to fill the tin can for Mother at the pump, I caught Samiqwas's eye and waved. He saw me wave, but no smile of recognition crossed his face. Puzzled by his reaction, when next I caught his eye, I mouthed, "What's going on?" He shrugged and turned away, pretending to be engrossed in the game.

My eyes followed his out of curiosity. His father picked up the dice cup from a swearing soldier and made the toss. Someone shouted a praise call as Ko bent to pick up his winnings.

Puzzled by Samiqwas's odd behaviour, I hurried to drink my fill when it was my turn at the pump, then rushed back to Mother with the brimming can. In my absence Thonna had joined the women. She sat with her arms resting atop her bony knees, gazing longingly at the people wandering about the open area in front of the store. Her long hair had come lose from her braids and floated about her pinched face in dark wisps. She looked bored and hot, but she brightened when she saw me come up to the women with the water.

When I handed Mother the can, I begged, "I saw Samiqwas by the pump, Amima, can I go talk with him a while before we have to go back?"

Thonna glared at me, then swallowed her pride and mouthed, "Take me with you." I pretended not to see the desperation in her eyes. She was my coshelah—I should rescue her—the women would only let her go walking about if I agreed to be her chaperone. But she was a girl—and Samiqwas was—special. I selfishly didn't want her with me for my reunion with him.

Mother glanced around and finding Chief Eagan and Uncle talking with some other convert Elders and Intercessor Karl, she smiled at me and nodded. "Go ahead, son, but don't be gone too long. Give my nephew my love, too. Tell him to come see us some time."

Come see us some time? As I walked away I thought how unlikely that might be. The longer we stayed on the Preserve the divisions between the Qwani'Ya people had only widened, not healed.

Unlike Uncle Tli, Ko and his brother had never taken much interest in the larger affairs of the People. Gambling and finding another waskyja bottle occupied most of their time. If Samiqwas was living here at the agency—as I feared—I could guess why.

There'd been a time when I knew my cousin-brother's mind and heart as well as I knew my own—but that was before his sister died, his mother had run away with a soldier and he had gone to live with his father's kin in the Chamuqwani fashion.

Matoqwa and his brother Cohasi were nowhere in sight when I found him still observing the gambling. With a friendly smile plastered to my face, I joined him and the desert boys by the fence. I nudged him with my elbow to get his attention. He grunted when he saw it was me, then turned back to the game without a word. Though dirty and skeletally thin, he seemed to have grown taller since last I'd seen him. The yellow-eyed wolf that was his guardian, watched me from the smoky depths of his aura, its lip lifted in a silent snarl.

I stared at the back of his head for a long moment, before I asked, "I saw your father gathering in his winnings when I was getting water for Amima—she told me to give you her love—who's winning now?"

He snorted and moved a little farther down the fence. "Not Father that's for certain," he muttered still not looking at me. One of the desert boys said something to his friends in their own language and another laughed, looking at us. Feeling the heat rise into my face, I ignored their rudeness and turned to watch the gambling, still keeping an eye on my cousin out of the corner of my eye. What was wrong with him today? He was behaving like I was a rude stranger—or like I had dog shit plastered on my face.

I hadn't seen Samiqwas in moons because of my illness—surely someone had told him—if he'd asked—why I hadn't come to the agency. His coolness towards me that day hurt me deeply. He was snubbing me, hoping I would leave maybe, but I couldn't. He was my best friend. I continued to watch the gesticulating men shake the cup and throw the dice.

Ko had a brown bottle beside him and he drank from it often as he played. The big pile of script I'd seen beside him on the blanket earlier was nearly gone. I looked up as someone hailed Samiqwas. Matoqwa and the rest of our friends were returning pieces of greasy brown bannock clutched in their hands. I hadn't eaten yet that day and my mouth watered at the sight.

When Matoqwa saw me his mouth hardened. He said something to the others and they stopped their joking and fell silent. Coming up to Samiqwas he handed him the last piece of bannock, then turned to face me his hands balled into fists at his side.

Matoqwa and I had always had an uneasy friendship, but looking at him with my Spirit-Sight at that moment I was startled by the murderous intent I could see radiating from the Bear in his Spirit Fire.

I glanced at my cousin, begging for some explanation for my friends' odd behaviour. His aura told me that he wasn't angry with me, but he made no move to stick up for me either. He ate his bannock with a focussed intensity as if I were invisible. Swallowing down the fear knotting in my gut, I took a step backwards. I had no friends here—not anymore.

"What's wrong? Why are you looking at me like that, my relatives?"

Matoqwa lifted his lip in a sneer. He took a step towards me, the rest, including the desert boys—all but Samiqwas—edging round to try and encircle me.

"Relative? You are no kin to me, traitor," he snarled and took a swing at my head. I ducked and dodged another blow from Cohasi.

Before they could totally surround me, I backed around the corner of the fence, to put the stable wall at my back. "What do you mean I'm no kin to you? Of course we're related—second cousins. And wasn't it you who always said that all us boys from Big Ice Lake had to stick together?"

"That was before you turned traitor, dog turd," Cohasi snapped and aimed another punch at my head.

He was too slow; I blocked it easily, but the accusation ignited my temper, so I raised my own fist in answer to his threat. "You're as crazy as old aunty Deer Mouse was before she died. I'm no traitor, smelly fish guts."

"Oh no?" Matoqwa sneered. "Then what's that piece of silver I see hanging around your neck, hmm?"

"Yeah, what is that, convert boy? You trying to spy on us for that new half-breed pal of yours?"

"No! Charlic and those convert brats aren't my friends—I hate them."

"Sure you do—liar!" the pack closed ranks about me. I could feel the splintery wood pressing into my back.

I glanced towards my cousin who hadn't joined the others, but spoke no word in my defence either. "Tell them, cousin-brother. I'm no convert traitor. Like Grandfather I'm true to our traditions."

I saw the swirling colors of indecision raging in his aura, but his voice was as cold as a wind off a glacier when he spoke, "Where have you been the last few moons? And why are you wearing the Thunderer's token if you aren't a convert now, hmm?"

"If you had bothered to ask someone, you would have learned that I've been ill with a bad fever—you can ask Amima or Grandfather if you don't believe me." I grabbed the silver lightning bolt in my fist, its sharpened edges biting into my palm. "I'm only wearing this because Grandmother and Uncle want me to. I have to respect my Elders don't I?"

Blood moistened my palm and snaked down my forearm. A burning sensation flowed up my arm and a wave of dizziness blurred my vision. In the back of my mind I heard once more the spectre that wanted me and fed off Chief Eagan, mocking me with its laughter.

"Liar. You haven't been around because you were too afraid of what we might do to you," Cohasi taunted.

Matoqwa cracked his knuckles and smiled like a wolverine, ready for the kill. "As he should be."

I said a bad word in the Chamuqwani language and raised my fist. "I'm not afraid of you—any of you. I'm no convert—see." Before I could give myself time to consider the consequences of my actions, I ripped the hated talisman from my neck and threw it into Matoqwa's face.

The unexpected throw startled him, and I took advantage of his momentary distraction to try and escape. I was no coward, but even if Samiqwas stayed out of the fight, there were eight of them against me. I was no fool and the odds weren't in my favor.

I didn't get very far, however, before I was tackled from behind. I stumbled to the ground and curled into a ball as someone heavy fell on top of me. Then my one-time friends and the desert boys shouted encouragement to each other as they kicked and pounded me with their fists.

Called dog turd by my former friends and witch boy by the convert brats I was caught in the middle of warring factions with nowhere to turn.

I don't know what might have happened to me—maybe they would have killed me—or just gotten bored and wandered off to find someone else to torment. But praise my ancestors, someone made them stop, before they'd inflicted too much damage.

Through a black and red haze of pain I saw red blood suddenly blossom on Cohasi's face and he backed away, clutching his cheek and howling. Someone was shouting Chamuqwani curses at them and then they were backing away and I could see daylight and the cruel hot sun above me.

Grabbing onto the fence, I staggered to my feet. I spat blood from my aching mouth and looked around, my sluggish mind trying to figure out why they'd stopped pounding me.

Then I saw my rescuer and my eyes widened. Thonna red faced and wild eyed, had Matoqwa backed up against the stable wall, her balled up fist slamming into his chest as she scolded him like a toddler.

"Dog turd, mouse piss drinker! Leave him alone." She left off her punching to wave a hand at the other boys who were as stunned as I was. "Does it take all of you mighty warriors to battle one person? Cowards all of you. You shame your mothers and your ancestors! Are you maddened animals or people? He's been ill for moons with the spotted fever sickness—barely well enough to walk to the agency—and now look!"

The hunting pack was liberally splattered with horse dung and blood, as witness to her accuracy with stones and other such lethal missiles. To my surprise no one had challenged her or tried to defend themselves from her assault. Instead they dropped their eyes as if embarrassed by her scolding.

Inwardly I groaned as humiliated as the others, but for a different reason. By next ration day the word would be all over the Preserve that I had needed my coshelah girl cousin to rescue me. I made the mistake of glancing at Matoqwa and saw my worst fears take shape in his mind. Behind Thonna's back he smirked and drew his hand across his throat.

Next time I wouldn't be so lucky. I sighed and pushed myself off the fence. "Coshelah, stop; let's go."

But Thonna wasn't listening; she'd just spotted Samiqwas lurking at the edge of the group and turned the full force of her ire in his direction. Marching right up to him she poked him in the chest, and snarled, "You and your friends dare call Tasimu traitor! I say it is you who are the traitor—traitor to your own blood—your family. He is your brother-cousin. How could you let those rabid animals attack him and not help him. You are a coward and—and-and disgusting!"

Though to her way of thinking her attack on Samiqwas was justified, I could sense his shame and her shouting at him was only making him feel worse. I hated the barrier that had grown up between us. I mourned the loss of his friendship, but I still loved him. And for the sake of our childhood spent together, I wasn't going to let anyone hurt him more.

Fighting back the dizziness that was still clouding my mind, I lurched forward and took her roughly by the arm. "Thonna! I said enough. Let's go." Like a deer caught in torchlight, she stared up at me uncomprehending. Before she could gather her wits enough to make a protest I pulled her after me around the stable and headed for the pump. I needed to wash off some of the dirt and blood before Mother saw me.

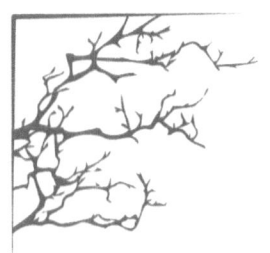

Chapter Fourteen

Once we were out of sight of the others she jerked her arm out of my grasp and stopped, her hands on her hips. Tears were pooling in the corners of her eyes, but her voice was harsh with anger when she spoke. "What's wrong with you? Ungrateful boy, I was only trying to help."

"I know you were, and I'm grateful—truly I am. It's just Samiqwas—we are—well, there's a lot you don't understand about Samiqwas."

She snorted and folded her arms across her chest. "So tell me."

I put my hand to the pump and gave the handle a couple good strokes. Feelings twisted like a whirlwind in my chest. How could I explain? "I will—I promise—someday soon, but right now will you help me with the water so I can get cleaned up?"

I held my hands under the spout and motioned for her to pump. She sighed and lifted the handle. The cool water splashed over my hands like a healing balm. The white sun was baking the ground, even though it was only early spring—there would be another two moons at least of snow back home—don't think about home.

I took off my tunic wet it, wiped off my face and chest, and then rinsed it in the water again. I would have done a more thorough job, washing the grime from my hair as well, but an Elder shouted at us to stop wasting water, so we left the pump and I put my damp tunic back on.

As we headed back towards the trading post, I was still nursing the humiliation of being rescued by a girl, so to taunt her, I asked, "What were you doing over by the stable? I thought your aunty told you not to wander off or someone might think you were a cloocha-whore, looking for men."

She flushed and muttered something uncomplimentary about me under her breath and looked at me out of the corner of her eye to see if I'd heard. Refusing to be baited, I smiled to let her know that I had, but was far too mature to fall for such a childish ploy.

She scowled, then in a normal tone of voice, she said, "My aunty was busy elsewhere, so your mother told me to go find you, because my father said we would be leaving soon—which, I might add, was some time ago."

An unexpected reprieve from the scolding we both feared came in the form of a dust cloud growing on the southern horizon. By the time we reached our family, the news that wagons were coming had spread like a forest fire through the agency. Everyone was excited; the promised treaty goods had finally arrived.

Giving Thonna and me a passing glance that took note of her flushed face and my dishevelled appearance, Uncle Royston turned to confer with his father-in-law, Grandfather, and the Elders of our party. It was decided that a few of the men and most of the women and young people would return to the settlement with most of the food ration to make sure the people waiting wouldn't go hungry for another day. The rest of us would wait until the wagons arrived and were unloaded.

Thonna, to her disgust, was forced to go back to the settlement with her Aunty Ashiqwa, but when I asked Grandfather if I could stay, he surprised me by agreeing. Mother too stayed to cook in case we had to remain overnight.

The wagons were still some ways off, so there wasn't anything to do but wait. Mother asked to use someone's cook fire in the camp and made us some mush with some dried berries in it. The gluey mess was bitter because of the resinous berries, but it helped fill the emptiness in my gut, for which I was grateful.

Considering what happened later, I should have pleaded a weakness from my illness and gone back with Thonna and the rest, but I foolishly wanted to gloat over my girl cousin, flaunting the superiority of my freedom. It was childish, but my budding male pride still was injured by her rescue, and I knew my staying would gall her no end.

Fearing my former friends from home might be waiting in ambush for me should I venture exploring on my own, I kept close to Grandfather's side, hoping to avoid more trouble. When after the meal he rose to walk around the encampment to see if anyone needed his services as a healer, I rose, too.

Before I could follow, however, Uncle Royston stopped me. "What have you and my disobedient daughter been up to?"

"Nothing, Uncle, I went to see Samiqwas and Mother sent her to find me. She did and we came back. That's all."

Well, that wasn't all and we both knew it, but I really didn't want to explain to him. I'm not sure what my face looked like, but it must have been bad. My shirt had dried by that time, but it had gotten torn on one sleeve and dirt and blood from my nose streaked its front. I probably looked a mess.

"Who were you fighting?"

"I wasn't fighting." *No, I was getting the shit pounded out of me.*

"Don't try to lie to me, boy," uncle snapped. "The proof is there on your face for all to see. As one of the Great God's Chosen you should be setting a good example for others, not brawling like some drunken heathen."

Once more I heard the creature's rasping laughter in my mind, sparking both my fear and my anger. It was because of this uncle and his god that my friends all hated me—called me traitor and spy. "I wasn't fighting. They attacked me. And I don't care about setting a good example, because I'm no damned convert, anyway!"

The words were barely out of my mouth, before I found myself sprawled in the dust once more that day. Uncle Royston's shadow looming over me, I spat out more blood and stared up at him.

Reaching down, he grabbed a fistful of my shirt and jerked me to my feet. "I'll have none of your sass. You are my adopted son and you will show me and the Great God some respect, do you hear me?"

Mother had abandoned her cleaning up chores and now stood beside her brother, begging him to calm down, telling him that I meant no harm. I wished she'd be quiet—I did mean what I'd said—and more.

"Well, maybe I have no wish to be a traitor's son. Nor am I a willing convert to the ways of your god." The pain of his slap fueling my rage, I opened my shirt and showed him my bare chest where the Thunderer's talisman no longer hung.

Royston's face darkened with his fury. He raised his fist and might have done me serious harm if Grandfather hadn't stepped between us and grabbed his arm. "No, my son, I can't let you hurt him any further. It isn't the Qwani'Ya way to beat a child. Remember the teachings of your youth and master yourself. Nothing will be gained by further violence here today."

When Uncle had quieted enough to see reason, Grandfather released his arm and motioned for me to follow him into the encampment of our sick and despairing relatives. As we wandered among the shelters, he watched me out of the corner of his eye, and finally asked, "Tell me what happened, Grandson. Who has hurt you?"

His tone was so gentle and understanding, that I felt the tears pooling in the corners of my eyes. I blinked hard to keep from bursting into tears, like some silly baby. Oh how I longed to crawl into the protection of his arms as I'd done as a child back home....

But I was no longer that innocent child, and he was old, no longer the man I trusted above all. I did, however owe him some explanation for my behaviour. Taking a deep breath, I told him about finding Samiqwas. How he had acted like I was his enemy, and how my former friends had called me a convert traitor and beaten me until brave Thonna stopped them.

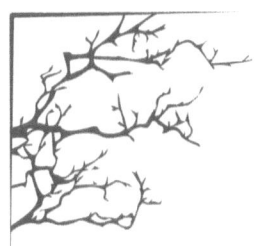

Chapter Fifteen

The wagons arrived while Grandfather and I were treating a young mother and her baby who both had bad coughs. Grandfather prayed over the little girl, drawing up the Qwakaihi of Fire from deep within the ground to aid the little one fight off the foreign infection. He handed the mother a small cloth tied with grass in which he'd placed willow and aspen bark. He told the girl's mother to gather more from near the creek when she ran out.

She nodded and thanked him, but I could see she was only half listening to his instructions. Everyone was shouting and running towards the stable yard where the wagons were being unloaded.

Grandfather and I looked at one another then headed back to the agency. The encampment had come suddenly alive. People forgot about their coughs and pains and smiled at one another, exclaiming about the big feast they planned to cook that night.

The gayety reminded me of the days back home when the steamboat arrived, bringing with it a cargo of wonders. We were just as curious and excited as everyone else, so we followed our friends and relatives back into the agency grounds.

I was disappointed to find that only five wagons were parked in the open area between the stable yard and the back of the trading post's warehouse. Chief Eagan had always implied there would be as many wagons bringing our treaty goods as stones on a hillside.

As we drew near, a large gathering of people were milling about shouting at the men unloading the wagons to hurry, so they could have some of the promised goods that day. The fat agent was there as well, making things worse. Red-faced and bawling he demanded that the people go away, so the men could work. "You will get your share later—maybe by the next ration day."

No one paid him any attention. Even the few unkempt soldiers posted to the agency to keep order, weren't doing much to keep back the anxious and excited people.

The trouble started when someone too eager to help, grabbed for a crate that the man on the wagon was holding over its side. The man on the wagon tried to ignore the outstretched hands and give it to a trader instead. He missed and the wooden crate slipped to the ground and split open.

Everyone crowded round to see, but to our horror the box was empty. There was a moment of stunned silence then several of the young men, Uncle Tli among them, climbed onto the wagons and began throwing down all the boxes they found.

Though the boxes had the Chamuqwani writing on them, most were empty, and the ones that weren't contain small shiny glass mirrors, not the promised farm tools or other supplies. None of the boxes that the angry men opened before the soldiers restored order contained food.

Amid the cursing and struggling men, a woman's high-pitched wail for her dead, pierced the tumult, causing us all to pause and stare.

"No food, no food! My baby is going to die. This fat Chamuqwani is killing my baby," she shrieked. I peered through the taller bodies blocking my view. Who was that crying—Shilshigua? "He grows fatter while our children starve." She let out a mournful wail, and was answered by other women in the crowd.

"Kill the fat Chamuqwani," a deep-voiced man in the crowd shouted. "Let's roast and eat him like one of his pigs. He will taste just as good."

There was a chorus of agreement to that suggestion, but by that time Commander Forggal had surrounded the frightened agent and was trying to escort him through the shouting people back to his office. In a quavering voice, the agent cried, "Go back to your homes—or I will have the soldiers put you in jail."

Uncle Tli laughed. "Let them try. There are only twenty of them. They can't kill us all. Then we come for you, fat man." He might have said more but two of the soldiers tackled him and he disappeared under a rain of blows. A woman screamed and someone hit a soldier with a piece of fresh horse dung.

Both Qwani'Ya and Kukiya desert tribesmen shouted their agreement to my uncle's plan. All the different people's earlier rivalries forgotten, they were united by this new threat to their families' survival. Children cried and women screamed, adding to the chaos.

"Your promises mean nothing," one of Tli's friends from Blue Lake shouted. "They are like water poured onto the sand. They disappear without a trace in the hot sun."

From behind his guarding soldiers, we could hear the fat agent, blubbering, "Please stop! Listen to me. This has all been a big mistake. I will do all in my power to find the bad men who tricked you and stole your treaty goods—I swear—I will get them back for you."

"Liar!" Amidst a chorus of angry shouts, a hailstorm of dung and other missiles thundered upon the men.

Knowing they were outnumbered many times over, Commander Forggal retreated to the agency porch and lined his men up with their weapons drawn and pointed at the crowd. Losing patience with us, Commander Forggal shot his thunder weapon into the air and threatened to call for reinforcements from Black Rock Fort if we didn't settle down.

His black coat rumpled and dirty, Agent Daglish peered from the safety of his office doorway at the angry people. When the soldiers once more had the crowd under control, the fat agent lost his fear of us and came out onto the porch. He pointed his finger at the people, his voice angry and accusing, blaming us for the misery of our lives.

"Why are you people always complaining? I'm sick and tired of your whining. If you take the mirrors and make fancy willow basket frames for them, I will have the traders sell them in the big towns of the Empire. These mirrors are a good thing. They will make money for you. Tell your lazy women to make pretty beaded designs for the mirrors' frames. We have a whole shipment of beads in the store we will sell to you cheap. Then you can buy what you want with the script you will be given when the mirrors sell."

"Our women have no experience in making such things," an Elder from Broken Shell Mound Village said. "We need food for our children and ourselves now, not shiny bits of glass. People can't make anything if bellies are empty. Take mirrors back."

"What good are these pieces of shiny glass? We can't eat them," someone shouted. "Take them back and give us food or thunder weapons so we can hunt and feed ourselves."

"True enough, those shiny pieces of metal can't be eaten," Chugai murmured to a man with a long scar on his cheek standing near me. "But they can catch the sun's Qwakaiva and focus it to make fire—lots of nice big fires." The man I didn't know looked about the agency his expression thoughtful. He smiled and nodded.

Unable to stop myself, I glanced about the agency too. There were many wooden buildings here, the dusty barn where the horses and mules were kept, the Chamuqwani trading post, the agent's office and homes, the half-finished temple with the bare golden ribs of its wooden frame bleaching in the harsh desert light. Yes, the mirrors' Qwakaiva could make many beautiful, bright fires.

Though the soldiers were obeying the agent, they didn't look happy about their jobs. Commander Forggal said something in a low voice to Agent Daglish that made his face blanch, but from fear or rage I was too far away to tell. The agent's further demands to disperse the angry men and crying women, met with a stubborn reluctance on the commander's part.

Seeing that he had little support from the few soldiers stationed at the agency, and guessing that this time the people weren't going to be satisfied with just talk, Agent Daglish finally instructed some of his men to slaughter a few of the fat smelly pigs he kept in the pens behind the stable.

"Don't worry about your missing treaty goods. I will give some of my own food to make up for the loss."

"And probably charge us for it, too," someone muttered.

"We will all have a feast tonight, a big party. You would like that, yes?" he knew we would. And though some of the People continued to grumble, things quieted down when the animals were killed and the smoky-rich smell of roasting meat filled the air.

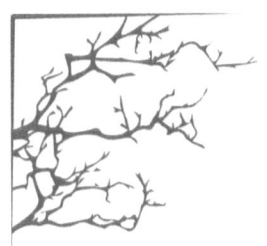

Chapter Sixteen

I think Grandfather must have had a talk with Uncle Royston sometime during that night of feasting at the agency, because no more was said about my throwing away the god's talisman. And truth be told, I was glad for it. Perhaps it was only the first good meal I'd had in a while lulling me into a new feeling of well-being, but I felt as if a burning weight had been taken away. My Spirit felt as light as cattail down on the breeze, my body renewed with strength and vigour.

With some of the freshly killed meat and a box of the despised mirrors among our belongings, we left for the convert settlement early the next morning. Deciding to take the agent's advice, Chief Eagan took the mirrors and a few other trinkets from the post store to see what might be made of them for sale in the Empire.

Though they would have never admitted it if asked outright, by chance I overheard them talking that evening and I knew that the incident with the empty boxes that should have contained farming tools had upset the Convert leaders deeply. All through the long cold winter of starvation, they had prayed to the new god and kept their faith in the Empire and its promises strong. Such a betrayal had come as a shattering blow.

Still suffering with the aches and bruises of my recent fight with Matoqwa and his friends, I couldn't sleep that night. When I stepped outside I saw our women's cook fire still alight, and so I headed in that direction, hoping for some hot willow bark tea.

While still in the shadows, I noticed that the hunched figures round the fire weren't my new aunties, but Chief Eagan, Uncle and Charlic's father Samith. I paused, before they saw me, uncertain what to do next. I should have gone back to my blanket, but I did want some tea, and this secretive meeting sparked my interest. I crouched in the shadows, daring to listen and hoping they would leave soon.

Samith was saying, "...This lord's agent is stealing from us I fear. My son read the words on the empty boxes. They said they had hoes and shovels inside—but they didn't. What happened to the tools, I want to know."

"And will they charge us for the things we never received? That's the question I would like answered as well," Uncle added.

Chief Eagan grunted and placed another stick on the fire. The light flared, revealing his scowl. "I never have liked to look of that fat man. He is weak of nature, but he may not be the thief. Any one of the traders—or even some of the soldiers or wagon men could have taken the good somewhere along their journey and sold them elsewhere for their own gain."

"I agree, father-in-law, that we must be careful and not make accusations that we can't prove, but something isn't right and we can't ignore that either. Our people are starving. We can't continue much longer as we are. We signed the treaty in good faith—but did the Chamuqwani?"

Eagan's scowl deepened, but before he could reprimand my uncle, Samith spoke again, "I agree with our brother, Elder, we must find out the truth about what the Chamuqwani intend for us. Maybe we should journey east to talk to the Father Emperor."

"And how do you plan to get the agent to give you a pass to leave the Preserve?" Eagan asked, "He isn't likely to give us a pass to spread the news of his thievery, now is he?"

Samith seemed taken aback by his angry tone of voice, but he soon had a solution to the problem. "No, he won't. So, we will have to find other Chamuqwani who will help us make arrangements for the journey."

"But in the meantime," Uncle pointed out. "We should seek out those among the foreigners who can speak on our behalf, tell the Father Emperor we want a new agent, a man who won't steal from us, or let us go hungry."

Eagan nodded and rose. "All right, I see the wisdom in your counsel, brothers. I will walk back to the agency in the morning. I will seek out Intercessor Karl and ask his advice on this matter."

The others rose as well, but before he left them, Samith asked, "And if the Intercessor won't agree to help us, what will you do?"

"We will send a delegation to the fort at Black Rock—with or without a pass," Eagan said,

"We should have the clerk at the fort write a letter to Intercessor Raymonel," Uncle suggested. "I know he will help us."

Chief Eagan snorted and gave his son-in-law a baleful glare. "If he is well enough to help us, and not dead from the evil that your family brought down upon him. The good intercessor would be here among us now—and maybe none of this would have happened, if not for that heathen witchery."

Uncle reeled back as if Eagan had struck him. Though I couldn't see his face in the darkness, by that time they'd stepped away from the fire, I *could* see the streaks of red anger shooting out from his aura. When he spoke at last, his voice was even and controlled, however, as it should be when speaking to an Elder. "With all respect, Elder, neither my father—nor my adopted son—was the cause of the good priest's misfortune."

He turned to Samith for confirmation. "Our brother here has told us that another Qwakaihi travelled south with the people for much of the journey. He is the one who did the evil—not any of my kin."

"So you and some others have told me," Eagan muttered, sounding unconvinced, "now good night to you both."

Eagan headed for the unfinished stone house. Samith and Uncle wished each other "God's Grace" and left to find their own blankets.

I waited for a long moment in the shadows till I was sure they were truly gone, then approached the fire. The days in this new land were growing increasingly hot, but the nights were still brutally cold. I huddled in my blanket and tossed another bundle of twigs on the fire. I picked up the blackened pot beside the fire and shook it. Hearing a satisfying slosh inside, I poured the remaining liquid into a battered cup and sipped it, listening to the night sounds around me.

For the first time since Intercessor Raymonel left us, I wondered if Uncle's conclusions were true. If I hadn't helped Chumco place that charmin the priest's tent, would our lives have been different once we had arrived in this place? Could one man alone have turned back the evil stalking us?

I would never know the answer to that question. And to dwell upon it, would only twist the cord of guilt tighter around my heart. I put down my empty cup and rose. I would try to sleep. The whir of a snake's rattles a faint memory in my mind, called me to my dreams.

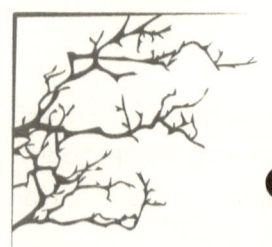

Chapter Seventeen

As he'd promised Uncle, Eagan set off to talk to Intercessor Karl just after the morning meal next day. He returned late in the afternoon grim-faced and sweating, his mouth set into a hard line. I was unable to eavesdrop on the council meeting he held that evening, but judging by the headmen's expressions after the council ended, no one seemed very happy with the results of his trip.

I thought no more about the incident, but ten days later when the desert moon rode full and high in the night sky, Samith, Uncle and two young men from the settlement slipped away from the Preserve without permission, heading for the fort at Black Rock. During their absence I became an unhappy ghost about the settlement, showing up for meals and doing my assigned tasks, and then retreating once more into the solitude of the desert hills on the other side of the creek.

I felt unusually vulnerable with Uncle gone to the fort and Grandfather often away on his own affairs. I doubted if Uncle had told anyone about my discarding the god's talisman, but I was wary of that fact becoming common knowledge. I feared Eagan's wrath if he should discover the loss while they were gone.

Though the spectre's voice was less insistent in my mind since I'd removed the Thunderer's pendant, I was certain it hadn't given up on devouring my Qwakaiva and my soul. If I was seen too often by the bitter old chief the spectre that haunted him might whisper in his ear that I no longer wore the god's sign just to make trouble for me.

But in truth it was a joy to be out upon the land. Though so different from Big Ice Lake, I was growing to understand and yes, maybe even love my new home. Since my illness, its spirit had touched my heart, giving me a fragile sense of peace.

The warmer weather had given the desert new life. In the cool morning, doves cooed and sage sparrows sang sweet whistling songs in the thickets along the creek bank. When not checking my snares, I would lie like a snake in the sagebrush, looking up into the blue sky, watching eagles soaring on the wind.

Sometimes when she could sneak away undetected Thonna would seek me out. She seemed to have an uncanny sense of where I was, no matter how hard I tried to hide. And after a while I gave up and let her find me.

I could see the muddied colors of her Spirit Fire and I knew she was unhappy. Maybe she missed her little brother. Maybe she felt guilty for living when she knew how much her parents had favored the little boy. Girl children weren't valued as much as boys among the Chamuqwani or those of my people who had converted to their religion.

Lost in her own musings, she rarely spoke on the occasions she found me, seemingly content to drink in the peace of the desert. We would lie near each other watching the eagles, in silence. Sometimes we would dig wild roots or check my snares for game. If there were many birds or rabbits we might stealthily cook and eat some of our findings before returning to camp.

Though she never spoke openly of what tormented her, I could read the signs in her Spirit Fire and suspected I knew the cause. I'd heard Mother and Grandmother talking when they didn't know I was around. Uncle was thinking of sending her to live with her betrothed's family. Charlic's mother was pregnant and Thonna would be a blessing to the woman once the child arrived.

Setting aside my own problems with him, Charlic himself was no great prize in my opinion. He was a braggart and a bully, who flaunted the fact that the priest in his northern village had started teaching him the Chamuqwani magic of reading and writing, before they left the North.

I didn't understand why Uncle couldn't see what a dog turd he was—even with his education. I wished I could do something to save her, butI was still considered a child and my Qwakaiva was insufficient to aid her. So I did what I could, let her come with me out onto the land when possible and listen to her angry talk when on the rare occasion she did voice her thoughts and needed someone to lend a sympathetic ear.

ESCORTED BY ARMED SOLDIERS, Uncle and Samith returned exhausted and famished the night before they were due to appear at the agency for ration day. As we walked to the agency the next morning, they related the gist of their story. Though the men put a brave face on their talks with the fort's headman, Commander Rossman by name, the chaotic patterns of their auras told me that much about their meeting troubled them.

Uncle had brought with him the half empty box of mirrors as proof of what he claimed. He learned while at the fort that the writing said the box was supposed to contain hammers and other small carpentry tools. Which was a lie—the tools had been stolen and the useless mirrors sent in their place.

The Chamuqwani commander knew he spoke the truth, but he refused to blame anyone or admit any wrong doing on the part of Agent Daglish. The commander did, however, promise to look into the matter, and then returned the men to the Tribal Preserve.

Since my fight with Matoqwa and the other boys, I'd dreaded going to the agency for rations, but my youth and strength were needed to pack supplies, so I dutifully went with the men and carried my share. While at the agency, I usually stayed near Uncle or Grandfather and was glad when Chief Eagan called for our return to the settlement.

That day when we arrived to collect our rations, however, there were soldiers waiting for us. They arrested Uncle Royston, Charlic's father Samith and the others that had gone with them to the fort. As they were being hauled away struggling to the wooden hut the agent used as a jail, Chief Eagan, face as dark and forbidding as a thunder cloud stomped onto the agency porch, demanding to see the fat agent.

"Go away or you will join them," the soldier on duty growled.

"No, I will not go away. I want to know why you are doing this—and I'm not leaving till the Agent tells me why he has ordered this terrible thing!"

The commotion was starting to attract a crowd of board onlookers eager for any kind of entertainment. Normally the little hut was used for confining soldiers or Qwani'Ya people who got too drunk and started fights. It was almost unheard of for one of the Chamuqwani god's converts in Chief Eagan's settlement to be singled out for such a punishment.

"Arrogant traitors," Somebody in the onlookers shouted. "Finally figured out that you're just another dirty zaunk like the rest of us, eh?"

"Why don't you ask your mighty god to save you, stinking traitor?" I heard Gagayii call out.

"Pray harder, dog turd, your god's not listening," someone else shouted. The crowd began to laugh, but the noise soon stopped when the Commander shouted for quiet and his men leveled their weapons at the crowd.

In the silence that followed, Eagan demanded, 'My son-in-law and these others are good, god-fearing men who don't drink or cause trouble. Why are you arresting them?"

With the agency's soldiers now here to back him up Agent Daglish crept out of his office onto the porch.Still hiding behind the soldiers he whined, "I don't care if they are converts. They left the Preserve without a pass; they broke the rules and I can't allow that to go unpunished.

"But they had a good reason to go." Samith's brother Lucaseph shouted. "Someone is stealing our treaty goods."

"I don't care what the reason was; you broke the law—and I'm not stealing from you," the Agent shrieked. "Now, be quiet and line up for your script or there will be no food given out today. I will send you back to your huts with nothing till next ration day."

"What is the punishment you intend for them?" Grandfather asked in a calm voice devoid of emotion, as the people began lining up.

"For leaving the Preserve without permission," Commander Forggal said, "three days in the jail and ten lashes with the whip."

"And that is just for the first time. The next time anyone leaves without my permission it will be worse—much worse," the agent said and smirked at our horrified expressions.

During all this I had been scanning the crowd looking for Uncle Tli, afraid he might get involved in the trouble, but to my relief he wasn't there, which, when I had time to consider it was equally worrisome.

He should have been there with everyone else to collect the supplies his wife and daughter would need, so where was he?

My worry goading me, I decided to risk another fight when I saw Samiqwas by himself for once. He was standing by the soldiers' barracks watching them pushing Uncle and the other chained men into the jail. He silently acknowledged me but continued staring at the drama going on across from us.

"Where is Uncle Tli; do you Know? I didn't see him in the line for rations. He isn't in jail, too, is he??"

Samiqwas looked at me then and shook his head. "Uncle Tli is gone."

My mouth dropping open I gasped, "Where?"

He shrugged. "He and some of the other Qwani'Ya and Kukiya men left—no one knows where."

My wits having a hard time understanding his words, I finally stammered out, "But what about Shilshigua and his daughter? I know he loves the little one. What will they do for food if he isn't here to collect their rations?"

Samiqwas snorted and pointed with his lips to some women sitting on the porch of one of the smaller wooden houses in the row built for the agent and his traders. "Shilshigua is fine; she's right over there. She and her daughter have plenty to eat and she doesn't need uncle anymore. She's a trader's woman now."

My mouth fell open again. "You mean she finally divorced Uncle Tli and is married to a Chamuqwani?"

He snorted again. "She's not married—Chamuqwani don't marry zaunks. She's only his cloocha-whore."

Though I'd heard it often enough since coming South, I wasn't sure exactly what that bad word meant to the Chamuqwani, but like zaunk it wasn't a good thing to be called. "When did all this happen?"

"Sometime after the wagons came with no food."

I would have liked to ask him more questions, but I heard Matoqwa calling to him and I reluctantly left, fearing another confrontation with my old hunting pack.

Knowing the few of us from the convert settlement left free were going to be hard pressed to carry all our supplies back Chief Eagan decided to pick up only a portion of the supplies then come back for the rest with the old mule the next day. I heard him telling one of the other convert men that he planned to speak to the priest again in secret when he returned.

I saw the sparks of anger and desperation in his Spirit Fire, though his face showed little of his turbulent emotions. <<So if you are so powerful, why aren't you giving your host the Qwakaiva to help rescue the God's people? Are you too weak, Spirit?>> I taunted the demon clinging to his shoulder.

The creature snarled, showing its fangs. <<Have a care, little human, or one day you will pay for your insolence.>>

I shivered and its toothy smile widened. I resolved in future to keep my smart mouth shut, in case it could follow through with its threat.

WHEN WE ARRIVED BACK at the settlement Aunty Marika and Samith's wife fell to the ground, rocking and wailing. Tearing at their faces and clothes with dirty fingernails they mourned as if their husbands were already dead.

No amount of comforting and soothing by Grandmother and the other women could stop their wailing until Chief Eagan had had enough, and roared, "Stop this foolishness right now, Stupid Women, or Mighty Djoven will punish you. Don't bring more trouble down upon us with your evil yowling. What if a malicer heard you and decided to make it true? Your men aren't going to die; they are just in jail."

He angrily gestured at the abandoned pots simmering on the cook fire coals, that were starting to give off a burnt smell. "Go back to your cooking, all you foolish hens before you add wasted food to your sins," he snarled.

Stifling their sobs, Aunty and the others silently went back to their cooking.

The meal that night was a silent affair, no one feeling much like talking. I realized as never before how out of touch the converts were with what was really happening to our people. They believed all the lying priest's promises, and thought themselves "different", protected by their god once they converted to the Chamuqwani's new religion. But as Samiqwas put it earlier that day, we were all the same to the invaders, just savages, "dirty zaunks."

When I looked with my Spirit Sight I could see the currents of fear and despair swirling in chaotic patterns about the meeting house. My own worry goading me, myeyes were drawn to Thonna to see how she was doing. She was sitting by her mother and her mother's sister, glumly eating her portion.

Like the others, her Spirit Fire radiated fear and worry, so I resolved to find her later and do what I could to assure her that her father wasn't going to die. The food, as Chief Eagan predicted, had a scorched flavour, but I wolfed it down anyway.

I waited till I saw Thonna pick up a couple buckets later that evening, grabbed my own, and then followed her up stream to get water from the deep pool where the creek ran clearer than the shallow muddy flow closer to camp.

She filled her buckets and would have walked past me without speaking, but I set down my own load and put a hand on her shoulder to stop her. "They won't kill him as your mother fears," I said, trying to assure her.

She stopped and set down her buckets and folded her arms across her chest and glared. "And you know this for certain? How do you know; does your Qwakaiva tell you such things?"

Did my Gift know for certain that he would be all right? Not really. I dropped my eyes and scuffed a bare toe in the dust. "No," I finally admitted, "but I have a feeling that it's not his time to die."

"Can your Qwakaiva help him escape?"

I sighed and shook my head. "I'm sorry I would like to, but that's not my Gift."

She snorted and picked up her buckets again, her expression one of contempt. "What *can* you do with your 'Gift' then?"

I sighed and picked up my own buckets. "It's complicated." She snorted again, so I hastened to add, "I mostly just see things from afar—and sometimes I know—things, but I had to stop my lessons when the soldiers forced us to come here."

She stopped again and turned to me, and demanded, "What do you mean see things—what things—how?"

Sorry I'd started down this path I took a deep breath and touched the cord around my neck. "If you promise not to tell anyone—even your parents I will look into the Seer's Pool and check on Uncle if it will ease your mind."

"Seer's Pool?"

"It's a pattern I make with the cord—like Sled Dog Running or the Aseutl's Teeth that we make to amuse ourselves or younger relatives. Only, the Seer's Pool has Qwakaiva."

"Show me—"

"First promise."

"All right—I promise. Show me... and teach me how to make it."

I laughed and picked up my buckets. "I can show you how to weave the pattern, but if you don't have the right kind of Qwakaiva all you will have are diamond figures in a loop of string." I motioned to a grassy patch off the path where we could sit.

When we were seated close to each other on the grass I took the cord off my neck and looped it over my hands and looked up. She was watching me with an expectant expression. "I'm not sure how much your father has told you about the old traditions, but it is customary for a supplicant to offer something to the Spirits in exchange for the gift of their wisdom."

Her eyes opened wide at that. "What kind of gift?"

I shrugged. "I don't know.Anything you value, some food, smoke, some pretty cloth, or other medicine, whatever."

Her eyes narrowed, her mouth hardening into a grim line. "Food, eh? Are you trying to get me to steel some food for you, stupid boy?"

I jerked back as if she'd slapped me.

"No! It's for the Spirit Helpers who will come when I call them for you."

I was deeply offended by her accusation and could have said more angry words, but then I realized that growing up as a convert child uncle and her mother probably spoke little of how they were raised. She was ignorant—didn't know—anything.

Instead of jumping to my own defence as she probably expected me to do, I surprised her by saying in a calm voice, "The gift you choose isn't for me but the Spirits. I am only a channel for their power. If you want to offer them food, then leave it along the creek, or burry it under a stone if you are worried I'm being greedy and want it for myself. That's what I will do with your gift—whatever it is—if you give it to me."

Thonna dropped her eyes and twisted the folds of her shawl in her hands. 'I'm sorry... it's just I'm so worried. If father were to die mother couldn't protect me. They would make me marry Charlic right away."

I patted her hand before putting the cord back over my hands. "Charlic is a dog turd. We will run away together before I let that happen."

"You promise."

I glanced in the direction of the settlement. It was getting late; we would be missed soon. "Yes, if I ever leave I'll take you with me—satisfied?"

"Yes." She motioned to the cord across my hands. "Do it so I can see."

I dutifully took a deep breath and focused my eyes and my Qwakaiva on the large diamond in the center of the pattern.

With a little effort a picture of Uncle Royston and the others formed in my inner awareness. It was dark in the hut so I couldn't tell much. Uncle being a relative I centered my Qwakaiva on him. "He is in some discomfort and pain, but Uncle and the others haven't been whipped yet—he thinks tomorrow maybe. He heard the soldiers talking," I told her.

"How do you know that?

"I can see them."

"I can't see anything but your dirty shirt in that diamond," Thonna grumped, breaking my concentration.

I jerked up, the pattern slipping from the string. Her disbelief had triggered my defences, tumbling me out of the communication. Taking in a deep breath, I said, trying to be patient, "I already told you it takes a special kind of Qwakaiva to see into the Pool. Uncle Royston isn't going to die though he is in pain, and will be in more pain if they whip him tomorrow as he thinks."

When she still looked skeptical, I added, "When you see him again he will have a long gash on his right arm where he slid down the wooden wall in the jail after they shoved him inside." I showed her on my own arm where it would be. "Ask him how he got it, if you don't believe I truly saw him."

Shewas quiet for a long moment gnawing on her lip at last she said, "Thank you.You were looking into the Seer's Pool that first day when I found you, weren't you?"

"Yes."

"Who were you trying to see?"

Samiqwas and Uncle Tli, like now, I was worried about my relatives."

"Why?"

"Uncle Tli has a bad temper and he hates the Chamuqwani. When we were coming here they put him in jail and beat him too, because he tried to stop some soldiers from cheating us out of our script."

Thonna's eyes bugged wide at that revelation.

"And Samiqwas," I continued, "we grew up together, in the same house like brothers. All my life he was my best friend." I shrugged placing the cord back around my neck and standing. "But now his mother is gone, and we live in the Chamuqwani way. He's no longer my brother—barely a relative." I took another deep breath, and rubbed at my eyes. I wasn't going to cry—I wasn't. "And-and I miss him."

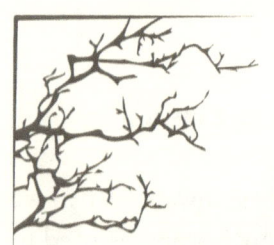

Chapter Eighteen

Agent Daglish was a little more generous on the ration days following Uncle Royston's trip to the fort and the mirror incident, but the promised goods were still slow in coming. A few bony old horses and mules—formerly owned by the soldiers were given to us as part of our treaty goods. The beasts were supposed to be for ploughing our new fields, but neither the seeds nor the ploughs materialized by early summer. Most of the beasts were too old and sickly for heavy work. We had no oats or hay to feed them, so many were killed and eaten by their allotted owners and their hungry relatives.

Some of the healthier ones, Chief Eagan and other appointed headmen on the Preserve kept in their settlements to enhance their prestige and to use when sending messages from one encampment to another. This was how we learned the news of the terrible fire so quickly.

One night as we were about to return to our lodges for the night, the boy named Kiethrap came rushing to the doorway of chief Eagan's stone meeting house. Clinging to the doorframe, he took in great gulps of air, trying to catch his breath. The family had just finished our evening meal and we stared open mouthed.

"What's wrong, boy," the old man grumbled. "It grows late, why aren't you at home with your family up the creek?"

At last regaining his powers of speech, he blurted, "Elder, come see! There is a strange red glow in the southern sky. Mother says it is a sign from the Great God. Come see.—everyone." Chief Eagan snorted, but rose and followed Kiethrap, the rest of us trailing them out into the night.

It was impossible to see the southern sky clearly under the trees sheltering the house, so we all trooped to the path connecting the settlements along the creek for a better view. To the north along the path I could see the distant light of campfires spread out along the valley and the dark silhouette of the brush and forested hills beyond.

To the south the creek wound through the starlight, until it curved sharply to the east about the distance a man could walk in two hand-marks of the sun. As if the sun had changed course and would soon climb back into the sky from a new direction, the southern horizon glowed bright with an unnatural orange hue. By that time other members of the community had noticed the light and had come out onto the path to gawk and speculate about its cause.

The Willow Agency lay in that direction....

"Is it indeed a sign from the God?" someone among the gathering people asked.

Maybe, I remember thinking, but whose god was offering up the evidence of his power? *Those mirrors can make fires, lots of nice bright fires.* Chugai's words came unbidden into my mind and I shivered. But that wasn't possible—it was night—there was no sun for the mirrors to steal its Qwakaiva and make fire.

I wasn't the only one whose mind had swam down that terrible channel, for I heard Eagan tell Uncle to bring out one of the horses and send one of the young men to the agency to find out what had happened.

Soon after that I saw Charlie's older brother galloping off in the direction of the agency. There wasn't much to see or do after that, and the night was growing colder. Still discussing the phenomena, most of the people soon drifted back to their homes to wait for news and maybe catch some sleep.

Though trembling with both fear and the cold I was one of the last to return to my hearth. I stared at the angry red light, my mind tumbling in a whirlwind of chaotic images and thoughts. From somewhere far away the whir of an angry snake sounding a warning echoed in my mind. At last when mother's insistent calling penetrated my turmoil, I reluctantly turned away and returned to my own hut.

With the murmur of my relatives' low-voice talk a lulling presence in the back of my mind I drifted off into uneasy sleep. Sometime later, the pounding of a horse's hooves roused me. The sky outside was still dark, but paling near the eastern horizon. An owl hooted from the darkness. The morning doves roosting in the branches of the cottonwoods stirred restlessly, murmuring an occasional soft coo.

Grandfather was sitting by the sleeping fire, feeding it new twigs to awaken its hunger. When he saw me watching him, he motioned for me to get up and go fetch water for tea. I tossed one of my blankets about my shoulders and stepped out into the dawn.

Over by the stone house the messenger was in low-voiced conversation with Uncle and Chief Eagan. It was growing too light by then to risk sneaking up to listen, so I gathered up the skin bucket and headed for the creek. When I returned the messenger was gone. Spotting Thonna by the wood pile, I hastily sat down my burden and headed in her direction. Maybe she knew the latest news. And if I chopped some wood for her she might be nice and even tell me.

Picking up the axe off the ground, someone—probably Tomson again—had left to rust unsheathed by the wood pile, I put a juniper round on the stump and lifted the axe. "Did you hear what the messenger told your father?" I casually asked in a low voice.

She looked up from placing kindling in the sack she'd just made of her apron and grinned. "Maybe. How badly do you want to know?"

I sighed and split the round with more force than I needed to. She was playing games with me, so the information must be good. "What do you want?"

Her grin widened. "Go fetch water for me and I will tell you—maybe."

"Maybe? Maybe I'll just wait and ask my grandfather. Chief Eagan may not like him, but he is an Elder and will surely be included in the morning's council."

She stuck out her tongue at me, then relented, and murmured as she passed me, "It was a fire—a big fire. The half-finished temple burnt down." I dropped the axe just missing my foot.

I brought her the water she asked for.

The news had spread through the settlement before the mush had cooled in our bowls. The Thunderer's temple had been turned to ash. Many of the soldiers' horses had been stolen from the stable while people were fighting the temple fire. Then the stable too had been set ablaze to mask their escape. Some weapons and other supplies had also been looted during the chaos.

Who had done it? That was the question on everyone's lips. I had watched Grandfather from under half-closed eyes all during the morning meal. I feared I knew the answer to that question and I guessed he did too. Tli, Chugai and Matoqwa's older brother Qwati had made no secret of their contempt for the convert traitors and the lying Chamuqwani agent.

He caught me watching him just before the meal ended. Our eyes met and a silent communication passed between us. The food I'd just eaten lay like a rock in my stomach. I knew what he wanted from me, even if he couldn't force the words past his lips to ask.

He feared for his son, and only one gifted with Qwakaiva from the Great Aseutl could tell him what he wanted to know. A prick of resentment tempted me to deny him, but I banished the evil thought from my mind.

I too was worried about Uncle Tli. I would do what I could to ease his heart, and so I put a finger to the braided hair cord about my neck as I walked outside. He nodded slightly and followed the rest of the adult men into the council.

We would meet later out on the desert.

As a child I wasn't included in that meeting, but I didn't have to be inside to know what was happening. Everyone in the settlement that morning probably heard Chief Eagan's angry shouts. Knowing that the temple had been singled out for destruction enraged him to the point of madness.

He, or the skeletal Spirit guiding him, seemed to view the raid on the agency as a personal attack upon him and his God. He raged and shouted curses in the meeting until he fell into a fit and had to be carried senseless to his bed. The meeting broke up soon after that with nothing much decided. More messengers were sent off for news, and this time Uncle Royston was among them.

The big question that no one dared voice was what were the soldiers and the agent going to do about the destruction of their Lord Joper and the Empire's property? Throughout the rest of the day everyone talked in hushed voices, as if listening for the sounds of more bad news. Even the little ones wore frightened expressions and played half-heartedly with their stone and twig toys.

It was nearing evening, the purple shadows of the trees long across the sagebrush flats when Grandfather and I were able to slip away into myspecial sheltered thicket of aspen and pine, over the hill across the creek. I'd come here often both by myself and with Thonna. I'd already dug a small fire pit and lined it with grey stones from the creek bank.

I lit the fire while I waited for Grandfather. When the fire glowed bright and strong, I sprinkled dried juniper leaves over the flames. Inhaling the fragrant smoke, I sat cross-legged upon last summer's leaves and tried to compose my thoughts.

Insects clicked and hummed in the underbrush. I heard the baby growls and the yip, yip of young coyotes at play. A grouse drummed an alarm call in the rabbit brush. Grandfather slipped silently between the trees and squatted across the fire from me. I took the cord from around my neck and looped it over my hands before looking up.

"What do you want to know, Elder?"

He drew out a small pouch from inside his tunic and laid it on the ground beside me. I let the loop rest across my arm and picked it up. The leather was old and greasy from his sweat and body oils, but I could still smell the strong scent of the herbs and resinous pine needles inside it. He had just gifted me with medicine from home, maybe all he had left.

This was medicine that would be irreplaceable. I glanced up, studying him cautiously. This was indeed a precious gift—a true gift of power from one Qwakaihi to another. Tears stung my eyes; I felt humbled by his acknowledgement of my Qwakaiva.

Oh, I knew the pouch's content wasn't for me personally. By giving me this he was honoring my Benefactor Kunai. I was only the channel through which the Unseen Ones could work their influence in our physical world if they chose to do so. I bowed my head in acknowledgement of the honor paid my Benefactor and settled the loop across my hands. Taking a deep breath I repeated my earlier inquiry.

"Tell me about my youngest son. Where is he? Is he alive—is he safe?"

Slipping deeper into my trance my hands formed the pattern known as, The Seer's Pool. I peered into the central diamond of the figure and allowed the images to form....

"...Tli is alive and well for the moment" I told him softly. "I can see him sitting round a fire with several young men and a few women. They are joking with one another, and eating fresh meat—deer maybe. I hear horses stamping outside the firelight. Chugai is there... and Slylum, Tigali and some other young men from home and the villages down the Socanna River are there too.

"I can't see all their faces, the light is too dim. ...Some of the Kukiya tribe's young men are with them as well. One named Golannah is their leader."

Grandfather took a deep breath, and asked, "Where are they?"

"They have ridden far on the stolen horses. I see the shadows of tall trees beyond the fire, so I think they are in the mountains."

"To the north? Are they planning to go back home?"

I took another deep breath, trying to focus. He was asking for more of my gift than being a ghostly observer. To answer his question I would have to touch the mind of at least one of the men clustered about that far away fire.

<<O Spirits, help me. He has honored you with his faith; don't let my weakness and inexperience dishonor you,>> I prayed.

As I peered harder into the pool I felt a long sinuous body wind its way up my arm. I held perfectly still, unsure if the one who had answered my request had appeared in physical form as well as a spiritual essence.

A forked tongue flicked out and touched my ear and a voice said into my mind, <<Your kinsman goes north, but not back to the Big Ice Lake. He follows the Desert's Child, the cunning one who brings them to a holy place to hear the words of one who has battled the darkness and holds the lightning in his hand. They go west, to the Broken Land, where the soldiers never follow.>>

"No. The warriors will head west once in the mountains. They go to a holy place where someone who will give them a message waits for them."

Going to a sacred place. As I spoke those words I felt such a longing in my heart to be with them, that the feeling nearly dragged me from my trance. The snake's tongue touched my skin once more. <<Have patience, young one. It is not your time, but it will be soon.>>

"What of the soldiers, Grandson? What will they do now? Will Tli be in danger?"

"I have no way of touching the minds of those men," I heard myself say and knew it was the snake speaking through me. "Danger stalks all who take on mortal flesh, old man. Surely you of all men know this? Your son is a man who has chosen a warrior's path in life. He will be bound by its pattern and neither a father's love nor a Qwakaihi's power can change that. Only he can re-braid the cord of his fate if he so chooses."

"I see. Thank you, Spirit. I will consider your wisdom, but is there nothing I can do to dissuade him from a path that will surely be his death?"

"All will die," the Snake repeated impatiently. Rattlesnake raised her flat triangular head and fixed the old Qwakaihi with hard yellow eyes. Her tail whirred a warning rattle. Grandfather met her gaze and stared back unblinking.

She hissed and finally added, "If you would aid him you must choose. Perhaps it is all the ones you love that are in danger. Journey into the desert, old one, and seek out the one who is called Iyantsha, the Prophet. But if you do so, have a care. All actions have power. Death stalks all your children."

By the time she had finished with me, I was trembling so violently that the cord slipped off my hands and the pattern disintegrated. Flowing down my arm she slithered away into the brush, leaving me spent and exhausted. As I slipped into a dreamless sleep, the last thing I saw was Grandfather's haunted eyes.

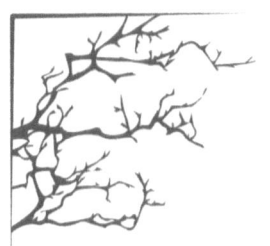

Chapter Nineteen

A large number of people asked to come with the party going to the agency for our supplies on the next ration day. Grandfather, mother and I were going in the hope of hearing news about Uncle Tli, but like the rest, I also was curious to see the damage done by the outlaws.

When I learned Thonna, her mother, and Charlic were also included in the party I had mixed feelings about going, however. Thonna was bossy at times, but she was also intelligent, loyal and fearless when defending what she felt was right.

I supposed I admired her—and I wasn't going to let Charlic hurt her, but I never thought for a moment about wedding her. So I couldn't understand the dog turd's growing jealousy. It was disgusting—unnatural and I tried to avoid both of them when I had to remain in the settlement. Fearing another confrontation with Charlic that morning I kept close to Grandfather and refused to meet Thonna's eye every time she looked my way.

But when we sometimes met in the desert, when she could sneak away, that was a whole different matter. I was teaching her how to set snares and other things about the Qwani'Ya way of life I had learned from my Elders on the Big Ice Lake. They were a part of her heritage, too, but she was sadly ignorant of those teachings, being raised as a Convert child closer to the Chamuqwani settlements down river.

BEFORE WE EVEN TOPPED the hill overlooking the agency we could smell the odor of charred wood and scorched hair and meat. I coughed, pulling the cloth around my neck over my nose and mouth. It didn't help much and I remember wondering how the people living there could stand it.

As the messenger had told the Elders the nearly finished temple to Mighty Djoven was totally destroyed. An untidy pile of charred timber and blackened ground was all that was left. Next to the temple was the priest's house. It had been badly damaged, but still standing. A dirty blanket was hung over the hole where a door had recently hung, the wall nearest the destroyed temple was a sooty black color, and all the house's new glass windows were smashed and broken.

Charlic had been surveying the destruction, as well, and amidst the low angry cursing of the other converts I heard him ask his father, "Where is the priest; was he killed or injured when heathens attacked the agency—do you know?"

"No, the Intercessor, praise the Great God, wasn't killed by the heathen scum," Samith answered, his mouth hardening as he surveyed the destruction, too.

Charlic glared at me, as if I had burnt down the temple myself. He drew his finger across his throat, promising pain. I looked my tormentor in the eye and lifted my lip in a mirthless smile, and then had the petty satisfaction of seeing him turn away with a shiver.

"And they will pay for this evil," his brother Lucaseph snarled also staring at the wreckage as we passed.

Samith glanced at him sharply, and hissed, "Keep quiet, ptarmigan brain! Someone might hear you."

I shivered, as I saw Lucaseph's chest explode with blood. I heard Rattlesnake's whir in my mind as the foretelling hit me. Blood and war were coming to the Qwani'Ya people and there was no escape.

I must have staggered, because the next thing I knew Grandfather had put a hand on my shoulder. "Are you all right, Grandson?"

Startled I looked up into his concerned eyes. He had probably sensed the power of the Sending. I don't know what he saw in my face, but he tightened his grip and slowed our pace to walk a bit behind the others. Mother glanced back at us, but he motioned with his chin for her to continue on with the rest of the women.

Without him needing to ask, I blurted, "There is more trouble coming, Ati, and I'm afraid. I think the convert men are planning some sort of revenge—and there will be more blood spilled on both sides because of it."

Grandfather patted my arm, but I could tell his mind was focusing on my news instead of offering me comfort. At last he said, "Thank you for telling me, Grandson. Be at peace and don't worry. I will speak to your uncle and see what can be done to avert more trouble."

It won't work. All the talking you or Uncle Royston may do won't stop what is coming, I silently told him in my mind.Still I childishly hoped I would be proved wrong and his Qwakaiva would be strong enough to turn aside the disaster.

We could see more damage to the agency as we drew nearer the trading post. There was a large hole in the post's warehouse that some soldiers and traders were trying to close with salvaged lumber. Through the gaps we could see empty shelves and scorched sacks.

The barn too was gone. The horses left behind by the outlaws were pastured in hastily-built pens scattered on the slope behind the agency. As I watched two soldiers and a couple Qwani'Ya boys were taking the horses and mules in small bunches down to the creek for water.

To my private amusement Agent Daglish's house had also been singled out for Fire's special attention. Though not burnt to the ground its windows were gone and the door and walls on three sides blackened. I could only guess what it looked like inside. His little garden and his smelly pigs were also either burnt or gone.

When my relatives and I arrived some people from the more distant encampments were already there, milling about scanning the destruction and talking to one another in low frightened voices.

Unlike my other trips to the agency there were no gambling games in progress by the soldiers' barracks and no clumps of gossiping women by the trader's cabins. I glanced around for Samiqwas and the other boys from home, but could see none of them.

I was hot and thirsty and hoped we could get our rations and leave soon, but my wish would go unfulfilled that day. When the people gathering in front of the post were starting to grumble about the wait, the fat red-faced agent came out of his office, accompanied by several grim-faced, well-armed soldiers.

"I know it's ration day, but I have no supplies to give you," he whined. "You will have to wait till the wagons with more supplies come from the East."

"No food?" someone shouted. "Our children and old people are starving. What do you expect us to feed our families then?"

"It's not my fault there's no extra food," he complained when Abe translated for him what the people were saying. "Blame the outlaws for your troubles not me. There are no rations till the next shipment comes from the East."

"Then give us weapons so we can hunt and feed our families," a convert man from down the creek from Chief Eagan's settlement shouted.

Agent Daglish shook his head. "No weapons. It's against the law to give you zaunks weapons."

"Then order the soldiers to hunt for us," a woman cried. "My little ones are hungry."

"We signed your treaty in good faith," a convert Elder shouted. "Did your great lords and the Father Emperor do the same? We only want what the treaty says is ours."

"There would be plenty for us, Fat Man, if you weren't so greedy,"another woman screamed holding up a tiny baby for him to see. "I have no more milk in my breast to feed my baby.Give us your rations if you have nothing else. See what it feels like to starve for a change,"

As Abe translated more of the People's angry words the fat agent's face turned a dangerous shade of purple. Finally he had had enough and made a cutting motion with his hand, speaking sharply to Commander Forggal. In the next moment a soldier shot his weapon into the air, silencing the growing clamor.

When the people were silent, Agent Daglish said in an angry voice, "I have nothing left to give you and all your threats and protests won't change that fact. Go back to your settlements. I will send a message when the new supplies come."

When he finished speaking the agent turned and entered his office, slamming the door with a loud bang.

Though some still remained to protest or plead their case for special treatment neither the agent nor the grim-faced soldiers listened. We had had nothing to eat that day, only cups of tea to fortify ourselves for the journey and now not even that for the hot trip home. My stomached cramped in anticipation of the hungry days to come.

Before leaving,Chief Eagan and a few of the convert headmen sought out the priest to plead their need for food and the promised farm tools and building materials.Intercessor Karl promised to write to his superiors in the temple, but told chief Eagan he had no power to issue rations. After that there was nothing to do, but return home.

It was a solemn party that returned to the settlement that day empty-handed. No one sang songs to the Thunderer to help pass the time, or laughed and joked with each other as was the usual custom. When I looked about me all I saw were despairing frightened faces, and I suppose my own expression was no different.

Though I had begun to hate the Chamuqwani mush and salty bac'con, I knew we had to depend on their supplies, as long as we were forced to remain near the agency and had no gardens, or weapons to hunt for ourselves. I knew my skills with snares and traps would be needed even more in the days to come, but after many moons of living by the creek the little ones were getting wise to my snares and stayed away. I had to travel farther and farther from the settlement to bring home anything at all.

Glancing to the northwest where snow-capped mountains rose high against the azure sky, I remember thinking, *"If the agent isn't going to feed us, why stay here?"*

All over the Preserve after the agent refused to feed us people were afraid. Angry words were spoken between the different factions if men from opposing groups met upon the path, or when hunting out on the land. Chief Eagan and other Elders, Grandfather among them, made more trips to the agency to plead with the priest to help us.

Looking back, I don't know if he was just overwhelmed by our suffering, or he was also a part of the corruption as some Traditionals claimed, but nothing ever came of their trips to ask for his, and his god's help. It was after one of these frustrating visits that Grandfather left the settlement for good.

Before he left he pulled me aside and told me, "I'm going west to prey and seek the one the Spirit told me to find, Grandson."

I looked west toward the distant peaks and my heart sank. Without his some-time presence here I would be even more alone, tempting prey for Charlic's malice and Chief Eagan and his hungry demon. "Take me with you, Ati, please."

He shook his head and patted my shoulder. "No, Grandson you need to stay here and take care of your mother and grandmother in my absence."

"Uncle Royston can do that, maybe better than I can, Ati, please." But his answer was still no, and in my childish way I hated him for his refusal.

DURING THE TERRIBLE time that followed his departure I was only vaguely aware of what was going on in the convert settlement. Claiming that I had to go farther and farther away to bring back enough game to help feed so many people I tried to stay on the land as much as possible. No one questioned me, as long as I had food when I returned.

It was during this time that Grandmother became more and more troubled in her mind. Without Grandfather there to anchor her spirit in the present she began to spend most of each day reliving her youth in our village along Big Ice Lake. Sometimes she couldn't remember who I was, and I had to explain to her our relationship. She would nod her head and smile and then a while later she would ask me the same question of who I was once again.

I hated to see my strong, out-spoken grandmother so feeble in her mind. Mother and Uncle's wife and aunties were kind to her, but I wished Grandfather would come back.It hurt my heart to see her like that, but I knew my Qwakaiva couldn't heal her, and Grandfather's continued absence just added more fuel to my growing resentment. But to be fair, if he *had* been there, her healing might have been beyond even his great gift.

It was while I was returning back to the settlement late one evening that I noticed Charlic's older brother, his uncle Lucaseph and several more young Convert men quietly leaving the settlement. In the dim light I couldn't see all their faces, but I did notice that all of them were carrying some kind of weapon.

The secretive way they were moving through the brush sent a shiver down my spine and the hair on the back of my neck rose in fear. Not wanting them to see me I flattened myself among the sage and rabbit brush, ignoring the hidden cactus spines that were now jabbing into my side. In my mind I could hear Rattlesnake's whirring tail, warning me to keep still. There was danger; Death was hunting in the desert that night.

I counted about fifteen men and older boys pass my hiding place. Silent and grim they headed up the creek road in the direction in which I knew there were other camps belonging both to Converts and Traditional peoples. An owl hooted somewhere in the willows; wherever they were going trouble was waiting for someone.

When I was sure they were gone I picked up my kills, and taking a round-about way I crept back to the settlement, coming in from another direction from the one where the men left. I had eaten while still in the desert, feasting on roasted grasshoppers, low-growing plants with soft leaves, and a couple little brown burrowing animals I dug out of their holes. I wasn't hungry, so I didn't care that I'd missed Chief Eagan's prayers and the meager evening meal.

Spying Thonna chopping wood outside Uncle's shelter I walked over and handed her my catch. Taking up the axe, I asked in a low voice, "What's going on?"

She cocked her head, pretending to be puzzled. The northern jay in her aura imitating her movementsperfectly its bright bird's eyes laughing at me. "I'm chopping wood; that's what's going on, stupid boy. Where have you been?"

I paused the axe in mid swing, and snorted. "What is that you are holding? I've been hunting, stupid girl." In an even lower voice as I completed the swing, I said, "I saw some convert men with weapons heading up the creek as I was coming back. So I ask again, what's going on?"

Thonna's eyes widened at my news. Also keeping her voice low she murmured, "I'm not sure. Many of the men have been meeting in secret, but they are always meeting to pray or talk about how the agent is stealing from us. So I thought nothing of it. I didn't know anyone had left the settlement tonight."

Growing thoughtful she then added, "Charlic has been boasting to me that the heathens were going to pay for burning down the Thunderer's temple and making the agent so mad. I try to ignore dog turd and his boasts, so I wasn't really paying attention to what he wanted to tell me—now I wish I had listened."

I wished she had, too, but that couldn't be helped now. "Where is Charlic now, do you know?" I was wondering if he was one of the shadowy figures I had seen with the Convert men.

"I don't know and I don't care."

"What does your father have to say about these meetings? Do you think he knows what they plan?"

"He hasn't mentioned anything. Do you want me to ask him?"

I thought about it as I chopped through a few more pieces of wood, finally I shook my head. "Better not. Whatever they are doing this night they want to keep it secret. Even if your father knows he probably wouldn't tell either of us—and will be angry with you if you ask."

Frowning in concentration as she thought it through, she finally nodded, seeing the truth in my words. As I finished the wood for her and turned to go she stopped me by asking, "Tas, can you find out by looking into the Pool?"

I froze, then glancing around to make sure no one was paying us any attention, I came close and hissed, "You promised not to tell about that. Do you want to get both of us in trouble, stupid girl?"

Unbothered by my annoyance she met my glare without flinching. "And I won't tell anyone—I keep my word—but can you, stupid boy?"

Could I? "Maybe—but not while I'm in the settlement I will go up the creek to my spot later and try. I will tell you in the morning what I discover—if anything."

She wasn't happy about my answer, but I left her then, still muttering to herself about stupid boys and even stupider men.

In my own shelter Mother was happy to see me and sat me down by the fire and handed me a cup of warm tea. I sipped it gratefully, my throat dry from chopping Thonna's wood. As I sat I drew my last rabbit from under my shirt and handed it to her. "For you and Ami," I said.

She took the rabbit but frowned as she stroked its soft brown fur with her hand. "You should have given this to the chief's wife to be put with the supplies for our next meal, my son. You know it is our Qwani'Ya way to share. The women are planning to do a pit-cook tomorrow with the roots the convert desert women showed us how to gather. They can cook the rabbit that way as well."

I glanced over at the bundled figure of the old woman, sleeping on the bedof sage and rushes across from us. She was snoring softly, her breath coming in ragged gasps. "I gave the rest of my catch to Thonna to give to the chief's wife, Amima. They will have plenty for the pit-cook," I glanced back at the pile of blankets again. "I know it's the Qwani'Ya way to share, but Ami is so sick—I just wanted..."

I left the rest of my thought unvoiced. How much of Grandmother's illness was because of a convert malicer's curse or was it just a natural part of aging, and how much was due to our hard journey and the starving conditions in which we were forced to live? I didn't know.

Mother seemed to understand my intent. She smiled and patted my hand. "You are a good boy, Tasimu, my little Rock Squirrel." When I glared she only laughed. "You will always be my little Rock Squirrel, no matter how old and gray you get."

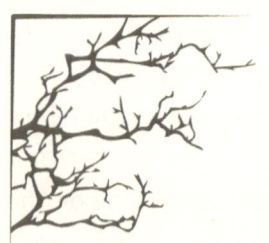

Chapter Twenty

Retreating to my own bed not long after that, I told Mother I was too tired from my hunt to talk more and forced myself to sleep for a time. When I awoke next, all was dark in our shelter. I lay still, listening to the sounds in the night around me. All seemed quiet outside—and safe. Inside our shelter I could hear Grandmother's soft snoring and the rustling of tiny creatures in the grass thatch above us. Even Fire was dozing, only a faint red glow shown from its nest of rocks in the fier pit.

Easing out of my blankets I gathered my things and crept out into the night. Desert nights are always cold even in the heat of summer, I'd learned since coming to this new land. So I wrapped my blanket-coat about me and tied the belt tight as I slipped out of the encampment and took the familiar path that led to the ford across the creek. The night air was heavy with the pungent smells of sage and cottonwood buds.

Once across I breathed a sigh of relief and moved easily through the darkness with only the stars' light to guide me. In the little clearing among the aspens and scrubby pines I used for my secret prayers I built a small fire in the nest of stones and sat down to compose myself for the work. Tossing a handful of dried juniper needles on to the fire I breathed in the sacred smoke and slipped the cord over my head, laying it across my hands.

Half into the Dream a rustle in the dark broke my concentration, sending me with a snap back into my body. I wasn't sure what had aroused me, but Rattlesnake would have warned me if there was danger.

Then as I opened my eyes, Thonna stepped out of the trees and came over to my fire and sat across from me. Annoyed, I scowled. "What are you doing here? Your father will beat you if he finds out you are here alone with me."

And Charlic will beat the shit out of me if he finds out you are here, too, I thought.

For her answer she took from under her shawl a small bunch of juniper twigs tied with a silken red ribbon like the traders back home gave to the women and girls on Chamuqwani holidays. Her expression uncertain she held it out to me. "I thought the Ones who talk to you—show you things might want an offering... and I want to help—I" she broke off, unsure what to say next.

I let her wait while I thought about her gift and what to do next. I didn't really want her here, but on the other hand, she had come with something she valued as an offering for the Unseen Ones, and I had no right to refuse her. Knowing the ribbon would be hard to replace in future, it was a gift worthy of the Spirits who guided me.

And yet, I still wasn't sure it was right for her to separate herself from her family and the traditions she had always known. If I encouraged her, she might regret this later. Looking her rudely in the eye I said, "Thonna, you know it's no secret that in spite of your father's baptism, I keep faith with our ancient traditions.

"I have been gifted with Qwakaiva—some even call me witch," I took a deep breath, "and maybe there is a seed of truth in that accusation. I have used my gift in ways I'm not proud of now, but you were raised differently—and I don't want to see you hurt. Or painted with the same brush of fear and malice that colors me, and that will surely happen if you set aside the beliefs of your family."

I sighed and added, "Maybe Grandfather is partially right when he told me the old way of life is dying and we need to bend with this strong Chamuqwani wind or we will be broken."

By the time I'd finished there were tears of frustration pooling in the corners of her eyes. She angrily wiped them away and growled, "And do those pretty words apply to you as well? If you believe following the teachings of the Thunderer is the right path for me, then why isn't it right for you, hmm?"

Well for a lot of reasons, which I had no intention of explaining at that moment, so I sighed and dropped my eyes, watching the tiny red flames hungrily curl around the wood I had fed them.

At last I took her offering and said in a soft voice, still looking her in the eye. "Thank you." I looked down turning the bundle over and over in my hands. "I know this gift is worthy of my Benefactor, so I accept it, but maybe you should go back now—before anything bad happens—before you are missed and get hurt."

She shook her head, getting that stubborn look on her face I had come to know so well. "No I'm not going anywhere. You might need me to watch here while you are—away."

Well, maybe she had a point. It would be safer for me if there was someone in the physical world to guard my body while I traveled in the Dream. "All right, as you wish." I shrugged, placing her offering within the fire.

The fire shot up, the ribbon burning with a blue-tinted flame. The sweet smoke of the juniper was now fragrant in the air. I placed my cord across my hands and began weaving the pattern of the Seer's Pool.

"I have no close connection with the few men I saw briefly from my hiding place earlier this evening, and I don't know where they were going, so I'm not sure I will be able to see much," I told her as I drifted deeper into the Dream. "Be patient with me. This might take a while."

<<Spirits of the Desert help me,>> I cried out to the Night as my trance deepened. <<I fear for my relatives and all my Qwani'Ya people. Death is hunting new prey and men with evil in their hearts walk dark trails tonight.>>

In the pine nearby an owl hooted. <<Come, Cousin, fly with me and we shall look for them,>> Owl said. Then she swooped down, grasped my spirit-body gently in her talons and flew away with me.

On silent hunter's wings she soared high into the dark sky. Below us the creek was a blue misted ribbon of Spirit light, winding off across the desert, growing wider and slower as it left the tree-covered hills behind.

Green auras of trees stood tall reaching for the sky. Here and there the glowing shapes of other living beings were scattered upon the land. <<We need to go closer to the Earth so I can find the camps of my Qwani'Ya relatives,>> I told Owl.

As she dipped lower an image of Grandfather's nephew, Lynx Hunting came unbidden into my mind. And then I was there, watching in the Seer's Pool through his eyes what was happening all around him. Fire, fire was everywhere, women screaming, children crying, and the clan's simple shelters in flames.

People were running everywhere confused and frightened, trying to hide—get away. Angry men shouted war cries and reached for anything to use as a weapon. The convert men attacked the unsuspecting people with a grim ferocity that left me stunned.

"Heathen Scum, you die tonight! This is Mighty Djoven's vengeance for your evil!" I heard someone shout—was that Lucaseph? Maybe, can't see. And then a man with black on his face and a white lightning bolt on his forehead rushed Lynx Hunting. As they grappled, the black-faced warrior thrust a spear deep into his gut.

At the same moment I cried out, feeling the lance thrust as keenly as if that unknown convert warrior had plunged his spear into my body as well. I doubled over, the cord slipping from my numb fingers as the connection was violently severed.

I must have blacked out for a time, because the next thing I knew a tangle-haired and wild-eyed Thonna was cradling my head on her lap. When she saw my eyes open she sat me up and offered me a cup of cool water from the creek. "You scared me, stupid boy. What happened?"

I shivered, drank the water, and gingerly touched my stomach. The vision had been so real I feared I might find blood when I pulled my hand away. I drank more water, trying to bring all of my Spirit back into my body and ground myself in this peaceful place under the trees.

"What happened; what did you see?" she repeated, a note of anxiety in her voice.

I snorted a laugh and replaced my special cord back around my neck. "See? I did more than see. I was there, smelled the smoke, and felt the spear plunge into my relative's gut."

"That's impossible!" She growled and looked as if she wanted to punch me. I was glad she didn't. I felt bad enough without her adding to my misery.

"You aren't making any sense. What are you talking about?"

"Lucaseph, Charlic's older brother, and several other Convert men have just attacked a Traditional encampment and are killing Qwani'Ya people—men, women—everyone."

"They wouldn't! Oh, I know some of the men are very angry about the temple burning, but they would never kill other Qwani'Ya people—they just wouldn't—"

"I *saw* Lucaseph and I heard a man say that it's a punishment for burning down the God's temple. Punishment," I laughed, but there was no mirth in the sound. "The problem is those people were innocent. Their only crime was not following the Chamuqwani god."

"No, no, not true," Thonna shook her head back and forth, denying the awful truth in my words.

"I was linked with our relative, Lynx Hunting, when a man painted black with the God's white lightning bolt on his forehead stabbed him with a war spear. It was terrible!" I took another long drink of water, unable to speak more.

By the time I finished, Thonna's whole body was trembling with horror. I knew she wanted not to believe me, but a part of her knew I spoke true and it both angered and sickened her. Well, I guess she got more than she'd expected when she gave me her offering.

I stood up, pulling her up with me. "It's late—near dawn. You will be missed soon. I'll walk you back to the edge of the settlement. You need to be safe in your bed before your family wakes and the war party returns."

As I started to lead her out of the clearing she pulled me around to face her. Her face was only a dim blur in the dying firelight, but I heard the desperation in her voice. "Tas, what are we going to do? Those people—the killings—"

I took her arm, urging her forward. Suddenly recalling some of the things my Qwa'Nayhi Seal father had told my mother when, at Chumco's urging, I spied on them by entering one of her dreams, I said, "There's nothing we can do for now. There are greater forces at work here than you and I can fathom."

"But—"

"Thonna, I know you want to help and it makes you angry. It does me, too, but what is done, is done. Be patient—and wait. Our time will come to war against the Evil stalking all our people, but that time isn't now."

We had come to the ford by the settlement by then and I urged her to cross.

"Aren't you coming with me back to your mother's shelter?"

I sighed and shook my head. "No. I need to be alone for a while—and pray. I will see you tomorrow." When she still hesitated I impatiently motioned for her to cross. "I will be all right. Truly." I chuckled and waved her on again. "And besides it will do your reputation no good if you are seen coming back to camp with me—alone—late at night." She made a rude noise and said a bad word. I smiled and told her good night.

Once she was safe in the settlement I faded into the brush, heading for the sacred clearing among the aspens. Though I dreaded using my Qwakaiva again I should look for Grandfather within the Pool. If I could find him, he would want to know what had happened to his relatives.

As I neared the clearing, focused on the grim task ahead, a horrible thought being whispered on the night breeze came into my mind. Had Lynx Hunting's encampment been singled out by the convert men in the hope that Grandfather would be there and be killed as well?

I shivered at the notion. As often as possible Chief Eagan made it clear that he hated him, taking every opportunity to show Grandfather and the others at the settlement how he felt. Grandfather mostly ignored Eagan and kept out of his way as much as he could—as did I.But in spite of the extra rations our presence offered the convert community, Chief Eagan wanted the "Heathens" gone.

It was only at Uncle Royston's insistence that he didn't demand that Grandfather and the rest of us leave. And with the demon's goading Eagan could have said something to Lucaseph and then hoping to please the Elder they would have singled out those innocent people for their vengeance.

If Thonna was right Uncle might not have known the full extent of what the warriors planned, but I was totally certain Chief Eagan, and his demon leach did. They welcomed the bloodshed and approved of the killings. I shivered, fearing what the future held for all of us. The night was cold. I would build up the little fire and hoped to share my warmth with Rattlesnake for I craved the comfort and reassurance of my new Spirit Helper that night of all nights.

Chapter Twenty-One

When I walked back to the settlement around midday with a few small birds and gophers in my sack, the people in the convert settlement were going about their usual daily chores as if nothing had happened the night before. Young children played catch the rabbit, under the trees. Women sat and gossiped as they mended clothing and prepared food for the pit-cook planned for the next meal.

Many of the men and older boys didn't appear to be around. Maybe they were hunting deer or antelope out in the desert, or maybe they were just asleep after last night's activities. I wasn't about to ask; I had no wish to let them know I had seen what evil they'd done the night before.

After handing my catch to Aunty Marika, I looked about for Thonna to assure her I was well. Not finding her I headed for my own shelter. I had no plans to stay here very long, but I needed to check on Mother and Grandmother before I left again.

To my surprise I found Thonna helping Mother with the old woman when I stepped inside our hut. I could tell right away that Grandmother was having one of her bad days. With Thonna's help Mother was trying to feed her some broth she'd made from the rabbit I'd given her last night, but Ami was refusing to take sips of the soup they were offering her.

"Go away and leave me alone, you strange people," she whined turning her head away when Mother offered her the spoon. "Where is my Tuulah? She should be home from berry picking with Esuli by now. I will eat nice fat crow berries when they get back. Go away and leave me rest."

Mother sighed and dipped the spoon back into the broth lifting out a chunk of boiled rabbit on the spoon this time. "Tuulah will be back later. Then you can have berries," she coaxed. "Please eat some nice rabbit now."

Spying me by the entrance, she added, "look there, Grandson has come back to visit with us. He caught this fat rabbit just for you. He will be sad if you don't eat some of this nice soup. Please eat, Amima."

"Grandson? That strange boy isn't my grandson. That boy is too big. My Samiqwas is just learning to walk. And little Tas is still in his cradleboard. I never saw that strange boy before. I want to rest now. Why won't you people let me rest?" she complained.

"Amima, of course he is your grandson. That's Tas standing there."

I came a bit closer so she could see me better in the dim light. Then plastering a big smile on my face, I said, "Asiya, Ami. My, that rabbit soup looks good. Please eat. Your daughter has worked very hard to make nice food for you."

Looking from one of us to the other Grandmother seemed confused. "Tas? Is that boy really Tas?"

"Yes, Amima, that's Tas," mother assured her. "Please eat."

The way she looked at me I feared she didn't know who I was, but maybe just to please us she managed to eat about half the bowl, before she said she was too tired and crawled back to her blankets to sleep.

"Who is Tuulah?" Thonna murmured as she handed me a cup of tea.

"Your father's other sister," I answered.

"Is she dead?"

I shook my head. "No, she married a Chamuqwani and left us after her little daughter died on our way here."

When the old woman was snoring peacefully Mother and Thonna came over and joined me by the fire with their own cups of tea. Glancing once more at my sleeping grandmother, and fearing what Thonna might say to her, or anyone else in my absence, I asked, "Amima, has Thonna told you what happened last night?"

Mother looked at Thonna, then shook her head. "No, what happened that you two want me to know about?"

Did I want her to know about Lynx Hunting and the rest of it? Not really, but I'd opened my big mouth and now I needed to finish it. So I told her about the Convert men making war on Grandfather's relatives. By the time I'd finished there was a horrified expression on her face and tears in her eyes.

Covering her head with her shawl while she grieved for our relatives, she finally let the shawl fall to her shoulders and asked, "Was your grandfather there—is he—"

'No he isn't dead—he wasn't there," I assured her. "When I searched for him in the Pool last night I saw him sitting in a circle praying with some of the desert people a few days walk west of here."

Mother frowned, a troubled expression appearing on her tear-stained face. "Why is he so far away; Tas, has he left Amima for good? I was hoping he could ease my mother's mind with his Qwakaiva.Is he coming back soon?"

Glancing over at my still sleeping grandmother, I doubted that even he could help her, but I tried to reassure Mother. "No, I don't think he has abandoned us, but I don't know when he is coming back. He's gone to seek out a great Qwakaihi among the Desert People as one of my Spirit Helpers directed him to do. He will come whenever that work is done I'm sure."

Last night when I finally was calm enough in my mind to find him within the Seer's Pool I had seen him with the one Rattlesnake called Iyantsha and his followers. They were circled round a fire among high red cliffs somewhere to the west. I had tried to touch his mind, tell him of the trouble among the Qwani'Ya People, but just as I thought I made contact with him Eagle and other fierce guardians of the Kukiya People noticed my spirit hovering just outside their circle of power and attacked.

I tried to explain that I was no enemy, but they wouldn't listen. <<Go away,>> Eagle said. <<You can speak to your Elder later. I cannot allow you to break the power of their prayers now. The work they do here is more important than avenging the ghosts of a few dead people.>>

Well, vengeance wasn't what I had in mind, but I wanted no trouble with them, so I retreated as they commanded me to do.

I finished my tea and rose to go soon after that. Still troubled, Mother stopped me. "You brought me terrible news, my son. Have you spoken to your Uncle Royston about what you saw?"

I shook my head. "No, and I don't plan to. He will ask me how I know about it—and that might bring up accusations of witchcraft again. I don't know if he knew about the raid, but I think it will be very dangerous for anyone who speaks openly about this."

I could see the stubborn look on Thonna's face and knew she was preparing to argue with me. "Thonna, think! Those men did what they did, in secret, in the darkness of night. No matter how justified they feel they were, they killed innocent women and children in that raid.

"To the Chamuqwani we are all just zaunks. Fighting and killing each other—it won't matter to them. Someone broke their laws and must be punished for it. Lucaseph and the others will fear the soldiers coming after them if someone tells them who is responsible for the deaths. So I caution you to be very careful, or you might be badly hurt—or worse." I made eye contact with both of them. "Very, very careful—both of you."

"Where are you going, son?" mother asked as she saw me gathering my blankets and other necessary things for a journey. "Are you going to find father?"

"No, I'm going to Lynx Hunting's encampment—to see if I can do anything to help those people—maybe hunt for them—I don't know. I'll come back in a few days—tell Uncle if he asks that I am just hunting. It is getting hard to find my prey this close to the settlement."

And there's no reason to stay since the agent isn't giving us food anymore, I thought privately.

Before heading to my relatives' camp I took some time to hunt, begging the little ones to help me feed the survivors of such a brutal act, and I was grateful the four-legged and winged ones had pity on me and filled my sack to overflowing. Heavy laden with food, It was midmorning the next day before I finally walked in to Linx Hunting's encampment.

Except for the ghosts hovering by their relatives, the camp was much as I'd seen it in my vision. Smoldering shelters sent lazy plumes of blue smoke into the sky. Grim-faced people with tears still running down their faces sifted through their scorched and blackened belongings, looking for what was salvageable. Young children were sitting alone among the ruins unattended and crying.

Away from the destroyed shelters up the slope, a few stick-thin men were making slow work of digging a shallow grave in the hard ground. Not far away several bodies covered with grass mats lay waiting their final resting place. Older children and women not busy elsewhere gathered stones and laid them by the grave to be placed on top after the men finished entombing their loved ones.

I walked into camp, searching for Pretty Shell Woman, Lynx Hunting's wife and at last found her nursing her youngest in the shade of a scorched scrub oak. Nearby a girl of about four years stared up at me with wide frightened eyes. I smiled as I approached, hoping she would understand that I was a friend and wouldn't harm her.

Pretty Shell Woman was singing a low prayer-song to herself with her eyes closed. Lynx Hunting's ghost stood nearby, the gash made by the spear in his gut still dripping blood down his leg.

As I crouched in front of her she opened her eyes and stared blankly at me.

"Is his body up there?" I motioned with my chin to the bodies awaiting burial.

It took her a long moment to recognize me, but at last she did and nodded. "Yes. How did you know?"

I dropped my eyes, ashamed of my inability to stop the killing. At last I said, "I saw with my Qwakaiva what happened here." I touched my stomach. "My Spirit was with him when it happened; I felt the spear thrust as if it had pierced me, too."

Her face crumpled as I finished, the tears rolling unnoticed down her soot-coated cheeks. At last she took a deep breath and asked, "Is his uncle coming? Some of the men are injured. We could use your grandfather's healing herbs and prayers."

I shook my head. "Grandfather was given a task by the Unseen Ones a few days before this happened. He will come—eventually, but at the moment he is several days walk to the west," I reluctantly told her.

"And what of you, young hunter, can you help them?"

I shook my head, once more ashamed of my helplessness. "I'm sorry, but no; I have no Qwakaiva to heal the living. That's not my gift." I took a deep breath and then at the ghost's urging I added, "Your husband is nearby and he wants me to tell you that he loves you and is sorry he couldn't protect you and the children from the evil last night."

It took a moment for the meaning of my words to sink in, but when it did she covered her face with a part of her dirty shawl and began to cry.

I let her morn for a time in what privacy she had. The ghost drew near and put his arms around her, but I couldn't tell if she knew. The little girl I thought might be able to see him, because she crawled to her mother and leaned against her side. Still crying Pretty Shell Woman threw an arm around her shoulder, drawing her close.

Finally hoping to distract her I pulled the full sack from my back and showed her its contents. "I planned to stay a few days and help with anything I can do before I must go back to my mother and grandmother—who is not doing well herself. I will hunt and set snares to catch food, and I have followed Grandfather around enough in the past to know how to use and gather simple medicines, but that's the best I can do."

She took the sack and nodded. "Well, that is something, and I thank you for your gift of food and for coming to help." Pretty Shell Woman stood and laid the now sleeping baby on a scorched blanket next to her older daughter with instructions for the girl to watch the baby."I need to find my aunty and a fire to cook your gifts for the people." As she passed me she gave me a sad smile and patted my shoulder, thanking me again.

After she left I walked up the hill to see if I could lend a hand to the men making the mass grave for their dead. I helped gather stones for the rest of the afternoon, and then near evening when the people were called away to eat I remained by the site, still troubled in my heart and mind by this senseless tragedy.

I sat by the grave mound and breathed in the sadness of recent death. I made a small fire and sprinkled sacred juniper and the last of Grandfather's gifted herbs from home over the flames. Breathing in the fragrance I prayed, <<O Unseen Ones hear my prayers and help your Qwani'Ya People. If I am found worthy, give me the strength and wisdom to help them—both the Living and the Dead.>>

A soft breeze caressed my face, bringing with it the scents of sage and pine resin from the land around me. The little wolf dogs the desert people called coyotes yipped to one another out in the brush. An owl hooted from somewhere among the pines farther up the slope. The dark silhouettes of desert bats venturing out from their caves in the cliffs soared high into the mauve sky. In the deepening shadows the restless dead gathered around me to convey their last messages to their living relatives.

The ghosts seemed so confused, unsure of the way back to our ancestral resting place so far to the north. A lump in my throat I wished I was older—better trained so I could help them.

As if divining my thoughts, an older hunter came over to stand by me as I listened to a frantic ghost, worried about her young children speak to me. He silently watched me for a time, finally he said, "You can see them, can't you, Grandson?"

Startled, I looked up. A man with more white than black in his long braids was standing beside me. There was a bloody bandage wrapped about one arm and a jagged old scar running down one cheek from eye to chin. I thought I knew him, but couldn't remember his name. He was one of Grandfather's cousins from a village down river from my home on Big Ice Lake, so we were related—sort of. "I can see them, Elder."

"And can you speak to them as well?"

"Yes," I admitted.

"And what are they saying to you?"

"They are angry, lost, and confused. They are also worried about their relatives left here among the Living with so much Evil conjured among us." I looked down, once more ashamed of my ignorance. "But I can't help them much.I don't know what to do, or the proper songs to help them find the way home—and my grandfather... He is far to the west at the moment."

The Elder thought about my words, and at last he put a hand on my arm, urging me to stand. "Then it will be up to you and me to do the best we can to help them and ease the suffering of those left behind. I know some of the old songs and with your Qwakaiva to help me we will manage." When I was standing he motioned with his chin down the slope. "Come, Grandson. You must rest and eat something before we begin."

With the wailing ghosts still calling to me, I followed him down the hill and ate the food offered me without tasting it.

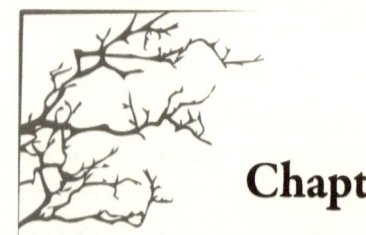

Chapter Twenty-Two

My Elder must have told his relatives about my Gift, because everyone was very kind to me, thanking me often for coming to them when my grandfather was unable to be there.

Back in the ruined encampment I also learned that I wasn't the only one who had heard about the raid. During the afternoon and over the next few days, other men and women related to these people drifted in and out of the camp, bringing what food and supplies they could spare. That evening and the ones that followed, I heard lots of angry talk around the camp fires as men and women discussed the unprovoked attack and what to do about it.

Ignoring the talk after I had eaten that first night, I crept back to a spot near the grave site. I didn't feel much like talking—to either my relatives or the ghosts. As I rolled into my blanket I looked up into the starry sky and prayed, <<Spirits of this land guide me, so I can help my People. There is no one else and I am young and know little of what is needed, but my people both living and dead need help.>>

Lying there fearful and uncertain about tomorrow I at last felt Rattlesnake come and curl herself up against me. I lay perfectly still as she crawled up my chest and touched my ear with her forked tongue. <<Share with me your warmth on this cold night, young Seal Brother, and I will lend you my guidance and Qwakaiva in the morning.>>

<<Willingly I will keep you warm and safe this night, Honored One,>> I told her. When she was settled to her liking in the hollow I made between my arm and my side, I covered us both with my blanket and drifted into a peaceful sleep.

Next morning as the eastern sky lightened I was awakened by Rattlesnake's angry hiss. Coiling for a strike she raised her triangular head out of my blanket; her rattles making a menacing whirr. The Elder I'd met yesterday and another man were standing above me, their eyes going wide when they saw my bed companion.

Stroking her head gently to calm her I said, <<Peace, Honored One. These men will not harm us.>>

I sat up slowly so as not to frighten her further. "Is it time?" I asked them. I yawned and shifted my companion to a more comfortable position. With much of her bulk now coiled around my chest inside my shirt and only her head and a loop of her coils around my neck, I rose to my feet.

The men stared at me for a long moment without speaking, at last the Elder said with a note of awe in his voice, "Ye-ess, Grandson. It is time to do what we can to ease our people's suffering."

I nodded, continuing to stroke rattlesnake as I walked with them to where the survivors and other relatives were gathering around the mounded grave. "Don't be afraid; this honored one has come to help us," I explained to them.

The People had formed a large circle enclosing the mound on all but the west side. The ghosts of the recent dead hovered by family members, or floated above the piled stones, looking lost and forlorn, their bloody death wounds visible for any with the Spirit Sight to see. We took our places in the East where someone had made a fire. A young woman added bundles of sage and juniper to the flames when we joined them. I breathed in the resinous smoke and followed its blue cloud up into the azure sky where Eagle already floated, waiting to guide the ghosts through Death's Portal.

And, it would be my task to create that portal with Rattlesnake's help.

I shivered. Hopefully, no convert malicer knew of this working and would try to interfere, because I doubted I or anyone else in the circle was strong enough to stop them if so.

<<Fear not, young Seal. Eagle and Cougar keep watch in the Dream so no malicer can harm anyone of us,>> Rattlesnake assured me before I could ask.

<<Thank you, Spirits and Guardians of this desert land.>> I breathed in a sigh of relief. It would seem that in spite of my inexperience the Unseen Ones of this land had thought of everything. <<O Mighty Kunai thank you, may I be worthy of your trust. Help me to guide my people well, now and in the future,>> I prayed.

Rattlesnake touched my ear with her tongue to reassure me. <<I am here to guide you right now, little Seal. Do not doubt your Qwakaiva. Trust in your Benefactor and the gifts of your heritage.>>

When all were gathered the Elder beside me unwrapped a hand drum and began to sing, others who knew the chant quickly joining in. The young woman with the smoke bundles lit one in the fire, then passed it to another hunter who walked around the circle, bathing the People in the cleansing smoke. Giving way to the sound I felt my body relax as Rattlesnake and I swayed in time with its ancient rhythm.

Since the earliest beginnings my people had drawn both comfort and power from the songs given to us by the Ancestors and the Unseen Ones. When it was my turn to receive the sacred smoke I held out my hands, pulling the Smoke and its Qwakaiva to me like a drowning man. I bathed my face, my heart and the other centers of Power in my body as I'd been taught, by both Chumco and Grandfather.

When the songs ended I sank to the Earth, Rattlesnake shifting her position with the change. My legs trembling from the excess of Qwakaiva I was gathering to myself for the portal opening, I was grateful to sit. Around me others were sitting as well. Ignoring the whispers and stares directed my way I closed my eyes, opening myself to the communication with the Dead.

Grandfather's cousin remained standing. Bending to pluck from the ground a peeled stick decorated with a few feathers and other ornaments, he held it up for all to see. "It is time to say our good byes to our kindred. Anyone wishing to speak can take the Sharing Stick and tell us about their relative."

He pointed to me, sitting beside him. "My Grandson has a powerful Gift as all can see. If you have questions or the Dead have messages for you he will translate for us."

It took most of the day to finish the ceremony. Lots of tears, lots of songs and prayers, lots of messages back and forth from the Living and the Dead that I needed to translate. Without Rattlesnake to help me, I'm not sure I could have done it.

Sun had passed his zenith and was turning a bright gold in color when all was said, and I rose to make the final portal that would show them the way to go home. Eagle screamed overhead and flew towards the lowering sun. Cougar growled a warning at any ghost who thought to linger.

Framing the Sun between my two thumbs and forefingers I poured the Qwakaiva I had left into widening the glowing circle. Rattlesnake slithered up my arm and bit the soft flesh between my left thumb and forefinger. I gasped with the shock and almost lost the portal as I felt her venom enter my blood.

<<Don't be afraid,>> she said. <<I am just adding more of my power to yours for the portal opening. Kunai has given you the Qwakaiva to withstand my bite. You will not die of this. Continue; your relatives are waiting!>>

Blood streaming down my arm I took a deep calming breath, ignored the pain and channeled her added power into the working. Trust, it was all about trust. I had pledged my life and my Qwakaiva to the Master of Enigma when we ran Drown Canoe Rapids on our journey here. Kunai could do with me as he chose. I just had to trust that he wasn't done with me yet and complete the task given me.

The golden aura of the Portal grew as I channeled our combined power. Eagle screamed again, and then I saw Lynx Hunting and some of the others pass through the gate. Somewhere amidst the glowing Qwakaiva I heard a northern Raven welcoming them back to our ancestral lands. A part of me wished I could go with them, but I resisted that temptation. I was needed here.

<<You will return to be with your ancestors someday,>> Rattlesnake assured me.

As Sun disappeared in the red and mauve clouds of evening I let the Power go and sank like a child's rag doll to the ground. Uncoiling herself from around me Rattlesnake touched her tongue to my ear one last time. <<I go to hunt now. When you recover I will expect several nice fat rabbits as payment for my help,>> Rattlesnake told me as she slithered away into the shadows. <<And have your relatives brew you some tea from the plant with little white flowers for the pain of my bite.>>

<<You shall have the rabbits, Honored One, thank you.>>

DURING THE FEW DAYS I remained with Pretty Shell woman and her people recovering from the Work, they took care of me like I was an invalid when my fever was high. They made me the tea Rattlesnake spoke of and shared with me the little they had. I was vaguely aware of the talk about me spreading throughout the Preserve and the news only added to my fears about returning to Uncle Royston's settlement. If he or Chief Eagan heard the news that I had performed a ceremony for the murdered dead, they might hurt or kill me or those I loved.

I also knew someone had sent word to the outlaws hiding from the soldiers up in the hills, because near the end of my recovery I was sure I saw Chugai in the shadows by one of the fires where many young men were talking in low voices. Hearing Rattlesnake's warning in my head, I continued on to the privy hole through the darkness as if I was unaware of the talk or his presence.

Caught in the middle between two now warring groups of Qwani'Ya people, I decided that it would be prudent for me to leave next morning and go back to my mother's hut. I was feeling much stronger and I'd been gone several days longer than I'd originally planned. I knew that I and the food I provided would be missed by now, and people might start asking Amima uncomfortable questions.

If the Converts didn't accuse me right out of being a malicer when they next saw me, they might think I had joined the outlaws like so many young men from back home and then take out their spite on mother and grandmother. I hoped Grandfather would come back soon....

RETURNING TO THE CONVERT settlement in late afternoon two days later with a string of rabbits and grouse over my shoulder to sweeten what I suspected would be an angry reception, I found the settlement in turmoil, my arrival barely noticed. From inside the meeting house I could hear women wailing and Chief Eagan's thunderous shouts.

Hanging my catch in the tree near Uncle's shelter, I crept to the big meeting house and peeked inside. Not wishing to make my presence known just yet I staid only long enough to see that most of the convert community was there. Two covered bodies lay near the altar mound with Chief Eagan standing between them with hands raised in prayer and supplication. Fearing the demon would see me and alert its host I quickly withdrew, throwing up a protective shield against its malice.

Unsure what to do next I retrieved a grouse for Grandmother from my string and drifted without much thought to my mother's hut. I didn't know who lay dead, but I was afraid for my female relatives and wished, once again, that Grandfather would come back.

To my relief I found both mother and grandmother inside. But even in the dim light given off by the fire I could tell that something was wrong. Mother sat by Grandmother's blankets, gently sponging her face with a wet cloth and singing softly to the unresponsive old woman.

Placing my blanket roll and other things on my usual pile of sage and grasses I went over and crouched beside them.

When she became aware of my presence mother looked up and smiled. "I'm glad you're back, my son. I was worried about you."

"What's happened, Amima? Who is dead in the meeting house—and what's wrong with Ami?"

She sighed and wiped the old woman's hot face again. "Several men were attacked on their way home from talking to the priest yesterday. Lucaseph and Tomson were killed and your Uncle Royston and Samith were injured."

I sat back on my heels stunned. So the war between the factions had begun in earnest. "How badly is Uncle hurt?"

She rose, motioning me to come away from Grandmother's bed and back to the hearth. Feeding Fire more sticks she set the big can we used as a kettle to boil and placed powdered juniper leaves in our cups. When the water steamed she poured the liquid over the tea and set the cups to steep.

"He isn't hurt too bad, so Marika tells me. He was hit on the head early in the fighting and must have fallen unconscious, because the warriors left him for dead. Charlic hurried back to the settlement to get help and the outlaws ran away, before there were any more deaths."

Taking my cup at last I took a grateful sip and asked, "Is he all right now?"

She shrugged. "Other than a few cuts and bruises and a bad headache I think he is doing all right, but I wish Appi was here to look at him."

Glancing over at my ailing grandmother I wished he was, too. "What's wrong with Ami? I know she was having a bad day when I saw her last, but she seems much worse now."

"She is," Mother agreed. "In the last couple days she's developed a fever and I fear it may kill her, if it doesn't go away soon."

Shocked I stared at her wide eyed, unable to believe such terrible news. "How could this happen, Amima? I know she isn't always right in her mind, but other than that she seemed fine—wasn't she?"

Mother shook her head and gave me a pitying look. "Not really, Tas. You are gone so much hunting for the People you probably weren't aware of how much she has changed since she became ill during the blizzard.

"Recently she is worse, because I think she misses her husband. And with so many strange and terrible things happening to our people it both frightens and confuses her with him not here to comfort her. And now her oldest son has been injured..."

She left the rest of her thought unvoiced, but I understood what she was trying to tell me. "Amima, we need to get away from this place and these terrible people."

"My son, I would like nothing better than to leave here, but I can't leave your grandmother in the care of strangers who aren't family—and Marika and her sisters and aunties aren't our kin—not really. No I must stay and care for her until she leaves us for her final Spirit Journey north."

"But Uncle is family," I protested. "She is his mother, too. Surely he would take care of his own mother—not let anyone hurt her now that she is so ill. But you and I... you know the Converts hate us. I don't think Uncle would protect either of us if Chief Eagan spoke against us. And with Grandfather away so much of the time I fear for you—I fear for all of us."

"I am aware of the risk, but nonetheless I must stay."

I sighed, resigned to her decision. "Then I must stay, too," I told her, and held out the grouse for her to cook.

A few days later when I finally did encounter my uncle when hauling water for the men working on the thatched roof of Chief Eagan's meeting house he asked me half-heartedly about my long absents days before.

I showed him the nearly healed snake bite on my hand. I told him I had been bitten while hunting, but Grandfather had shown me the plant to use if I should ever be bitten, so I was fevered for a while, but didn't die.

Knowing that his father was wise in the ways of healing he didn't question my answer. Maybe his head was still hurting him, because he next asked me if I knew where Grandfather was. I shook my head, then without him asking I told him that boiled willow bark was what I'd seen Grandfather use for pain and I didn't know any other remedy.

Over the next half-moon I stayed close to the settlement and tried to show Uncle and his wife and mother-in-law how useful it was to have me and my family around. I didn't know if the converts had heard the rumors about the death ceremony I'd been a part of, but I continued to bring back as much game and wild edible plants as I could find using my Qwakaiva, in the hope that Mother and grandmother wouldn't be bothered or turned out while I was away hunting.

During that time Chief Eagan and other Elders made several trips to the agency, pleading for food and the promised farm tools and other supplies. Always they were told by the fat agent that he had nothing to give them. And to add to our worries, the Desert People living on the slopes above the creek warned that the snows in the mountains were melting and some years the creek by their settlement would flood.

Once again during that time there was an attack by the outlaws in reprisal for the Convert raid on Lynx Hunting's innocent encampment. Chief Eagan was also ambushed on the road to the agency. He had gone to beg the priest to write to his superiors back east for their help. He wasn't hurt much, but the horse he prised was stolen, and he was foot-sore and furious by the time he made it back to his house. After that if he ventured out of the protection of the convert Settlement he went with a well-armed body guard.

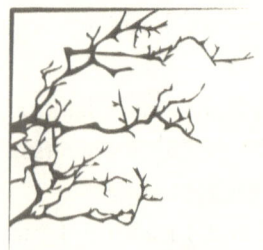

Part Two
Chapter One

One afternoon before heading back to Mother's hut I was checking my snares and mulling over the recent eventsin my mind, when suddenly there was a rustle in the brush behind me and a small rock hit my shoulder. Cursing my stupidity I spun around, fearing another ambush from the ever-determined Charlic and his pack. Picking up a few stones, I snarled, "Come out, Charlic, you cowardly pile of fish guts!"

But instead of my hated enemy a smiling Samiqwas stepped out of the brush to greet me. His mix of Chamuqwani and Qwani'Ya clothing was dirty and ragged, and his tangled hair needed re-braiding, but there was also a new air of confidence in his bearing I could sense before he even said a word. Still grinning he walked closer, eyeing the rocks I held. "Are you going to throw those at me? At this distance even a poor shot like you could hit a big target like me, eh?"

When I just stood there with mouth agape, he chuckled. "Close your mouth, Tas, before a bug flies inside, and you eat it."

Making a sound somewhere between a laugh and a sob, I dropped the rocks and grasped him by the shoulders. Staring into his amused dark eyes I swallowed hard several times, but my words were stuck in my throat and I couldn't speak. It had been several ration-day cycles since I'd seen him on our visits to the agency.

His father Ko was usually gambling or lying drunk by the soldiers' barracks, but no Samiqwas—or any of my old hunting pack were around. When I asked her, Amima said she'd heard a rumor that he was with Tli and the other warriors wanted by the soldiers, but no one knew for certain where the boys were much of the time, so I didn't know for sure what had happened to him.

When I'd gotten over my shock enough to speak, I said, "How did you get here—are you by yourself?"

Samiqwas glanced around furtively before answering. "Do you see anyone else?" Then, "Tas, is there somewhere private we could go to talk?"

I glanced back across the creek. The grass covered shapes of some of the convert dwellings were visible through the big cottonwoods on the bank, but I couldn't see any people. If anyone was bothering to look in our direction they might be able to see us, but most people would be gathering outside the meeting house awaiting the evening meal. Still I sensed that he had no wish to let our relatives know he was here.

I motioned with a jerk of my head up the creek. "Come on. There's a place I go sometimes. Nobody will see us there, but I can't stay long. I will be missed."

He followed me up the creek to the willow and aspen grove where I often went to pray, or just escape my tormenters back in the settlement.

When we were settled around my unlit fire pit I smiled at him. "I've missed you. Are you and the others well? Amima heard a rumor that you had gone to be with Uncle Tli and the outlaws."

He dropped his eyes and nodded. "I've missed you, too."

"If you came looking for Grandfather he isn't here—and before you ask, I don't know where he is. He left on a Spirit Quest after they put Uncle Royston in jail and Uncle Tli joined the outlaws."

Samiqwas nodded, trying to hold back a grin. "That fat agent sure was angry when we threatened to kill and eat him that day."

"Yes, he was and still is, only now he is worried, because some officials from the Father Emperor are coming, some say to examine the agency and how he has been treating us."

Samiqwas snorted. "The lying fat pig. Somebody should jail him for what he has done to us."

I chuckled. "I think that's what he's afraid of. Maybe Uncle Royston should join his brother and the outlaws," I joked.

To my surprise he didn't join me in my mirth. "I'm not sure he would be welcome. Many warriors are just as angry at the ones they consider traitors as they are with the Chamuqwani."

Sobering, I said, "I know. Charlic's Uncle is dead—some accuse the outlaws or other Traditionals for the deed. But I was joking. He wouldn't go anyway." Glancing around at the lengthening shadows, I said, "As good as it is to see you, I will have to go soon. Did you want me to give Grandfather a message; is someone ill?"

Samiqwas glanced around too, then shook his head. "No message, it was you I came to see."

Startled I touched my chest. "Me—why?"

For answer he handed me a small cord-wrapped bundle of fragrant gray-green leaves. I knew the Kukiya threw such dried plants onto a fire when they prayed, but I couldn't understand why he had come all this way to offer them to me.

"What's this for?"

Samiqwas shrugged, looking somewhat embarrassed. "It's for you. Uncle Tli and The war leader said to give it to you."

I turned the little bundle over and over in my hands. Its pungent scent blossomed in the air between us. I took in a deep breath, feeling its Qwakaiva spinning round inside my head. "To me? But why; what am I supposed to do with this?"

Samiqwas blinked. "What are you supposed to do with that—I don't know, porcupine brain? Do whatever you Qwakaihi do with such an offering—how should I know? All I do know, is that we need your help and Uncle Tli said to give it to you." He folded his arms across his chest and waited. "So, are you going to help us or not?"

Well, I was making some progress, as I'd suspected from the beginning he wanted the aid of my Gift, but I still was confused. "Before I can answer that, I need some more details—don't look at me like that! Until you tell me what you want, I won't know if I can do it. So, I repeat, what kind of help do you need?"

Samiqwas glanced anxiously around to make sure we were still alone. Finding nothing to worry him, he said in a low voice, "The warband is planning a big raid to get meat for the People from some of the Chamuqwani settlers who have claimed Kukiya land near the Preserve. The war leader said we need a Qwakaihi to guide us for such a big mission, but the prophet's people are still in the west and can't help. Uncle Tli and I told the others that you have Qwakaiva. We want you to come join us."

"Your war leader, that's Golannah, the Kukiya man who is now leading the outlaws that you're talking about, yes?"

Samiqwas stared at me open mouthed. "H-how did you know that?"

I smiled but refused to answer. I couldn't deny that I was flattered by his confidence, but a Qwakaihi like Grandfather, I wasn't. Once more the old longing shot through my heart like a knife thrust. My apprenticeship was no more. Chumco was far to the north and I was only half'-trained.

"You and Uncle shouldn't have done that, Cousin, you know I'm not—"

"Don't start in again about not being trained. You have the Gift, so why not use it and help us defy our enemies. We are doing this to help the People. The agent has promised us food and our treaty goods, but nothing ever comes of it. We only take from the Chamuqwani what is rightfully ours. Will you help or not?"

I wanted to help, but they needed so much more than my puny gift of foretelling. What if someone was hurt? I had no healing talent, nor any power to confuse an enemy sent to hunt them. No it was impossible—as much as my heart longed to leave the Convert settlement and go with them. "What about Grandfather? He could be of more use to you than I would be. Have you thought about asking him?"

Samiqwas sighed, looking exasperated. "Tas, Grandfather won't help us and you know it. He's too old for the war trail. Will you come or not?"

Oh, I desperately wanted to run away from this terrible place, leave the sickness, the despair, all the fighting, and especially Chief Eagan's rules and his fearsome demon, but I also didn't want to go to them with them having false expectations of what I could do for them. I took the bundle and tucked it inside my shirt and stood. Taking one of the rabbits from my string, I handed it to him for his next meal.

"I accept the offering. But before I know whether I can help you with this, I must pray about it. If I think I can aid the warband, I will sneak away from the settlement three days from now and meet you in this grove after everyone is asleep."

When I returned the evening meal was an unsettling affair, everyone still upset from the recent killings. Misbehaving young children, weeping women and grim-faced men ate the tasteless meal, their spirit fires mingling in a chaotic turmoil to my inner sight. Hiding my head with my blanket I focused my Qwakaiva on not drawing any attention to myself. Conjuring an image of a white hare standing hidden against a snow bank in my mind, I ate my portion quickly and slipped out into the shadows heading for my bed.

I wanted to get a little sleep before I slipped away later. With Eagan's ever-watchful demon nearby, I didn't dare go into the Dream while in the settlement. I would go back to the grove and hope that would be far enough away for my protection.

THE NIGHT WAS QUIET save for the wind rustling among the cottonwood trees when I tossed my blanket over my shoulder and crept out of the hut I shared with my failing grandmother and Amima.Moon shone down on the trees and dry ground, muting theircolors to grays and blacks.

By the creek I paused. I looked up into the night sky searching for the familiar Spirit Lights, to tap their power as I used to, but I had forgotten, this far south there were no Spirit Lights. Only the stars looked down upon me with their cold, alien stare. I shivered, so far away, so cold, would they grant me some of their power if I flew up to them while my Spirit traveled within the Dream? I hesitated. What if my soul got lost along the way? No help for me there, I decided.

I glanced down at the creek as I crossed to the other side. Could I swim home along its murky channel? No, that wouldn't do either. This stream flowed west over the snow-capped peaks on the horizon to the distant ocean. It traveled in the wrong direction.There was no other way, my Spirit Body would have to sink down into the flinty ground, swim the dark currents of the black rivers under the Earth.

My heart quailed at such a thought. Chumco had warned me not to venture into those dangerous currents alone, but I had no choice now, if I wanted to help the outlaws secure food for our starving people.

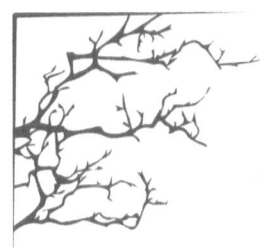

Chapter Two

As I made a fire and placed the war band's offering upon its glowing coals, I prayed some kind being would come to my aid, before some of the monsters of the depths discovered my Spirit and came to devour me.

Letting go of the image of myself as human, my Spirit-Body became a stream of water, sinking down through plant roots and soil, sinking down ever deeper through the porous rock of the earth's crust to merge myself with the black water of the underground rivers. Just before my consciousness would be forever lost and I would become one more drop merged into its mighty current, I shape-shifted into a seal and began to swim north.

As my head emerged from the dark water into a hidden cavern I heard a startled squeak and the flapping of wings overhead. In the next moment a tiny furred creature flew down from the rocks above and perched atop my head. Shifting one flippered arm back into a human hand I patted the little creature. <<Greetings, Little One have you come to guide me,>> I asked.

<<I don't know—maybe—where are you going?>> Bat said.

I thought about it for a moment as I stroked her soft fur and pointed ears. <<I don't know where I am going. Warriors in the world above made an offering. They seek guidance, asking help from the Unseen Ones, so they in turn can protect and feed the People. I want to help, so I came into the Dream, searching for my Benefactor—but I don't know where to find Him. Can you help me?>>

Bat thought about it for a while, and finally said, <<The Great Kunai will be found only if He wishes to be found.>>

My heart nearly falling from my chest I said, <<Oh. Thank you for telling me. I guess you or no one can help me. I'll just keep on swimming till I find him.>> I wouldn't be discouraged—I wouldn't give up—I wouldn't.

As I started to swim away, she flew after me, calling, <<Wait, Crazy Siyatli boy, where are you going? It is dangerous to travel the dark rivers alone!>>

I paused. <<I've been warned of the dangers, Honored Spirit, but I can't go back without searching for Him. My people's need is great. I must try to find Kunai on my own if you are unable to help me.>>

Growling in frustration she flew after me once more. <<I didn't say I wouldn't help you; I merely said the Great One cannot be found unless He wants us to find Him.>>

<<Oh.>>

<<Come, Siyatli boy, we will try to find him together.>> Sending her squeaky calls echoing off the rock walls she flew down the black river ahead of me.

Unable to see in the blackness I swam for a long time, my seal whiskers brushing against the rock bed of the channel my only sense of something solid and real. I had no idea where I was, or where Bat was leading me. I kept my intent to find aid for my Qwani'Ya People foremost in my mind and prayed that I would be found worthy of the Great Aseutl's notice. As Rattlesnake had told me once before I must trust, in myself and the Benefactor to whom I had pledged my life and service.

Tiring at last I slowed my swim. In spite of my desire to help I began to doubt the wisdom of this journey. Bat might not be the one to guide me through these dark caverns. And I was starting to fear I had been gone from my sleeping body in the world above too long. Maybe I needed to go back—try tomorrow night—ask Rattlesnake for her help.

I called to Bat to tell her what I planned, but she had flown too far ahead.I couldn't just leave her so I continued swimming down the black current, calling to her from time to time, hoping to catch up to her before my strength gave out.

Suddenly I heard a loud roaring, and then a frightened shriek from somewhere in the tunnel's blackness ahead. I was sure it was Bat. Normally she wouldn't have ventured this far into the depths on her own. The only reason she was in trouble was she was trying to help me. I hurried forward. Without giving myself time to think I remembered one of Chumco's many lessons and created a ball of glowing light from my Qwakaiva, tossing it in the air to guide my way forward.

Around the next bend in the channel where a long rock ledge hung over the river's flow, a large many-tentacled creature with glowing red eyes had pulled itself half out of the water and onto the ledge. It had caught Bat in one of its tentacles and was pulling her towards its open toothy mouth. Bat was shrieking and struggling, but the creature was unfazed.

Shape-shifting into a body half human and half seal, I created a spear of light and raced to help her. Intent on its meal the creature didn't notice me until I had come close enough to plunge my war spear deep into its gaping jaws.

<<Eat this if you are hungry,>> I cried.

The many-tentacled being roared waving its arms and tossing Bat high into the air. Churning the water around its lower body into a phosphorescent foam, it choked on my spear. I saw nothing of her after that, because the beast of the depths now focused its malice on me instead. As I let go of the spear and tried to swim away it spat out the spear and wrapped me in several of its long sinewy arms. Instead of Bat to appease its hunger I now found myself, being pulled closer and closer to that wide toothy mouth.

I shouted a war cry and hacked at the scaly tentacles confining me with a knife I created. In my mind I heard demonic laughter and wondered if Chief Eagan's demon had discovered me and alerted the creature to my presence in the Dream.

Determined not to make me and my Qwakaiva an easy meal for the beast I kept slashing with my blade. I might not survive this battle, but I wouldn't give either of the foul creatures the satisfaction of breaking my will before I won—or died.

Brave words, but I was tiring. Too long, too long away from the waking world. I would have to be clever if I wanted to survive the trap I was now sure the skeletal demon of Eagan's had set for me. Hadn't it warned me it would make me pay for my refusal of its patronage and power?

Pretending to be exhausted, I banished my knife and allowed the monster to confine my arms with another of its tentacles. I didn't resist its attempt to draw me into its open mouth. I trembled.

So near those gaping jaws, I would only have one chance to free myself. If my plan didn't work I would be eaten and Samiqwas would find my dead body when next he came to the clearing for my answer. With Eagan's demon's laughter roaring in my mind the many-tentacled creature drew me closer...

Then, just as it would have plunged me into its waiting hungry mouth, I shape-shifted into a form I was familiar with from my time with my mentor as we played among the northern lights. I became a snake-like dragon and blew a flaming burst of Qwakaiva into the closest of the monster's red eyes.

The beast let out a thunderous roar that loosened rocks from the cavern ceiling above. Falling from the darkness, they splashed into the river like deadly hailstones. Slithering out of my attacker's grasp, I ducked beneath the water and swam for the bottom of the channel, hoping to avoid the lethal rain.

As I dove I saw a large jagged stone hit the creature on its head. With a loud rumble it sank under the surface of the water with a mighty splash that sent me crashing into the stone bottom of the channel, even though I was by then some distance away from our combat.

When I recovered enough to think clearly, I shape-shifted into my seal form and blindly swam as fast as I could away from the monster and the sounds I could still here thundering in my wake. Though I had no idea where I was, and how to find my way back to the Surface World, it sounded like a part of the ceiling had come down and I was glad I had escaped the destruction. I kept swimming until all was quiet around me.

My Spirit Fire tingling from my narrow escape, I finally lifted my head out of the water and found myself in the middle of a black pool. Where was Bat? Hopefully she had escaped, too, and was safe. Above me glowing rock formations like giant teeth hung down from the ceiling of a dark grotto. A cool breeze brushed my face, smelling of dust and minerals.

I swam to a flat rock ledge, changed back into my human form and climbed out of the water. I had no idea where I was. <<O Spirits of this place, Mighty Kunai, someone have pity on me—help me,>> I prayed.

Then ahead of me in the grotto the glowing form of my former mentorChumco appeared. A torrent of relief and joy overwhelmed me. All would be well. My mentor hadn't abandoned me; I was saved. I called out to him and he turned to look at me.

"It's me," I shouted, "your, little Seal, see I am here." I hurried to catch up with him, but no matter how hard I tried to come near the distance between us only lengthened. <<Mentor, please, I'm truly sorry for denying you and your wisdom. You were right. Much of what you predicted has already happened. The People are scattered and hungry. Please help me to save them!>>

No matter how I called out how much I begged or what I promised him in return for his help, his manner remained cold and indifferent to my pleas. He wouldn't speak to me or acknowledge me in any way, and that hurt my soul to the core.

Oh a part of me knew by then that Chumco had used me ruthlessly, but better to be loved and used than be abandoned and alone I reasoned. I wanted only to remember his gifts of power and the pleasure he could give me.

Grandfather'sprediction that Chumco would have drained my Qwakaiva to the death of me meant nothing compared to the fear and emptiness that had entered my soul to take its place.

Fearing to stray too far from the water that I suspected was my pathway out of the Dream, I sank down to the stone and buried my face in my hands. If Chumco wouldn't help me what was I going to do?

<<stop your crying. That's not your old mentor,>>a voice said.

<<What do you mean? Who are you—show yourself if you are friend to me.>>

Bat chuckled, showing sharp white teeth as she grinned at me from her upside down perch in the rocks above. <<Look closely with your Qwakaiva past the illusion He has assumed to fool your eye, young Seal. Quickly now lest you be perceived as unworthy of His regard.>>

I wanted to argue with the little creature, but changed my mind as the words formed in my mind. Instead I did as she instructed. I opened my shields...And was nearly engulfed in the Aseutl's power. Unsure what to do next, I rose to my knees and folded my hands across my chest as I had seen my uncle and other converts do to show reverence to their god. I had realized by then that it wasn't my former mentor standing before me, but the Great Kunai cloaked within Chumco's shape.

The luminous being came closer, and stood over me. <<So, you would worship me in the Chamuqwani fashion? Should I be amused or insulted, I wonder?>>

<<I-I am sorry, Great One,>> I stammered I mean no offence, but I haven't been taught what is proper.>>

<<You think you know me then, little Siyatli boy?>>

This time I looked into his eyes without flinching. <<Yes, Master of Enigma, I think I do.>>

He motioned for me to rise. <<You are very clever, little human. At your birth I predicted to your father that you would be powerful, and once more I have been proven right.>> Kunai said, a note of smug satisfaction coming into the deep rumbling voice.

<<Yes, clever, brave, and a fool, like most of your kind,>> he continued. <<Clever to guess how to come here, brave to try and swim the black currents alone, but still a fool in so many ways.>>

<<You speak to me of my father, Great One, can you call him to us?>>

<<Perhaps I could, but why should I? You could do it for yourself, if you hadn't spurned the mentor I sent you.>>

At the mention of my father, the old longing once more flooded my soul. I wanted, no needed to know him—have him love me. A stupid wish. The Aseutl was right I was a fool like most of my kind.

Could a creature of the otherworld feel towards me the tenderness and love needed by a human child? I didn't know. Would it hurt more to know him and find out he was incapable of loving me in the way I craved? Perhaps, I wasn't sure. Maybe I was better off with my dreams.

But keeping in mind what Chumco *had* taught me I faced Kunai boldly; I wouldn't be discouraged. I had pledged my life to Him and to the protection of my People. And to my eternal gratitude, the great Aseutl had answered my summons—in spite of my ignorance.

<<I was foolish perhaps to abandon my mentor, but that is water gone down stream now,>> I said. <<Chumco is gone, my father is gone, and I will have to live with that. I didn't swim the black water to change the past. I take responsibility for that decision. Tell my father whatever you like.>>

Kunai rumbled a laugh. Still keeping Chumco's form he motioned for me to resume my seat and came over to sit on the ledge facing me. <<Very well,

I shall. Now since you have gone to all the trouble to summon me, what do you want?>>

<<I came searching for power, because warriors of the People have sent a spirit offering. They request my help for a raid against our enemies.>>

<<Power, eh? You want me to gift you with some of my power; and what will you do with such a gift, I wonder? You may use my Qwakaiva to help the warriors now, but what will you use this power for later? Do you want to become a big chief among your people when you are older?

<<If it is just power you crave, the specter that stalks and taunts you can give you that. Surrender to it and I will release you from my service. Since you have already abandoned one teacher I have sent you, why should I bother to give you another? Better you remain just a half-trained Qwakaihi. Maybe you will cause less trouble that way.>>

Half-trained, I thought as my temper ignited, unable to help anybody even myself. Why are Grandfather, and now Him, always throwing my ignorance back into my face? <<I seek none of your Qwakaiva for my own selfish reasons—now or in the future. I only want to fight the evil that is devouring my Qwani'Ya people and the Earth! I will die first before I let that evil creature have me,>> I hotly declared.

<<Die, eh? As you almost did when Waluukba had you in its embrace at the specter's urging.>> He shook his head in mock reproof. <<So much fire, so much passion, your bravery is—impressive, little human. But have you no fear of my anger should your bravado annoy me?>>

He knew about my narrow escape? Why was I surprised? Of course the Great Aseutl knew. That thought cooled my temper like a fall into a snow bank. And now that I could once more think clearly, the thought of his punishment was sobering. <<Yes, Great One, I do fear your wrath—I'm foolish at times, but I'm not a total fool. In spurning your teacher, maybe I *have* forfeited any claims to your favor for myself, but I don't ask for myself. I come seeking aid for my people.>>

<<Please help him, Great One,>> Bat said from her perch.

Kunai seemed to think about our request for a long time, finally, he said, <<I have looked into The Pool of the future. Your request has merit and may prove interesting. See and remember what I now show you.>>

Still cloaked in Chumco's form, Kunai pulled out a loop of cord from a pouch around his waist. He looped it between his fingers and held out the pattern to show me. <<Did your mentor teach you how to make this?>>

The pattern within the string resembled the diamond design of the Seer's Pool, but the angles and curves that comprised the outer frame of the central diamond were different. And yet, I was sure I had seen its working before.

<<It looks familiar, but I don't know how to form it. What is its purpose?>>

Kunai's rumbling laugh came again. <<Yes, it should seem very familiar.>> Moving his forefinger, Kunai pulled on one of the intertwined cords and a pleasurable warmth began to build in my groin. His golden eyes alight with amusement, he tugged on the cord again, this time a little harder. The warmth became a rhythmic stroking that nearly laid me flat upon the stone.

Trembling like a leaf in a gale, I resisted the golden dance of pleasure threatening to engulf me. <<Please, Great One, stop.>>

Kunai raised an inquiring eyebrow. <<Stop? You don't like that? Then perhaps you would enjoy this more, hmm?>>

Kunai tugged at another cord and the sharp sting of pain mingled with the sweet taste of pleasure. This time I did fall, writhing on the cold stone. The Aseutl was toying with me, letting me know who was master of my Destiny, punishing me with a glut of both pleasure and pain for defying his will and abandoning my studies with his chosen teacher for me.

I screamed, I cried, I begged for him to stop and finally he let go and I lay quivering in a tangled heap. He left me alone for a time, Bat flying down and clumsily trying to comfort me. At last he grew impatient with my blubbering and told me to get up.

Kunai made no comment about what had just occurred between us. He only held out a hand on which a loop dangled. <<Now come sit by me and I will show you how to create the pattern known as The Aseutl's Gift. If you wish to help those who sent you an offering, then you will need to know how to make this design.>>

He gave me a mocking smile. <<As you have just learned, when part of the pattern is plucked what is shown in the center diamond is affected by a

Qwakaihi's will.Observe.>> Kunai took out his string again and reformed the pattern. <<Look into the diamond.>>

I did, and in the center I saw a rocky hillside similar to many I saw everyday in the Waking World. <<Now watch.>> Kunai plucked a cord and a rock detached itself and went rolling down the hillside, kicking up plumes of dust in its wake.

<<When you invoke the power, form the pattern, and project the wanted image, you will change what can occur in the Physical World. You can move objects and create illusions for a time. How long they last will depend on the strength of your power.

<<If you are worthy I will teach you more—later. What I show you now is enough to aid the warriors who sent the offering.>>

I was suitably impressed; my mind whirled with the possibilities for using such a power in my world. <<I would be honored if you would teach me how to make the Aseutl's Gift, Great One?>>

<<Its possibilities are tempting, hmm?>> Kunai gave me that enigmatic smile again. <<Sit here beside me and I will show you. If you are clever and can remember once you return to the Waking World you will have my permission to use this. But understand this too, young one, your Gift is great and so you may be able to accomplish much in your world that will be to my liking.

<<But know this too; just as you discovered when I sent Rattlesnake and Eagle to help you send your relatives home, there is a price to become one of my favored. For each time you draw on my Qwakaiva to work some conjuring in your world, you will taste some of the pain I also have shown you this night. That will be my price, so have a care how you use my Gifts.>>

Recalling Rattlesnake's bite during the portal opening and the payment Kunai might inflict in future was sobering. All thoughts of exacting revenge on my uncle, or Charlic and his friends with acts of petty trickery were forgotten. Knowing that I would suffer each time I invoked the power would ensure that I only called upon it when absolutely necessary for the good of the People.

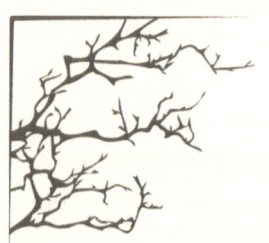

Chapter Three

Sun hot on my face, it was late morning when I finally awoke in the aspen grove by my dead fire pit. My body aching I stumbled to my feet. Water, I needed water but the can by my hearth was empty. I folded my blanket and put it over my shoulder. Tucking one end into the belt at my waist I went in search of a cool drink at the creek.

Then, to my disgust, when I checked my snares before going back to camp, I found that Coyote had stolen all but three of the rabbits caught in them while I overslept. Still not fully grounded in the Physical World after my ordeal, I was not having a good morning. Hoping to sneak back into the convert settlement and get more sleep in Mother's shelter, I headed in that direction.

I made it back into Mother's lodge without a problem and was just settling into my soft nest of sage and grasses when Mother returned with Grandmother and a weeping Thonna. Stifling a groan I sat up, bracing myself for more trouble.

The women seemed surprised to see me lying atop my bed. When she saw me Grandmother let out a startled cry, trembling and clinging to Mother. "Who is that stranger in our home, Tuulah My Girl?"

Her once stout body now skeletally thin, and nearly bent double with the weight of the many hardships of her life, she resisted at first Mother and Thonna's attempts to settle her by the fire pit. "No, no I don't want to. That stranger will hurt us. We need to find my husband to make the stranger go away."

Not bothering to remind the old woman that she wasn't her oldest daughter Tuulah, Mother continued to urge her forward. "That's Tas, your grandson. That's not a stranger who will hurt us. Come sit down and I will make you some tea. Maybe Grandson has brought you another fat rabbit and I can cook you some nice soup, too. Wouldn't you like that, Amima?"

"Tea? Yes, I want some tea," she whined. It took a little more coaxing but they finally got her settled by the firepit wrapped in a dusty blanket. Thonna built up the fire while Mother was settling Grandmother. I rose and picked up the water buckets near the entrance. Pouring the last of the water into our big can to heat for tea, I refused to meet their eyes and headed for the creek.

Judging by their strange looks in my direction I wondered if I had been gone in the Dream longer than just one night. As I passed through the grass covering to the outside, I turned and said to Thonna, "There are three rabbits in my bag. Tell Aunty I'm sorry it isn't more. A coyote stole the rest of my catch before I could get to them this morning."

She glared at me, the many questions she wanted me to answer alight in her eyes. Before she could voice them, I said, "I'll get more water now," and then I was gone.

I hurried down the trail to fill our buckets in the deep pool up from the settlement, my thoughts in turmoil. The herbs I had gathered for Grandmother's fever seemed to have helped the fire burning inside her, but the sickness gobbling up her mind I couldn't cure. Even in the last few days she seemed to have gotten worse.

How could I leave them now—how could I not...

My worries a heavy burden on my back I nearly ran into Charlic as he stepped out of the brush to confront me. I sighed. "Charlic, I haven't got time for this. My Mother needs this water. Grandmother is very ill right now. If you must fight with me again please wait till I finish bringing her the water."

As I tried to walk past he blocked my way. Looking down his long Chamuqwani nose at me, he sneered. "I wanted to be the first to tell you, Heathen Scum."

I sighed again. "Tell me what?"

"In a few more days it will be official—she will be mine. Your Uncle has agreed to send Thonna to live in my parents' home. And after that I won't allow her to see you. If she tries, I will beat her—as the Great God says a husband can do to a disobedient wife. The formal announcement will be made at the next Prayer Day when Intercessor Karl will tell everyone about our betrothal and coming wedding."

He folded his arms across his chest and smirked. "I'll let you live—this time, witch boy, because soon you will be gone—for good—and your uncle won't care."

Now I understood Thonna's distress, and his smug attitude sparked my anger. I gave him a toothy smile. "Uncle Royston might not care, but I have two uncles, don't forget, and Uncle Tli just might care to avenge me if you should succeed in getting rid of me. And he already knows what a dog turd you and your brothers are."

As he thought about my threat his face reddened, his anger showing like a deep bruise on his pale yellow skin. "Maybe we won't wait that long. Maybe I will give my bride to be a present of your head on a pole."

I snorted and curled my lip in disgust. "So, brave warrior, you and your pack of scavenging dogs plan to ambush me and kill me this time—hmm? You're going to kill me, like your relatives killed the innocent women and children who died in Lynx Hunting's camp?"

Charlic's face paled and his mouth dropped open. "Surprised I know? Didn't you just call me, witch boy? What else might I know, eh?"

That had been stupid—I had just ignored the warning I had given Mother and Thonna. I was leaving soon anyway—I hoped it wouldn't matter. While my words still had the power to stun him I brushed past him and hurried back to my lodge. The anger still bubbling inside me I refused to look back.

BY THE TIME I RETURNED Grandmother was asleep in her bed and Mother and Thonna were sitting by the fire with their own cups of tea. I set the buckets down and placed the gourd dipper back in one of them, then I came over to join them. I glanced longingly at my bed, but sleep would have to wait.

I sat beside Mother and she poured the last of the tea into a cup and handed it to me. My stomach rumbled. I sipped my tea. "Charlic stopped me on my way back with the water. He told me what Uncle has done," I quietly told them.

Thonna's face reddened with anger, but she also looked like she was going to cry again. "I won't go I won't marry him," she declared. "I've told father—all of them. No matter how much they beat me I won't marry him—I won't."

She got that stubborn look on her face that told me she meant it. She might do herself harm—even kill herself, as she swore she would, if they forced her. I wanted to help her—truly I did. My guts twisted in knots as I wondered what to do. And, once again I wished Grandfather was here.

I didn't think of her as a potential wife as the jealous Charlic accused; she was just my girl-cousin, but Thonna was an enigma to me. I found her both fascinating and discomforting. Sharp-tongued and quick witted she reminded me a lot of my bossy older cousin, Samiqwas's sister Esuuli, who'd been lost to us when we were forced from our homes. Like the matriarchs of my Qwani'Ya People in the past, she had a fierce and unquenchable spirit. Her misfortune was to have been born into a time when the roles for women among us were in transition.

"When do they plan to make the announcement? Charlic said on the next prayer day when the priest comes, but I don't know when that is."

She shrugged. "I don't know either—a few days, maybe. With the roads not so safe with all the fighting, the Intercessor doesn't like to leave the agency—and we have no extra food to feed him and the soldiers when they come, anyway."

"I will try to talk to Uncle, if you think it will help," I offered.

"Don't bother," she growled. "He won't listen, to you or anyone—" she broke off and stood as she heard Aunty Marika calling for her. "I've got to go. Amima needs my help with the evening meal."

When Thonna was gone Mother set her cup down. Glancing at her now sleeping mother, she asked, "I should go help them as well. Can you stay here and watch your grandmother while I am away?"

As she started to rise, I said, "Please wait. Now that we are alone I have something I need to tell you."

For just a moment I saw fear in her eyes as she sat back down. Taking up her empty cup, she pretended to drink. "All right; what is it, my son? I noticed you haven't slept here for a couple nights. Has something happened to my father?"

So caught up in my own maelstrom of conflicting emotions I never considered her interpretation of my strange behavior. "No, I don't think so. He is still a few days walk to the west with the Kukiya—the last time I checked on him."

I turned to look at my sleeping grandmother and choked down the lump forming in my throat. I had to leave the convert settlement, but grandmother was so ill—and as Amima had already told me, she wouldn't leave her. I didn't want to leave her, either, but after Samiqwas's visit, the offering I had accepted, and my recent confrontation with Charlic, I couldn't stay.

Suddenly finding the plumes of lazy smoke rising from the few glowing embers left in the fire pit fascinating, I wouldn't look at her when I said, "Samiqwas came to visit me. He brought me an offering from Uncle Tli and the warband. They want me to join them. They have need of a Qwakaihi."

As I finished I glanced up to see how she was taking my news, but I saw little change in the calm expression of her still lovely face. As she used to do so often before when I was younger and needed her comfort, she had retreated into her private dream world where no evil or unpleasantness could harm her.

Frustrated, I reached over and grabbed her hand and gave it a little squeeze to get her attention. "Amima, I have to go, but I'm afraid for you, too, if you remain here alone without me or Grandfather to protect you. Please reconsider, let Uncle take care of his mother and come with me."

"I will be all right, and of course you must go." She patted my hand, trying to reassure me. Then she chuckled, an amused smile curving her lips. "My brother will probably try to marry me off to one of his convert friends, but like brave Thonna I will resist his efforts. Don't look so horrified, my little Rock Squirrel. I won't let him. If my father hasn't returned after my mother passes, I will leave and find Pretty Shell Woman or some of our other relatives to stay with until you, or father come for me."

Well that did ease my mind somewhat. Now what to do about Thonna? I had promised her I would take her with me if I left, but now how could I, when I was leaving to join a band of hunted outlaws. Even though marriage to Charlic was a fate I wouldn't wish on any poor woman, what I could offer my coshelah cousin wasn't any better—might be much worse.

Knowing what she would say if I told her I resolved not to say anything, take the coward's way out and just go. Mother could tell her after I was gone.

"When are you leaving," she asked breaking in on my thoughts.

I laughed softly. "That depends on how long I have been gone this time, but it will be soon. Tonight or tomorrow, Samiqwas is coming back to fetch me."

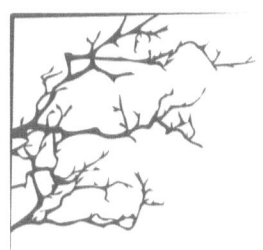

Chapter Four

I managed to say my good byes to mother and grandmother the next night when we returned to our shelter after the evening meal. I planned to sleep for a while, then slip out of the settlement undetected without attracting unnecessary attention. All went well—or so I thought until I was nearing my meeting place in the aspen grove when Samiqwas stepped out of the brush and confronted me.

I couldn't see his expression in the dim light, but his body language told me there was a problem. A shiver running down my spine, I murmured, "What's wrong? I was careful—I don't think I was followed."

He snorted a quiet laugh. "There is someone else waiting for you in your secret place besides me and Uncle Tli,"

Had Charlic or one of the other Converts discovered my plan? That shiver shifted to become a knife of fear in my gut. "I told no one but Amima of my plan and she wouldn't tell—who?"

For answer he waved me on, taking up his sentry position again. Guts churning and my thoughts in turmoil I brushed aside some hanging branches and stepped into the clearing. Someone had built a small fire and three people were sitting round it talking quietly.

Hearing my approach, Uncle Tli, a Kukiya man I didn't know, and Thonna looked up. My mouth dropping open I stared. At last I stammered out, "Thonna, what are you doing here?"

"My niece says you promised her she could come," Uncle Tli said. His expression was unreadable in the dim fire light and his voice gave me no clue as to how he felt about her being there.

Turning to the men I shook my head. "N-no I didn't tell her—Thonna you can't come—it will be too dangerous."

As I was speaking Thonna rose and came over to where I was standing, that grim expression I knew so well on her face. Bracing myself for an argument I was caught off guard when she punched me so hard on the jaw that I nearly fell down.

"You promised, dog turd—you promised that if you left the settlement you would take me with you! And now you are leaving—leaving me here where I will have to marry that other dog turd, Charlic—and you didn't even have the courage to say good bye. Mouse piss drinker!" and she raised her fist to hit me again.

Hastily I stepped back out of range, before she could land another blow. "Thonna, don't! I know I promised, but this is different than us just running off to live with other relatives—you might die."

"I will die if I stay here," she snarled and tried to hit me again. "Or I will kill him—and then the soldiers will kill me too. So whatever way you look at it I'm going to die if you don't take me."

She swung at me again, but this time I grabbed her arms and held them as she swore and tried to get to me. "Thonna, please. I know I behaved like a coward. I just didn't want you to get hurt."

"Hurt? Stay or go I might get hurt. Don't try to tell me how to live my life. I'm tired of everyone doing that, my mother, my father, dog turd, and now you! I will make up my own mind, follow my own path, and-and—" she broke off, calling me a bad Chamuqwani word. Wrenching an arm out of my grasp she swiped at her eyes and then tried once more to punch me.

A soft laugh from the other side of the fire made both of us pause and stare in that direction. The Kukiya man was smiling at her his eyes a light with amusement. Addressing Uncle Tli, he said, "I like this niece of yours, brother. She has a warrior's fiery spirit. We bring her, yes?"

The Kukiya was tall and thin with a jagged scar on his chin. He had painted black and red lines on his face, and wore his long hair loose, held back by a cloth of some colorless fabric across his forehead. On the belt at his waist were knives and a quiver of arrows. Over his shoulder he'd hung an unstrung bow in a leather case.

"Maybe." Tli frowned and gave me a disgusted look, as if it was my fault things were getting complicated. Speaking loud enough for me to hear, he grumped, "I hope you are worth all this trouble." Then he asked, "Niece, if Tas didn't tell you he was leaving tonight, how did you find out?"

"Your sister told me. She said she couldn't leave her sick mother, but I should get away—and Tas had promised..." she broke off and dropped her eyes under Uncle's intense glare.

"My mother is ill? How bad is she?"

"She's bad," I told him. "Amima says she doesn't have long now."

Unable to keep the bitterness out of his voice, he next asked, "And where is my father? He goes to all the camps with his medicines to help other people, why isn't he taking care of his own wife—or has he divorced her now?"

"No, he hasn't divorced her, but it's hard for him in the convert settlement—and Grandmother won't leave. He doesn't know how bad she's become in the last few days after she caught another fever." I sighed and dropped my eyes. "I did my best—but it isn't enough. I found herbs that helped the fever, but not her mind."

"Where is he then?"

"Last I checked on him he was still several days walk to the west," I told Uncle. "He made an offering and the Unseen Ones sent him on a Spirit Quest for the people."

He thought about that for a long moment and finally sighed. "I wish I could go to her—see her one last time, but I don't dare."

"It wouldn't be worth the risk," I told him. "She probably wouldn't recognize you even if you *could* go. Her spirit is already half in the other world. Most of the time she doesn't even recognize me—and I live with her. She's often frightened when she sees me in our shelter and starts crying. Not knowing what she was doing she might alert the settlement to your presence," I explained.

Still lost in thought, Tli agreed not to try.

Glancing up into the night sky, the Kukiya studied the position of the stars through the branches. Nodding to himself, he picked up his blanket roll and handed it to me to carry for him. "It grows late; we go now." He pointed north with his lips and started back down the trail towards the convert settlement. "I will send your nephew to join you. Take them, my brother, to where the horses are hidden and head back to our camp. I will catch up to you later."

"Uncle, where are you going>" I asked.

He looked over his shoulder and smiled. "To get another pony, of course."

UNCLE TLI LED US WEST through the cactus and rabbit brush of the rocky desert hillsides all the rest of that night. As the light was beginning to pale the eastern sky, he left the path we'd been following and took another game trail into a deep gully and then into a small sheltered canyon. There among the tall grass and thorn with high red cliffs sheltering us from view a younger Kukiya man waited with three horses. Samiqwas whistled a desert bird call and he put down his bow as we pushed through the last of the rabbit brush.

His eyes scanning the people coming into the clearing I saw the fear on his face when he didn't see the Kukiya man with us, and then in the next moment his expression became unreadable. "Where is Utsiyonti?

"Went for another horse," Tli said. "Your brother will be along soon. We go back to camp now." Leaving Samiqwas to do further introductions, he headed for a hobbled spotted horse on the other side of the little hollow.

Samiqwas glanced at our retreating uncle's back and sighed. "Tuumaz, these are my cousins Tasimu and Thonna. They have come to join us."

Thonna was wearing Mother's old tunic dress from home and a pair of Chamuqwani trews she must have taken off a washing line instead of the long skirts the convert women all wore. I'm not sure Tuumaz had realized she was a girl till Samiqwas introduced us, because his eyes widened when he realized his mistake. Before he could comment on that fact Tli rode up and scowled down at us. "Why are you standing here? Get on your horses."

Reaching down a hand to me, he motioned for me to climb up behind him. I hesitated, looking at Thonna. "She can ride with Tuumaz or Samiqwas. I want to talk to you while we ride."

Eyeing the horses the Kukiya youth was bringing over Thonna said with a slight quiver in her voice, "I've never ridden one of the Chamuqwani beasts before."

"You will have to learn if you want to be with us," Samiqwas said. He glanced at me and smirked. "As will Tas. We all ride as much as possible; it's the only way to keep ahead of the soldiers."

Uncle growled impatiently when she still hesitated. "You wanted to come; now get on a horse or we leave you here."

"I'm coming, don't worry about me," she growled, giving Uncle an angry look. Thonna's expression turned grim, as she looked from Samiqwas to the desert man, trying to decide which of them to choose.

"You can ride with me. I am the more experienced horseman. That one might drop you on a cactus if you ride with him," Tuumaz said and held out a hand to her smiling. Samiqwas snorted and said a bad word which made Tuumaz chuckle.

At another impatient growl from Uncle my cousin helped boost her up and she settled herself a bit uneasily behind the Kukiya, holding on to his waist. Then Samiqwas took the rope halter of the last horse and pulled himself onto its back with a bit of effort.

Hiding a grin, I grasped Uncle's belt as he urged the horse into a fast trot.

As we rode throughout the morning, Uncle Tli questioned me thoroughly about the people and conditions in the convert settlements and at the agency. I told him everything I could, but when he wanted more specific details than I could supply, I suggested, "Uncle,the rumors that I was a malicer followed me to the Preserve. I wasn't well liked among those people.

"Thonna's betrothed and Chief Eagan, your brother's father-in-law, know I keep with the old way and they hate me for it. I've been trying to stay away from the settlements as much as possible, hunting in the desert for meat which the converts were more than glad to take from even a 'witch boy.'

"You should maybe ask Thonna some of these questions. Her parents and other relatives rarely let her escape their watchful eyes to seek me out for what I could share with her of the old teachings. She would have been around the settlement to hear the gossip much more than I."

He grunted, thinking about my words for a time, as he guided the horse through a difficult passage up the rock-strewn hillside. When we had crossed over the ridge and were well below the sky-line on the other side, he said, "There is a rock over hang not far ahead, and in its deepest shadow is a small pool that should still have water for us and the horses at this time of year. We will rest there during the midday heat.

"I will take your suggestion and talk to her then. You can ride with Tuumaz when we start up again. She can come with me so I can get to know her better and learn more of the latest news."

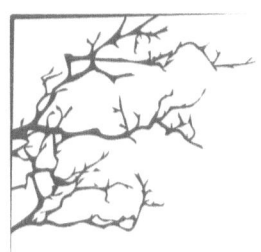

Chapter Five

It was late afternoon the shadows lengthening into purple streaks across the gray sage when the sound of horses coming at a fast pace made Tli pause. Reaching for the long thunder weapon he'd hung in a case on the horse's side, he looked down the slope behind us. A lone horseman leading two other horses was coming up fast behind us, kicking up a pale dust cloud in their wake.

As the rider drew near we could see it was a grinning Utsiyonti. Motioning for us to keep going, he quickly caught up and passed us, taking the lead. "How far are they behind you?" Uncle Tli called after him.

"Too close. We ride now talk later."

Catching up to his brother with me clinging on breathless at his back, Tuumaz took the lead ropes of the two spare horses, giving one of the lead ropes to Samiqwas and handing me the other.

I gripped Tuumaz's horse tight with my knees and held on to the warrior's belt with one hand while keeping a hold on the lead rope with the other. I prayed the loose horse wouldn't pull me off into the dust if it took it into its mind to start back for home.

At sunset we came to a creek that was running fast with the first of the mountain snow melt. The horses were tiring by that time, and Utsiyonti slowed our pace. He led us up stream for a time, paying close attention to water levels. At one point he got off his horse and stepped into the creek, bending to allow a hand to float in the water. My eyes widened when I saw with my Spirit Sight how he tested the current's strength by using his Qwakaiva.

Blue water Spirits rose up from the waves to greet him. Swirling around his chest and shoulders, they leaned close to whisper in his ear. Though I didn't understand their private communication with him I was sure he asked them questions about the safety of our intended route which they in turn answered. As he stepped back out of the stream, he saw my startled expression and smiled. He knew I must have seen the Water Spirits surrounding him.

"In the desert, water is life," he told me. "The Akiyazi, Water Spirits come to me and bless me with their gifts sometimes, when I have need of them."

Though I doubted if Uncle Tli had seen the Spirits, he must have known what the Kukiya warrior was doing from witnessing earlier events. "Will it be safe for us to cross?" he asked as Utsiyonti mounted his horse again.

"Safe? For a time yes," he said, "but at my urging, by morning Water will be too angry to let the soldiers follow us."

Tli grunted. "So we go back to camp now—tonight?"

"No not yet I think," Utsiyonti said, stroking the scar on his chin as he considered our next move. "In case the ones that follow are too clever for Water's tricks, we will go further north and hunt—maybe catch an antelope or three before we go west to our camp. Always good to bring food, yes?"

Tli and Tuumaz agreed and we headed north, allowing the horses to drink as we walked through the swollen creek for a time before climbing out on the opposite bank.

When we reached the top of the slope overlooking the stream, I touched Tuumaz's arm, handed him the lead rope, and slid off the horse's back. "What are you doing, Crazy Qwani'Ya boy? This no time to stop and pee," Tuumaz grumbled.

"I don't have to pee," I said, "but I think I can make it a little harder for those who follow to find us." He said a bad word but held the horses still and waited to see what I planned to do.

Murmuring a prayer for strength and guidance under my breath, I took the cord from around my neck and formed the pattern of the Aseutl's Gift for the first time. Focusing my Qwakaiva I created in the center diamond a picture of the portion of the creek where we had just walked out of the water. Seeing the horses large muddy hoof prints plainly marked in the mud heading up the slope towards us, I knew they left an easy trail for anyone to follow if they got this far. I plucked one of the pattern's cords as Kunai had shown me, hoping I was strong enough to change things in the Physical World as he said I could.

To my great relief a wave of water rose out of the creek bed and followed us up the path for some distance. And then as Water sank back into its rumbling bed, it washed away the marks of our passage. Then I noticed there was still a trail of hoof prints following us further up the slope in the dust, but I was unable to make Water climb any higher, no matter how I strained or coaxed.

Gasping I let the image in the center diamond fade. What to do now. Tuumaz would become impatient soon if I didn't do something more.<<Rattlesnake, are you near; can you help me?>>

<<Share with me your warmth tonight and hunt me a nice fat rabbit, and I will ask Master of the Air, Eagle, to call the wind for you,>> she said into my mind.

<<Willingly, Honored One, I will do that.>>

When I heard the scream of an eagle overhead I formed a picture of the trail in the diamond, then I felt Wind touch my cheek and with my Qwakaiva I directed Wind to blow away all traces of our passing from the dry sandy ground.

Satisfied that our trail could no longer be detected I allowed the pattern to fall apart at last. Slipping the string off my hands I replaced my special cord around my neck and held out my hand for Tuumaz to help me back atop his horse. Still staring at the path up the slope bare of any trace of our passing, it took him a moment to understand what I wanted. Finally he reached down and helped me up.

Wind followed us for a time, continuing to erase our tracks, but as the light dimmed and the desert twilight faded into night, Wind lost interest and left us for good.

Utsiyonti led us deeper into the desert by starlight until we came to a cluster of scrub pines near the top of a high ridge. There we made a dry camp, using some of the water we had carried with us from the creek to give ourselves and the horses a drink. As we fell to doing the simple camp chores I saw Tuumaz pull his brother aside for a talk. When they glanced in my direction I suspected he was telling his brother what I'd done to erase our back trail.

Samiqwas laughed at Thonna and me as we hobbled around the pines collecting wood for a small fire. Dropping her last load of branches by the fire

Uncle was starting Thonna faced our tormentor with hands on hips. "Laugh all you want, Coshelah Cousin, but I bet you were just as sore the first day you spent on horseback, too."

Tuumaz chuckled as he added his pile to hers. "We call him Granny, we laugh when he stagger and complain how his ass hurt, for long time after he join us."

"Hah, you don't call me that any more since I punched your nose for you," Samiqwas joked. Tuumaz laughed and aimed a blow at his head, which Samiqwas easily dodged.

The horses hobbled and staked out to graze we sat around the tiny smokeless fire and someone put a sooty can in the coals to heat water for tea. The scent of pine and sagebrush was strong on the breeze radiating up from the cooling land. Tiny rustlings and squeaks punctuated the darkness just outside the firelight. On a nearby ridge Coyote yipped and was answered by another of its kind from a farther hillside.

Trying to keep my eyes open long enough to eat, I took the strips of dry meat handed me and dipped them in the clay jar of grease someone brought from their pack and passed around. No one wanted to talk much. Utsiyonti divided the night sentry duty between the four outlaws, and Thonna and I took our blankets and made beds for ourselves under the trees.

It was getting cold and I would have liked to sleep nearer the fire, but knowing I would probably be sharing my blankets that night I dared not. So, scooping out a nest for myself in last year's pine needles I curled up with my back against a tree's scratchy bark.

Her belly swollen with a recent meal, she nestled in beside me not long after the camp quieted. I placed my blanket over both of us and drifted into a dreamless sleep.

Next morning as the east began to pale Utsiyonti had us up and moving again. Sometime as I slept, Rattlesnake had crawled out from under my blanket and slithered away into the brush to avoid being seen by the others.

Using his gift Utsiyonti found a deep pool of water under a sheltered overhang when we stopped in the midday heat. There we could fill our water jars and let the horses have a good drink. When we resumed our journey we continued north for the rest of that day through the sage brush and pine thickets. Nearing sunset Utsiyonti led us to another fast moving mountain stream. We decided to camp up the slope so the Kukiya men could take their bows and hunt before the sky became too dark to see.

I owed Rattlesnake a meal so I told Uncle that I was going further up the slope to set some snares for our evening meal. While Thonna gathered firewood and set about other camp chores Uncle Tli and Samiqwas took care of the horses.

Leaving my offering for rattlesnake on a flat sun-warmed rock I returned to camp in the deep twilight with a few grouse and a couple rabbits.

As I stepped into the firelight Samiqwas looked up and then joked, "Oh, there you are. I thought maybe you got lost and I was going to have to leave my cozy spot by the fire and go find you."

I snorted a laugh and tossed him my sack. "No, I didn't get lost, nor was I trying to get out of helping with the horses like I heard you call after me. Here you can finish preparing these for our meal—since you're sitting there doing nothing."

He called me a bad name in the Chamuqwani language and started to toss the bag back to me. Before he could throw it Thonna came over and plucked my catch from his hand. "Toss the meat around like a game ball! You two ptarmigans are going to spoil the meat and nobody will eat it. I'll prepare them, because neither of you know how to behave—and probably don't know how to fix them correctly anyway."

Samiqwas turned red and opened his mouth to snap at her, then realized she was joking with him, smiled and let her take the meat.

Over a meal of my catch and some tough sweet-tasting roots roasted in the ashes that the Kukiya called Clamisa I learned that the hunt for antelope had been successful, as well. They had killed two nice fat bucks. Not wishing to take the time to dry the meat, however, Utsiyonti and Uncle Tli decided that we would head west to the outlaws hidden encampment in the morning.

And with the morning came me and Thonna's first horseback lesson. Knowing which of the horses would be the easiest for us to learn upon, Utsiyonti chose the two oldest mares in our little herd for us. Mine was a deep brown in color with two white feet and a white patch on her forehead. I was very nervous that first day and can't say I ever became a comfortable rider during the time I spent with the outlaws. Thonna, on the other hand, was the best rider among all of the outlaw Qwani'Ya once she too got over her nervousness and had more experience.

With our long narrow shadows leading the way, we headed west into the dry country of the deep desert, arriving at the outlaw camp on the afternoon of the second day. Long before we actually reached their base hidden away among the caves and rocky ledges of a dry and empty land, we were spotted by sentries posted in the rocks who gave warning of our arrival.

Knees aching, my lips dry and cracking, and needing desperately to pee, I was relieved when I could finally climb down off the mare and hand her reins to a boy who led her away with the other horses. At a motion of his chin Thonna and I followed Uncle Tli and Utsiyonti up a steep trail that ended under a heavy overhang. In the shadows that seemed to lead deeper into the mountain, several men and women were sitting around a fire talking quietly. They looked up at our approach.

As we stepped into the firelight, a dark-skinned man with piercing black eyes, a big nose, and powerful shoulders rose to greet us. I recognized him right away; I had seen him before in my vision. In the next moment Golannah focused his penetrating gaze on us. When he turned to me, I let him continue his exam without looking away. As the war leader of the outlaws he had the right to know who he was inviting to join them, I reasoned.

Finished at last, he said to me in a strongly accented version of our language, "You young. Me no expect dat—still a child you, me think."

Once more I hated my short stature and wished I'd grown taller like Samiqwas. Even though he was only a year older than I was, no one would think him a child. Unable to help myself I let out a mirthless laugh, and told him, "Looks can be deceiving, War Leader Golannah. My childhood was over when the Chamuqwani forced us from our home on Big Ice Lake."

Golannah scowled at Uncle and Utsiyonti. The warriors shook their heads. "We said nothing to him," Tli finally said as Golannah continued to glare.

"They told us nothing about this camp or the people staying here," I assured him. "They didn't need to, because I already knew who you were. The Unseen Ones who guide me showed me in a vision after the fire at the agency."

Golannah grunted, studying me once again. At last he nodded, and then turned his attention to Thonna, asking Uncle, "You spoke to me of your nephew, but you said nothing about another family member. She is too young to be your sister, Qwani'Ya Cousin, so who else have you brought to join us, another Qwakaihi perhaps?"

"This is my niece, Thonna," Uncle said and placed a heavy hand on her shoulder, as he pushed her forward into the firelight. "My nephew seems to have promised her she could come, but as far as I know she has no special Gifts. She came because she doesn't like the husband my traitorous convert brother has chosen for her."

Raising his brows Golannah returned his black gaze to me. "You promised her?"

"Not exactly. I promised her that if I left the convert encampment to go live with other relatives I would bring her with me. At that time I didn't know the war band had need of a Qwakaihi and you would send for me."

"When you did know you still agreed to bring her?"

I fingered the swollen bruise still discoloring my jaw. "Not exactly. She—"

Utsiyonti chuckled and gave Thonna an approving smile. "This young warrior woman invited herself and gave our new Puhani a solid punch in the face when he tried to send her back." He shrugged and held out his hands. "So we bring her, too."

Golannah snorted a laugh. Returning his attention to Uncle and Utsiyonti he said, "Is good you come today. Come sit with us. My brother and the scouts also return. We need to discuss our plans." Dismissing Thonna and me Golannah added for my benefit, "Get food and rest, but don't go far away, young Puhani, I need talk to you, too."

I nodded, then noticing that Samiqwas had come up to join us Uncle Tli said to him, "Show your cousins around and ask Sagila to find you some food and the newcomers a place to put their things."

As we walked away, I whispered, "Who is Sagila?"

"Uncle's new Kukiya wife."

"Oh." A Kukiya woman, marrying outside the clans, things were truly changing for my people, I thought as Samiqwas led us back into the daylight. "He called me Puhani; what does that word mean, do you know?"

"We speak a mix of languages around here," Samiqwas explained. "Our language, of course, some Chamuqwani and the Kukiya tongue. As best I can tell a Puhani is a person with power, like a Qwakaihi among us."

"Oh."

We passed several people as we walked along the broad ledge under the overhang.Though they nodded to us no one stopped to talk and continued on with their daily chores. As we walked Thonna hovered as close to me as she possibly could. I realized with some surprise that in spite of her show of bravado, Thonna must have been worried about her reception among the outlaws.

This was her first time away from her family, which alone might make her nervous, and to add to her troubles, she had no Qwakaihi's gifts to ensure her acceptance here.

With the good smells of meat roasting growing stronger in our nostrils Samiqwas led us to an area where several women were grinding roots and roasting our antelope over several small fires. Calling out to a short round woman with smiling dark eyes near the edge of the cooking women's area, Samiqwas relayed Uncle's message to her.

Her eyes widened when she recognized that there was a girl among us. Sagila waved for us to sit near a tiny fire where a sooty pot steamed in the coals. "Welcome my relatives, and a special welcome to you, Little Sister," she said to Thonna and held out her hands to her before she could sit. Thonna gave her a tentative smile and took her offered hands. "Thank you, New Aunty."

As our new aunty served us a mush made from pounded seeds, wild onions and slivers of drymeat. A woman carrying a heavy willow basket passed by us then stopped and came back for another look. The woman was about my mother's age with long braids, hard eyes, and a wide mouth. She was wearing a ragged tunic dress that hung on her bony frame as if it had once fit a much larger woman. She studied us for a time, then said, "Thonna, is that really you, My Girl?"

Startled Thonna put down her spoon and looked up from her bowl. She studied the newcomer and then smiled. "Aunty Ashiqwa? W-what are you doing here?"

Ashiqwa snorted a laugh. "Doing here? Same as you maybe, I didn't like being beaten by that fish guts of a husband Chief Eagan and the rest of my family married me off to, so I decided to join the outlaws. And you/?"

Thonna laughed. "No marriage, just a betrothal, but I didn't like the dog turd they chose for me, either."

Ashiqwa shifted her heavy basket and pointed with her lips to another fire where a young girl was trying to amuse a fussy baby. "Come see me when you finish eating, my girl." Then grunting under the weight of her load, she called back, "Got to go. The little one is getting restless and this basket is heavy. You can tell me the family news later."

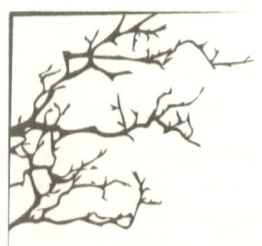

Chapter Six

When we finished eating Samiqwas offered to show me more of the encampment, so we said thank you to our new aunty and headed down the steep trail towards where the horses were kept. As we walked he pointed out where the sentry posts, and the cavern where we filled our water gourds were, and on a side path where the privy was located.

If we passed someone I didn't know from our travel to the Preserve Samiqwas introduced me, telling the ones that didn't know me that I was his cousin and I was the one the war leader had sent for. When he mentioned that, I dropped my eyes suddenly shy, because most gave me a speculative look as if they already knew what Golannah had in mind for me.

A little hesitant about the horses, and maybe looking for an excuse to put off spending time with them again so soon, I hesitated about half way down and asked him if we should go so far when Golannah said to stay nearby.

He snorted and kept going. "They will be a while yet. The councils can go on half the night sometimes."

"Shouldn't we put off seeing the horses until later? You could just introduce me to the people up here—just in case I'm wanted." I motioned to the ledge behind me.

He gave me a knowing look as if he could read my mind and knew I was nervous about the horses. When I wouldn't look at him he laughed. "They aren't so bad; think of them as extra-big dogs—and you know how to care for sled dogs, right? That's what I did when I first came here; I thought of them as big dogs.

"While there is still daylight and free time I need to show you what is required of all of us," he explained, "because after today you will be expected to help out caring for the horses—especially the little mare Utsiyonti has gifted you."

"Oh, I hope you will show me, because I know little of how to care for such beasts," I said with a nervous laugh. "They don't eat fish I could catch for them," I joked.

He snorted. "No, they eat grass and sometimes you will have to gather it for them. But of course I will help you, but ask Tuumaz or any of the dust eaters. They have been stealing horses from the Chamuqwani forever. They know best how to care for them, and can ride them even better than most of the soldiers."

"Dust eaters, why do you call them that? Grandfather says that's a bad word."

Samiqwas shrugged and then chuckled. "You should hear what they call us when they think we can't hear them, yellow snow eater, dog fucker to name a couple of the more complimentary ones."

My mouth fell open, and I stopped on the trail. "But we don't do that!"

"Of course we don't, ptarmigan brain, and they don't eat dust either." He thought about it a moment longer then laughed as a new thought came to him. "In fact they should call us the dust eaters, because that's what we are doing when we ride with them—eat their dust."

I could tell there was no real malice in his comment about the Kukiya, but I had heard the words used by the Chamuqwani and when they used it, like the word zaunk, it was used to hurt and shame. I hated to hear my cousin copying the Chamuqwani so thoughtlessly, but that wasn't the time to talk to him about it, because we were coming up to a group of tired and dusty Kukiya and Qwani'Ya warriors who must have just ridden into camp, and were heading up the trail towards us.

When we got to the little grassy hollow by a willow thicket containing a shallow pond fed by the same spring we used further up the slope, we checked on our animals and helped the boys and men already there, care for, and brush the beasts. My little mare seemed fine, and happy to have the attention I gave her when I borrowed a warrior's grass broom and combed the dirt and seeds out of her coat.

Engrossed in my work I paid little attention to the comings and goings of the people around me, or the lengthening shadows of the coming evening. Talking softly to my little mare, I tried to get over my nervousness and get to know her.

Touching her gently with my Qwakaiva I let her know that I wasn't going to hurt her or be mean to her. She nuzzled me as if she understood my good intentions. When Samiqwas called, saying it was time to go, I let her return to her friends in the outlaw herd.

When I went to return the grass broom to the Kukiya man who had lent it to me, someone grabbed my arm roughly from behind and spun me around. "What are you doing here, dog fart of a traitor?"

Yanking my arm out of Matoqwa's grasp, I looked rudely into his angry eyes and snarled right back, "I'm no traitor, smelly fish guts! And I'm here because I was invited by the war leader to come."

The Bear in his Spirit Fire lifted its lip and silently snarled. Matoqwa scoffed, threw a punch at my head and called me another bad word when I dodged and he missed. By then his ever-present shadow Cohasi had come over with a sneer on his face to back up his brother.

Not daring to take my eyes off the pair, I was somewhat relieved when I felt someone at my back, and Samiqwas spoke. "Leave him alone, dog turd. Tas is telling the truth. The war leader did send for him."

Cohasi snorted in disgust. "And why would Golannah do that—if it's true—and I still think you're lying."

Samiqwas came up to stand beside me and glared at them both. "You know he isn't a traitor; Tas has always kept faith with our traditions. Think about it, you two, why would the war leader want him to come join us?"

"Yeah, he probably isn't a traitor—maybe," Matoqwa said, agreeing half-heartedly on that point, "but I still don't understand *why* he's here."

Why? Because he has Qwakaiva, ptarmigan brain—Qwakaiva we need. That's why my Uncle Tli and Utsiyonti risked going all the way to a convert settlement to fetch him. If the war leader hadn't wanted him to come, they wouldn't have sent us to get him. And he certainly couldn't have found his way here on his own, right?"

Matoqwa glared right back, then giving me a withering look, he finally said, "I guess he couldn't have found his way here on his own, so you and your Uncle had to bring him, but I still don't understand why he's here—lots of the Kukiya, and some of our own people among the outlaws have Qwakaiva. There was no need for him to come here—if that's your reason."

"That *is* the reason, truly. Golannah needs him, because Tas's Qwakaiva is special."

"Special? Ha!" Cohasi made a rude noise and glared at me.

Samiqwas folded his arms across his chest and curled his lip into a lop-sided grin. "What did you used to call him back home, Matoqwa, think!"

Matoqwa scowled thinking, then his eyes opened wide as Samiqwas's meaning came to him. He shook his head. "No I don't believe it—you're lying."

A little slower to catch on Cohasi frowned and asked his brother, "I don't understand; we used to call him lots of things like witch boy and Siyatli boy, but we didn't mean anything by it; we were teasing him. We just wanted to make him mad, or feel ashamed—"

"Well it's true; Tas is a Siyatli," Samiqwas cut in, "and, because he needs a Qwakaihi with a stronger gift than what people have who are here at the moment, the war leader sent us with an offering for Tas's Spirit Helper—so we bring him, too."

Still shaking his head as this new revelation sank in Matoqwa studied me with a new intensity. I met his stare without flinching.

Back home Qwa'osi the Otter warrior was beloved by my people and Co'yeh the Lake Seal was seen as evil, because they were often rivals for the same school of fish. I had been horrified and a shamed when Matoqwa and his friends taunted me by calling me a siyatli, but no more.

I now knew that the Qwakaiva I'd inherited from my father Star Swimmer, a Qwa'Nayhi Seal man, wasn't evil as most people used to think. It was a blessing. And when I called upon my father to help me save my people from dying in Drown Canoe Rapids, he had revealed himself to me and saved us from destruction. At that time as well I had pledged my life to his Benefactor Kunai, and my service as a Qwakaihi to the People.

"I still don't believe it," Cohasi said, folding his arms across his chest in an unconscious imitation of Samiqwas.

He had that stubborn look on his face, the one he got when someone tried to change his opinion. Once an idea was fixed in his mind I knew from the past it was hard for him to let go of it. I sighed, tired of always being caught in the middle and having to defend myself. "Believe what you want

Cohasi—I really don't care—as long as you and your brother leave me alone,"
I said.

"You should believe," a new voice said from behind me. Tuumaz stepped
forward so I could see him. "You should believe, and maybe be afraid, too,
if you make angry him, hmm? I see things he can do with his power. Yes,
me think you should be careful—very careful how you make angry, little dog
fart—very careful."

When Tuumaz's meaning sank in Cohasi's face became ashen and his
eyes grew wide with fear. "I wouldn't do anything to harm you—no matter
how mad you make me," I hastily assured him. "I want only to do good—for
the People."

Ah but what does good truly mean, hmm? A soft voice inside my head
whispered. Recalling how I thought I was doing good when I placed
Chumco's pouch of bad Qwakaiva within the priest's tent that nearly cost
him his life, I shivered.

"I want only to use my gift for good and to protect our People," I said
again, trying to reassure myself that it was true.

Tuumaz gave a noncommittal shrug and motioned with his chin back up
the cliff trail. "We go. Golannah want talk to you—now."

Leaving my cousin and the brothers staring after me I nodded my
agreement and followed him.

Golannah and the war council were sitting around the same fire I had
seen them at earlier that afternoon. The only difference was that the war
leader had been joined by more people than earlier. Uncle Tli and Utsiyonti
were there as well as a few of the dusty men I had seen coming up the trail
when Samiqwas and I were heading to the horse meadow. But there were also
a couple Qwani'Ya women with streaks of gray in their hair and hard eyes,
sitting among the men.

Then I saw a pale-skinned Chamuqwani with long yellow braids sitting
among them and stopped abruptly, my mouth dropping open. Though
sitting like the rest I could tell he was a tall man with powerful shoulders,
and scarred muscular arms. His cheeks were tattooed with a series of black
dots. He was bare-chested except for a leather vest that bore painted Kukiya
designs. When he noticed us watching him from the shadows he fixed me

with cool green eyes. In his Spirit Fire a Cougar stared at me with the same yellow-green intensity.

Guessing my shock and its cause Tuumaz chuckled softly. "Surprised see a Chamuqwani here, young Puhani?"

"Y-yes," I murmured just as softly. "Who is he?"

"That is Nachoga, Golannah's brother." Putting a hand on my shoulder Tuumaz urged me to take a seat by Uncle Tli when the man holding the Talking Stick noticed us and stopped speaking. Feeling suddenly shy, I moved forward and took my place next to Uncle as he moved over for me.

Golannah fixed me with his penetrating stare for a moment then motioned for the man with the talking stick to continue his report.

At first I was only half listening to the talk going on around me as I tried to put my nervousness aside. Gazing into the flames of the council fire I took several deep slow breaths. I wanted to help, but I was so young—and to my own way of thinking still only half-trained as a Qwakaihi. I was afraid I couldn't do what they needed me to do. I was afraid I would fail—and warriors would die, because I made the wrong decision or because I wasn't strong enough to channel the Qwakaiva needed to aid them.

<<Oh, Great Kunai, Spirits of this land, help me to be worthy of the trust given me by these warriors,>> I prayed silently.

Taking more deep breaths, I focused my attention on the colors in the flames and watched the tiny Fire creatures play among them.

<<You are just a channel for the Unseen Ones,>> they sang to me as the Fire popped and groaned.

Channel for the power of the Unseen Ones, I repeated to myself. That was my true purpose here. The Spirits would help the warriors—or not—as they chose, and I had little to say about it. As I calmed myself I realized that I had no reason to be worried or afraid, for it wasn't the me, that was Tasimu, that Golannah would be asking for help. It was my Benefactor and his Spirit Helpers who would offer their aid and advice. I was only the physical channel by which they could manifest their will in my world. I need only relax and let them enter. I felt much better after I realized that.

Feeling the presence of Spirits gathering at my back I returned my attention to the Council and when everyone had finished speaking and

Golannah turned to me, I didn't need Uncle's jab in the ribs to alert me to that fact. I was ready to speak.

Summing up Golannah said to me, "You have heard what my warriors say, young Puhani. There is a grassy valley over the mountains three day east of here. The Chamuqwani call such a place a rancha, my brother tell me. It have lot big fat herd beasts—and it near the Preserve.

"We go there and take lots cai beasts. We feed the People still on Preserve and take some meat west when we go find the Prophet—like some my people want." He lent forward and fixed me with his piercing stare again. "So after we go fetch you, how you gonna help us, eh?"

I took a deep breath. "I won't know exactly how to aid the raiding party until we are there, but as Utsiyonti and Tuumaz may have told you, I can call upon my Spirit helpers to erase our back trail so the Chamuqwani soldiers will have a much harder time to find us."

I wasn't sure the Kukiya war leader understood everything I'd said in my Qwani'Ya language, so when I finished I turned to Utsiyonti, who seemed to know my language pretty well, and he spoke briefly in their tongue to clarify what I'd said and what I'd done on our way here to stop the men following us.

Golannah nodded his approval. "So when soldiers chase us you can hide us, eh?"

"For a time, yes."

"How long?"

I shrugged. "I don't know. I will do my best, but I am not a man grown with a man's Qwakaiva."

He thought about that for a long moment, then changed the subject and asked, "You say you see me and know me before you come. How you do dat?"

For answer I took my special cord from my neck and showed it to him and the council. "I make special patterns with the string. The patterns have—power." I didn't know the word in their language and I glanced at Utsiyonti or Uncle for help.

When he understood what I needed, Utsiyonti said, "Puwa."

"Thank you, Puwa. When I saw you I had been asked by my grandfather to find Uncle Tli. He was worried about his son after he heard about the fires at the Willow Creek Agency. I found Uncle in the pattern. He was sitting around a fire eating meat, somewhere in the mountains north of the Preserve. You were there too."

"How you know is me?"

"I knew who you were when I briefly touched my uncle's mind." Uncle gave me a withering scowl, but didn't interrupt. Later I suspected he would have much to say to me about my spying on him.

"Can you see in the pattern you make, the rancha and its beasts now?" a scarred older warrior asked.

"No I cannot, because I have never been there, so I will have no image to focus my Qwakaiva upon."

Golannah frowned, considering my limitations and how to work around them. At last he said, "What else can you do with power? Can you show me something?"

I took the cord I had been holding loosely over my hands and formed the pattern of the Aseutl's Gift. "I can create a picture in the center diamond and with my Qwakaiva—Puwa I can change something in the picture that will also happen in our world. I can do this, but if you don't have the right kind of power to see it all you will see is my dirty shirt in the diamond."

Golannah grunted and a couple of the others laughed. "I no have the Puwa to see, but some here can see maybe they have right kind Puwa. You show, eh?"

Utsiyonti, one of the women and, to my total surprise Nachoga stood up and came around the circle to look over my shoulder. "I haven't seen much of the land around here," I told my audience when I got over my shock, "so it will have to be something simple and close by."

Recalling Kunai's warning and knowing I was probably going to suffer for this, but unable to resist the temptation, I formed an image of Matoqwa and Cohasi down by the horses, in the central diamond. After all, I was doing the war leader's bidding, wasn't I? Golannah needed a demonstration; I wasn't toying with them for my own amusement—not really. I hoped my Benefactor would see it that way. "Can anyone see what I have placed in the center of the pattern?" I asked.

"Two Qwani'Ya boys caring for the horses," my three observers answered.

"Good, now watch." Picking up the grass broom Matoqwa had dropped I focused my Qwakaiva upon it. On its own the broom rose into the air and began combing Matoqwa's matted and dirty hair.

My audience began to laugh as he batted at the flying broom and then tried to out run it. I chased him for a short time around the grassy hollow, then spying Cohasi staring with his mouth open I had the horse broom start combing his hair, too. I couldn't hear their frightened yelling, but I watched as they raced up the cliff trail back to camp. I let the image fade and dropped my hands into my lap.

Still chuckling Utsiyonti went to check on the boys when he heard a disturbance outside on the ledge. Taking their seats again in the circle, Nachoga was still grinning when he related to the rest of the Council what they had seen.

Not long after that a grinning Utsiyonti pushed Matoqwa and his brother into the firelight, Samiqwas, Tuumaz and several others trailing behind.

Golannah gave them a fierce stare and demanded, "What happened? Why you make so much noise?' dropping their eyes they stammered out a story about being chased by a horse broom that confirmed what Nachoga had just told the council.

Tuumaz saw the grin I couldn't keep off my face, and as Golannah dismissed them with a warning to keep quiet, I heard him say, "See I warn you, dog fart. Next time Puhani hit you with more than horse broom, maybe."

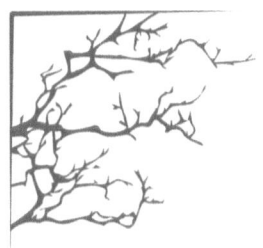

Chapter Seven

The Council dismissed me not long after Matoqwa and the others left us. With a stern warning under his breath to stay out of trouble, Uncle Tli told me to go find his new woman Sagila, and wait for him. I rose and picked my way through the clusters of people sitting around small fires eating and talking in low voices, searching for Sagila or someone else I knew who could direct me to her fire.

Night had come while I sat with the war council and the smells of cooked antelope and baked seed cakes made my mouth water and my stomach rumble. Then I heard Samiqwas laugh and found him, most of my old friends from home, Thonna and her aunty, sitting around Sagila's fire.

When she saw me Sagila rose and came over with a cry of welcome. Pulling me to her plump chest she hugged me then held me out at arm's length to look at me. "Oh, poor boy, so thin you. Don't nobody feed? Just like my husband when he come, you too skinny. Come, I fix dat. Make fat you—like me. You hungry, me feed. Sit, sit."

Suddenly shy with all her motherly attention, I felt my face heat with embarrassment and took a place beside the fire as she directed me. Not daring to look at Matoqwa and his brother, I glanced at Samiqwas instead. I saw his smile and dropped my eyes refusing to look at anyone else. In the next moment Sagila handed me two flat seed cakes wrapped around pieces of roasted antelope meat. They tasted wonderful and I wolfed them down without shame.

Not long after I finished eating Uncle Tli joined us and I was grateful when Sagila turned her motherly attentions on him. As most of the boys rose to seek their beds Uncle stopped them. Swallowing a mouthful of meat, he said, "We will be leaving in two days and we will take some of you with us to help with the butchering of the Chamuqwani beasts, and with bringing meat to some of the encampments of the People on the Preserve. So gather your things, pick your best horses, and be ready."

When he finished eating Uncle and his new wife left to be together in the darkness, and that gave me a chance to talk to Samiqwas alone. As we sat by the sleepy fire I asked him to tell me more about the outlaws and what had been going on since he'd left the agency.

One of my first questions was to ask about Uncle Tli. "Uncle seems in better health since he left his wife and daughter. He's not coughing and spitting blood like before. Has Grandfather been here to heal him?"

Samiqwas shook his head and laid another piece of dried dung on the fire. "No, we haven't seen Grandfather. Uncle's new wife got her Aunty Betsiya who can heal to look at him. She gave him some bad tasting teas to drink for a while and he got better. People say she is a powerful Kukiya Qwakaihi like Grandfather and sometimes goes with the warriors on raids."

"That's good to know. Point her out to me tomorrow."

"I don't need to. She was the woman sitting at the war council tonight that had red cloth twined in her braids."

"Yes, I remember her now; she was one of the ones with Qwakaiva that could see the pictures I formed and what I did with my string."

Recalling how I'd used my Gift to get back at Matoqwa he chuckled and rose to find his bed.

ALONG WITH MY COUSIN Thonna I spent much of my time as the preparations went on around me with some well needed riding lessons, which I was not too proud to accept from Tuumaz and a Kukiya Elder. On the night before we left Thonna caught me returning from the horses and held out to me a blanket-wrapped bundle.

"I know you will ride with the warriors where there will be the most danger, unlike Samiqwas and the rest who are just going to care for the horses and do other camp chores. May the Unseen Ones who guide you keep you safe. And thank you for bringing me to this place," she added, suddenly shy.

Smiling and hoping to put her at ease, I said, "I had no choice, because I didn't want anymore bruises—and you would have kept beating me until we let you come."

Then becoming serious, I added, suddenly worried and afraid for her safety if the soldiers found this place. "Will you be alright here among all these strangers? I hate to leave you here—in case the soldiers come."

"We will be leaving this hideout soon as well. Golannah wants to go hear what the Prophet and his people are saying about the Chamuqwani. At present they are further west where the soldiers never come, so we will be safe.

"I can stay with Aunty Ashiqwa, her new man and her adopted children when we go. And your Aunty Sagila is very nice, too. Don't worry about me—just keep yourself safe, and I will see you when you meet us in the west." She said, and swiped at her eyes with a free hand. Holding out her bundle impatiently, she urged me to take it.

I took the bundle and asked, "What's this?" She motioned for me to open it, so I untied the rawhide cord holding it closed. Inside I found a leather vest with painted Kukiya designs similar to the one Nachoga wore.

When she saw my puzzled look, she said, "It's for your protection. The Kukiya women say the designs have Qwakaiva. They say their prophet showed them how to prepare them. They claim the Chamuqwani can't harm the warrior who wears one—so the prophet says. Aunty Sagila made one for Uncle and I made this one for you."

Though I wasn't sure if the design had enough power to protect me from the Chamuqwani thunder weapons, it did have Qwakaiva, and its intent was to protect the wearer from evil. I also could feel the love and well wishes Thonna herself put into the vest as she made it. I was moved and felt tears pooling in the corners of my eyes.

"Thank you. I will wear it with pride." Then noticing the little clay jar that was also in the blanket I held it out and asked, "What's this?"

Her wide mouth curved up into a grin. "It's for your legs and backside after a long day on horseback." I laughed and thanked her once again.

WE LEFT BY STARLIGHT the following morning, heading towards the paling eastern horizon. To my surprise when we gathered our horses and supplies for the journey it was Nachoga who was leading the band of Qwani'Ya and Kukiya warriors, not Golannah as I had assumed.

Uncle Tli was coming, of course. To keep an eye on Samiqwas and me—to make sure we behaved, he claimed. Though he gave me a stern look, I think he was also afraid for our safety, but didn't know how to show it.

I didn't know all the warriors by name, but Utsiyonti and Tuumaz were coming, as were two other young Kukiya warriors I recognized by sight but not by name. From Big Ice Lake Matoqwa, Cohasi, Tigaliand Uncle's former brother-in-law Chugai were coming as well as a couple hunters from down the Socanna River.

That first midday we rested out of the heat in a strange cave-like tunnel on the side of a barren mountain that rose unexpectedly out of a dry rocky valley. Inside its cool shade the sides of the tunnel were smooth and slightly rounded, like the inside of a big blowgun.

Noticing my interest Utsiyonti came over to me. "It is a strange place, eh? Some of the old ones among my people say that one of the Aseutl deep in the earth was angry and burned away the rock with its fire to make this place."

I ran my fingers down the walls smooth side again. Thinking of my Benefactor Kunai I nodded. "I can believe that. They are very powerful beings."

I had noticed that all the men in the raiding party were well armed, carrying thunder weapons, not wanting to ask Uncle or one of the other men about them, I waited and then cornered Samiqwas when we were bringing our horses to drink. "I see the men all have thunder weapons as well as their bows. Where did they get them?"

"From the Chamuqwani, where else, ptarmigan brain."

I gave him a withering look and he relented and explained. "Some came from our raid on the Willow Creek agency, but most come from Chamuqwani who trade with the Kukiya."

When I stared incredulous he laughed, but there was no mirth in the sound. "It's true some of the Chamuqwani are so greedy they will trade even with the outlaws—if we pay their price."

"But the warriors could kill their people with those weapons. Why would they do that?" I said.

He shrugged. "Because they are greedy bum-fuckers and don't care who we kill—as long as it isn't them."

Still pondering over this new revelation I left him to apply some of Thonna's salve and rest in the shade while I could.

When we began travelling again in late afternoon Nachoga led us over a pine-covered ridge and down into a narrow sided canyon in which a fast moving creek had cut a channel. We followed the creek until it became too dark to be safe for the horses to travel further, then we hobbled them so they could graze, and made a fireless camp higher up the slope.

Unable to control my curiosity any longer I pulled Samiqwas aside again when we were finished with our horses, and asked him what he knew about Nachoga.

"I was surprised to see such a pale-skinned man among the Kukiya when I got here, too," he admitted. "At first I thought he was a mixed-blood zaunk with a trader for a father, like Kutima back home, but that isn't so. He is a true Chamuqwani."

"How is that possible," I wondered.

"When he was a small child Golannah's father stole him in a raid to replace a son who died from the Chamuqwani spotted sickness. He adopted him as his true son and Nachoga grew up alongside Golannah, knowing nothing of Chamuqwani and their ways."

"Hmm, I don't recall seeing him on the Preserve or hearing anyone talking about a pale Kukiya.'

'That's because the soldiers made him leave his family when they put us zaunks on the Preserve," Samiqwas said and spat on the ground in disgust. "Aunty Sagila said that his wife and young son died last winter when there was little food and no one to hunt for them."

"That must have been terrible for him. Torn away from his family and those who loved him and who he loved. Did he even know how to talk to the Chamuqwani who took him away, or where to go?"

Samiqwas shrugged. "All I know is that somehow he knew when we fired the agency and returned to fight alongside his brother."

As Samiqwas headed up the slope I said, "Do you know he also has Qwakaiva?" when he turned to stare at me I nodded. "Powerful Qwakaiva, too, and that is amazing to me, because I thought only our people were gifted with that kind of power."

He grunted and continued on his way.

By the end of the next day the land we traveled through had changed. It was still drier than our home in the north. But compared to the Preserve or the country around the outlaws' stronghold further west the land we now traveled through had more water and more green trees and grass. There were also more signs of the Chamuqwani as well, so we had to be extra careful. Nachoga sent out scouts both in front of us and behind.

Once a scout hurried to tell us that soldiers were traveling on the other side of a nearby ridge. They were still unaware of our presence, the scout assured the war leader, but Nachoga decided to take no chances in case they changed direction.

Telling the warriors to hide in a grove of scrub pines he had me use my Gift to erase our back trail so the soldiers wouldn't be alerted to our presence if they came our way. When they were gone, we came out of hiding and continued our journey.

Next day Nachoga seemed to have some idea of where we were going. He led us down a well-traveled trail in the gray dawn until we came to a tree-covered slope that overlooked a wide valley. Down below we could see the dark silhouettes of Chamuqwani houses spread out along a winding stream. In some, lamp light glowed in their glass windows, the people already up and preparing for the day's work.

When we were safely hidden within the trees, Nachoga assigned his sentries and warned the younger warriors to stay out of sight and keep the horses quiet. Next he took from his pack dirty and patched Chamuqwani clothes which he put on over his vest and Kukiya things.

Undoing his long hair from its braids, Nachoga twisted his hair into a knot which he tied with a cord on the top of his head. Over that he placed a dusty and sagging broad-brimmed Chamuqwani hat. To disguise his tribal tattoos, he had Utsiyonti rub grease and dirt on his face to partially cover them. Then to finish off his disguise he took a small flask of waskyja from his saddle pack and sprinkled some of its contents on his dirty Chamuqwani clothes.

When he was ready Tuumaz brought over the old brown gelding that I wondered why we had brought with us, because it looked as tired and beaten down as the Chamuqwani Nachoga had transformed himself into right before our eyes.

Just before he left us he came over and looked down at me from his seat atop the old horse. "See me, young Puhani?" When I nodded, he said, "Watch me in your Puwa Diamond. If I no come back by tomorrow night I will be dead—maybe." He gave me a crooked grin. "Then I will have to come to you in the Dream and lead the raid from the Ghost World, eh?"

I hesitated, then smiled and nodded, understanding that he was joking with me. "I will watch, War Leader. And guard the others as best I can." He grunted, moved out of the thicket, slouching over his horse's withers as he headed down the long road into the enemy's valley.

I dozed through much of the day when I wasn't needed. I took a watch as sentry and helped to feed and water the horses when it was my turn. Sometime during the heat of the afternoon Utsiyonti found me and asked me to check on the war leader with my special string. I sat cross-legged in the leaf debris under a tall fir and formed the pattern of The Seer's Pool in the center diamond.

"He is riding up to a big Chamuqwani house painted red with white around the windows," I told him as Uncle and a few other warriors came over to listen. "A big bellied Chamuqwani and two other, younger men with thunder weapons have come out of the house to greet him."

"Can you hear what they are saying?" Utsiyonti asked.

"No." I paused, going a little deeper into my trance. "Our leader is aware now of my watching. He has let me touch his thoughts. He is asking them about work. The men are cautious, as anyone would be of a stranger, but they aren't overly hostile at the moment.... They say there is no work for him, but he can go to the long house where the men who work there eat and sleep.

"Someone will feed him and then he must go. He will eat their food and ask about their herd beasts and where they keep them... and if other

Chamuqwani need someone to work for them. After that he will leave and go further into the valley."

Nachoga hadn't returned to us by nightfall, but I told Utsiyonti and Uncle that he was fine. He had been hired by another Chamuqwani rancha further up the valley. The next day he and the other rancha men would be moving many of the beasts they named cai to another safer place further east.

As I slept that night, a tawny cougar surrounded by Spirit Light padded into my dreams. The big cat fixed me with its yellow-green eyes, and Nachoga's voice said into my mind, <<Come, little Siyatli Seal, come into the Dream so I can show you the way you will lead the warriors for me. I will wait for you by the cliff that has a bear's head shape. I don't dare come back down the valley lest the Chamuqwani grow suspicious if their cai go missing so soon after they hired me.>>

<<When should I bring the warriors to you?>> I asked.

<<Tomorrow when you wake will be good. Leave the pine thicket, but keep undercover. Head south-west back into the higher country near the Preserve. This rancha is farthest away from other Chamuqwani ranchas. The fat agent has warned this Chamuqwani to move the beasts he sold him further east, because of the trouble we make for him on the Preserve and rancha boss-man is angry. Many of these cai were part of our treaty goods. So before they go on Train, we take back what is ours, eh?>>

<<Yes, we have a right to take back our own cai beasts—and fuck the Chamuqwani Ranch Boss-man,>> I said, tasting the bitterness of his words in my mouth.

The cougar's eyes gleamed with his own turbulent emotions as he agreed with me. <<Fuck all Chamuqwani, eh?>>

Before he left me he showed me an image of a high cliff that resembled a bear's head. <<Keep on the east side of that cliff. We will be herding the cai in that direction. Tomorrow evening I will come to the war band in person or to you in the Dream. By then I will know what we need do next.>>

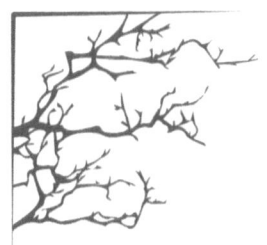

Chapter Eight

When I woke the next morning I reported to Utsiyonti what Nachoga had told me during the night. He and Uncle decided that while there was still a morning fog rising off the creek to mask our journey we would move camp. Fog... Before we left I took some time to form a vision of the stream in the pattern I hastily made in my string. In the central diamond of the Aseutl's Gift, I thickened the fog and encouraged it to follow us down the valley.

With scouts ahead and behind us we led the horses through the trees in a south-westerly direction. As Sun climbed higher into the blue sky its heat made it impossible for me to make Fog stay with us. Finally I gave up and allowed Sun to finish burning away the protective mists concealing us. By that time we were far enough away from the more settled portion of the valley that there was less of a chance we would be spotted from below even without Fog to help us hide.

The bear's head cliff now visible to the west we kept it on our right as we traveled. To be safe we moved slowly and kept within the trees as much as possible. Under my breath I murmured a prayer to the Unseen Ones, <<Master of the Air, oh Eagle lend me your keen sight and help me to keep my People safe from any enemy.>>

A short time later I heard an eagle scream overhead and looked up to see Eagle floating on a high wind current. I called to Samiqwas to take my mare's reins for a while and stay close. He looked at me puzzled, so I explained, "I want to check to see no one is following, or that other enemies are near."

"Don't you need your special string for that?" he asked.

"Not this time." I pointed with my lips to Eagle soaring overhead. Then I slipped into a light trance and let my Spirit see through Eagle's eyes.

In the valley and nearby slopes there was no sign of soldiers or other Chamuqwani. But further south a large dust cloud with dark riders along its edge moved up a long slope heading for a fenced area near the base of the bear's head cliff. They must be the cai and Chamuqwani sent to move and guard them. We were safe as long as we didn't get too close and were spotted by those riders.

When I opened my eyes and reached for my reins I was startled to see Uncle Tli riding on my other side. When he noticed I was back, he asked, "What did you see?"

"The cai and the rancha's herders are nearing a fenced area near the base of the cliff the war leader told us to go to," I said.

Uncle grunted "That cliff is one of the boundary markers for the preserve, I believe," he told us.

Later when we were running out of tree cover we stopped for a council in a sheltered hollow among the rocks that had a decent sized seep where we could get water for ourselves and the horses. Directing Matoqwa and Samiqwas to take charge of the horses and see they kept quiet. Utsiyonti motioned for me to follow the warriors to a sheltered spot among the rocks.

"We will have to leave the horses here until dark, or till we hear different from the war leader. I will send scouts to watch for Nachoga," Utsiyonti said.

He next turned to me. "Can you let him know where we are and that we will stay concealed till dark allows us to come closer."

I nodded and removed the cord from around my neck and formed the pattern for the Seer's Pool. "I have told him we are near; he says it's good to wait. He will come to us during the night. All is well."

That evening as we waited Utsiyonti gathered us together, and raising his hands to the starry sky asked the creator to bless our work that night. "Keep us safe from our enemy's weapons, Unseen Ones of Earth, Air and Water. Evil surrounds us. The People are starving. There is no malice in our hearts; we wish only to do good for the People. We want only for our children to survive these terrible times."

When he finished he dismissed everyone to make their own personal prayers and preparations for the coming raid. I took a deep breath suddenly realizing that I, or anyone I knew and loved in the war band could die that night. During the long march and while living on the Preserve Death was always hovering near, but that night the specter seemed especially close. In silence the warriors left to ready themselves for victory—or death.

I sat among the rocks in a place where I could look down and watch the men and beasts in the valley below. I ate a couple balls of the drymeat and wild onions mixed with fat that the women had sent with us. Slipping into a light trance I prayed, <<Spirits of the Night, Rattlesnake, are you near? I must help these men feed the People. Please lend me your strength and Qwakaiva this night. I don't want to fail them. They are depending on me; please help me.>>

In the night as I dozed she came to me and crawled up under my shirt and twisted her long sinuous body around my chest, laying her head on my shoulder. <<The Great Kunai has sent me. He favors your venture. I am here, brother. I will help you.>>

Not long after that the Cougar came to me again. <<It's time, young Puhani. All is quiet here most of the Chamuqwani are sleeping. Awake the warriors and bring them to meet me near the cai pens.>>

As I stood Uncle and Utsiyonti resting nearby opened their eyes and rose as well. "The war leader says to come now. He will meet us when we are near the cai beasts."

Realizing my mare wasn't going to be happy with me when she smelled my companion I stopped down wind of her trying to figure out what to do.

Uncle Tli came over impatient with my delay. "What are you doing? It is too late to be afraid. Get on your horse."

"I'm not afraid, uncle," I murmured. "I just don't think the mare will let me near when she smells my helper."

"What are you talking about, foolish boy? Get on that horse."

As he drew near Rattlesnake raised her head and whirred a warning, looking him straight in the eye. With a curse Uncle leapt back as if she had indeed bitten him.

<<Peace, Honored One. You just surprised my uncle. He won't harm us.>>

Utsiyonti came over, frowning. "What's the problem, Puhani?"

Still stroking Rattlesnake to calm her, I said, "I will need the help of this one once we near the cai, but how do I get there? I will be too slow if I walk, but I don't think my mare will let me ride her now."

Utsiyonti's eyes widened as he recognized Rattlesnake. He thought about the problem, than told me to wait, motioning Uncle and the others to get their horses and mount up. Returning to his saddle he rummaged in his pack for a moment and pulled out a small clay jar.

As he opened it he called to Matoqwa to saddle and bring my mare to him. When he brought him the mare he put some of the jar's contents around her nostrils. At first she tried to jerk her head away, but he soothed her with a gentle crooning chant and she relaxed and let him touch her.

I wasn't sure what was in the salve, but even from some distance away I could smell its pungent scent. Still holding her head and talking to her he motioned for me to come and mount. It was a little awkward for me to mount with Rattlesnake squeezing my middle but I managed and my mare didn't seem to mind her other rider.

THE CHAMUQWANI HAD planned for this trip well. The cai were penned in a small box canyon where there was some sage and grass and a little water collecting in a pond at the base of one rock wall. A short distance away from the beasts' pen the men had laid out their blankets next to a dozing fire the bulk of a wagon parked at the edge of their camp. Separated from the cai, the men's horses were also confined. Only one mounted man was guarding them.

Also mounted, Nachoga was one of the two guards, watching the cai. I couldn't tell in the dark how many of the horned shaggy beasts were crowded into the canyon behind the wooden fence. Many were calling to one another and all were restless as if they sensed our presence and knew their coming danger.

<<I can sometimes speak mind-to-mind with Utsiyontias I do you, so tell him to pick a couple men to circle behind the horse herd. I will signal him with my Qwakaiva, like we are talking now, when we release the Cai. Then he must scatter the horses before the Chamuqwani can catch them and follow us. Your Uncle and Chugai can help me open the gate,>> the war leader said to me. <<You can go with the younger warriors guiding the cai and later I will need you to erase as much of our back trail as your strength will allow.>>

<<War leader, no one will need to risk the Chamuqwani discovering them at the pens,>> I told him, <<because I think I can open the gate with my Qwakaiva, if you let me try. And, my Spirit Helper Rattlesnake is here with me. If we get closer she can frighten the beasts and they will want to run away without our warriors risking their lives to free them.>>

<<Hmm... That is a daring and dangerous plan, young Puhani. Are you sure you want to risk yourself that way?>>

I took a deep breath and touched Thonna's protective vest, feeling its love and protection surround me. <<Yes. I want to help feed our starving people and using my Gift so no one is hurt is the best way to do that.>>

<<Hurt, eh?>> I caught the trace of amusement in his thoughts as he considered my offer. << All right, have your uncle bring you closer, and tell Chugai to have the others ready to herd the beasts westward when we release them.>>

In a low voice I relayed Nachoga's orders to the war band. Uncle Tli scowled when I told him we were to go down and meet Nachoga by the cai pens, but he didn't say more than for me to watch myself—and behave.

The warband split up after that. Giving Utsiyonti and his men some time to creep around to the other side of the encampment, Uncle and I made our way slowly through the brush down the slope on foot, leaving our horses with Samiqwas.

Sensing our nearness Nachoga spoke once more into my mind, <<Tell your uncle to stay in the brush and cover us with his thunder weapon. I will meet you near the gate.>>

With an image of Fox crawling silently through the darkness to kill his prey foremost in my mind, I made my way slowly towards the cai pens. Standing in front of the gate the other Chamuqwani rider sat his horse, lazily talking and joking with Nachoga. As the war leader moved in my direction the other man stayed by the cai.

When Nachoga stopped a little ways in front of where I crouched, I could see that he was no longer riding the old gelding I had last seen him on. This horse he must have borrowed from the rancha. It was a fine young animal, gray with a black mane and tail—one worthy of a powerful war leader.

As the Chamuqwani by the gate lit a smoke I got my first close look at the gate I had boasted I could open. My heart sank when I saw what a difficult task it was going to be. I was expecting a simple metal latch of some kind but that wasn't what I saw.

To confine the cai these Chamuqwani had stuck two tall posts in the ground on both sides of the opening. In the posts were four big holes, and through each hole they had placed long poles. To open this gate I would have to push each pole back through the holes so they could fall to the ground.

Sensing my dismay perhaps, Nachoga said, <<Now that you see the gate, is your Puwa strong enough to move the poles, young warrior? There is no shame in this if you can't. Go back and send your Uncle to me and together he and I will do it.>>

Could I open the gate with my gift....?

Yes, but not in the way I had originally planned.

<<I can't lift the poles out of the holes, war leader, but I can weaken their centers enough with my power that the cai themselves will break the gate down when Rattlesnake frightens them and they run,>> I said. <<I just need a bit of time to focus my Qwakaiva on the problem.>>

Nachoga grunted and moved his horse away from me so as not to draw attention my way by staying too long in one place. When he was closer to the other man I heard him yawn and then say, "I grow sleepy. Maybe I go back to fire get some kafa. You watch Cai for little time, eh?"

The Chamuqwani snorted. "Make sure you don't get somethin' more than kafa. Boss don't want nobody drinkin' on the job."

"Just kafa. No have nothing else now boss-man take away."

The man chuckled, then waved his hand in dismissal. "Go then—and hurry up about it. Cause when you come back I'm gonna go get me some, too."

Nachoga moved away into the darkness, but once out of the man's sight he headed up the slope to where the warband waited. I took off my special string and hastily formed the pattern for the Aseutl's Gift.

I took in a deep breath and let it out slowly as I created an image of the gate in the center diamond. I directed my Qwakaiva to go deep, deep into the hard strong center of the wooden bars. I tugged on a strand of the pattern and focused on the power becoming long snaky grubs, hungrily eating their way through each pole, their bellies becoming bloated and round as they burrowed, leaving an empty core in their wakes. Eating, hungry fresh green wood, sweet, sweet—so good—so hungry—eat, eat.

Before I could get too deep into my conjuring, Rattlesnake touched my ear with her tongue. <<The enemy has moved away. We go now,>> she said. <<My relatives have come to help us.>>

I looked up from my conjuring. She was right; the way down seemed clear. Nachoga was up the slope concealed within the trees, probably giving uncle or the warriors some last minute instructions. Tired of waiting perhaps, the other guard had moved away from the pen and it looked like he was heading back to their camp for his kafa and to see what was keeping his partner.

I rose and sprinted down the rest of the slope, trying to be as quiet as possible. When I got to the gate I crouched and opened my shirt, allowing Rattlesnake to crawl out. <<Be careful, Honored One,>> I called as she slithered into the grass on the other side of the post. <<I will wait for you here and pull you out of danger when the cai run.>>

The cai milled about, nervously dropping fresh pats of dung and lowing their distress to one another. I peered into the pen. They didn't seem to be aware of her presence yet.

Maybe she was waiting to reveal herself when her relatives had had a chance to crawl behind the cai. Or, maybe she was waiting till she got further among the beasts before she would sound her rattles and start the stampede. "Please be careful, they might trample you if you go too far," I murmured under my breath as I tried to see through the gloom to follow her progress.

Intent on the cai, I remained with my arms and upper body inside the enclosure, hoping to pull her out of danger when she came back to me. The night about me hummed with Qwakaiva. Fear slithered down my backbone like an icy river. Above the cai's moaning I heard an owl hoot in among the pines. I swallowed, trying to clear the lump that had formed in my throat. <<Oh, Great Kunai, keep us safe tonight and bless us with success,>> I prayed and reached in my belt pouch to scatter a bit of sacred herbs upon the land as an offering.

Suddenly a rough hand grabbed the back of my shirt and hauled me up to my feet, then turned me to face him, so he could get a better look at me."Hey what'cha doing?" Wearing clothes that smelled like the cai he tended, he also wore a dusty broad brimmed hat. Below his angry light-colored eyes, he had grown a shaggy tangle of curly hair on his face that reached nearly to his chest.

He looked at me in the star light and swore. "Mighty Djoven's balls, you're nothin' but a kid—a filthy zaunk kid." Getting over his shock, he demanded, "Did somebody send you to spy on us?" When I didn't answer, he shook me hard enough to make me bite my tongue.

"Come on tell me the truth, you thievin' little zaunk bastard." He shook me again. "You spyin' on the rancha?"

Spitting my blood in his face, I snarled in the Chamuqwani language, "No spy me, and no thief either. Chamuqwani thief you. Take cai from my people." And then I called him a bad word in his language.

He hit me that time, but I didn't care my anger over all the injustice done to my people was at that moment making me fearless. "Chamuqwani dog turd!" Behind me the cai were snorting, stamping their hooves, calling to one another and bunching up as if they would run at any moment. The man had noticed the agitated cai, too, and was looking around for his partner maybe.

"Damn where did that no-count drifter get too? I got ta' take this little brat to the boss. The boss will get the truth out o' him. Damn where's that drunken tramp gone?"

"I'm right here, Chamuqwani," Nachoga said. Letting go of me, the man turned to face the new threat. As he reached for the small thunder weapon holstered at his hip, Nachoga plunged his long knife into the man's side burying it hilt deep between his ribs. The man choked on his own blood and sagged to the ground at my feet.

Grabbing the dying man by an arm the war leader pulled him to lie in front of the gate. At all most the same moment I heard the familiar whirr of Rattlesnake and her relatives within the cai pen. The beasts let out frightened bellows and thundered towards the weakened gate.

Atop his horse again, Nachoga shouted to me over the din, "Quickly now, Puhani, before you are trampled. Get up behind me," Nachoga leaned over and held out a hand to me.

I hesitated, still worried about my Spirit Helper's safety. "But Rattlesnakeisn't here—" Nachoga swore and roughly pulled me onto his horse, then kicked the gray hard and the horse leapt away as the first of the Cai burst through the gate.

"Spirit Helpers can take care of themselves. They live or die in this world as the Unseen Ones will. Don't worry about her now. We ride."

From the other end of the Chamuqwani camp came the wild whoops of Utsiyonti and his warriors. Then I saw flashes of light and heard the thunder weapons roar. Horses screamed and ran off into the night with the warriors right behind them. Most wakened from sleep by the noise, the rancha men shouted to one another and stumbled about, not understanding at first what had happened.

In the confusion we managed to gather most of the Cai and many of the horses and hurry them back into the mountains, heading for the Preserve. Chugai, Uncle Tli and some of the hunters from down the Socanna River lagged behind to kill or discourage any of the rancha-men who tried to follow.

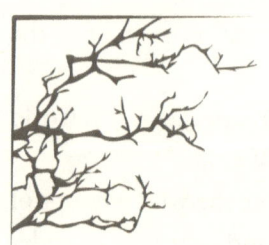

Chapter Nine

By day break we were deep into the mountains. The warriors, the horses and the Cai were growing tired, so we stopped by a shallow creek to let everyone rest and eat while Utsiyonti attended to our few wounded. Too tired myself to eat, I lay flat in the tall grass and rested my head on an arm and closed my eyes. I had used a lot of Qwakaiva and I was exhausted. My mouth and cheek hurt anyway, so I didn't mind missing the trail rations the men hastily grabbed from their packs.

I might have dozed off, for the next thing I knew someone was standing over me. As I opened my eyes, Uncle Tli crouched beside me and handed me a cup full of berries he or someone had picked down by the creek. I sat up and took the cup, gingerly putting a berry in my mouth. Its sharp acidy taste stung my raw tongue, but its sweet cool flavor was worth the discomfort. I thanked him and he nodded.

"You did well last night, nephew. The war leader has spoken to me of your power and bravery. I am proud of you."

Startled I looked him boldly in the eye. I couldn't ever remember Uncle Tli praising me so highly before. "Thank you, Uncle your praise means a lot to me."

Tli grunted and pointed to the half-eaten cup. "Finish that; Nachoga wants to talk to you." I poured the rest of the berries into my mouth. I handed him back his cup and rose to follow him back to the fire.

As I sat down someone handed me another cup—this time filled with pine and willow tea. I sipped the warm liquid and waited for the war leader to tell me what he wanted. Setting his own empty cup down he fixed his cougar eyes on me for a long moment, and then I felt his power reach out and touch me. I resisted the impulse to shield and allowed his study. I sensed he was only checking to see I was doing all right.

Finally he said, "I sense that you are still tired, but if you are able to do a bit of scouting for us with your power, your Puwa, I need to know how far behind us the Chamuqwani are.And, I'd rather not risk anyone being spotted if they went back to find out."

I glanced up searching the sky above. "If I can find and persuade Eagle or Hawk to lend me their keen sight for a time I will hunt for you, war leader," I said. "If not I will try with my special string."

"Good. That eases my mind somewhat."

Finishing my tea I rose and walked to an open space where I could see the rocky cliffs and the sky above them. I searched and at last found a young hawk perched on a rocky ledge overlooking the creek. <<Winged Brother, fly with me and lend me your sight. My people have need. Our enemies follow. Please help us and I will hunt a nice fat rabbit for you,>> I prayed.

It took a bit of coaxing on my part, but at last Hawk took flight, soaring high above the creek and with me looking through his eyes we headed down the wide trampled trail the cai and our horses had left in the brush and sand.

I saw with dismay that the trail of so many beasts traveling together was like a bright beacon in the dark of night. Even a small child could follow it. Hawk and I flew back as far as the west side of the Bear Head Cliff. I spotted three Chamuqwani riders coming slowly along our back trail. They were being careful, looking all around and studying the ground before them. I suspected they were waiting for a larger force to catch up and then they would be after us at a much faster pace—and with intent to kill.

The sun had passed its mid-point in the sky when I reported my findings to Nachoga and the warriors.He grunted and waved for me to sit. Someone handed me a seed cake wrapped around some fresh deer meat.

"The Chamuqwani scouts that follow are waiting for the soldiers," a scarred Kukiya warrior grumbled."Maybe we should ambush and kill them before they can tell them where we are."

"Maybe, but the trail is easily followed even without the scouts to guide them," Uncle said.

"We will have to split up the cai and butcher them," Chugai said. "They leave too big a trail this way."

"Golannah will have people meet us once we get into the rough country west of here," Nachoga said as he turned his cougar eyes on me again. "But getting them into the deep canyons is the problem that concerns us now."

I knew what he wanted—needed, but I was so tired by that time my hands were trembling so much I could barely raise my cup to my lips.

Studying me as well, Utsiyonti said, "I think I may be able to help with that, brother." He pointed to a ridge of dark clouds forming in the south. "I will speak to the Akiyazi on our behalf. I will ask Water to send rain enough to raise the creek and wipe out our tracks once we cross to the otherside."

"And if Rain comes this whole area will flood I suspect," Chugai said.

I let out a deep sigh of relief. "I will help as best I can once I rest," I offered.

"Mm, that will be good, but you will have to do your resting on your horse," Nachoga said. "We need to get ourselves and these beasts up to higher ground, because Chugai is right. If my brother does persuade Rain to come this far north, where we now are, will be under water. So, get your horses. We go now."

"You can ride behind Samiqwas," Uncle said as I started to get my mare. "I will tie you on; then you can sleep a little maybe. Cohasi can bring your mare on a lead rope for when you need her."

I dozed behind Samiqwas until the rain began pouring down in midafternoon. Then there was no way I could rest with water dripping down my back, so I called to Cohasi to bring my mare and I rode her until we stopped to rest.

Seeing Hawk following after Rain blew away, I risked leaving my body to take a quick look through his eyes at the country we'd traveled. The flat land at the bottom of the valley where Creek lived was now a broad impassable lake, the surface churned up by Wind into muddy waves. Even the slope we had just climbed ran with little streams cascading into the new lake below, erasing our passage.

With the Unseen Ones' blessing, by the time the Chamuqwani made their way around the flood we would be far away and the cai gone to feed many hungry people.

AS THE WAR LEADER PREDICTED Golannah had sent word to trusted people on the Preserve who met us by the next day. With the added help the beasts were split up into groups of two or three animals each that soon disappeared into the mountains for the butchering, and then the distribution of the much needed meat.

Keeping aside four cai for the people waiting for us the warband headed west back to our hideout in the barren lands. I don't remember much of that trip, because along the way I became feverish and spent a couple days dozing tied to my horse with Samiqwas leading her.

I had been feeling bad about losing Rattlesnake and expecting—hoping for some type of reminder from my Benefactor of his conditions surrounding the use of his Qwakaiva. So when I developed stomach cramps and a fever I welcomed them—in a strange sort of way. My suffering was a chance for me to let go my guilt.

It did surprise my companions, however, because I had forgotten to warn them about what I must pay for my helping them. Kneeling beside me that night when my fever raged and the cramps bent me in half with pain, Nachoga placed a hand on my forehead and frowned.

"What's wrong with you, young Puhani? Did the ghost of the Chamuqwani rancha man I killed or another among them sicken you with his evil Puwa?"

"No, war leader, I don't think so. I will be all right in a few days," I assured him. "This happened before at the camp of my relatives when they were attacked by malicer converts and I helped the ghosts find their way home. It is the price I agreed to, and must pay for the gift of my Benefactor's power each time I call upon it."

He thought about it for a moment then nodded. "Harsh conditions, but I can see the wisdom in them. Do we need to stop to take care of you?"

I was unable to answer him at that moment as I grabbed my gut and doubled over gasping. Uncle Tli had come over by that time and held me as the spasm passed. "My nephew Samiqwas and I can stay with him if needed until he recovers," Uncle Tli said. "This close to the Preserve border it wouldn't be wise for all of us and so many beasts to linger here longer than necessary."

Motioning for Uncle to lay me on my side I vomited a foul tasting liquid into the dirt until my gut was empty. When I covered up the mess and sat up still feeling a little dizzy, Nachoga handed me a drink of water. "My Benefactor favored the warband's request so my sickness won't last too long."

No, just long enough to pay for the loss of Rattlesnake—a death for which I was truly sorry and knew I deserved to suffer for—in spite of Nachoga's comforting words.

Looking at all their concerned faces, I tried to reassure them. "I will be able to ride by morning most like. If not just tie me to my horse." I attempted to smile. "I don't want to miss the feast we will have when we butcher the cai at last."

"Hmm..." motioning for the others to leave us alone for a while, his green cougar eyes seemed to look into the depths of my spirit. At last he said, "There is more to this sickness than what you are acknowledging even to yourself maybe. You just admitted that the Unseen Ones favored our raid, so why would you sicken because of it?"

I dropped my eyes; I didn't want to admit—even to him, that I blamed myself for Rattlesnake's death. I deserved to suffer.

When I didn't speak he seemed to understand what was really troubling me. "I think you blame yourself for the snake's death, and I think you yourself are making your payment to the Unseen Ones harsher than is necessary. It is one thing to acknowledge their Gifts and offer a gift in return, to remain humble and show your gratitude for their favor, but it is only arrogance for you to decide how much to offer."

At his words my head shot up, my mouth dropping open in surprise. He chuckled softly and laid a scarred hand on my arm for a moment, then withdrew it as if he had surprised himself by the gesture.

"You are only the physical channel for the Unseen Ones' puwa in our world—as was the snake that came to help us—as am I—as are we all in some way. Rattlesnake isn't dead. If She is your chosen helper then you will see her again when She is needed. I truly believe that—as should you."

I dropped my eyes again, ashamed now of my lapse. I knew in my heart Nachoga was right. Tomorrow it might be my life that would be sacrificed for the Good of the People. "You are right, war leader. I am sorry—I had forgotten my teachings."

He patted my arm again, letting me know he understood. "You are young, and this raid is the first time you were called to go to war. You had hard lessons to learn, but you have done well." He stood and looked down at me, his expression solemn. "Do pay what is owing, young Puhani, but don't add more to what is owed the Unseen Ones than they require of you."

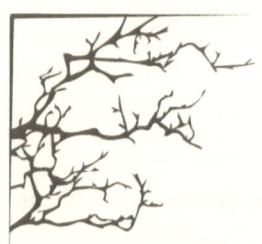

Chapter Ten

By dawn my stomach cramps had subsided and though I was still feverish I was able to sit my horse. Uncle told Samiqwas to stay close and I saw him turn to check on me several times throughout the ride that day.

We traveled at a slow pace, keeping the cai moving ever westward into the rocky and arid lands of the desert. In this part of our Preserve the land was cut with brush-covered hills and steep ravines where in spring and early summer snow melt transformed nearly dry winter stream beds into raging torrents.

When we stopped in the afternoon heat to feed and water the animals, I nearly fell off my mare. I had been hearing spirit voices talking and singing to me all morning and I felt like I stood on a cliff's edge between two worlds. Still dizzy and weak I sprawled in the shade of a large boulder staring up at the cloud people dancing as Wind tossed them about the blue sky, trying to catch my breath.

After a time I became aware of someone standing beside me. When I focused my gaze in that direction I saw it was Matoqwa looking down at me with an unreadable expression on his broken nosed face. His Spirit Bear too watched me with a thoughtful expression. I hoped he wasn't angry and wanting to fight, because I was too weak to put up much of a battle if he did.

"I'm sorry for chasing you with the horse broom—and I'm sorry for not helping with camp chores right now. I'll get up in a moment and help with the horses. I just need to—" as I started to sit up he snorted and pushed me back to the ground.

"Don't worry about it. Everything is taken care of."

Matoqwa and I had always had an uneasy friendship and I wondered what was on his mind, because he continued to stare down at me and it made me uncomfortable. "What?" I finally asked. "I said I was sorry, didn't I?"

He snorted a laugh. "Yeah, you did—though I don't know if I believe you, Siyatli boy." Then after another long moment mustering his courage he asked, "When we were back home, Tas, did you know you were a Siyatli—I mean could you do all those things with your Qwakaiva like you did during the cai raid?"

I sat up and shook my head. "No, I didn't know who my father was until I called the Unseen Ones to help us when we might have died at Drown Canoe Rapids and he answered. And also no, about me knowing how to use my power, not until the warband sent Samiqwas with an offering for my Benefactor and he showed me how to aid the warriors did I learn how to use my Qwakaiva in the manner I did on the raid."

Looking him rudely in the eye so I knew he understood me, I added, "I also meant what I told you and your brother that day among the horses. I want only to do good with my power. No matter how angry you and Cohasi make me, I won't hurt you like a malicer." I touched my chest for emphases. "There is a price exacted each time I call upon the Unseen Ones for their Qwakaiva. My weakness and fever right now is the price I'm willingly giving them in return for letting me help feed the People."

"Mm," shaking his head he wandered away without another word.

My fever persisted for the rest of the day, and that night as I slept She came to me in my dreams. Slithering up my side, Rattlesnake coiled her long body upon my warm chest and raised her head to look at me.

<<Ah, little Siyatli boy, I am moved by your concern for me and mine. So to honor your tender human heart I will give you a gift for which you have not asked. Come, leave your sleeping body and I will show you something that you will want to know and act upon—before it is too late.>>

<<What gift is it you would give me, Honored One?>>

<<You will understand when I show you. Now come.>>

I was relieved and honored by her visitation, but her words also sent needles of worry and fear running down my spine. But Rattlesnake refused to answer any of my further questions, so I at last slipped the bounds of the Physical World and drifted into the Dream, shape-shifting into my half man, half seal form to join her. Through the dark and the swirling colored mists of the Dream we swam for a time, Rattlesnake leading, me following close in her wake.

Then ahead of us the mists cleared and I saw the familiar site of the convert settlement. Instinctively I held back reluctant to come so near the evil spectre that had attached itself to those people. The evil one had tried to kill me more than once since I refused to become its slave. I had no wish to give it another chance to torment me.

Once more Rattlesnake wound her sinuous body around me and touched my ear with her tongue. <<Have no fear, little Siyatli, I am shielding us with my Qwakaiva. The spectre cannot harm you. Pay attention; we go closer now.>>

With her wrapped around me I swam into Chief Eagan's stone meeting house where most of the settlement was gathered. The sunlight coming in a high window said that it wasn't a meal time, so I couldn't understand at first why they had come together to pray. Everyone looked sad some openly crying like Aunty Marika and Amima.

I next saw Grandfather standing beside a somber Uncle Royston. I was surprised to see him back in the settlement; I hadn't checked on him for a while, but I thought he was still with the profit's people in the west.

<<Why is he here?>> I wondered.

<<Look down—over by their stone altar,>> Rattlesnake directed, catching my unshielded thought. <<Then you will understand why he has come.>>

I looked down by their altar and saw a body wrapped in grass mats and bound with rope. Above it hovered Grandmother's spirit looking sad and confused. <<Oh Ami,>> I thought. In the Physical World I could feel salty tears pooling in my eyes and flowing down my cheeks, though I still slept.

Sensing me perhaps, Grandfather raised his head and focused his attention in my direction. I doubted he could see me through Rattlesnake's protective shield, but I was sure he was aware of me watching, and I suspected I knew what he wanted from me.

<<Honored One, can we help her find her way home?>>

<<No, if I unshield the spectre will become aware of us and either attack us or try to destroy her spirit out of spite. See the dark cord around her neck?>>

<<Yes, what is it?>>

<<It is the trap hidden in the lure set to catch you, Siyatli boy, do you see why I bring you here instead of allowing you to discover her fate on your own? This woman chose her path when she listened to her oldest son's entreaties and accepted the lightning bolt charm. Now it binds her to the invaders' god as surely as there is snow in a northern winter. I brought you here to warn you, Tender-Hearted One. There is nothing you can do for her now. If you try on your own the spectre will ensnare and eat you.>>

<<But Kunai—>>

When She next spoke there was a new hardness to her spirit voice I hadn't heard before. <<The Great One will not help you. If you are stupid enough to ignore the warning I was sent to give you, then he will leave you to your fate.

<<In this you cannot allow your soft human nature to rule your actions. You have chosen to become a part of a dangerous game for the survival of your world. This is but one of the many hard lessons you will need to learn.>>

Feeling like my heart was going to shatter, it took me a while to ignore Mother's tears and Grandfather's stricken face when he realized I wasn't going to help her. Finally mastering my turbulent emotions, I said, <<I understand and will heed the warning you have been sent to give me, but isn't there anything we can do to help her, Honored One?>>

<<Not at the moment. Perhaps later when the spectre and those who direct it have their attentions focused elsewhere you may be able to guide her ghost back to your ancestors. We shall see.>>

With the sadness welling up inside threatening to overwhelm me I finally agreed to leave that terrible place. I needed to wake up and tell Uncle and Samiqwas what had happened, I told her.

<<I know you are eager to tell your relatives, but first I am also directed to show you a vision from the near future. Should you choose to act upon what you see you will have Kunai's blessing.>> Uncoiling herself from around me She once more led me through the mists and close to another glowing light.

This time the vision was of the Willow Creek Agency. A mixed crowd of Chamuqwani and "hang around the agency" Kukiya and Qwani'Ya people had gathered in the yard outside the fat agent's office. They were expecting a show of some kind; I could almost taste their excitement as I watched.

This time there was also sounds as well as the pictures. I could hear the people muttering and cursing. "The old bastard and the cloocha-whore are sure gonna get what's coming to them." A bearded Chamuqwani with a red nose said to a gray-haired man beside him.

"Yeah, when the Intercessor and the commander finish with them there won't be nothing left but raw meat for the buzzards," the man agreed.

"Damn right!" Another Chamuqwani interjected, "One of the zaunks who is always losing at the dice game says the old man used to be his father-in-law till his whore of a wife ran off with a soldier. Word is the old man's been going around spreading talk of rebellion."

"And the cloocha ain't no better. My woman says she convinced a sweet young girl to run away with the outlaws," another man said.

Red Nose snorted with disgust. "All o'em ain't no better than animals. We should kill'em all if you ask me."

"Well nobody did, bum-fucker,"a mixed-race trader-man that I hadn't seen before said in our defence. He had a shell earring and his black hair cut short.

Before the two men could carry their insults further and come to blows, the fat agent, the soldier's commander, Intercessor Karl and Chief Eagan stepped out of the agent's office and onto the porch. A soldier hollered for quiet and the crowd fell silent.

"We have called you here to witness the punishment handed out to anyone—young or old—who tries to convince others to break the Father Emperor's law, no matter the reason, peaceful or otherwise, it isn't allowed," the agent said. "Leaving the Preserve, even to just pray and dance, as this lying bastard claims, is against the law and won't be tolerated."

"Do you understand, or do I need to get the interpreter to translate my words for you?" the soldiers' commander asked Grandfather.

"Me understand," Grandfather said in his best Chamuqwani. "Me no tell People make war, just want to pray and dance. No want kill Chamuqwani."

The soldier snorted as if he didn't believe it for a moment.

"Heathen dancing and praying may not be against the Emperor's law, but it is against Mighty Djoven's law and it won't be tolerated even here on the

Preserve," the intercessor said. "It is time to set aside your backward heathen ways and embrace the Thunderer's teachings and become civilized at last."

"We all time cee-bil-ice," Grandfather said and lifted his chin proudly. "Qwani'Ya Kukiya just different no bad, no good—different is all."

Then changing the subject he glanced at his daughter then asked, "Me understand why Chamuqwani want punish me. You afraid Qwani'Ya power. You afraid me. Why punish daughter? Good she, no hurt Chamuqwani, no tell people go dance. Why you want hurt womans?"

"Because of the missing girl," he answered.

Mother spoke up then focusing her gaze on Uncle Royston leaning grim-faced against a scorched porch post. In our language, she said, "Amima told me once, before she became sick in her mind, that she was very sorry she listened to the clan mothers and married you to the people down river.

"You have changed, brother; you aren't the same brother I grew up with. What happened to you among those people? How could you forget everything your family taught you? Why didn't you come home if it was so bad among them?

"Over and over I tried to tell you. Thonna is gone because you wouldn't listen to her. Neither I nor Tas encouraged her to run away. In fact Tas didn't even tell her he was leaving. He figured she would be safer marrying someone she hated rather than joining him among the outlaws."

"If you and your son didn't help her then why is she gone?" Uncle snapped.

"Because like most Qwani'Ya women Thonna is smart and no beaten down slave to obey rules she knows in her heart are wrong. She threatened to kill herself rather than marry a young man she so fiercely hated. Did you know that?"

Uncle waved his hand in a dismissive gesture. "I heard her spout that nonsense, but it was idle talk. She needed only a few good beatings and a firm hand and she would have settled down and become a good wife and mother."

"A few good beatings, eh, Brother? Listen to yourself. Since when is beating someone to make them agree with you the Qwani'Ya way? Our ancestors are shamed to hear you talk like that."

Uncle snorted his face contorting with his contempt. "Well, maybe I don't care what a bunch of drunken, dirty savages think. Maybe I'm ashamed of them, too."

I saw tears pooling in the corners of Mother's eyes, falling slowly down her cheeks. "Oh, brother, I'm so sorry. I will pray for you."

"Don't bother. I don't want your heathen prayers," he snarled, interrupting her.

Ignoring his rude behavior she continued, "I believed her when she said she would die before she married Charlic, and that's why I told her the warriors had sent for Tas. She herself took the food and clothing and knew exactly where to find Tas and the outlaws, because I didn't even know that myself. Thonna is her own woman and does her lineage proud—no matter what you think."

Then unable to contain his rage any longer Chief Eagan snarled in our language to make sure they both understood. Addressing Grandfather again, he raged, "you and everyone here just heard the woman condemn herself. She is guilty of bearing a child out of the God's holy marriage and defying Mighty Djoven's holy laws set down for women to obey.

"She will deserve the lash and worse, as do you, Heathen Pond Scum! Along with your crimes against our Mighty Djoven, your daughter encouraged an innocent girl to defy her father's will when he betrothed her to a fine young convert boy."

His face purpling with the intensity of his emotions, Eagan shouted, "Filthy whore! She helped the girl so she could follow the whore's witch-bastard son when he ran away to join the outlaws now plaguing the law-abiding people on this Preserve. That's why she is going to join you in the God's torment."

"Is that you yourself saying these terrible things, Qwani'Ya Man, or are you only repeating the venomous words the evil spectre perched on your shoulder is telling you to say?' Grandfather nodded focusing his gaze on a point over Eagan's shoulder. "Yes I can see you, Evil One. And it's time you were gone. You've caused enough trouble for my Qwani'Ya people."

Raising his manacled hands Grandfather drew a symbol with his Qwakaiva in the air between them. His power enveloped the creature in a ball of flames. With an ear-piercing screech the spectre disappeared, and in the next moment both Eagan and Grandfather fell senseless to the ground.

Shaken and frightened I saw no more after that. <<It is enough, Siyatli boy. I have shown you what the Great One wishes you to see. Now it is up to you to decide what to do with the visions.>>

Then she returned my spirit to my sleeping body and disappeared.

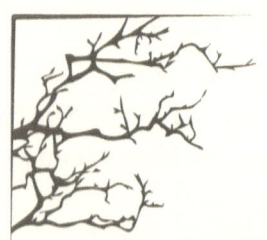

Chapter Eleven

Tears still streaming down my cheeks, I sat up with a gasp and cradled my face in my hands. During the night my fever had abated, but I felt no better, my grief threatening to overwhelm me at any moment. Though it was still dark a faint grayness on the eastern horizon told me dawn would be here soon. In the nearby grass those not on guard with the cai still slept. I shivered and pulled my blanket about my shoulders. How was I going to tell Uncle Tli and Samiqwas about Grandmother's death and Grandfather's capture?

And, more importantly, what was I going to do with the information Kunai had sent me about Mother and Grandfather's pending punishment by the Chamuqwani? I knew in a way the Great One was toying with me, testing me to see if I was worthy of his regard—I just hoped I was, for everyone's sake...

With my blanket still wrapped around me, I fed the dozing fire and sat to feel its warmth. Sometime later Uncle Tli stepped out of the darkness to join me. Crouching by the fire he set down his thunder weapon and reached for the sooty can, nesting in the warm ashes. When he lifted the can over his empty cup only a thin trickle of tea poured out. Glaring over at me he muttered something uncomplimentary about lazy boys.

Needing another moment to gather my thoughts and tell him about my visions I murmured an apology, grabbed the flattened skin bucket, and went to fill it. When I returned Nachoga, Chugai, and the older Kukiya warrior with the scarred face were also sitting by the fire. I filled the can, put in some fresh leaves and placed it to heat in the flames. Sitting myself, I allowed the quiet talk to continue on around me, still mulling over what to do about Mother and Grandfather. Then a jab in the ribs startled me out of my reverie.

"What's a matter with you, nephew? Wake up. The war leader just asked you a question," Uncle growled under his breath.

Ashamed of my laps I turned to Nachoga and stammered, "I-I'm sorry, war leader, I wasn't listening. What did you need?"

Nachoga waved a dismissive hand in my direction. Then in an unexpectedly gentle voice, he asked, "Never mind that for now; it isn't important. What's troubling you this morning, young Puhani?"

Unable to hold back my grief any longer, I said through my tears, "Rattlesnake came to me in my dreams last night." ThenI told him and the others about her visions.

When I finished Tli muttered a vile Chamuqwani curse and stomped off into the darkness. Some of the others who were now awake and who had just joined us stared after him. In low whispers the word of what had happened quickly passed around the circle. Men and boys poured tea and ate then quietly went about their chores to prepare for the journey that day.

When I rose to join them Nachoga waved me back to my seat. "Stay a moment." When I settled back he leaned forward and fixed me with his cougar eyes. "I sense there is more to your telling than you mentioned, can you recall the visions clear enough to show me with your Puwa string?"

Could I? "I-I don't know, but I will try." I lifted the cord from around my neck and scooted closer to him. As I looped the cord around my hands in the now familiar pattern, I said, "I've never tried to recall something within the Seer's Diamond."

"I would like to see for myself if you can manage it." He shrugged. "If not then we will just talk about what can be done to help them."

With his calm assurance giving me hope, I formed the pattern of the Seer's Pool and used my Qwakaiva to recreate Rattlesnake's visions for him. I wasn't able to duplicate the words that were spoken, but I could recall enough of her visions that he could form a picture of what had, and would take place if something wasn't done to change the future.

When I finished and allowed my string to slip off my hands I looked up letting my eyes ask the question my lips were afraid to speak. Nachoga was silent for what seemed a long time, but probably wasn't. At last he said, "What do you want to do about this, young Puhani? I am willing to offer you my aid, but it is up to you—and your other relatives here to decide our course."

As Rattlesnake had said, this problem was being left up to me to solve.

I opened my mouth to speak when the clop, clop of a nearing horse's steps silenced me. In the next moment Uncle Tli, packed and mounted, rode his horse up to the fire and looked down at us.

"I am going to do what I should have done long before now," he announced.

Taking a sip of his now cold tea, Nachoga asked in a calm voice, "And what is that, Qwani'Ya brother?"

"Kill my traitor of a brother, and as many convert turds as I can before they kill me," Tli snarled.

"Uncle no," I gasped. "I agree we need to save Amima and Grandfather from the priest's and the fat agent's punishments, but running off to get yourself killed isn't going to help them escape Chamuqwani vengeance."

"You should listen to your nephew, brother," Nachoga said as he rose to his feet.

By this time Chugai, Utsiyonti and a couple Kukiya men had ridden over and surrounded Uncle. Unless he wanted to fight them, he wasn't going anywhere at that moment.

"War leader, stop this stupid dog turd," Chugai said. "Qwati from back home and I said we would go with him, but he told me no. He says he plans to carry out his vengeance alone. He says we are needed here to help with the cai."

"You *are* needed to help with the cai and bringing meat to the starving families," Nachoga agreed, "which is why the young Puhani and I are going with him—not you."

At his revelation everyone who was near enough to hear froze, staring. "No, this isn't your problem. They are my blood kin. I will do it; and kill my brother as I swore I would do when we came to this terrible place," Tli said and tried to jerk his horse's reins out of Utsiyonti's grasp.

Without raising his voice Nachoga said, "No, brother, you are not going alone, because Chugai is right you are a stupid dog turd—who isn't thinking clearly."

"What about the damned cai," Uncle Tli growled. "Aren't you needed to stay with the beasts?"

"My help, as is yours, would be useful at this point but not needed. Utsiyonti can take over from here. There is little need for my Puwa and my other skills now, but you, on the other hand, will need me if your riding off is anything more than a suicide attempt." Uncle bristled at his implication, but kept quiet, as Nachoga continued, "You are grieving the loss of your mother right now, so I am willing to ignore your insulting behavior, but have you stopped to consider that this is only a trap designed to capture anyone foolish enough to try and rescue them?"

Uncle's mouth dropped open, but he stopped trying to guide his horse out of our circle. At last he said, "I don't understand; what are you talking about?"

"While the others pack up camp and start the cai and our extra horses moving, get down off your horse and we will talk about what I saw when your nephew showed me the Spirit's visions with his special string."

Motioning for me to leave them and help pack up, Nachoga poured Tli the last of the tea and the two men resumed their seats by the fire.

As I was saddling my mare Samiqwas came over to me, a determined expression plastered on his face. "I'm going with you," he stated. "Grandfather is my grandfather, too. And-and your mother is my aunty."

DURING THE MORNING ride Uncle Tli, Utsiyonti, and Nachoga discussed what to do with the remaining cai and made plans for the rescue attempt. I was consulted on occasion when they needed clarification on a particular point I'd seen in the Dream, but mostly I did what I'd been doing since we left the Bear Head Cliff. I spied on our back trail with my Qwakaiva and herded the cai and horses, like the rest of the boys and younger warriors.

At the afternoon break I learn that Uncle, Nachoga, Samiqwas and I would head south into the preserve when the rest break was over. Herding the cai and the loose horses, the rest of the warband would go west into the dry mountains and head for the stronghold.

Travelling ever southward, we headed deeper into the preserve. If my Dreams were to happen in the near future Nachoga knew we had to travel swiftly, but he also knew we needed to be cautious and not be seen if possible. Often we hid by day when my spying, through a helpful bird's eyes, detected soldiers or other mounted people on the same trails we were following. Since Moon was nearing her fullness we usually continued on deep into the night, stopping only when the horses needed to rest and feed.

The news of our part in the cai raid and the distribution of the butchered meat had spread before us so on the few occasions we did approach an encampment of Traditional people carrying fresh deer meat and asking for news and a hot meal, we were welcomed with smiles and a warm place by the fire.

We learned when we stopped at the camp of Uncle's former in-laws that there were more soldiers than usual on the Preserve. Our informants said they were hunting us and searching for the stolen cai. We had been warned, but our first sign of trouble came without me sounding an alarm and from an unexpected source.

We had hidden ourselves among the pines on a grassy slope so the men could get some badly needed sleep. Samiqwas and I were left on guard taking turns dozing and watching over the path below. I was tired, still recovering from my fever, but pushed on anyway and let Samiqwas sleep longer than I should have maybe. I'd been unlucky in finding a friendly eagle or hawk to help me spy from above, so I'd had to rely on my human eyes and my string—in which I placed too much confidence and my Qwakaiva failed me that time. I didn't see what was coming.

All seemed peaceful with no soldiers or riders nearby, I told Uncle and Nachoga when they woke in late afternoon. Leaving Samiqwas and me to do camp chores and water the horses, the warriors decided to split up and do a bit of hunting before we headed on after dark. By tomorrow we would be too close to convert settlements and the agency itself to risk hunting for fresh meat.

I had built a small smokeless fire and Samiqwas had taken two of the horses to water at the creek. I was alone and just putting our big can by Fire to heat when a sudden unexpected noise made me look in the direction of the trail below. Then I heard one of the horses down by the creek cry out a welcome which was answered by another beast somewhere just out of sight in a bend in the trail.

Leaping to my feet I grabbed my mare and uncle's spotted gelding and wrapping a bit of my Qwakaiva around their mouths to keep them quiet I backed them into the darker shadows under the pines. Straining my ears to try and hear what was going on below, I said using the mind talk, <<There's trouble, war leader, are you near?>>

Then I heard a gruff Chamuqwani voice call out to Samiqwas. He answered, and then another man spoke. Two men and Samiqwas alone, an icy chill ran down my spine. Leaving the horses tied to a sturdy pine, I crept down the slope, heading for the creek and grabbing several good-sized rocks as I went.

At the creek I crouched and peered through the berry bushes. I saw Samiqwas standing defiantly in front of our horses, facing two mounted Chamuqwani. I couldn't hear what they were saying, Water was singing too loudly as it danced over the stones in the creek bed, but it was clear that the two Chamuqwani were angry about something.

The men wore the same broad-brimmed hats and leather trousers as the rancha men I'd seen that night by the cai pens. I wondered if they were scouts for a larger party of Chamuqwani searching for us and their missing beasts. The one with the black hair on his face pointed to the branded mark on the gray horse that Nachoga had claimed and asked Samiqwas a question. Samiqwas shook his head and gave the angry man a puzzled look as if he didn't know what he was talking about.

The other man atop a spotted pony said something and urged his horse forward, reaching for the gray's lead rope. Shaking his head, Samiqwas moved to block him. The black bearded man was reaching for the thunder weapon holstered at his waist when I stood and hit his hand with a rock. Being a notorious bad shot, fortunately for us I had had the presence of mind to touch the rock with my power so it hit its target. He dropped the weapon with a curse into the creek before he could aim and shoot it.

The man on the spotted horse too was reaching for his weapon when Samiqwas leapt onto his horse and headed up the slope away from the creek, still clutching the gray's lead rope. Before I could throw another stone or the man could raise his weapon, a red flower blossomed in the middle of his dirty shirt and Uncle Tli stepped out of the brush on the other side of the stream. Clutching at the arrow now lodged in his chest, the Chamuqwani toppled from his mount, making a loud splash in the shallow creek.

The dead man's horse shied and would have run, but I was able to grab him and hold on as he tried to buck. I could see the whites around his big brown eyes so I ran a hand down his neck to calm him.

Seeing that he was outnumbered and weaponless, the black bearded one jabbed his heels hard into his mount's flanks and the brown horse leapt for the trail. He didn't get very far, because Nachoga, like the big cat who shared his Qwakaiva, dropped from a tree limb onto the horse's back. Grabbing the Chamuqwani by his hair, Nachoga yanked his head back and slit the man's throat with his long knife.

Allowing the body to slide off the horse's back Nachoga slid forward into the saddle and wheeled the horse around and headed back up the stream towards me. He motioned up the slope "Go back to camp and help your cousin pack up our things we need to leave here—now!"

In spite of his command I was slow to move, still staring at the two bodies staining the creek water red. "What about the Chamuqwani? If the soldiers find them—"

"No one will find them. Cougar is coming. There are hungry kittens to feed at this time of year."

By this time Uncle Tli had crossed the creek and come up to us. As he went to strip the bodies of all usable weapons and supplies Nachoga motioned with his chin to the trail "Take that horse your nephew is holding and check to see if there are any more rancha-men behind us."

Uncle climbed on the horse and headed back down the men's trail. Seeing me still standing there when he rose with the two men's weapons and clothing in hand, Nachoga scowled. "I-I'm sorry, war leader, for letting this happen. I should have seen—"

He shook his head and motioned with his chin for me to take some of his load and precede him up the trail. "It is of no consequence. As you once said you are a boy and don't have a man's power and strength yet. And it is also my fault for forgetting that."

Leaving the stripped bodies hidden in the brush for Night's predators, we left that place as soon as uncle returned and reported that no other Chamuqwani were following.Though no one blamed me for the near disaster, I felt terrible. Hoping to make amends and prevent another mishap

I persuaded Owl to watch for enemies on our back trail that night as we hurried south into the more settled areas of the Preserve near the agency.

When we camped just after dawn in a thicket of aspens Uncle approached me with a bundle of sacred leaves in hand. Before giving it to me he took out his knife and opened a gash on his arm, dripped his blood onto the bundle and then offered it to me.

"I realized during our ride that we had, neither given thanks for the successful raid on the rancha, nor asked the Spirits who come to you, for their help on our current mission." When I hesitated he proffered the bundle again. "I offer my blood in thanks, and as a prayer for their aid in avoiding all enemy snares set for us, and rescuing our relatives from the undeserved Chamuqwani vengeance."

I took the offered gift, thanked him and said I would place the bundle in the flames when next I prayed.

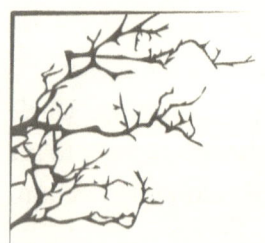

Chapter Twelve

By daybreak we were within a short distance of the agency and could go no farther till dark. We hid ourselves and the horses among the pines on the eastern side of willow creek. Below us a ragged camp of the lay-about agency people sprawled among heaps of refuge. As we watched ragged men and women rummaged through the agency's garbage, searching for something to eat or trade. The smell wafting up the hill towards us was horrible.

When we had made a fireless camp and rested for a time Nachoga called us together for a council. Sun was nearing the midway path in his journey across the sky by that time. Crouching in a small circle with the lacy branches of a juniper overhead Nachoga said to Uncle, "I think your nephew there," he pointed with his lips to Samiqwas, "is worried about his father. He wants to go check and see if he is doing all right. Is that not so, young warrior?"

Startled Samiqwas glanced up from the design he was idly drawing in the sand with a twig. "Me, war leader?"

Nachoga smiled, showing lots of teeth. "Yes you. Didn't you tell me once that your father has a problem with drinking too much of the Chamuqwani waskyja? Well, as a good son I think it's time you check on him. And while you are doing that you can listen to the agency gossip and learn if the events shown to our Puhani here have happened yet."

Nachoga leaned forward and fixed him with green cougar eyes. "Can you do that for me, young warrior? Don't give yourself away by asking too many questions, but we need to know first where your grandfather and aunty are, before we risk going down there to rescue them and find ourselves caught in a trap."

Before Samiqwas could answer Uncle Tli declared, "If my nephew is going to the agency then I am going with him."

"No you are not! Is your wish to commit suicide stronger than your Fox's cunning? Listen to the one I see hovering in your Spirit Fire that is trying to talk to you. No one is going to take much interest in a dirty ragged boy who has come around looking for his drunken father. But you—you are known to be an outlaw and will be recognized.

"Someone will tell the soldiers." His lips twitched as if he was about to smile. "And I don't want to have to rescue you along with the rest of your family." It took a bit more arguing, but eventually Tli saw the wisdom in the war leader's plan.

"Maybe I should go with Samiqwas," I suggested when all was settled. "I could speak to you mind-to-mind and tell you what you and Uncle need to know."

"That is a good suggestion and speaks to the honor of your lineage and bravery, but I suspect that it would be as dangerous for you to go down there by day, young Puhani, as your uncle. No it wouldn't be wise. You will remain here—and rest. We will need all the Puwa you can conjure for us later."

Nearly as ragged and dirty as the people we could see in the camp below us it didn't take much of a disguise for Samiqwas to look the part of just another boy who hung around the agency looking for handouts and able to do small chores for anyone willing to pay him. Leaving his horse with us Samiqwas headed down the slope for the agency, by-passing the camp and coming to the agency from a different direction.

Giving him time to be well on his way Nachoga then put his own plan into action. Donning his disguise as a Chamuqwani tramp, he took up the saddle of one of the dead men, and studied the horses with a critical eye.

"Though he is a fine horse and I like riding him, I think it would be best to leave the gray with you, brother, and take the brown. If one man could recognize him then maybe others will too."

"If you were planning to go to the agency yourself, why did you send my nephew?" Uncle grumbled as he brought over the brown horse for Nachoga.

"I wanted to give the young warrior a sense of confidence in his own skill and wit, but I had no intentions of letting him do all the scouting alone."

Tli thought about it for a long moment, and then grunted his agreement. "What will you tell the soldiers about why you are there?"

Climbing atop the horse Nachoga adjusted his Chamuqwani hat and smiled down at us. "Why, I will tell anyone who asks that the rancha boss-man sent me to scout for his cai." He took out the small waskyja flask from inside his dirty shirt and shook it to show it was empty. "And, searching for the lost beasts is thirsty work, so I come to find more drink and hear the news."

KEEPING AN EYE ON THE horses, Uncle and I took turns sleeping throughout the rest of that day and into the evening. I used a touch of my Qwakaiva to keep the horses quiet so they wouldn't give us away to people passing along the road below. Uncle was growing impatient when Nachoga finally spoke into my mind.

<<Your relatives are here. I witnessed the scene you were shown in your special string, Puhani. They plan to whip your mother and maybe hang your grandfather. I think the agent and the soldier commander want to use him as an example to discourage others from defying their laws. Not sure but maybe they will do this terrible thing day after tomorrow. So we come just in time.>>

Recalling how Grandfather had collapsed after trying to destroy chief Eagan, I asked, <<Is my grandfather all right?>>

<<He was unconscious when they dragged him and your mother into the hut they call their jail. I had Samiqwas check on them a short time ago. He is conscious now and will probably recover soon.

<<The convert traitor is in much worse shape, so they say. He is abed in the priest's house with many people standing around outside praying for his recovery. Samiqwas says your uncle Royston is among them, but it's better if you don't tell Tli. He will only complicate our escape attempt if he knows. I don't trust him not to try to kill his brother—even though as the war leader I told him no.

<<Some of the soldiers and traders are already celebrating by drinking. The word has gone out and there are many people here—and more coming tomorrow. I am sending your cousin back to you. Bring our horses to the hill

where the agency horses are kept. It may take a while, but wait there until all is quiet. I will tell you more then.>>

Samiqwas showed up as deep twilight turned into full night. Together we managed to slowly make our way through the dark to the hillside above the horse pens. It didn't look like much more had been done on the various rebuilding projects than the last time I had come with my relatives to the agency.

The Thunderer's temple had two new walls—of stone this time, but the stable hadn't been rebuilt, the horses still being kept in hastily built pens on the hillside. I studied them as best I could in the dim light, wondering if I should try to use my Qwakaiva to weaken their gates if Nachoga wished to stampede the horses before we left.

When I asked, he said, <<The army's black smith has made iron clasps for them so we can release them later without using your Qwakaiva. But stay alert, young Puhani. You can best use your power to make sure no convert malicer is near and waiting to pounce when we come for your relatives.>>

When I assured him I would, he added, <<Leave Samiqwas with the horses. I don't want him to be seen with us in case we need him to spy for us again. You and your uncle move closer but don't come to me at the jail until I call you.>>

I relayed his message and then Uncle Tli and I crept down the slope towards the agency. As we approached Uncle threw his blanket over his head and added a bit of a stagger to his walk, leaning on my shoulder from time to time, as if he too had been drinking. We stopped by the wall of a trader's house and crouched in the shadows unable to go further. The open space in front of us was lighted by torches, with several people awake and wandering around. Inside the trading post I could hear drunken singing and the laughter of men and women. On the far side of the open area by the priest's house, a group of converts were loudly praying to their god.

Then I touched Uncle's arm and motioned to the Chamuqwani lurching across the open area stopping to drink from a flask of waskyja. He was making his way slowly towards the jail hut and the guard on duty there. "That's the war leader," I murmured so only he could hear.

We watched as Nachoga staggered over and began talking to the soldier left on guard by the door of the jail hut. At first the man was suspicious but as Nachoga talked they began sharing the flask and joking with one another as if they were old friends.

"I hope he doesn't get too drunk to ride his horse," Uncle grumbled.

"He's not drinking," I whispered back. "The war leader is only pretending to drink when it is his turn."

As we watched the soldier seemed to become very drunk, very fast. <<Circle behind the hut and come up on the side most in the shadows,>> Nachoga said to me.<<This one will be too sleepy to stand much longer. I will need your uncle to help me carry him away into the darkness while you see if your Puwa can open the door.

<<This man doesn't have the key.>> A mental chuckle, <<It seems the fat agent is keeping the key with him, so that no one can steel his prisoners away.>>

We waited for a group of soldiers to pass, heading for their barracks with their arms about several Qwani'Ya women, and then crept to the side of the jail hut in the deep shadows of the trading post.

It didn't take long for the guard to slump forward into the war leaders waiting arms. "Quickly now, Brother, help me drag him into the darkness and strip him of his coat," Nachoga called. Tli appeared in the next moment and they carried the drugged soldier into the shadows. As Tli dragged the drugged man deeper into the night away from the hut, Nachoga returned in another moment wearing the man's dirty soldier coat over top of his other clothes.

With his hat pulled down to shade his face he fumbled with the buttons on his clothing, as if he had gone to take a quick pee and now was back at his post again. <<Come.>> Nachoga said. <<See if your Puwa will open the lock.>>

I came near while he stood in front of me. I studied the door for a moment then I disappeared into the blackness again. I took off my string and quickly formed the pattern of the Aseutl's Gift, placing an image of the door and its lock in the center diamond.

<<O Great Kunai, lend me your Qwakaiva this night so I can help my people,>> I prayed. <<A blood offering has been given. Bless our work and protect us from the evil sent to entrap and kill us.>>

I took several deep breaths and drew in the power from the Earth beneath me and the Night all around me. <<All about me is Qwakaiva,>> I sang in my mind. <<All about me is the power of the Unseen Ones. I come with no malice in my heart, wishing only to use my Qwakaiva for the good of the People. Please help me.>>

I plucked the pattern with a forefinger and allowed my intent to guide my Qwakaiva into the heart of the lock. Letting my spirit hand touch its inner workings I tapped and twisted and at last felt the lock's grip give way and open.

I was about to tell the war leader of my success when I became aware of another person approaching the hut and hastily crouched in the shadows once more. Peering around the corner of the hut I saw it was no soldier, but a Qwani'Ya man wearing Chamuqwani clothing like most of the converts did.

And when he spoke to Nachoga I knew him. It was Uncle Royston. I shook like a leaf in the wind, knowing Uncle Tli was near and fearing what he would do next when he discovered that fact. Hastily I made my war leader aware of who had come calling.

Nachoga raise the soldier's long thunder weapon and growled, "Halt!" just as any other soldier would.

Then in his best Chamuqwani Uncle Royston said, "Please, Sergeant I want talk prisoner beg woman tell where my daughter. I want daughter come home—where she belong."

Still pointing the thunder weapon at Uncle Royston Nachoga repeated, "No talk with prisoners. I got orders. You go way now." He motioned with his weapon for Royston to leave, but Uncle stood his ground.

"Please. Have children you? Maybe you understand how me worry if you do. Me just want talk."

For a long moment Nachoga remained silent red spears of anger shooting from his Spirit Fire. I sensed his raw emotions as he struggled to gain control. At last he said in a voice as cold as the ice in winter, "I had children; they are dead now. You go."

"Dead? Oh I sorry hear that. I pray for them. Were they baptised in Mighty Djoven's sweet smoke before die?"

"No and I don't want or need your prayers," Nachoga growled and made a threatening motion with his weapon. "Go. Now!"

Surprised by his anger Royston stepped back. Taking in a deep breath he finally said, "I sorry all I want is talk with my relatives. If sister tell me truth and father ask priest and agent for mercy, no one need die. Maybe only send to prison over mountains. I no want relatives die."

Then a disgusted snort came from the darkness behind me. "Should have thought of that before you turned traitor once again and betrayed them to the Chamuqwani and the malicer priests, brother," Tli said and stepped out of the shadows. Nachoga growled a bad Chamuqwani curse.

Startled, Royston's mouth dropped open. Tli laughed but there was no mirth in the sound. "I told you once I was going to kill you for your treachery and now I've come to do just that." Tli drew his knife and took a swipe at his brother.

"Uncle Tli, no," I said and rushed to grab his arm. "It is the worst of evil Qwakaiva to kill blood kin."

With a snarl he pushed me to the ground and made another pass with his knife at his brother, this time cutting a long gash across his chest which soon blossomed red. "This traitor is no kin to me—even the fat agent says so."

"Yes, I'm glad Agent Daglish gave you a different name, because I don't want to be related to a murdering outlaw like you either," Royston said, his voice rising with indignation. He touched his chest and seemed surprised when his fingers came away dark with blood. Eyes wide and pleading, Uncle Royston glanced at Nachoga, taking him for a soldier who would help him. "This man outlaw. You put in jail. I tell agent," he said switching languages.

When he turned to get the soldiers, Nachoga hit him in the jaw with his thunder weapon, silencing Uncle Royston and dropping him to his knees. Hurriedly, the war leader glanced around to see if so many people clustered by the jail hut had attracted the attention of anyone else awake.

Nachoga gave Tli a disgusted look. "Why you do this now? I tell you we here to get sister and father, not take revenge on brother."

Leveling his weapon at Tli, more red spikes of rage shooting out from his Spirit Fire, Nachoga growled, "Weapon make too much noise or me kill you—both you right now, stupid dog fucker. You want everybody here die cause you mad at brother?"

I shared my war leader's worry. There were few people awake by then, the drunken reverie almost silenced, but Uncle Royston might be missed at the praying vigil and a worried convert come looking for him. And the growing conflict between the two brothers could gather an audience of soldiers at any moment.

By this time Royston had gotten to his feet. Realizing that Nachoga wasn't the soldier he'd thought him to be, he drew his own knife and made a lunge for his brother.

<<Puhani, open that door and get your relatives out of there—now. I will deal with these stupid dog turds.>>

I needed no further urging, and flung open the door as Nachoga ignored the drawn knives and stepped between them, cursing them both in several languages.

Hearing the talk outside, Mother and Grandfather were awake and standing just inside the door. They blinked in the growing light but came out at my whispered urging. When she saw it was me, Mother hugged me and whispered, "Oh, my son. I knew you would come for us."

When Grandfather saw a wounded Royston and Tli's red knife he staggered and would have fallen if Mother and I hadn't caught him. "Oh, my children, please don't do this to each other," he cried. "I would rather hang from a Chamuqwani rope than see you hurt one another. Please for the sake of your dead mother's ghost, don't do this!"

I saw that by this time Tli too had a gash on his arm and Royston another across his middle. Nachoga too was bleeding. At their father's words both men paused long enough for the war leader to step in and deliver a powerful blow of his fist to each man dropping Tli to his knees and Royston to the ground.

Retrieving both weapons Nachoga stepped back. Breathing hard, he yanked Tli to his feet. "What fuck is wrong with you, dog turd? Do you want get us all killed?" he snarled and gave him a hard shove in the direction of the horses that almost dropped Tli to his knees again. "Take your relatives to the horses. Your father isn't well. You need to help him. Never mind your vengeance now."

Tli staggered but remained defiant. "What about my brother? If we don't kill him he will sound the alarm."

"No he won't; leave him to me. Go—now! Puhani, go with them—help your mother. She frightened and confused right now."

<<And stay in touch with me. Tell me right away if your uncle tries to do anything else stupid.>>

I didn't want to leave him, but I knew he spoke true. So I quickly took Mother's hand, while Tli threw Grandfather's arm over his shoulder and half pulled, half carried his father up the slope into the darkness.

Samiqwas met us with the horses when he saw us coming. Tli climbed on his spotted horse and reached down a hand for his father. "Come on, climb up behind me. Samiqwas, help your grandfather."

Still hesitating Grandfather said, "I don't understand, Son. What are you and the boys doing here?"

"Did you think I was going to let them hang you, old man? Now get on this horse! We ride. Talk later."

Samiqwas helped him and he straddled Tli's horse, grabbing onto his waist. Next my cousin turned to me, seeing I was leading the gray, and already atop my own horse, he said, "What are you doing, porcupine brain?"

"Go with Uncle and take Amima with you. I need to bring the war leader his horse. He may need it. That brown wasn't a very good mount."

"There's trouble then?" he murmured as he started to help mother onto his horse.

"Yes, and Tli started it—almost got us killed—Amima can tell you about it as you go. I will try to speak to Grandfather with Qwakaiva and let you know Nachoga's orders and what's happening."

"Be careful, my son," Mother said.

"I will," I promised her.

"I love you, little Rock Squirrel."

Samiqwas laughed.

As they rode away I heard mother ask, "Who was that Chamuqwani that helped us—and who is Nachoga?"

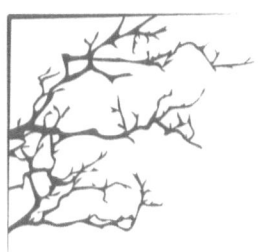

Chapter Thirteen

Nachoga met me as I came near the horse pens. "Where is my uncle Royston?" I asked as he took the reins of the gray.

Swinging into his saddle, he said, "I left him unconscious over there." He pointed to a half-covered body lying in a pile of stinking dung and debris outside the nearest pen. Riding to the gate he flipped up the latch and the gate swung open. Moving to the next he motioned for me to get the other one.

I had just opened it when a man tasked with guarding the horses saw us and shouted a warning. Nachoga drew his thunder weapon and fired. There was a loud boom and a flash of light, but I couldn't tell if he had hit his target, for at almost the same moment a horse screamed and plunged for the open gate beside me.

My mare frightened by the noise cried out, too, and then jumped sidewise as the panicked horse and the others in the pen ran past us. I pulled hard on her reins then gave up and let her run, trying desperately to keep from falling off her back.

Behind me a cougar screamed and the night burst into chaos as more thunder weapons exploded and men shouted. Nachoga and his Spirit Helper answered with another enraged scream, challenging the enemy. By that time hearing the weapons and thinking a cougar was there to eat them, the rest of the agency's panicked horses were thundering out of their enclosures to scatter into the night.

When I gained control of my mare at last I headed away from the agency. <<War leader, where are you? I'm on the creek road, heading north. Are you all right?>>

Nachoga didn't answer, but soon I heard a horse pounding down the road behind me. A few moments later he caught up and passed, my mare willingly falling in behind him as we raced on through the night.

It was starting to get light in the east, we had little time to escape before the soldiers caught their horses and came after us. <<Young Puhani, you know this area better than I do,>> Nachoga said when we had ridden a while longer. <<We need to cross the creek and head west into the desert. Where is a place where we can ford the creek?>>

<<The nearest one will be just north of the convert settlement where I lived with my mother and grandparents,>> I told him. <<But it may not be safe to cross there. We could be seen from the settlement.>>

<<We will have to take that chance. Maybe most of them are already at the agency and those who aren't won't see—follow us.>>

Pulling his horse back he allowed me to take the lead. As I passed him I noticed in the growing light that in spite of the soldier's dark coat to mask it, there was a red stain on his left shoulder that seemed to be getting larger as we rode. I made no comment but wondered how bad his wound was. Swallowing my panic I urged my mare forward, my eyes scanning the brush for the game trail leading to the ford.

As we passed the convert houses I saw that a few people were awake and must have seen us, but no one challenged us and no thunder weapons boomed. Few Qwani'Ya people had horses at that time, so maybe Nachoga's Chamuqwani hat and clothes fooled them in the dim light. I hoped so.

I found the trail soon after we passed the settlement and we turned off the main road. I would have stopped to mask our trail, but he shook his head. "Don't waste your Puwa. If this is the nearest ford those who follow will know we went this way."

We crossed and headed into the brush, then in a rocky patch past my aspen thicket refuge, Nachoga told me to turn and retrace our path back to the ford. Entering the water again we walked the horses up stream for a while and then crossed and headed back into the brush. This time he did let me stop long enough to erase our tracks.

It was nearly full day and I could see he was tiring. "We need to stop soon so I can wash and bind your wound." When he would have argued with me, I growled, "You are bleeding and soon will be leaving a blood trail for men and dogs to follow. So before you get too weak to stay on that horse we need to find shelter and rest."

He stopped but didn't get off the gray. "All right, I will let you clean and bind the wound, but no more. I want to reach the hidden canyon where Tuumaz met you and your uncle with the horses when you joined us. That's where I told Tli to wait for us."

At the stream I had allowed my blanket to drag through the creek to clean and wet it. Getting off my mare I cut a couple strips off it and also picked some broad flat leaves I knew were good for stopping blood. Still atop his horse he waited for me. Climbing back on my mare I chewed them to a pulp in my mouth. Suspecting he wouldn't be able to remount if he got down for my doctoring I washed the wound then spat out the green leaf paste and rubbed it in, then wrapped the damp cloth around his shoulder and chest to stop any blood from marking our trail. It was awkward to clean and bind his shoulder on horseback, but I managed.

He neither flinched, nor cried out as I worked, though I knew the wound was giving him a lot of pain. It was deep and there might still be some of the little iron pieces inside his flesh. I hoped Grandfather was well enough to help him when we caught up to the others.

In spite of his assurances to the contrary I sensed when I touched him how truly weak he was, so I shared some of my Qwakaiva with him as I sometimes had done with my old mentor when he had need of my youth and strength for his own conjuring. Nachoga's eyes widened as he felt my Qwakaiva, but accepted my gift without comment.

During the long ride that fearful day I let Nachoga go on alone a few times while I used my Gift to mask our back trail, and I borrowed Eagle's keen sight to watch to see no enemy followed. I was also able to contact Grandfather and have him relay a message to Uncle Tli about what had happened.

And though he hadn't told me to do so, I searched out and found Utsiyonti. I briefly told him Nachoga was wounded and asked he come with some of the warriors to meet us, and help in case the soldiers caught up to us.

But in spite of my gift of Qwakaiva, the war leader was barely able to stay atop his horse by the time we reached the little hidden canyon in early evening. Fortunately the others were there to meet us, and Uncle helped me get the grumbling and cursing Nachoga off his horse and onto a blanket by the fire.

After helping Samiqwas take care of our horses I returned with him to check on the war leader. Lifting the can from the rocks by the fire, I poured myself some tea. Across from me, Mother was bathing and dressing the minor wounds on his arms and chest, while Grandfather focused his attention on the more serious wound in Nachoga's shoulder. With his own minor wounds already bandaged, Uncle Tli was drinking a cup of tea and watching the proceedings,with a grim expression.

I gave him a disgusted glare. Like Nachoga and Chugai had said, Uncle was a stupid dog turd—and our near disaster was his fault. As if my strong emotions had the power to actually cut him, Uncle met my gaze, then dropped his eyes and stared into the flames. Returning my attention to the healers, I shivered as fear ran down my spine. With a shock I realized that I admired this strange Chamuqwani-Kukiya man, who treated me like a valued member of his warband and not just a child to be ignored.

If Nachoga sickened and died of his injury, what would I do? He was a fearless and experienced war leader who fought for the protection and the good of the People. What would happen to all of us if he wasn't here to protect us...

Swallowing down my dark musings I went over to them and crouched beside Grandfather. Putting down my nearly empty cup, I asked, "What can I do to help?"

Still deep into his conjuring, Grandfather remained silent with hands atop the gaping wound, his whole being centered on the healing. I could see in his Spirit Fire the Otter who lent him power flickering in and out, as his Qwakaihi tried to draw strength from such a distant source.

Breaking in on my observation mother finally answered, "Appi says that there are still pieces of iron in the wound. He is trying to draw them out without cutting and injuring the shoulder more. The healing will go faster if he can do it this way."

Ah, but could he? Grandfather had used a lot of his Qwakaiva in his battle with the convert specter back at the agency. And Qwa'osi The Otter from whom he drew his power lived by Big Ice Lake to the north, far away from this dry desert country.

Breaking another of our ancient laws, like with Nachoga, I didn't ask his permission to give him power using my Gift. I simply moved over, put my hands on his back and drew up Qwakaiva from the Black Waters under the Earth, as only one favored by Kunai could do.

He resisted me at first, until I snarled into his mind, <<Don't fight me, Otter's Qwakaihi. You need what one of Co'yeh's kin can give you if you want to help this man survive his wounds.>> At my words he mastered his revulsion for taking aid from one who was fathered by a Qwa'Nayhi Seal man, the Otter's rival, and let me continue pouringQwakaiva into his failing human body until the healing was complete.

When he had finished and fell exhausted backwards into my waiting arms, five tiny pieces of iron were clutched in one hand.

NEXT MORNING I WOKE with Sun's light on the eastern horizon. Thinking we would be moving on as soon as we cooked and ate a hasty meal, I threw off my blanket and headed to help care for the horses. I was still exhausted, my head ached and my hands shook as I pulled out my twig and peed.

I took my little mare to drink then stumbled back to our camp and flopped down by Fire's stone nest. Mother looked up from feeding hungry Fire some branches and smiled. Two blanketed, unmoving lumps lay nearby. "Sit, my Son you look tired," she said in a low voice. "I sent Samiqwas to get water further up the canyon, away from the place the horses have muddied. When he returns, I will make everyone breakfast."

I brushed hair off my face and stared at the light coming through the trees and listened to the pounding drum in my head. "Where's Uncle? When he wakes the war leader will want us to go—"

"Oh, we aren't going anywhere today," she told me in that firm no-nonsense voice that Grandmother used to use when she would stand no arguments to her will. "And I told your lazy uncle to go hunting. Sick and injured people need fresh meat so they can get better faster."

My mouth dropped open. My dreamy gentle mother had never been so forceful, or talked like that before.

"Your Grandfather is far too ill to go anywhere today—and you don't look much better." She announced. Glancing at the other wrapped bundle, she frowned. "And as for him, even if he is the war leader, he will lose this fight, if he tries to argue with me about leaving so soon after all the work we did to save his life."

She nodded to herself. "He may try, but he will lose that battle." Her eyes lost in a distant memory she smiled to herself as she continued to feed Fire. I wondered if she was recalling another time and another injured warrior she had cared for. The Qwa'Nayhi Seal man she had found wounded and nursed back to health, my father.

Samiqwas came back then and Mother poured water into a big can and set it by the happy fire to heat for tea. Rummaging in our stacked saddle bags she found a sack of pounded coussa root and mixed it with water and berries she'd gathered from some bushes growing near the seep. Adding a couple of balls of dry meat and fat that were our usual rations to the pot she set the mush to cook at the edge of the flames.

The good smells of her cooking at last aroused the sleeping men. When she noticed Grandfather was awake Mother crouched beside him, helped him sit up, and then handed him a cup of tea. Though unmoving, Nachoga was awake and watching her through half closed green eyes as still as the big cat who was his Spirit Helper.

When she turned to dish Grandfather a bowl of her mush from the big can Mother noticed him and smiled. Nachoga started to return her smile then grimaced with pain as he got awkwardly to his feet, using only one arm. When he returned from a trip into the trees he sat once more by the fire and Mother handed him a bowl.

Taking the bowl he focused his gaze on me and asked, "Where is your uncle?"

"Hunting, so Amima told me. And Samiqwas is up on the cliff watching for enemies," I said, before he could ask. "I'll go and relieve him after I finish eating." He grunted and returned to his meal.

All was quiet for a time then Grandfather set down his bowl and asked, "Did you kill my son, war leader?"

Nachoga paused with spoon half way to his mouth. Looking Grandfather straight in the eye, he said, "No, Honored Elder, I did not. True,

I made it so that he couldn't tell the soldiers how to follow us, but I left his fate up to the Unseen Ones to decide. He was alive when we left the agency, as your grandson will tell you."

"Thank you." He took a few more mouthfuls then said, "I don't know how much you can remember of what happened after Tas brought you to us last night; I know by then you were in much pain and your great strength was nearly gone. I managed to remove the iron pieces from your shoulder, but the muscle is still quite damaged.

"You may lose some movement in it permanently if you don't take time for it to heal properly."

"Mm, and what does that mean exactly, Elder?"

"It means giving your body time to rest. It means not taking the war trail until the wound has time to grow new blood and muscle, or you may never be able to draw your bow or use those other things again." Grandfather motioned with his chin to the pile of weapons someone had laid near the war leader's blankets.

Nachoga snorted a mirthless laugh. "That is a task easier spoken of than accomplished, Elder. Both our peoples are starving and surrounded by enemies who lie and steal from us. Years ago I pledged my life to the protection and service of my People and our allies. Whether I live, or die heal or not is up to the Unseen Ones. I must continue."

"Your purpose is a noble one, warrior, but I don't think the Cougar I see in your Spirit Fire or the others who guide you would want you to risk your life or injury unnecessarily. I am not saying to change your life's path, I am only saying give yourself time to heal."

"Mm." Nachoga went back to eating while he thought over what Grandfather advised.

"I've been in the western desert among the prophet's people. I might suggest you go there and take my relatives with you. Listen to his words from the Great Ones who watch over our troubled world. He will show us the way to rid ourselves of the Evil that has come among us." And as an added incentive, Grandfather said, "Maybe he can heal your injuries better and faster than can I."

As I rose to my feet to relieve Samiqwas, I said, "I have already contacted Utsiyonti. He is coming with a warband to help us."

When Nachoga opened his mouth to protest—argue—whatever, Mother took his empty bowl, wrapped his blanket about his shoulders, and then firmly urged him to go back to his nest and rest.

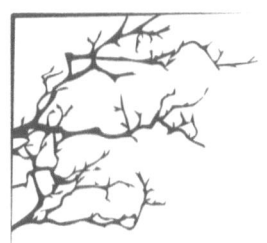

Chapter Fourteen

O n the morning of the fourth day after our escape from the agency Utsiyonti was able to contact me. <<How is the war leader doing?>>

I had just relieved Uncle on sentry duty and was perched on a high outcrop where I could see the rocky passage to the hidden canyon and the open land and brush covered slopes beyond our refuge. Using Hawk's eyes I saw the warriors as they passed from one juniper thicketto another on a nearby slope. Soaring higher I saw no soldiers or other enemies on their back trail.

<<The war leader is grumpy, but healing. That looks like a big war party for an escort, trying to hide itself among those junipers. You aren't being followed, so come in, but disguise your tracks just in case,>> I said.

He was still too far away for me to see his expression with my human eyes, but I sensed his surprise. <<Look up.>> He did and I sensed the amusement in the mental voice as he took note of the hawk floating nearly above them.

<<These men haven't come as an escort. Most of them are heading east to raid the Chamuqwani for meat and other supplies—as am I. Two among us are the Prophet's initiates who will go into the Preserve to speak to others about his teachings. Only Tuumaz, and a healer and her apprentice, will escort you, the wounded Nachoga and the others of your family back west.>>

Thanking Hawk for his aid, I left him to hunt and returned to my human body. <<I will tell them you are coming.>>

<<Good.>>

Still perched in my hiding place I told Nachoga of our visitors then watched as they crept closer. As Sun climbed toward the midpoint of his journey, seven people approached the narrow passage and slipped into our hidden sanctuary. The rest of the warriors hobbled their horses and made camp within the junipers on a nearby slope. Getting permission to leave my post, I jumped down to help care for the horses.

Arriving back at camp I received some surprises that I wasn't counting on. The first came when I joined the people caring for the horses. I had expected Tuumaz but not Thonna. Dressed in a long tunic and leggings with her hair held off her face with a cloth headband, I thought she was another Kukiya youth till she spoke.

Suddenly rooted to the spot, I stared with my mouth dropping open until the spotted horse I was leading nudged me hard in the shoulder, impatient to get to the water. Remembering my task I hastily lead him to the pond, then hobbled him and released him to graze on the long grass and rabbit brush nearby.

Catching up to my friends, I blurted, "Thonna, it's good to see you, but what are you doing here?"

Thonna turned and smiled, then seeing my expression, she put her hands on her hips and scowled. "What does it look like, stupid boy? I'm here to help the warriors when they hunt the Chamuqwani's cai."

"But-but you can't!"

Her scowl deepened and she took a step closer to me. "Why not?"

"B-because you might get hurt—or die!" I stammered, feeling foolish.

By that time our conversation had attracted the attention of a grinning Samiqwas and Tuumaz. "She gonna hit Puhani, if talk more he. Me got pretty green stone me bet."

Samiqwas chuckled. "No bet. Tas isn't smart enough to know when to keep his mouth shut. She's gonna hit'em."

Focusing her glare on them she growled "And you two are next if I start hitting. I have every right to be here. Aunty Ashiqwa gave her permission and my new uncle Talulsit is with the warband out there, so just shut up—all of you."

Pretending to be frightened, the others hurried away still grinning. Thonna swore a Chamuqwani soldier's oath and returned her attention to me.

"Thonna, I'm sorry; I met no offense—I just..." I let my voice trail off unsure how I wanted to continue.

She glared at me for a moment longer then her expression softened. "My name isn't Thonna, Tas. I left that accursed Chamuqwani name behind when I left my father's home. My relatives among the rebels have gifted me with my true name. I am called Xyilaha now."

Xyilaha, the name didn't sound like a name in our language, so maybe she had received it from the Kukiya family her aunt had married into. "Xyilaha, I will try to remember, but if I forget can I still call you, stupid girl instead? Ow!" she hit me, then we both smiled as we walked back to the fire together.

As I took my place in the outer ring around the council fire with the younger people and reached for the hot tea Samiqwas was handing me, I said under my breath, "Good thing you didn't bet him. She *did* hit me."

The corners of his mouth twisted as if he wanted to grin, but thought better of it when he saw Uncle Tli scowl at us.

Looking around the council fire I saw Uncle, Utsiyonti, Nachoga, Mother and Grandfather, as I'd expected, but then I got another surprise. The woman with gray streaks in her long black hair who had seen the images I could make with my string, named Betsiya, sat next to a scar-faced veteran and another seasoned warrior. Thonna, or should I say, Xyilaha, went and sat behind Betsiya.

I hadn't paid much attention to Betsiya back at the outlaws' stronghold. I had too much to learn in too short of time, but I had heard that, like Grandfather her Gift was healing. Betsiya smiled at me then returned her attention to what Grandfather was saying.

"I have no wish to return west with your people, war leader. I have done all I can for you. But my people need to hear the Prophet's message and learn the prayer songs I can teach them. If you have a horse you could lend me, I would be grateful so I can continue my journey."

"Appi, no!" Mother said from her place beside Nachoga. "You are still too weak. When you are rested and have regained your strength then think about continuing your work—" Turning moist, pleading eyes on Nachoga, she begged him to agree with her.

"No, Daughter. I am rested enough. It's time I go on my way. On horseback it would be easier for me, but I will walk otherwise."

"We have extra horses, Elder, that won't be a problem, and the one called Sheikai is with us. I believe his mission is the same as yours," one of the newcomers said.

Grandfather smiled. "Yes, I know him. He is another of Iyantsha's emissaries, as am I. it will be good to travel with him for a time."

Nachoga leaned forward to better see him as he focused his cougar eyes upon Grandfather. "It will not be as easy for you to slip among the enemy's camps as before. When you let yourself be ensnared in the trap set by the Evil Ones, you became an outlaw like the rest of us, and the soldiers and the agent's men will be looking for you. They will hang you as they promised if they catch you. Do you understand that, Elder?"

"Yes, I am sure that is so. Still I must go and trust that the Unseen Ones who have sent me, will also protect me."

When Mother opened her mouth to argue, Nachoga shook his head and put his uninjured hand on her arm and squeezed gently. After another moment she closed her mouth and dropped her eyes.

"Ahho, I pray that it is so," Nachoga said, and dropped the matter.

For the rest of the afternoon the men sat around the fire talking war and safe routes through the dry lands to and from the west. Eqwohi, the tattooed veteran warrior who was leading the raid among the Chamuqwani, asked many questions about the valley where we had stolen the cai, and the other Chamuqwani held lands Nachoga had seen while away from the Preserve.

Then after a meal of deer meat and coussa root and berries I got my last surprise of the day. When the warriors rose to gather their horses Uncle Tli rose with them. Seeing me stare after my retreating uncle, Tuumaz said so only I could hear, "Nobody make him go war now, but Golannah mad him. Better when uncle come back with meat and gifts for People. Then Golannah be happy again."

Well, he had a point. I loved Uncle Tli but I was still mad at him, too. And I wouldn't be sorry to see him gone for a time, either. The only problem was that now we would be left with only three youths, three women, and a wounded warrior if we ran into trouble on our own journey west.

As it turned out, however, only one woman was returning west with us. Betsiya and her apprentice Xyilaha were going with the warband after all.

When Nachoga asked her where she was going Betsiya put her hands on her hips and said, "I'm going with my husband, of course. He will want me to warm his blankets, help with butchering the cai they take, and healing stupid men who get injured. He will need me more than you will, Kukiya brother."

"But, sister, what about my shoulder? Didn't you come to take care of me?"

"I did, but you don't need me now." Betsiya pointed with her lips to Mother standing at his elbow. "Just listen to that one—and do what she tells you. She can care for you as well as I can. And you, I think, will like it better if she does." Betsiya gave Mother a knowing look and the two women shared a secretive smile.

Unable to hide his own grin, Nachoga looked into Mother's eyes, then said, "Maybe I will. Go on then."

Eqwohi chuckled and through an arm around Betsiya and walked her to her horse. Over his shoulder he called, "I will send Dotsuwa and Jenaitsi back to see you get to your brother safely."

Nachoga snorted a laugh. "Dotsuwa isn't going to be happy with you."

"No, but he *will* be happy later, because you are going to give him two new horses when you next go raiding. And as for his son, he is in love and afraid the woman will find another interest while he is gone—so he won't mind when you give him a horse, too."

Nachoga laughed. "You have thought of everything. Maybe you don't need me anymore. Maybe I just stay with the prophet's people, eh?"

Instantly throwing all teasing aside, Eqwohi said, "Rest and heal, Nachoga, Pride of the Kukiya People. We will always need your wisdom and protection."

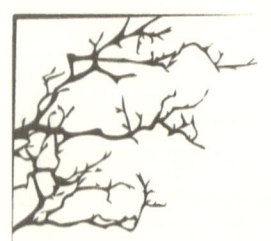

Chapter Fifteen

Our escort showed up at our fire not long after the others left us. I didn't like the muddy colors I could see in their Spirit Fires, and feared we were going to have trouble with them from the beginning. Dotsuwa, the father, was a square-built man with streaks of gray in his wispy long hair. He had hard eyes and a haughty expression curling his thin mouth.

A couple years or so older than Samiqwas, his son Jenaitsi was a younger version of his father in looks, but was maybe a little afraid of him. When his father was near he rarely lifted his eyes from the ground and jumped to do his bidding, but at other times Samiqwas and I found that Jenaitsi tried to get out of his share of camp chores whenever he thought he could get away with it.

Thinking that as a Kukiya he was superior to a Qwani'Ya person, he looked down his nose at Samiqwas and me, and told us just exactly what he thought of such inferior people from the north at every opportunity.

I'd had lots of practice while living at the convert settlement, enduring Charlic and his pack of scavengers, so I just ignored him. But the wolf in Samiqwas bristled at every cutting jibe and I feared there might be trouble as our journey west continued.

Catching Samiqwas alone as we came back from caring for the horses one break time, I said, "Don't bother with the puffed up little grouse. It isn't worth the trouble you will make for the war leader if you give the dog turd the beating we both know he deserves. We only have to put up with him and his father for a few days, so let it go."

"Like a lake seal shedding water off its oily fur, eh?"

"Exactly."

Samiqwas smiled, then becoming thoughtful, he muttered, "His father Dotsuwa, I wish we didn't need him to travel with us for our protection, because he is a dust eating dog turd, too."

I agreed with him, but couldn't help wondering if Eqwohi had taken the opportunity to rid himself of such a disagreeable man at the first chance that presented itself—much to our misfortune.

The trouble began that first evening when we were caring for the horses. Dotsuwa wanted Samiqwas to carry his bag and blanket roll back to our fire. Samiqwas was busy and said he would do it when he finished, but that wasn't good enough for the man. Aiming a blow at Samiqwas's head when he finally bent to pick up the man's bag and blankets, he growled, "Lazy, rotten, fish eater, I tell you take my blankets and make me a bed under the trees by fire—now not in morning."

Samiqwas hopped back before the blow connected, said a bad Chamuqwani word then stalked to our camp without looking back, leaving a cursing Kukiya warrior, and his bags behind.

Finished with my mare I came over and picked up the blankets and bag still lying at the fuming man's feet. "We have been taught to respect our Elders, Kukiya warrior," I said as I lifted them to my shoulder. "He would have carried them, if you had asked him instead of yelling and trying to hit him. It isn't our Qwani'Ya way to beat a person to get them to do what we want, nor did I think it was a Kukiya way either. Only Chamuqwani do that."

I would have carried his things, but before I could take more than a few steps Tuumaz came over and took them from me. Tossing the bags at Dotsuwa's feet he said something to him in their language that soured the man's mood even more. Motioning for me to follow him, we headed back to our fire together. Looking back I saw Dotsuwa angrily gesture to his son to pick up the disputed things and follow us.

At the fire the rich smells of roasting meat and coussa flat cakes baking on a large flat stone made my mouth water. Mother and Nachoga were there already Samiqwas just sitting down to join them.

"The food smells wonderful, Amima," I said as I sat down beside Samiqwas, Tuumaz sitting on my other side.

Mother smiled at me then pointed with her lips to a grass mat where she had laid out a steaming pile of flat cakes and roasted deer meat. Reaching for the can to pour Nachoga some tea, she said, "You boys help yourselves. Everything is ready."

We needed no further urging.

After they had made their beds and unpacked Dotsuwa and his son finally joined us. Like the rest of us Jenaitsi came over and helped himself to cakes and meat, but Dotsuwa remained where he was—glaring at everyone.

I noticed that Mother had cut up Nachoga's meat to make it easier for a one handed man to eat. Smiling and joking with him she hovered near him, making sure he had everything he needed. Watching them seemed to sour Dotsuwa's mood even further.

When the war leader had finished she handed him another cup of tea then rose and announced, "That tea contains some herbs father left to help you sleep and aid the healing. I will change the wrappings on your shoulder now before you get too sleepy."

As she passed him, Dotsuwa looked to see if Nachoga was watching, then reached out a hand and grabbed her arm. "He can wait for that. Bring me food first, Woman, and be quick about it."

Startled, Mother stared mouth dropping open. Then her mouth shut and she jerked her arm out of his grasp. In a level voice, she said, "As I said, Kukiya Man, the food is ready help yourself. I am neither your wife nor your slave."

Dotsuwa curled his lip. "So you want to be only *his* slave?"

Mother stepped back in case he tried to grab her again. "I am no one's slave."

As she went to get the clean wrappings Nachoga chuckled and fixed him with his piercing cougar stare. "See that you remember that, warrior. The woman and the other Qwani'Ya peoples here around this fire are honored allies of the People. They are well-loved by me and my brother, so have a care and treat them with respect."

Dotsuwa snorted. "Some say, that unlike a true son of the People your brother has become too friendly with certain Chamuqwani and other *outsiders*. They say you and he have brought bad Puwa among the People and maybe brought these pale-skinned invaders to our land."

Even in the ruddy firelight I could see Nachoga's face turn red, but he took a deep breath before answering. In a hard voice he said, "Those who have nothing better to do with their time say lots of stupid things. My brother and I have strong Puwa that we use for the good of all. When those who chatter like noisy jays have fed the people and accomplished great deeds in war, then they will have the right to comment about what we do, and who we claim as allies."

WE HAD PLANNED TO LEAVE early the next morning, but during the night it rained and our leaving was delayed until the rain slowed next day. We spent a miserable night with only smoky fires for heat, tucked in hastily made branch-covered lean-tos among the pines. When we finally got started it was midmorning. Once outside the hidden canyon we found thick mud in the ravines and gusting winds on the higher slopes which slowed our progress further.

Utsiyonti and the warriors had left with us extra blankets and supplies, which was good, but still Dotsuwa complained about the weather, the slowness of our pace and anything else he could think of, whenever he returned from a scout to report.

Over the following days as we traveled ever westward Sun's heat became fierce, to our northern way of thinking, but the Kukiya seemed not to notice. The land dried, creeks shrinking to only muddy puddles when we could find them at all in the deep ravines. Sagebrush, scrub pine and juniper gave way to bunchgrass and long stretches of red sand on the slopes below twisted rock formations. Traveling in such open country was a challenge for people who wished to go in secret, so often we journeyed at night, or in the gray time before Sun awoke.

In spite of his injury Nachoga kept us going at a grueling pace. Still a newcomer to horseback riding, Mother usually rode just behind or next to Nachoga so he could keep an eye on her. When his attention was elsewhere I would catch Mother giving him anxious looks, worried no doubt that he might sicken before we could reach the Prophet's healers if he overexerted himself.

When I could persuade a friendly bird to lend me their eyes I did as much scouting as possible, Samiqwas leading my mare and me tied to her back.

I saw no soldiers, but on my last pass over the trail ahead that day I did notice two Chamuqwani with a pack mule over the next ridge, heading west down the same trail we were traveling.

As I released Hawk and settled once more into my own flesh, I heard Jenaitsi say to Samiqwas, "What matter that lazy boy? Him sick or just want nap?"

Jenaitsi repeated his taunt several times, before he got an answer. Through gritted teeth Samiqwas snarled, "He's scouting."

Jenaitsi snorted. "Look like him sleep to me. My father scout, Tuumaz scout, they good Kukiya men. No need stupid, lazy dog-fucking boy, scout."

At that point I opened my eyes and before Samiqwas could do or say anything, I said, "There are two Chamuqwani with a pack mule over the next ridge in front of us. I need to tell the war leader."

Leaving the dog turd with his mouth hanging open Samiqwas clucked to his horse and we moved to catch up to Nachoga and Mother.

They were walking their horses side-by-side and talking softly and looking into each other's eyes. At our approach they broke apart Mother dropping back at the next wide point in the trail so we could approach.

"What is it, Young Puhani?"

Wounded shoulder and arm in a sling and a blanket thrown around his back and pinned in place across his chest with a stick,he looked tired, but still had the Qwakaiva to look at me with his green cougar eyes as he had always done. "There are Chamuqwani ahead," I said.

His eyes flicked from side to side, evaluating the land for concealment or a place that could be defensible in a fight. There was nothing near to hand but a small thicket of nut pines. Moving off the trail he motioned for us to head for the thicket. "Soldiers? How many Chamuqwani?"

"No soldiers. Only two Chamuqwani, wearing clothes like—like yours when you go spy on rancha men. They have a pack mule with them."

He snorted in disgust. "Probably miners then. In spite of treaty, and this Preserve land, they come." He broke off as he saw Dotsuwa coming down the trail to report.

By this time Jenaitsi, too had joined us, and once again his mouth dropped open when he heard his father's report echo what I had just said.

"What you want do, war leader? I take Tuumaz and my son and we go kill them, eh? You can stay here with woman and children."

Outwardly Nachoga's expression never changed, but I could see the red spikes of anger at the man's implied insult, and frustration at his own weakness. "Or we could just stay out of sight until we see if they are going to cause us a problem," he countered.

Dotsuwa spat in disgust, then he snarled, "What! You think they are your lost relatives, maybe? They are invaders—enemy. Whether they make trouble for us or no, they need to die this is Kukiya land!"

Nachoga's expression remained blank, but he couldn't control the red flush that colored his paler Chamuqwani skin. His hand coming to rest on the butt of the small thunder weapon he still carried at his hip, he fixed the two warriors with his green cougar stare. In his Spirit Fire the big cat snarled. "If you are so unhappy to stay with us in spite of the horses you were promised, then maybe you go back to Eqwohi, eh? We will manage without you.

"True, those men shouldn't be on our land—Kukiya land, but right now there are also many soldiers on *our land*. If men are killed and soldiers, hear the boom of Chamuqwani weapons and find out we kill Chamuqwani miners, then more trouble for the People. I say leave them for now." I could feel his Qwakaiva gathering as he stared down the pair. "So, you and your son go watch the Chamuqwani—or go back to Eqwohi and forget about my horses."

Muttering a curse Dotsuwa wheeled his horse about and with Jenaitsi following they headed up the trail to check on the miners.

I stared after them for a time then broke the silence by asking, "What would you like me to do, war leader?"

He studied me critically with his Spirit Sight for a long moment, then said, "Nothing for now, Puhani. Tuumaz and your cousin can scout our back trail for a time. I may need your Qwakaiva strong later. Don't tire yourself doing tasks others can do now."

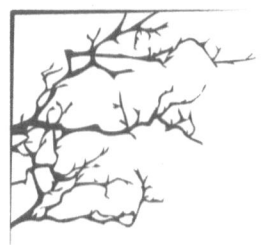

Chapter Sixteen

Two more days passed with no further sightings of an enemy. Moving ever westward into a broken land of rocky ledges and canyons we kept an eye on the minors, but they seemed oblivious of our presence. They acted like they knew where they were going, however, and that aroused our curiosity.

Instead of going around them Nachoga, Tuumaz and Dotsuwa took council and decided to move at their slower pace to try and discover what mischief they were up to. And so Samiqwas and the warriors took turns spying on them.

As we were about to stop for the mid-day rest, Dotsuwa and his son rode back to us, both men carrying new thunder weapons on their saddles and Jenaitsi dragging the miners' mule behind him on a lead rope.

Anger darkening his features Nachoga rose to meet them. When they stopped in front of him, he said. "I thought we agreed to leave the miners alone until we discovered what they were up to on our land. What happened?"

Dotsuwa smirked. "They saw us, so we had to kill them. And we know what they are doing on our land anyway."

"Oh? What?"

For answer Dotsuwa removed a small pouch from his shirt, opened its string top and displayed a palm full of yellow rocks and sand for Nachoga's inspection. "Digging for this is what the dog fuckers were up to."

Mother gasped. We all knew what it meant. These Chamuqwani had discovered the golden rocks they so highly prised. The golden rocks that had caused so much heart-ache and death for both our peoples—and now, here on Kukiya land, the nightmare was beginning again.

Nachoga's expression hardened. "I was afraid of this. These men must have discovered the golden rock then went to a Chamuqwani village to buy supplies so they could return to our land and dig more rocks."

"Yes, war leader, you speak true and that why we kill them," Dotsuwa said.

Nachoga grunted his agreement, thoughtfully stroking his chin where a golden stubble of hair was starting to grow.

"We can use the extra supplies but we should find their camp and send people back to destroy all evidence of them being here," Tuumaz added.

"It may be too late for that," Nachoga said pointing with his lips to the dusty mule. "They have already been to a Chamuqwani place. They probably didn't tell the people there where they found the yellow rocks, but the gold they had to sell would have made other Chamuqwani interested in finding more. And looking on our land will be one of the first places they come. Did you find their camp before you killed them, or do we need to waste time looking for it?"

Dotsuwa nodded. "We find it." Looking grim he pointed with his lips towards a tawny lump visible through the heat haze on the western horizon. "It is near the base of Red Rock Bute up the slope from Sandy Creek. They make a pit house, but not good, too close to Creek. It would have filled with water when floods come."

"I want to see it," Nachoga said. "Maybe they will have more yellow rocks there for others to find, if we don't take them away first."

"Pit house is not far; we can stay there tonight. It have water and grasses for horses nearby. Then we look around more in the morning."

When we arrived at the spot in late afternoon we saw how the miners had abused the Earth with their greedy search. Where grasses and shrubs once covered the lower slope of the butte, now the hillside was pockmarked with several bare patches where the rock had been exposed to the miners' picks and shovels.

Even to my poorly trained eye, the pit house seemed made by an inexperienced hand and ready to cave in at any moment. Garbage was everywhere, rusted cans, empty waskyja bottles, scraps of bone and other awful thrown together in untidy mounds or just left near the house to rot.

Adding to the bad smells and mess, the Kukiya hadn't bothered to drag away evidence of their slaughter. The miners sprawled in a mangled heap just outside their house. A pool of drying blood darkened the sand near the entrance already attracting a cloud of insects. Overhead a few vultures circled waiting for us to leave.

I saw the ghosts of the men watching us with mournful dead eyes, and I shivered as they called out to me, begging me to help them. Thinking of my own dead, I hardened my heart against them. <<No, I won't help you. Look where your greed and theft of Kukiya land has got you, stupid Chamuqwani?>>

They were confused and angry, but also so alien. Much to my regret later, at that time in my life I didn't know how to help them—nor did I want to.

Samiqwas grabbed Mother's horse as it shied at the blood sent. She must have felt the horses' unease as well because she said to Nachoga, "This is a bad place. Do we have to stay here tonight?"

"No we will camp up the creek. Tomorrow my warriors and I will come back and take away what we can use. Then we will go on our way to the Prophet's encampment."

Mother seemed relieved at that, but when she studied Nachoga her expression was still troubled. When the Kukiya and Samiqwas had wandered away to explore the area, she moved her horse closer and spoke to him softly, "I know you don't want to, but you need to take the opportunity to rest tomorrow. There is still blood seeping through the wrappings at night when I change them. You aren't strong enough to do everything you want to do—or think you should do—and if you catch a fever..."

Nachoga grunted and moved his horse away, calling for Tuumaz to scout up the creek for a good camping spot. Dismounting outside the pit house he bent and stepped inside.

Mother sighed and urged her horse to follow Tuumaz up the creek. To get away from the yammering ghosts I followed her.

Noticing the vultures still circling overhead I decided to do a little scouting and I wanted a protected place away from the disharmony where I could leave my body and search. With the warriors busy with other tasks I called to Samiqwas and Jenaitsi, who were just dragging away one of the bodies into the brush. I pointed to a grassy rock shelf down the creek on our back trail. "I'm going to scout. Tell the war leader."

I retraced my steps, then dismounted and hobbled my mare to graze on the tempting green shoots. Walking to a shady spot I dug out a hollow in the sand and lay down. I was surprised when Rattlesnake slithered out from among the nearby rocks and joined me.She tucked herself next to my side, and said, <<I will keep watch for you.>>

<<Thank you, Honored One.>> Relieved and grateful, I let my Spirit fly up to greet Vulture's kin soaring above.

<<Since you are just waiting around for my relatives to finish,>> I called to them, << how about one of you flying with me and lending me your keen sight for a while? I promise you won't miss the feast they are preparing for you.>>

With Vulture lending me his eyes we flew Creek's ravine in both directions. We saw no enemies, or other relatives. Not wanting to go back so soon, I stayed with Vulture and watched my mother and Tuumaz pick a nice sheltered spot up Creek's sandy bed that had a deep pool of clear green water among a stand of cottonwoods and willows. Circling back I saw Samiqwas bringing our horses to drink at the creek downstream from the cottonwoods.

Up the slope from the miners' house Dotsuwa and Jenaitsi hacked up the now naked bodies and scattered the remains on a nearby slope to make it easier for the deserts predators to carry away all evidence of what had happened to the minors. Nachoga, I assumed, was still inside the miners' dwelling sorting through their things. I could see a growing mound of usable gear piling up outside the entrance.

A while later Vulture and I were circling back from another pass down our back trail when Rattlesnake's angry whir sounded a warning in my mind. Leaving Vulture to his own interests I sprang quickly back into my vulnerable flesh.

What I saw when I returned was Jenaitsi standing over me with a big rock in his hand. An angry snake had risen from my side with head raised and fangs dripping, ready to strike. Remaining still so as not to frighten her further, I said, "If you try to smash my head with that rock she will get you even if you hit me. Toss the rock behind you and walk backwards slowly."

Eyes wide he did as I suggested. "I-I wasn't trying to hit you," he muttered. "The war leader sent me to get you and I saw the snake..."

He broke off as I sat up letting Rattlesnake shift her position to wrap around my chest as I stood. "Mm. Well, you have delivered your message. Best you go now."

He needed no further urging. Smelly fish guts, I wasn't sure I believed him, but now that he knew I was protected by powerful allies, it might give him pause in future if he sought another opportunity to harm me. Thanking Rattlesnake for the timely warning, I released her in the brush and went to get my mare.

The campsite Tuumaz and Mother found was restful, the ancient tree and the cool green water a true blessing in the heat and dryness of its desert surroundings. When I commented about it to Nachoga that night as we ate, he nodded and explained, "Sandy Creek is born from a spring deep under the mountain there." He pointed with his chin to a rocky butte glowing red in Sun's dying fire.

Another amazing thing I remember about that night was the sweet golden fruit packed inside one of the miner's big cans that Mother opened.Nachoga said the fruit was called peaches in the Chamuqwani language. They were amazing! Mother made the war leader a tea with herbs and some of the golden liquid that was also in the jar, and the rest she added to a tasty porridge the next morning.

There were more cans that we could have opened, but Mother took charge of them and later when Nachoga and Tuumaz were elsewhere trouble started when she refused to give Dotsuwa and his son some when they demanded them.

Samiqwas and I were just coming back from setting our nightly snares when we heard Dotsuwa's angry voice by the fire shouting at my mother. I would have rushed in blindly to defend her, when Samiqwas put a hand on my shoulder and pulled me back into the shadows.

"I want to see what this is all about before we rush in to help her," he murmured next to my ear. "Besides, Aunty is getting good at taking care of herself, these days."

"...We were the ones that killed those enemies all the plunder is ours by right," Jenaitsi snarled.

"And is it also a Kukiya custom to be selfish and not share?" Mother said as she stood boldly in front of her cash and put her hands on her hips. "When we go to ask for a healing for the war leader we will need gifts, both for the Prophet and the Unseen Ones who guide and aid him. I want to save them to offer for Nachoga's healing—and you want your war leader to be healed, right?"

Dotsuwa spat on the ground. "Maybe, maybe not. Why you always sit by and care for that one? Are you just another cloocha who wants to be a Chamuqwani's whore? He is no real man of the people, only a pretend Kukiya, a ghost. Better you find another man, a real Kukiya warrior. Maybe I kill him and take you be my cloocha-whore? Maybe you like that better, eh?"

When he reached for her Mother dodged, and then snatched up the digging stick Tuumaz had made for her that was resting against the cottonwood. "Don't touch me, you smelly piece of weasel vomit. You are no real man to talk to me like that."

When he would have lunged for her again Samiqwas said, "If you say bad things about my aunty again or try to harm her, I will kill you."

Turning Dotsuwa saw that Samiqwas had drawn his bow and was aiming an arrow at his chest. As fierce as the Wolf who claimed his Spirit, Samiqwas stared unblinking into the man's eyes, his hand and arm steady and unflinching.

Oblivious to the subtle game of power going on between the two, Jenaitsi scoffed. Looking for his father's approval, he joked, "Want me to take care of this sassy dog-fucking baby for you, Father?"

"I wouldn't try that if I were you Kukiya," I said and stepped out of the shadows to stand beside my cousin. "If either of you harm my mother or any of my kin, you will die—and most terribly—I promise you that."

Jenaitsi skin turned ashen, visible even in the dim light. He must have told his father about his earlier encounter with my protector, because neither man chose to continue the confrontation. Muttering curses under his breath and calling me a malicer Dotsuwa stalked off, followed quickly by his son.

When they were gone I rushed over to Mother who was trembling violently. Hugging her tight, I said, "Amima, are you all right? Did he hurt you?"

Mother took a deep breath as she tried to relax and control her trembling. "No, no, I'm all right; he didn't touch me—this time. I'm glad you two were here, but I thought you were hunting."

This time?

"We were.Tas and I were just coming back from setting our snares when we heard them talking to you,"Samiqwas said and lowered his bow.

"Oh, I'm sorry you had to witness that unpleasantness. How much did you hear?"

"Enough," Samiqwas said, the still snarling Wolf inside him lending his voice a harder and more mature quality than usual. "And that makes me wonder if this is the first time that dog turd has been bothering you."

"You said, 'this time.' I'd been wondering why you were always asking one of us to accompany you while doing simple chores. And why you ride or sit near the war leader as much as possible," I said. "Has he or his son been bothering you? Are you afraid of him, Amima?"

"No. I just don't want to give anyone an opportunity to make more trouble for the war leader," she said. Then, needing an outlet for her pent up agitation, she began picking up and packing away things people had left scattered by the fire.

"We need to tell Nachoga about his Kukiya warriors' disrespectful behavior," Samiqwas began, "He is their leader and—"

Mother whirled around clutching the can of peaches she was holding like a weapon, ready to hurl it at Samiqwas and me if we wouldn't listen. "No! You will not tell him I forbid you to say anything about this to Nachoga or Tuumaz!"

"But he is their war leader," I protested. "He needs—"

"He needs to heal," she countered, her expression stern. "That is the most important thing right now. Insults made by a stupid, ignorant man who his mother is probably ashamed she bore, don't matter."

Her glare was fierce as any mother bear when she next spoke. "Not a word—I mean it. If Nachoga were to find out, then he would have to do something about it. His warrior's pride and honor would demand it. He would be no match for father and son if it came down to a physical fight—and it probably would.

"He told me Dotsuwa has carried a grudge against him for many years so this goes far beyond the insults and petty annoyances of being sent back to Golannah as our escort. I won't add another stick to that fire if I can help it. Right now Nachoga is pushing himself, but he really isn't well, and I don't want to be the cause of..."

Her breath catching on a sob she broke off, took a deep breath and said firmly, "I will deal with Dotsuwa, in my own way—if I have to."

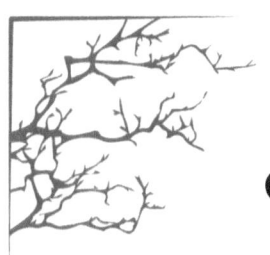

Chapter Seventeen

It was decided to tear down the miners' pit house next day and partially fill the hole with rocks and dirt, so it would appear as if it had been abandoned years ago. All the men's unsalvageable clothes and other items they agreed should be taken away and dumped. Tuumaz suggested that the things be tossed in a cave about a half day's ride south. "I can do that for you, war leader, if you want," he said.

"Hmm, perhaps we should give that honor to the ones who killed them," Nachoga said and stared grimly at father and son.

Dotsuwa gave him a stiff nod. "I will go, but not that far. There are deep clefts on the butte that will do just as well. No one will find them where I put them. My son can stay and help with destroying the pit house. Then we can leave this place sooner."

"All right, do what you think best. As long as they won't lead the soldiers or other miners to the diggings of the dead ones, it's good with me."

Turning to Tuumaz he next asked, "Do you know where my brother is right now? We need to find him as soon as possible to warn him about the new threat these miners bring to our lands."

"They will most likely be at Saluuli Lake by now," Tuumaz said. "Golannah told Utsiyonti that was where the Prophet and his followers would be camping so they can harvest cattails and other roots that are ready to eat this time of year."

"Good that's only a two or three days ride west of here," Nachoga said.

NEXT MORNING THE MEN finished their meal and had started back to the miners' camp, when Mother stopped them and announced to Nachoga that she didn't want to go with them to that evil place again.

Nachoga frowned; I could see that he wasn't happy with her decision not to come with us, but all he said was, "What do you plan to do all day, then?"

Mother gave him a smile, her eyes playful. "Oh, I plan to do lots of things. Cook, mend yours and the boys' clothes—rest, and even sleep, maybe," her smile widened, "you could join me, you know."

He chuckled deep in his throat, his eyes saying he would like nothing better. "Oh I could, could I? That is a very tempting offer." He touched her arm then his mood soured when he saw Dotsuwa and Tuumaz frowning at them. "But not today. You will have to rest alone—*today*."

Glancing at the others waiting for him her smile disappeared as well. "I don't really plan to lie about, but you should come back and rest at some point, so you won't tire yourself over much. And I do mean rest—because I won't be here to distract you. I actually want to wash clothes and your bandages up the creek, as well as gather willow bark and whateverfoods I can find for us to eat while we journey tomorrow."

He thought about it then grunted his agreement with her plan. "I will have one of the young warriors check on you from time to time to see if you need help."

As I started to follow them, Mother held me back with a touch on my arm. "Stubborn man! Try to keep him from overdoing himself if you can, my son. Sometimes he gets so frustrated with his weakness and does too much, and then the injury breaks open and bleeds again."

Annoyed, I grumped, "I'm not sure how you expect me, a mere child, to stop a grown man and my war leader, when you couldn't, Amima?" But then I heard the real worry and concern behind her words, and stopped my complaining.I shared them.

When she opened her mouth to get angry or maybe argue with me, I patted her arm and changed the subject. "I think you really like him, don't you, Amima? Is he the one you will choose to be my new father?"

Startled, Mother closed her mouth and stared at me as if I had grown moose horns on my head. She was silent for a long moment, then when I thought she wouldn't answer, she said, "Marry him? I don't know—hadn't really thought about him that way... Would that displease you, my little Rock Squirrel, my son?"

Would it displease me? I hadn't thought of their growing interest in each other in quite that way, before I opened my big mouth, either. I thought about it for a moment longer, then shook my head and said, "No. it wouldn't displease me at all, Amima. If you want him you have my permission. I would be proud to call him my new father."

She chuckled and gave me a big hug. "Not that I need your permission, as a mere child, of course, but thank you."

When I caught up to the warriors Nachoga, too, put a hand on my shoulder to hold me back. "What did your mother want?"

Grinning I said, "She wants me to keep you from being stupid and breaking open your shoulder again."

"Mm, and how does she expect you to do that?"

I shrugged. "She didn't say."

He walked on for a while, then asked, "She kept you with her a long time. What else did you two talk about?"

Smiling and wanting to joke with him, I said, "I asked her if she liked you, and if you were going to be my new father. I told her that if so, she had my permission if she wanted to marry you."

Nachoga stopped abruptly on the path and whirled to fix me with green cougar eyes. Startled I shrank back. He was shielding his thoughts from me so I couldn't tell if my joking had made him angry, but his intense stare made me nervous. At last he released me and continued walking. Without looking at me he chuckled to himself and then finally said, "What did she say when you asked her those questions?"

"I'm sorry, war leader. I-I was teasing with her when I told her she had my permission to marry you—I meant no disrespect to you or Amima. I would be honored to call you father," I stammered. "And-and she did say she liked you—very much."

He snorted a laugh and caught up to Tuumaz who had paused to wait for us.

Keeping mother's instructions in mind, I stayed close to him throughout the morning, helping the warriors and Samiqwas dig and hall rocks and debris to fill up the hole made by the collapsed pit house. Between Tuumaz and I we convinced Nachoga to leave the stone lifting to us and take charge of leading the mule back and forth while we piled rocks into carry baskets and the little cart we'd found by one of the digging sites.

Samiqwas and I checked on Mother a few times that morning, but she didn't need our help for anything. During the midday heat we all cooled off in the creek and rested in the shade of the willows. At one point I was sure I'd seen the war leader fall asleep—which would please Mother when I told her.

Our work was nearing completion in late afternoon when Nachoga walked over to where I was gathering my last load of stones and said to me in a low voice, "Have your Spirit Helpers given you a warning sign that something is wrong?"

Startled I hastily dropped the stone I'd been lifting into the basket and looked around. Seeing nothing amiss, I shook my head. "No, but maybe I wasn't paying enough attention. Have you had a sending?"

Nachoga stroked his chin, considering my question. "Not a sending exactly, but—something. Dotsuwa should have come back by now. Before you tire yourself too much, with the rocks, can you scout for enemies and see if you can find him?"

A prickle of fear sliding down my spine I nodded. "I will search."

Moving quickly away from that disturbed place I searched, with my own eyes, the cliffs for either a sight of Dotsuwa, or a friendly bird to help me. Vulture and his relatives were busy, but to my surprise a bored young eagle clung to a high outcrop, and he was willing to help.

Taking flight, we floated on Wind's currents high above the canyon and the surrounding cliffs. There were no soldiers or other enemies sneaking up on us, but alsono Dotsuwa on his way back to camp.

I told Eagle to fly a bit lower and do another pass...

There were Samiqwas and Jenaitsi bringing the horses to the creek for their last drink, before hobbling them near the cottonwood for the night...

At the miners' campsite, Tuumaz was holding up a burning clump of sage and circling the disturbed ground. As cleansing blue smoke formed patterns in the cooling air his chanting prayer echoed off the surrounding hills. Nachoga stood by the unharnessed mule, thunder weapon in hand, joining the prayer song, and scanning the hillsides for signs of trouble.

Seeing nothing amiss, I urged my friend to continue up the creek towards our camp. When we flew over, I was surprised that the evening cook fire hadn't been rekindled. Lighting in the cottonwood for a better look I could see no Mother busy preparing our meal. Starting to truly share Nachoga's worry, I urged Eagle back to the sky and we continued searching.

Heading up the creek to where I'd last seen Mother digging coussa root I saw only a tipped over basket roots falling out, a scattered tangle of cleaned bandages laying in the grass, but no mother. <<Help me, Brother Eagle. My Nest-Mother where...?>>

We circled, then a little farther up the stream Eagle's keen sight caught a series of violent movements in the rabbit brush. Pushing past my own turbulent emotions, I was at last able to translate the jumble of avian images Eagle's eyes were sending me.

Torn clothing, bruises, blood, Dotsuwa and Mother were struggling. She was fighting him, trying hard to defend herself with her digging stick, not making it easy for him, but she was losing her battle. Then as I watched he jerked the stick out of her hands and smashed his fist into her unprotected belly. Mother sank to the ground, and clutched at her middle. Throwing the digger to one side he loosened his clothing, rolled her over and tried to mount her like a maddened dog.

Rage goading me I conveyed my fear to Eagle. <<Help Nest Mother, Egg-Layer, Attack enemy, kill, KILL!>>

With a scream of white-hot rage Eagle folded his wings and plunged earthward.

Before Dotsuwa could complete his vile act, a heavy weight slammed into him, knocking him aside. Powerful talons bit deep into his head and neck while a hooked beak tore at his face. Blinded by blood and pain, Dotsuwa let out a piercing roar, and batted unsuccessfully at the winged demon trying to kill him.

Rolling out of the way Mother managed with the help of her discarded stick to pull herself out of danger and get to her feet. Wide eyed, and gasping for breath, she added her own shouts to the growing din, begging me to stop.

Eagle and I might have killed the man, and a part of me wished we had for all the trouble he and his son caused us, but the Unseen Ones had other plans for him. And at last Mother's frantic shouting to me to stop penetrated through the haze of white-hot fury clouding my reason. I released Eagle to fly away, leaving the bloody man sobbing and cursing in acrumpled heap on the ground.

Falling back into my body I swallowed my nausea at such a quick transition, staggered to my feet, and lurched for my horse. Once I was mounted I galloped down the path, heading for my injured mother. Already alerted by Eagle's scream and Dotsuwa and Mother's shouting, Tuumaz and Nachoga, still by the miners' destroyed campsite, had stopped working and grabbed up weapons.

"Are we being attacked?" Tuumaz shouted as I raced past him.

"No. You come—Mother..."

All the horses were at the creek with Samiqwas and Jenaitsi, but Nachoga needed no further explanation from me. Leaping bareback atop the startled mule, he slapped its rump with his quirt and pounded after me. Still afoot Tuumaz raced along in his wake.

Being closer to the trouble both Samiqwas and Jenaitsi had gotten to the site before us. When Nachoga and I arrived Jenaitsi had helped his father to his feet and was urging him to climb onto his horse and shouting curses and promises of revenge at mother. Still wide eyed and frightened she had retreated a little way up the slope and was trying to pull her torn clothing together while Samiqwas possessed by his snarling wolf stood protectively in front of her with his bow drawn.

I saw with grim satisfaction that though nowhere close to giving him dying wounds, Eagle's attack would leave him hideously scarred for life, and he might lose an eye. Long talon marks scored his head, neck and shoulders, streams of red flowing down his arms, back and chest. Only half-conscious, Dotsuwa was barely able to stay on the horse unaided. When he saw us coming, Jenaitsi took one look at Nachoga's face, leapt onto the horse behind his father and together they galloped off up the creek.

Beating the mule cruelly, Nachoga raced after them. Sensing its rider's urgency, the mule tried to catch up to the fleeing horse, but even carrying double Jenaitsi's horse soon left the exhausted and struggling mule behind.

At last the war leader gave up and rode the wheezing mule back to us. Sliding off its back he rushed to Mother. The back of his shirt was now stained red; the day's events had indeed opened the wound in his shoulder as Mother had feared.

Pulling her to him he hugged her then held her out to examine her injuries. "How badly are you hurt?"

"I'm all right, war leader, only cuts and bruises—I'm not hurt—truly. He just surprised me when I was digging for coussa. He claimed I'd been teasing him, wanting him to—but I've done nothing to encourage his interest," Mother protested, her eyes moist and pleading for Nachoga to believe her.

Grim-faced Nachoga nodded and stared at the dust cloud that was all that remained of the retreating men. "I believe you, Qwani'Ya Woman, I truly do. Because he has a powerful Puhani for an uncle that weasel piss drinker thinks he can get away with anything. For years he and his family have tried to destroy me, my brother, and all we care about at every opportunity. —but not this time. He has gone too far..." The fist on his uninjured side was clinched tight enough to crush rocks as he struggled to master his emotions.

I said, "His injuries are my doing. Samiqwas and I warned him last night what would happen if either of them bothered her again. I would have killed him this time if she hadn't pleaded for me to stop."

The war leader whirled to glare at me. "What are you talking about—this time?"

"Last night when we were coming back from setting our snares we heard the dog turd threatening her and calling her bad names," Samiqwas said. "I drew my bow and told him I, too, would kill him if he bothered her again."

Shifting his anger to Mother he said, "This has happened before?" When she reluctantly nodded he swore a terrible curse. "Why didn't you tell me, woman?"

Standing up to his ire, she snapped, "And what would you have done, eh? Get into a fight with him—injure your shoulder worse—or get yourself killed? And for what? You would risk your life over the mindless chatter of a scolding jay?

"I didn't tell you, and made the boys promise not to tell you, to avoid what I am seeing in your eyes right now. I thought I could handle him. And I didn't want you to get hurt—again."

He swore once more, his eyes flashing green fire. "And do you always protect your men and try to fight a warrior's battles for him?" he growled.

"Yes I do," she shot back. "If the warrior is injured—and behaving stupidly—like you are now. I did it for Tas's father and now I do it for you."

That gave him pause. Closing his mouth he stared at her, his fierce expression demanding an answer. "What do you mean? If the stories about your son's father being a Spirit warrior from the Unseen World are true, how could that be?"

"Because when I found him he had been badly injured. He was still in his seal form—too injured to change." She chuckled reliving the memory. "I thought I was the luckiest woman in my village to find such a big piece of meat unclaimed on the beach.Then he spoke to me and I realized my mistake.

"I dragged him back to my lodge and cared for him until he was well enough and had to leave me. But while he was still with me I twice fought off the evil monsters that were chasing him."

Caught up in her tale, but not sure if he totally believed her, Nachogasnorted. "You, a mere human woman, defeated creatures from Beyond, who hunted a Spirit warrior? I find that hard to believe. How did you do that, Qwani'Ya woman?"

Eyes defiant, she glared at him and the rest of her male audience and dared them to question her account. "I don't really care if you believe me."

"How?"

"I used my woman's magic to defeat them. The first time I was alone when those fearsome creatures found me. They were searching for him. Using my moon blood's power, I made them leave.

"The second time we were together, but he was still too weak to fight them. So, he showed me the glyphs and we painted them in my blood to protect us that terrible night," she said.

Defiant and angry now herself she used a soldier's bad word and folded her arms across her chest. "And I don't care if you men believe me or not. I speak true."

When the two continued to glare at one another Samiqwas diverted them, by saying, "Aunty, that is an amazing story." Turning to me, he murmured, "Did you know about this, Tas?"

I did know, but I wasn't going to admit it, because I had found out by spying on her dreams at Chumco's urging, and I was ashamed of my prying. So I just shook my head and gave him an enigmatic smile.

Mounted now with thunder weapon in hand, Tuumaz returned the topic to the matter of punishing the fleeing Dotsuwa. And asked, "Want me to go after them; kill the mad dog for you, war leader?"

"No. I will do it myself." Nachoga snarled. "Samiqwas, get my horse."

Mother clutched his uninjured arm and pleaded. "Nachoga, stop! You have torn open the wound again. Can't you feel the warm blood dripping down your back? Already you have damaged the healing my father gave you. Do you want to be a crippled warrior for the rest of your life?

"Please, stop and think. Take your vengeance—later—if you must but not now while you are so weak."

"Woman, don't try to tell me what to do! I won't let you rule me. A woman's blood Puwa can't resolve what has been festering between me and that weasel dung for far too long. It's time to lance the boil."

"Stupid, stubborn man!" she cried still holding onto his good arm. "How can I marry you if you get yourself killed?"

"They have no supplies with them," Samiqwas said, pouring a cup of cool reason onto their heating argument. "Maybe they come back. Better we wait and set a trap for them rather than chasing them now, and riding into an ambush." Nachoga considered and reluctantly agreed.

Then hearing the boom of a thunder weapon in the distance and then the noise of frightened horses running away both Kukiya knew exactly what had happened. Tuumaz took off in pursuit, Nachoga, ignoring his bleeding shoulder snatched up the reigns of my mare, and then he and Samiqwas raced after Tuumaz.

With only the poor tired mule left for us, Mother sighed. We looked at one another then started back to our camp among the cottonwoods. Leading the poor beast between us we paused at the creek for her to wash up, while I collected her fallen belongings and gathered a couple clay jars of water. We were going to need them.

We learned when we returned to our camp that while we had all been busy with other tasks that afternoon, Dotsuwa had packed up his and his son's things and hidden them away elsewhere in case he had needed a quick escape after planning his attack on my mother.

And leaving the horses as they had in such a hurry neither Samiqwas nor Jenaitsi had hobbled them. They had only left them to graze and drink as they pleased by the creek. So it had been easy for the fugitives to circle around, reclaim their things, collect another mount, then scatter the rest.

When the warriors returned later they brought with them most of the missing horses, but Nachoga's gray, that he was growing quite fond of, was not among them. Knowing what a blow that would be to Nachoga's pride, Jenaitsi had managed to steal him away before scattering the rest. And by heading east, to join the raiders into the Chamuqwani claimed lands the fugitives knew we wouldn't follow.

Stronger than Nachoga in speaking mind-to-mind my Gift made contacting Utsiyonti easy for me and that night I entered his dreams and told him what had happened to Mother and Nachoga. I didn't want the fugitives to be spreading lies when they caught up with the rest of the warband.

Rushton Archives: conclusion of second interview with subject 297

The End
Tasimu's story continues in Book Three, *Abandoning Memory*

ADDITIONAL INFORMATION for the books telling Tasimu's Story
Words in the Qwani'Ya Language:

Qwani'Ya Tsa'adi, or Fish People, what the Indigenous people living by Big Ice Lake call themselves

Qwa'osi the Otter Warrior, a guardian spirit protector of the Qwani'Ya

Co'yeh the Lake Seal, the Otter's rival, a spirit with both light and dark aspects

Siyatli, a child born to a human woman whose father is a lake Seal

Qwakaiva, a difficult word to translate in its full meaning, similar to what we might refer to as magic, chi, life force or shamanic medicine

Qwakaihi, a shaman, someone gifted with great power and uses the gift for the good of others

Aseutl, a snake-like dragon figure some say lives at the bottom of Big Ice Lake

Kunai, a shape-shifting magical being of great power, and benefactor of Tasimu

Qwa'Nayhi a shape-shifting being able to travel between many realms of existence, like the Qwa'Nayhi Seal man who is Tasimu's father

Amima, mother in the Qwani'ya language

Appi, father

Ami, grandmother

Ati, grandfather

Coshelah cousin, a person's patrilineal cousin. The Qwani'Ya claim their descent from their mothers, so the father's kin aren't as close and referred to differently

Wannigua, a little demonic spirit that often teases or taunts people

Shillsham Ceremony, the ritual period of isolation that all Qwani'Ya girls must do to prepare for womanhood

Chamuqwani, a term the Indigenous people use to refer to the Imperial invaders of their land

Asiya, a greeting like hello

UNFAMILIAR TERMS IN the Chamuqwani Language

Zaunk, a degrading term used by soldiers and settlers from the empire to express their contempt for all Indigenous peoples they discovered during their conquest

Bucki, a derogatory term for an Indigenous man or boy

Cloocha or Cloocha-whore a demeaning term for an Indigenous woman or girl

Words in the Kukiya Language

Kukiya, what the Indigenous people living in the desert and mountain country out of which the Empire created their Tribal Preserve call themselves

Puhani, a person with magical powers, the same as a Qwakaihi in Tas's people's language

Puwa, the magical power, like Qwakaiva, that a Puhani can use

Akiyazi, the magical beings that have power over the rain and the water in lakes and creeks

Don't miss out!

Visit the website below and you can sign up to receive emails whenever Celu Amberstone publishes a new book. There's no charge and no obligation.

https://books2read.com/r/B-A-YGQM-YRKDC

BOOKS 2 READ

Connecting independent readers to independent writers.

Also by Celu Amberstone

Rituals
Blessings of the Blood: A Book of Menstrual Lore and Rituals for Women
Deepening the Power: Community Ritual and Sacred Theatre

Tales of Tasimu
Taste of Memory
When Memory Dies

Tales of the Kashallans
The Dream-Chosen
The Hunted Kashallan
The Outlawed Bond
Uncertain Refuge
Prey of the Umwira
Blood Magic's Snare
Kashallan Alliance
Treacherous Campaign

Standalone
Refugees and Other Stories

About the Author

Celu is of mixed Cherokee and Scots-Irish ancestry. Celu Amberstone was one of the few young people in her family to take an interest in learning Traditional Native crafts and medicine ways. This interest made several of the older members of her family very happy while annoying others.

Legally blind since birth, she has defied her limitations and spent much of her life avoiding cities. Moving to Canada after falling in love with a Métis-Cree man from Manitoba, she has lived in the rain forests of the west coast, a tepee in the desert and a small village in Canada's arctic. Along the way she also managed to acquire a BA in cultural anthropology and an MA in health education. Celu loves telling stories and reading. She lives in Victoria British Columbia near her grown children and grandchildren.

About the Publisher

Kashallan Press is an independent publisher releasing books by author Celu Amberstone. Among her books are critically-acclaimed works now re-released by Kashallan Press, and new works showcasing her talents in writing both fiction and non-fiction.

www.ingramcontent.com/pod-product-compliance
Lightning Source LLC
Chambersburg PA
CBHW031211020726
47499CB00002B/544